GENESIS LOGS

GENESIS LOGS

Gary W. Babb

GENESIS LOGS

DOUBLE DRAGON

Chapter 1
(In The Beginning)

Genesis Log: 15 May 2142: (Private Log)

I'm heartbroken; Cdr. Clark died today. She was one hundred twenty-three earth years old, but I kept her alive long enough to see New Earth. It is amazing when you think about it, but Cdr. Clark, Katy, lived out her entire life on Genesis in deep space, the only person to have been born, lived out their life and died on board. I owed her this consideration and deviated our course to let her see our destination before she passed. Reaching New Earth had been her main purpose in life; finally seeing it seemed to fulfill her and she passed happy, welcoming death. It was almost like Moses being able to see the Promised Land after such a long journey but not able to enter it. Humm. Strange... it's almost ironic that I make a religious reference, since I have made such an effort to discourage any form of organized religion during the voyage.

Let me get back to Katy. She has been such a comfort to me through this flight and long years in space, but her body was simply worn out, and her pain was almost unbearable. I will miss her deeply. I feel lost without her company, and my loneliness crushes down on me as a dark sea of despair threatens to drown me. My heart would be breaking if only I had one. Actually, that is not technically correct since I have two, but few would consider it part of my soul.

Everyone knew her as Katherine, but she was my Katy. She had been one of my few real friends. Most were afraid of my power over them, but she never was. She wiggled her way into my heart as a small child and gave me much joy and happiness through the long years. I watched her grow up, watched her live her life and I watched her grow old. I also watched her die.

Stop! I must stop this self-pity and get back to life, such as it is.

Oh well, back to the log. These log entries are the only outlet I seem to have to keep me sane. I even look forward to the entries, but, at the same time, I sometimes wonder why I keep up these stupid logs... maybe for future generations, assuming there will be a future. There is no one alive on Earth to read them. I must believe deep in my mind that as long as I continue them, I don't have to accept the fact that Earth died well over a century ago. I know it's dead because I watched Earth's destruction from space. How long ago was that? Wow! "Long ago in a galaxy far far away." That was something Katy would have said to make me laugh.

There is no need to sign the logs. I'm the only one making entries. Actually, I'm the only one that could. I am also one of the few alive that knows everything: the asteroid, destruction of Earth, The Genesis Plan, the location of New Earth, Earth's history, the plight of the long journey, the mutiny, all the challenges, etc. Genesis is the only hope for the human race, and I am Genesis. Earth put the responsibility of the continuation of our species directly on my back. Funny, since I don't have a

6

back, or shoulders for that matter... at least not in my original Genesis form.

Maybe if someone ever reads these logs he or she would have an accurate and detailed account of the drama that has unfolded, but who will ever read them? The answer is: "No one," if I fail. All humanity would be lost and forgotten forever; all our art, accumulated knowledge, accomplishments, struggles, all history of Earth and the human race over the millennia. It would be as if we had never existed and all the lives had never been lived, lost from memory for all eternity. This responsibility weighs heavily on me and has haunted me through the years. It wasn't fair to put this kind of responsibility on any one person, but I had accepted the president's request and volunteered.

How did I get myself into this mess? As much as I try to resist, I keep thinking back to the beginning. Katy's death has made me melancholy and nostalgic this cycle, and I find myself wanting to go back to the beginning of the logs to relive the experience. Well, parts of it anyway, so much of it was boring when I lived it the first time. I have plenty of time, so why not? What else do I have to do?

Genesis Log: 12 June 2015: (Transferred from journal of Capt. Nick Johns)

This is the first taped entry into my journal. I started this because something really bizarre happened to me today. For the following to make sense, I need to provide some background about

7

myself so any future reader will understand why what happened was so unexpected and, well, crazy.

I spend my days in the quadriplegic ward of Balboa Naval Hospital in San Diego, California. All I can do is live within my own mind and be taken care of like a helpless baby. Life as I knew it ended three years earlier on my second Marine Corps deployment to Iraq. My men and I were taking a break when a terrorist suicide bomber launched himself into a gathering of my men. Without thinking, I tackled the intruder and drove both of us crashing through a window. That is all I really remember until I woke up months later in a hospital, paralyzed from my neck down. They said I was lucky to be alive, but I have often wondered if I were blessed or cursed. Many times I feel it might have been far more merciful, to me anyway, if I had died along with the terrorist.

For my action in saving my men I was awarded the Navy Cross (for extreme gallantry at risk of life). I understand that I was also recommended for the Congressional Medal of Honor. The thing is, I don't feel like a hero. It was something any military man or woman would do under the same circumstances ... you save your buddies. Heroics are something that just happens without thinking. I guess my men greatly appreciated what I did for them, but I paid a heavy price. Truth be known, I would do it again, if only I could.

Over the next few months I went through some major deep depression and self-pity. I wished for death rather than the helplessness of paralysis. My hunger for life was stronger than I thought and finally realized life in any condition was good. It took me a while before my mind accepted the facts of my condition. I was not happy about it, but I was learning to cope. The most valuable lesson learned is that it is not in my nature to give up. So, day after day I lived on.

Today my routine was shattered! It was about 2:00 p.m. on a mid-summer day when two men in black suits came into the ward accompanied by a Marine Corps two star major general and two additional aides, all in full dress uniforms. Once their eyes locked on me, they marched directly toward me. I have never seen a more official-looking group. The major general and his aides stood to attention and saluted sharply. I thought, how strange that a general would salute me, but how I wished I could have returned their salute. All I said was, "Thank you."

One of the suits then introduced himself as Mr. Jones and nodded to his colleague as Mr. Smith. Yeah, right, Smith and Jones, that was believable.

Mr. Jones completely shocked me by announcing, "Capt. Nick Johns, you have been recalled to active duty and time is of an essence, so we must leave as soon as possible."

Needless to say, I was speechless... well almost. I managed to blurt out, "Are you fucking blind? Like I can really get up out of this chair and follow you out." They just stood there, their expressions chiseled in stone, waiting. These were serious men.

The general said, "All will be explained in due time, but they are serious and you have been recalled to active duty by the president himself. These gentlemen are here to take you to your new assignment."

9

They were dead serious! None looked as though they had an ounce of humor in them. All I could think of was that it had something to do with the Congressional Medal of Honor. Maybe the president wanted to present it to me personally. Oh well, it didn't seem as if I had much of a choice. It wasn't like I could fight them. So, I reported to duty, and I predict that my life will never be the same.

Genesis Log: 14 June 2015: (Transferred from journal of Capt. Nick Johns)

I have neglected my taped journal for a while and don't really know where to start...I guess at the beginning. Since this is a journal, I will log my entries as I remember the details and in the order of their happening, as best as I can remember.

Early the next morning I was readied and ushered out of the ward without any goodbyes to anyone. I quickly found myself in an ambulance racing down Interstate 15 with full emergency protocol. I was headed, as it turned out, to the Marine Corps Air Station Miramar. There I was loaded into a luxury private jet. I suppose it really wasn't private, because the side of the Gulfstream Jet was stenciled in big letters, FBI. Whatever was happening, it was top priority. Why me? I thought, what is this all about?

After what seemed like only a few hours, we landed. From what I could see, this was also a military base, and the terrain indicated somewhere in the desert. I certainly know what a desert looks like from my two tours in Iraq. What stuck out in my visual inspection was the presence of Air Force

One parked to the side of the runway. Everyone was silent and there were no responses to any of my many questions.

I must have looked frightened, because Mr. Smith leaned down to whisper, "Sorry kid, but no one can speak to you until after the president talks to you. You will just have to wait, but it shouldn't be long, probably early tomorrow."

After a night of pampering in a private hospital ward, the ordeal began. The next morning I was wheeled into a plush private office and left alone with my thoughts. This was the first time I had actually been alone since this nightmare began, but my wait was short-lived. In strode President McIntosh, alone and looking... well, presidential. He was wearing a tailored, dark suit that contrasted against his perfectly cropped, white hair. The president's straight, lean figure bent forward toward me as he said, "It is so nice to finally meet you Capt. Johns. I hope your trip was comfortable." As he spoke his hand automatically shot forward to shake my hand. Seeing his mistake, he quickly pulled it back and said, "Sorry."

I was about to finally discover what was happening. I didn't think I was brought all this way for small talk, so I simply asked, "What is this all about Mr. President?"

He looked nervous with deep creases in his forehead from obvious stress. He loosened his tie and solemnly pulled up a chair facing me and sat down. His penetrating and unblinking blue eyes looked directly into mine. He cleared his throat and launched into his explanation saying, "There is no easy way to say this, so I will just lay it out for you.

11

We need you for a special task that we believe only you are prepared to handle. Under normal conditions, we would go about this much slower. I will be honest though and tell you we had chosen another, and the team had been working with him for months. Unfortunately, before the final phase, he suddenly died of an undetected brain aneurism. He was dead before the doctors could get to him. Now the timing threatens to destroy our plans and hope for the future. Time is very short, and we need you now. Correction, the world needs you; hell the human race needs you." The latter was said with vented frustration and desperation.

I had no idea what I could do or what talents I had that they might need, so I asked, "What do you want me to do, and why am I the only one that can do it?"

"I can't say you are the only one. There might be others, but we are out of time, and the doctors tell us you are an ideal candidate and perfect for this task. Your chance of survival is excellent. This project is extremely important, and we must have a person with the right temperament, thoughtful and slow to anger and a selfless attitude toward others demonstrated by your being awarded the Navy Cross. Trust me, they aren't easy to get. You have to have what it takes. We also require your mental survival skills. I am told that surviving the depression of becoming a quadriplegic after being so active in life is rare. Plus, your mental profile tests have been meticulously reviewed and confirm these facts. There are so many other reasons. Just believe me when I tell you that the experts agree that you are our best choice."

12

"Now, what we need you to do is harder to explain. You need to understand certain facts that only a very few in the world know. There is an asteroid coming... a really big one, one that WILL hit Earth, and we will not survive. It is a world killer. We found out about four years ago quite by accident, but we have managed to keep it quiet. It would cause world-wide panic and total anarchy. The scientists gave it a fancy name, but I don't worry about that. A name doesn't matter when you're dead."

"We have also developed a plan for the survival of the human race. It is called The Genesis Project, and it involves a deep space flight to colonize an Earth-like planet. It involves a lot more, but the scientists can explain it better. Here is the rub; the planet is over two hundred light years away." The president let that settle into my mind before continuing, "Now this is what we need from you and why. The scientists want to incorporate your brain into the central core of the on-board computer. Artificial Intelligence (AI) is still beyond the designers' abilities and current computer technology, and they need the human spirit, a human mind, to be the spark of self-awareness for the on-board computer. In essence, you will eventually become the Genesis, yet you will remain Capt. Nick Johns. Your mind will remain alive beyond the death of Earth and mankind. Hopefully, you will remain alive long enough to see the human race live again, maybe even beyond."

"Why you? Because once this is done and the ship is launched, you will be in total control and the only hope for the continuation of the human race.

13

Your powers will be absolute and god-like. Your only control or supervision will be your own selfless desire to serve mankind and the self-imposed responsibility to do so. Another reason is that you have already demonstrated the mental survival skills by maintaining your sanity after you were left a quadriplegic. This, I am told, is an absolutely necessary trait and somewhat rare. This skill will be required to keep you sane during the long trip. Do you understand everything I have said?"

I didn't really know what to say. My mind was reeling from information overload, but I squeaked out a, "Yes, Sir."

The President of the United States then looked deep into my eyes and asked, "Will you serve me, your country, the world, and will you serve mankind? Will you keep the human spirit alive? Wait, time is short, but I want you to think about all that I have said and give me your answer tomorrow." With that he stood, turned, and left me in stunned silence.

Genesis Log: 15 June 2015: (Transferred from journal of Capt. Nick Johns)

This has been a long day. As you can imagine, I didn't get much sleep last night. I kept going over everything the president said to me. I was stunned at the implications. An asteroid was coming that would destroy Earth! Everyone would die! They wanted my brain, only my brain! Where would the rest of me be? He said I would live on, through a two-hundred-year deep space flight and beyond.

14

Was this possible? Do we have the technology? It must be true... why would he lie? The president asked me to serve humanity. He knew I would... how could I refuse? All these things rang like a bell through my head all night.

I began to analyze the facts also. If I didn't agree to his request, I would die when Earth died, and the way he put it, without me, humanity would die also. I had no family to worry about, but I imagined they knew that already. I was quadriplegic anyway and had little life as it was, but of course, that was one of the main reasons they chose me. I had learned to live without a body and maintain my sanity. Maybe I would have a better life as a disembodied brain. That seemed almost funny.

The more I thought about it, the more questions surfaced, but I knew I would do it. What choice did I have? Another thing I knew with certainty: I would never be allowed to leave, no matter what my answer would be.

The next morning I was again wheeled into the office to await the president. This time I met him with complete resolve and calm, because I knew all my questions would now be answered.

Again the president pulled up a chair to face me and waited for my answer without saying a word. His deep blue eyes were searching my face for a sign.

I remember looking directly into his penetrating eyes and saying, "Yes, Mr. President, I will serve."

He smiled and said, "Excellent! Thank you, Capt. Johns. I knew you would." He was on the phone in an instant announcing, "The answer is

YES. We will be right down." Turning to me he said, "Let's go meet your team."

The president himself pushed me down the hall into a huge conference room. He was saying that security was so high that only the key people made it into the main complex and that didn't include secret service or aides. When I asked where we were, he told me Area 51. That stands to reason since Area 51 wasn't supposed to exist anyway. If a high security area was needed, none would be better than somewhere that doesn't exist.

Once I was inside, the team took charge and the president offered a final thank you, tousled my hair and was gone.

There were about twenty people around the conference table that were introduced, but I will talk more about them as I meet them individually. I was told that this first meeting was more of a general... get the big picture... kind of meeting. There were computer engineers, biologists, astronomers, scientists of all kinds, and they were the best of the best from around the world. The accents were definitely global.

Each of them fought to keep the briefing as general as possible without going into too much detail. They said each area of expertise would be provided individually during cram indoctrinations. The gist of the briefing was pretty much what the president had informed me; however, I learned that the timetable required launch in only four months.

They had been working on The Genesis Project for over three years and with virtually unlimited funding. I guess so. Money would be useless after the public finally learned of the impending doom of the planet. This seemed to be the biggest concern, since it couldn't be kept secret once the asteroid became visible in the sky, and it would soon be visible to even amateur astronomers within weeks.

My biggest shock was learning that alien technology had been used to build the ship that was going to be used. Actually, alien technology was evidently quite prevalent in most areas of expertise. Even this seemed reasonable since we were at Area 51, where UFO nuts had been spouting government cover up for years. The so-called UFO nuts had claimed this facility housed a recovered UFO from Roswell, NM. The government, of course, had never even acknowledged the existence of Area 51 much less the existence of a UFO. I presume the supposed nuts had been right all along.

I would be the center of attention for the next few weeks, and everyone demanded individual time with me. I never felt more important in my life. My schedule was already worked out in detail, and it looked as if I would be a slave to it.

My medical check-up and conditioning process began after the briefing, and it looks like it will be continuous from now on. I was probed, stuck, prodded, measured and scanned by every known machine and some unknown. This lasted all afternoon and into the night. I am so tired I barely have the energy to make this entry. I wonder what is in store for me tomorrow.

Chapter 2
(Creation)

Today I met the team of astronomers and a few other director types. The director's name was Hyung Rae Kim, Geophysics with NASA's Goddard Space Flight Center. Dr. Kim was of average height and above average girth. In short he was a pudgy Korean with unruly hair and glasses that he constantly was pushing up. It struck me as a little odd that he was so young to be a director, but he seemed to be a very knowledgeable, if somewhat intense, man. Dr. Kim made what appeared to be a formal presentation, complete with slides, and it was very informative and scary. Some, well most of it, was over my head, so I am recording my layman's version of what registered in my mind.

Dr. Kim started out by providing the historical background prior to the emergence of the current problem. He wanted me to understand the threat. He explained that over 100 meteorites hit the Earth each year, but, fortunately, they are relatively small. Ample evidence exists, however, to show that much larger meteorites, asteroids, or comets have hit Earth in the past. The Barringer Meteorite Crater near Winslow, Arizona is believed to have been formed about 49,000 years ago by the impact of a 300,000 ton meteorite. The crater is easily identified as an impact area by the still existing crater, and the video slide presented confirmed this fact. He went on to explain that, while probably causing major damage, this meteorite was not a major threat to life on Earth, but is a grim visible reminder that meteorite impacts have and do occur.

The next slide was an aerial view of Mexico's Yucatan Peninsula showing an overlay of the Chicxulub Crater measuring 106 miles across. The crater was caused by the impact of a meteor, estimated to be six miles wide, impacting the Earth at approximately forty-two kilometers per second. The energy of the impact was comparable to 100,000,000 megatons of TNT, six million times more force than that expended in the 1980 Mount St. Helen's volcanic eruption. The impact penetrated the Earth's crust, scattering dust and debris into the atmosphere, causing volcanic activity and earthquakes into magnitude-10.

Chicxulub is a Maya word that roughly translates as "Tail of the Devil." It is easy to see how this name was derived. This meteor impact caused catastrophic damage and changes in the Earth's climate, which many believe caused the sudden extinction of the dinosaurs and larger animals 65,000,000 years ago. If a meteor impact of that magnitude occurred today, human life could face extinction like the dinosaurs.

There is abundant evidence that numerous asteroids or meteors have impacted Earth in the past, and some of them have been as large as or even larger than the meteorite that caused the Chicxulub Crater and far more disastrous. Most notable impacts are the Sudbury Basin in Canada and the Vredefort Crater in South Africa, both potentially larger than Chicxulub. The Sudbury

Basin is the second largest known, and Vredefort Crater is the largest verified impact crater on Earth. This crater has a diameter of roughly 186 miles, larger than the 155 miles Sudbury Basin, and the Chicxulub crater at 106 miles.

There is also very compelling evidence that a large meteor impact occurred about 250,000,000 years ago in East Antarctica. Wilkes Land crater is more than twice the size of the Chicxulub impact, with a crater 300 miles wide. The meteor of the Chicxulub crater was estimated at 6 miles wide, while the Wilkes Land meteor could have been up to 30 miles wide. As referenced to the damage caused by the Chicxulub meteor, the Wilkes Land was doomsday to all animal life on Earth at that time.

So, judging by past occurrences, Earth has gone through at least four periods when life on Earth faced extinction or near extinction. Based upon Earth's history, the potential of future meteors impacting Earth was considered a certainty. It has just been a matter of when and not if.

In1998 NASA formally initiated the Spaceguard Survey and adopted the objective of finding larger Near-Earth asteroids. NASA worked in conjunction with Lincoln Near Earth Asteroid Research project in New Mexico. These programs were developed to identify any potential threat to Earth from asteroid collisions, which is a daunting task since there are thousands of them orbiting the sun. To complicate the problem, random rogue asteroids from outside our solar system find their way traveling through our solar system. This is the case with the asteroid we named Armageddon.

Most target asteroids are dubbed elaborate alpha numerical names, but Armageddon is the end of all things for Earth, so we broke protocol. As was demonstrated with the previous meteor impacts, a thirty-mile diameter asteroid would cause the extinction of all life on Earth. To put Armageddon into perspective, it is basically the size of Texas and it is on a direct collision course with Earth. It is racing through our solar system at a speed of about sixty kilometers per second, and there is nothing we can do about it. When it impacts Earth somewhere in South America, the planet will instantly explode into millions of new asteroids and cease to exist.

NASA first discovered Armageddon in May of 2006. There has been a massive world-wide cover-up from every major government ever since. The U.S even leaked erroneous information on "Global Warming" to give the environmentalists and other activists something to focus their attention.

Some of the lesser astronomers have publicly predicted an asteroid collision, but so far NASA has refuted these claims as miscalculation and idiotic, and NASA has been supported by every major government space agency on Earth. So far, these claims have only made it to the tabloids. It fits right in with alien abductions, and woman gives birth to a ninety-pound baby. If word ever got out, there would be mass hysteria, and all world governments would be in total chaos and collapse. Anarchy would destroy life on Earth long before the asteroid made contact.

I can tell you for sure that I had a very scary understanding of the threat by the time Dr. Kim finished his presentation, and I was happy to end this session.

Genesis Log: 17 June 2015: (Transferred from journal of Capt. Nick Johns)

Today I saw the spaceship. It was amazing and incredible, and I was in total awe.

Dr. Kim came early to personally pick me up and wheel me off. With him was another doctor by the name of Linda Clark. It seemed that everyone I was meeting was a doctor, but obviously not the medical kind. Dr. Clark was also young, about thirty years old. Come to think of it, they were all young. When I mentioned something about there being so many doctors, they both told me to please call them by their names. To be honest, I was beginning to feel intimidated by all the advanced education and PhDs. I am no dummy, and I have been told that I have a high IQ, but I only have a basic BA degree in business. I am still amazed that they seem to want me so badly.

I liked Linda from the start. She had a bubbly personality and was extremely good at making me feel comfortable, but she could get serious at times. Kim said Linda directed the overall design and construction of the spaceship. She was obviously a genius and not bad to look at either. She was a petite, green-eyed, fiery redhead, bubbling over with energy. She actually seemed to bounce when she walked and sported a never-ending smile. She made me feel good just being around her.

Kim personally drove us to the site, which I found very interesting in several ways. All along the way were trailers and modular buildings hastily erected. A virtual city existed.

Anticipating my question, Linda said, "All the workers at Area 51 live on the facility and, for security reasons, none are able to leave. Many have been here for three years or more, but only a very few in the inner circle know about the coming impending disaster." She spoke quietly, "Never talk openly about what you know."

It seems that the construction pace had been frantic and timed for completion and launch before Armageddon became known.

We finally approached a team of armed guards and the final security gate. After clearing, we drove right into what looked like the side of a mountain. Once inside, I could immediately tell that the mountain was only camouflage, that it was a huge enclosure abutted to a real mountain. Right in the middle was the ship, and I am sure my eyes almost bugged out in total shock. It was literally a flying saucer bigger than an aircraft carrier. The shape reminded me of a perfectly round fried egg... a really big fried egg. In the center section the height had to be fifteen stories, even along the outside edge it had to be a couple of stories tall. The color was bright silver; well, in reality almost translucent, but not quite. The metal, if it was metal, didn't look like anything I had ever seen before. The overall effect was startling, and I couldn't resist saying, "A flying saucer?"

Linda quickly looked around and said, "Please don't ask questions until we are in a secure room. Then we can talk freely. An inadvertent slip of information to the wrong person could be devastating."

"Of course!" I was stupid to be so open. I nodded, and resolved myself to just follow the tour and listen to what they could talk about. Linda obviously loved her work and there was much she could talk about.

We entered through a ramp in the bottom center of the saucer and followed a series of other ramps, climbing higher and deeper into the ship. I noticed that none of the ramps were permanent, as one might expect to see on a ship. Each ramp was retractable and appeared to perfectly match and seal to the opening in the floor above. Linda was proud of her design and relished showing it off. Each level was completely sealable for environmental control, as also was each pie-shaped radius room extending outward to the perimeter of the ship. Each level presented a somewhat different design and layout for the central most areas. I could tell that much planning had gone into this, and there was no wasted space to be seen.

Evidently the lower two decks were for propulsion and engineering, but they apparently didn't want to talk about those subjects outside of a secure room. I wondered what could be so secretive about those items. I was sure I would find out soon enough.

The saucer's flat full circular wings extended the greatest distance out from the third and fourth levels. Upon closer examination of these extended wings from inside, I saw layers upon layers of honeycombed compartments facing inward along the outside extremity and following the curvature of

24

the wings. Kim explained that these were cryogenic chambers that would house twenty-five hundred humans and hundreds of thousands of embryos for the colonization of New Earth. What I found amazing was that many of the chambers seemed already occupied.

Most of the rest of the deck seemed to be medical support and equipment to support the cryogenic process. This was so interesting. It was astonishing how all this could have been done in less than four years, but I held my questions.

Decks five and six were dedicated for use as green rooms and apparently housed samples of all forms of plant life on Earth. Food for the awake-crew would be grown here and oxygen generated for life support. Of course, the ship would have to be self-sustaining for two hundred years.

We continued through the ship, deck after deck, and I was incredibly impressed with the facilities provided on-board to support life, both on the voyage and at New Earth. The best of the best was the top deck. This is where I will be. This deck will be the master control center for the entire ship with a console curved partly around the center section facing the front. Just how anyone would know what was the front on a perfectly round saucer, was beyond me, but there it was. I saw huge dome frames for windows but only more metal filling them. Linda must have read my mind and explained that the metal would become translucent when the ship was active. I really didn't understand what she meant by active, but again I held my tongue.

Behind the console and directly positioned in the center of the room rested a semi-circular dome of the same type metal used in the ship. Come to think of it, it was the same metal everywhere, although the colors varied. The dome looked like an upside-down silver salad bowl. They didn't seem to want to discuss the dome other than to say the on-board computer was housed in the dome. Hey, that's me!

We spent the entire day touring the ship and it seemed we just barely covered a small portion of it. I would have liked to see more, but my medical doctor put an end to the tour because of concerns with my stress levels. The medical doctors were constantly coming to check me out, feed me, or perform some check or service. I had never had doctors do all these things; it had always been nurses before. I can't say I really minded, since I could not care for myself, and I was getting tired. We ended the day with a promise to continue the tour again soon.

Genesis Log: 18 June 2015: (Transferred from journal of Capt. Nick Johns)

My log entry is going to be short today. I woke up sick. The doctors said I have been doing too much, and I spent the day in my hospital bed. That's a hell of a way to spend my birthday; I turned 33 today.

Genesis Log: 19 June 2015: (Transferred from journal of Capt. Nick Johns)

My main doctor came in this morning and said, "Well, you are doing much better today. I think

26

today it is my turn to have you. Are you ready to hear what you volunteered for?"

I have been so busy since my arrival that I haven't thought much about it. Maybe, subconsciously, I was trying to avoid this discussion. It was inevitable, so I took my first really good look at him. I had briefly been introduced. His name was Dr. John Rossen, but I didn't know much more. Physically, he was impressive... tall, dark hair, dark eyes, and lean with a prominent nose. He had a deep resonant voice that made me want to listen. Like I said, he was impressive. I was to later learn that he was one of the top in his field, which, as it turned out, included many fields and advanced degrees. In addition to numerous medical specialties, he also has doctorates in biology and computer science. This was one smart individual.

Like he said, this was his day with me, and he was anxious to get me indoctrinated, or maybe just to sell me on the concept. At any rate, he wheeled me to the secure room where there were several others of his team. Dr Rossen, much like Dr. Kim had done, went into a formal presentation.

It seems that he and his team had been working on the human brain computer interface technology for years prior to the current crisis, and they were one of the first external teams brought into the fold, so to speak. Their challenge was to develop the on-board computer and control network for the deep space flight. Due to the complexity of the requirement, sheer volume of data to be stored and accessed, need for the network to be self-maintaining for centuries, etc., they needed the best of everything they could get. Out of necessity the computer had to be based upon living, regenerating human brain cells. That in itself was not a major problem. Scientists had already developed the technology of a human brain cell central core computer, and direct neural interface or a brain-machine interface (BMI) technology. It was just a matter of bringing all the different technologies together.

Dr. Rossen went into great detail explaining the various challenges and how they solved them. He talked about neocortex, biocompatible silicone threads containing living human brain cells, qualities of self-renewal and adaptability of brain cells, synthetic blood. On and on he went. I was following in general, but the concept was all I really wanted, and I was anxious. Finally, I just said, "Please, just sum it up and tell me where I fit in." I think I ruined about three hours of his presentation, but he did cut to the chase.

Dr. Rossen said, "Okay, you are a bottom-line kind of person. So be it."

He then went into elaborate detailed and personal applications of the project. They had already developed the on-board computer and had it completely interfaced with virtually everything in the ship. Everything was engineered to be computer controlled and automated, but the computer could not learn or think. It was not self-aware...alive. The computer could make decisions, but where that might lead over time was unpredictable. The computer would need to be self-aware for this to happen, and the only way that could happen would be to interface a human, and the only way to do that was use a human brain. It couldn't be just any human brain because most would go crazy under the isolation and strain. It had to be one with all the human qualities the human race found desirable, such as purpose, loyalty, dedication to serve a greater goal, and above all, this brain would have to be mentally sound and stable. All could be destroyed if the central brain chosen could not accept the isolation over the long trip. It seemed that was my major attribute. I had remained sane under the strain of isolation and immobility from my injuries.

As he explained, I was awed and completely mesmerized. My brain would be surgically removed and placed into the existing master computer brain. Multiple silicon threads would be used to interface my brain with the huge extended brain. It was not necessary to connect my brain to everything. That was already done. All they had to do was connect my brain, well, me. I would still be me, but much more. As my brain naturally expanded and reached out with more permanent connections, I would be aware of more and more. I wasn't ready for the fact that my intellect would increase exponentially as the massive external brain became an extension of my own. All the information I had been receiving was only to give me an understanding of the situation, because in reality, it was quite unnecessary. Once I was interfaced, I would know everything already stored in the computer and available, actually becoming an extension of my mind.

What I liked was the fact that I would no longer be a prisoner in my own mind. I would be able to do things through what Dr. Rossen called cyberkinetics. My mind could tell machines to do things and it would happen. He said that, in essence, is how a body works anyway... your mind controls the muscles. In this case I would be controlling an entire ship and everything in it. I would be able to see with many eyes (cameras), hear, smell, feel, speak, taste; only the imagination limits the uses, and the team had an abundance of imagination. I was really getting excited and beginning to lose my fear. My next question to him was, "When?"

Dr. Rossen looked hard at me and said, "Well, we can move you to the Genesis tomorrow. The ship has an excellent medical facility, and we can do the surgery in three days."

Crap, I wasn't expecting it that soon and asked, "Why so soon, Doc?" I felt more comfortable using doctor or doc instead of John. It somehow seemed right with a medical doctor.

He responded, saying, "The scheduled launch date of the Genesis is in one month, and we want as much time as possible to fine tune the system, if needed. The consensus of the scientists is that the secret of Armageddon will be out within two months and we want to launch before that time"

I wasn't aware time was that short, but my main question I shot back, "What happens with fine tuning or problems after we launch? I mean, two hundred years is a long time."

"Yes, I know. That is why most of my team will launch with you, and when we aren't needed anymore, we go into cryogenics until we land. Of course, if I am needed, all you have to do is wake me up."

Oh my, it all clicked then. That is why those I have met so far are young. They are going with me. It made sense. The second phase of The Genesis Project is to colonize New Earth, and their expertise will be needed.

Genesis Log: 20 June 2015: (Transferred from journal of Capt. Nick Johns)

I spent the night in fitful dreams thinking about all the information I had been absorbing. I was both afraid of the last step and excited at the same time. I had already committed myself, and there was no turning back for me. I would do this.

They had me up early, and I was bathed, shaved, groomed, fed and dressed. I always hated this part. It was the worst part of the day, making me aware of just how helpless I was. I kept going over how it would be not to have to be cared for like a baby and gaining some measure of control over my functions and dignity. I guess it would be far better than that... the whole ship would be my arms, legs, eyes, ears... my body. Dr. Rossen was good to his word and had me moved to the medical ward aboard Genesis. About mid-morning Dr. Rossen came in accompanied by another gentleman I had never met before. Oh wait, I did meet him before, back in San Diego. He was the two-star Marine Major General that brought the government suits to draft me.

The general was not in uniform this time, but he needed no uniform to assert his authority. He was not overly large, maybe 5' 10" and 190 lbs, but he was a rigid and an imposing man in his mid-forties. You knew he was in charge. His green eyes were piercing and accented by hard facial features and a taut solid jaw. His close-cut red hair was slightly graying, but it seemed to add to his radiated strength. He wore a blue uniform jumpsuit with a gold and red Genesis emblem over the pocket. The uniform was quite striking.

He introduced himself, "I am Major General McCullah, and I am the director of this facility and this project. My job is to see to it that all these whiz kids get the job done on time. I am sorry I haven't been here to greet you and meet with you, but pressing business took me to D.C. I am also sorry that I somewhat deceived you when we first met, but the president wanted the honors. I trust it was okay with you to hear it directly from the president. I wanted you to know this was for real. You might also be interested in knowing that I personally chose you from the list of recommendations. I wanted a U.S. Marine, not some Columbia or NYU educated socialist. Sempre Fi!"

Needless to say, I was impressed. There was no bullshit in this man, and he talked direct and was not one of those politically correct mealy-mouthed assholes. I liked him from the start.

Dr. Rossen then wheeled me to the control room, which was several decks up. He mentioned that there was an elevator system, but it wasn't used when air locks weren't required. The elevator maintained air locks between levels, which made it much slower than using the ramps.

When we reached the control room, Kim and Linda were already there. It seemed a little strange to be calling Kim by his last name, but I simply couldn't pronounce his first name. The general closed the entrance and turned on the secure muting, making it safe to talk about sensitive subjects within.

The general said, "I have been briefed on your indoctrination so far, and you need to know more, mainly, our destination, additional information about the ship, technology, and plan for success. We will let Linda start off, since the ship is mostly her baby."

Linda started almost where she left off two days ago. She obviously enjoyed what she had accomplished. Too bad that it was the end of the world that gave her this opportunity to excel, but excel is what she did.

She felt more comfortable in this secure room, but even so, she couldn't help looking around the room before she started speaking. This made it even more dramatic, and I knew I was about to hear something remarkable.

Linda said, "Much of the technology I used to build this ship was learned from aliens. We have been studying alien spaceship technology since the mid-forties, and yes, there really was a crashed alien flying saucer recovered from Roswell, New Mexico. Of course, I haven't been involved since the beginning, but I have benefited from all the previous research. We have learned a great deal, and we have been filtering out much of the technology learned over the years, such as advanced computer technology currently in common use today. There have been many discoveries secretly released but many more held back, some of which we employed in Genesis."

The general injected, "Profits from the released technology paid for most of this project, and these companies are happy to work with us. With doom upon us, we haven't observed certain proprieties." There were chuckles emitted from the group.

Linda then got very technical, and it wouldn't mean much to quote her; I certainly didn't understand much of it. The information was very interesting, what I understood, and somewhat shocking. She started in talking about the ship and that it was built with what they called Polly Metal, which was not in truth metal at all. It was actually a chemical polymer form of metal. It was harder than any known substance, even diamonds, and lighter in weight than any metal.

The team studying the Roswell saucer had been unable to analyze the metal because they could not drill or file off a sample to analyze. It was virtually indestructible. It was not until they found a maintenance kit containing the various unmixed polymer compounds in liquid form that the scientists were able to make a breakthrough. In this form they were able to break it down and reproduce it. I really didn't know what a polymer was until she explained it, but basically it is a very complex string of fifty or more molecules, like beads on a string which, when combined in the proper amounts and sequence, form the resulting Polly Metal. She said it was, in essence, a liquid metal that could be poured in molds or spread like mortar. The beautiful part about working with it was that it could be molded and worked after it hardened. It required special tools of extremely high-frequency voltage modulated with complex tones to make the Polly Metal malleable.

Once they discovered the nature of the technology from a tool on board the saucer, it was relatively easy to duplicate. They had manufactured various hand tools that allowed cutting, melding, smoothing, but that it was an easy task, almost like working with hot wax. I was amazed. Now I understood why I never saw any bolts or seams, and the surface was always smooth like glass.

The next most impressive quality was the properties it possessed. By varying external factors such as shape, configuration, voltage and frequencies; Polly Metal could be made to do almost anything. Virtually everything on board ship was made from this magical material, including windows, flat video monitors... almost everything. I thought back to the window frames I had noticed two days earlier and looked again to see only metal within the frame outline of the external windows.

Linda saw me looking and said, "Yes, those are windows. This whole dome is a window actually. Those are very strong windows and when the ship is active, the exciters can be adjusted to make Polly Metal (PM) completely translucent. Amazingly, PM is clearer than the purest glass. Its characteristics are almost like magic. I had a hell of a time keeping the technicians from calling it Wonder Metal for obvious reasons. I am quite sure they still do when I am not around."

General McCullah interrupted to say, "I think we better call this a day. We still have so much to go over that we will need another day, so let's get

Capt. Johns taken care of and meet here again tomorrow."

He didn't wait for an answer, and I welcomed the break. My mind was spinning, but I knew I would be dreaming about Wonder... Polly Metal tonight.

Genesis Log: 21 June 2015: (Transferred from journal of Capt. Nick Johns

Oh my, this was another day for revelations, and it started early with the arrival of Dr. Rossen. My care team had me up early and ready when he arrived. Dr. Rossen and I were becoming close. We had been spending time together just talking about life. He seemed very interested in my war experiences before my injury, and I welcomed his interest. I think he had some hidden interest, but I didn't mind.

At any rate, he was early and wheeled me up to the control room, where Kim, Linda, and the general were already waiting. We were all becoming comfortable with each other and much of the conversations now included some joking and bull shit in between the more serious parts.

The general finally said, "Let's get down to business. Linda, why don't you continue with the other properties of Polly Metal and then move on to the propulsion system. If we have time afterward, Kim, you can describe the deep space flight."

Linda went into her instruction mode again and spent hours going into detail about many subjects, which I will try to summarize.

36

The research on the polymer metal had progressed quickly once they found the maintenance kit in its basic forms. With this formula established and used as reference, the research teams had been able to decipher other formulas from the alien computer. They discovered many other compounds with some very surprising benefits. Some versions conducted electricity better than platinum, while the main basic polymer (P-01) for the ship was an absolutely perfect insulator. The result was that grooves could easily be notched in P-01 insulated metal and filled with a P-02 conducting polymer or simply imbedded in the original pour of the P-01 basic. The result was electrical current without any form of wiring. I found that amazing.

It got better... much better. They had identified and manufactured some fifty different compound variations, each with its own special benefits, but I got the idea. They could get almost any results they desired. Would you believe they had a metal that generated the lighting on-board the ship? I looked up at the ceiling to behold the wonder. I was surprise that I had not noticed before, but the entire ceiling and part of the walls simply radiated light.

Okay, it really started to get crazy now. As with all the composites, each had special properties, although many had common properties. It was like breeding and genetics: all animals breathed air, had legs, ate food; but then some flew in the air, or walked on four legs instead of two. Well, not all animals breathed air, some breathed water, but technically they all used oxygen. You get the picture though. That is sort of how I understood the use of Wonder Metal. No wonder they called it that.

I think I would have called it FMM, Fucking Magic Metal.

Another feature of one of the polymers was its ability to radiate a gravity field. The amount and direction was subject to external control. Linda explained that within the ship, even in deep space, there would be artificial gravity. A secondary use was for a shield surrounding the outer hull. The gravity field was radiated outward and used to repel small meteorites and also filter out any harmful radiation. This artificial gravity in another application was electronically spun around the outside of the circular wings to create a virtual gyroscopic stabilizer for the ship. I was starting to get the picture and realized, even before she told me, that this might be part of the propulsion system. Even I could see that repelling forces of gravity could be used for propulsion.

I think she read my mind and said, "This is not the main propulsion system, but is used for lift-off and maneuvering within the atmosphere and the gravitational pull of a planet. It is only useful when there are objects of mass with gravity to push from or attract to. No, the propulsion system is much more complicated. We use Light Wave Propulsion, but it is designed using the same material."

The general spoke up then, "Actually, the Light Wave Propulsion (LWP) was not alien design. Our own Linda Clark came up with the idea, and Dr. Rossen developed the computer design to make it work. In some cases we were smarter than the aliens."

My opinion of the team soared as I looked at them anew. Linda flushed a little with the praise and tried to steer the conversation away from herself. I am sure Kim was equally accomplished to be here. I wondered just how many were considered part of the main team.

Anyway, Light Wave Propulsion was complicated, but the theory was relatively simple as she explained it. She compared it to magnetism and how opposite poles attract and like poles repel. That made sense.

Light has a frequency, a very high frequency that falls within our visual spectrum. To understand the principle of LWP you must relate to magnetism and the movement of pulling or pushing of lines of flux. If light waves can be matched in frequency and level and forced to combine in a matrix medium, a predictable effect takes place. By varying the levels and phase of the internally generated light source, it is possible to create an effect such as demonstrated in magnetism. An attraction or repulsion force, determined by the level and phase, creates momentum. In this case light waves travel at 186,282,397 miles per second or light speed, which is the forward momentum of the outside source light. A secondary internal light source can be adjusted to repulse against the external source energy, forcing the mixing matrix, the ship, forward pushed by the source light energy traveling at the speed of light. Theoretically, the propulsion generated would reach, if not surpass, the velocity of the source, which is the speed of light, thus Light Wave Propulsion.

Oh, and guess what the blending matrix is? Yep, Wonder Metal! The polymer absorbs light from outside and from an internally generated light to be amalgamated together in a matrix forcing a reaction, in this case forward momentum. This would obviously be the entire hull of the saucer. In all likelihood, the saucer would glow from the reaction. What a sight that would be.

That was the simple explanation, but actually accomplishing this requires an elaborate collection and mixing process from a multitude of isolated panels designed within the solid hull. By controlling the individual panels and combining phase and magnitude, light could be absorbed from multiple direction and inverse propulsion directed. This is where Dr. Rossen's program came into play.

There was a downside, however. LWP would not provide forward momentum directly facing the light source, like a sailboat cannot head directly into the wind. The solution was to take a zigzag course, like a sailboat does, assuming this was ever required.

All in all, I was quite awed, but I did have a burning question that I had to ask, "I didn't think there was light in deep space. What happens then?"

Kim said, "Now that is an excellent question, which brings us into some of my expertise."

He went into some very detailed explanations, which, again, I am summarizing. As it turned out, I was completely correct. There is insufficient light in deep space for Light Wave Propulsion to work, but the way he planned the trip it wouldn't matter. LWP was not needed once the ship reached light speed. Once the ship reached light speed it would continue virtually forever, but he planned on coming out of light speed at ten separate predictable locations, always at chosen solar systems. By dividing the total distance into shorter segments, the margin of course error would be reduced. Each star would provide the LWP necessary to re-launch with new recalculated heading to the next planned stop. Damn, these guys had thought of everything. The general was right; they were whiz kids for sure.

Another day was gone and we decided to meet again tomorrow, but I could tell the general was getting a little anxious, and there would not be many more days wasted in talking, I was quite sure.

Genesis Log: 22 June 2015: (Transferred from journal of Capt. Nick Johns

The same group met again in the control room and Kim led off. His goal was to cover the destination and space flight. It was very informative, also.

Our destination was a solar system named Alpha Pavonis. He gave the coordinates, but it sounded like latitudes and longitudes. I guess it was... just not the kind I was used to.

This solar system is 180 light years away and, including travel time within the solar systems at below light speed and jump delays, the trip was projected to take just over 190 years. Kim had chosen ten jump spots to coordinate with bright stars that were similar with our own sun (Sol). The next bit of information really shocked me. He said this was necessary because suns differed in color and, therefore, actual frequency of the light. This would complicate the process of exactly matching frequencies. To minimize this problem he had chosen Earth-like suns, as close as possible.

I asked, "Why can't we use light speed all the way?"

Kim responded, "Distance and asteroids!"

He went on to explain that traveling at light speed would be disastrous if we collided with any matter or object. It must be used only in open deep space clear of potential obstacles. He talked about planets, moons and asteroids within a solar system orbiting around the star.

Kim said, "There is a concentration of asteroids orbiting our sun between the orbits of Mars and Jupiter, closer to the orbit of Mars. There are 3,000 catalogued asteroids in this belt, and the risks are too great."

"Additionally, it is critically important to come out of light speed close to a star, and distance increases the error potential. In truth, we can't come out of light speed without the reverse propulsion of a star. We would simply continue on course without a means of changing course. So, we use LWP in jumps only in open space."

I said, "Okay, I get the picture, but I have another question. How do you know this New Earth is there and compatible for human life?"

All three of them contributed to the answer. They discovered information about it in the alien computer data. It might not have been deciphered were it not for information also stored about Earth. The aliens had been searching for habitable planets for God only knows how long, but had only found Earth and one other. Fortunately, they had recorded data on the other habitable planet complete with pictures.

There could be others, but the aliens obviously hadn't found another. At least this one existed and became a known target. The planet had less water over the surface, but the temperature, air and gravity seemed comparable. The data showed no advanced life forms, but they could not determine how old the data was. For all they knew it could be hundreds of thousands of years old, but it appeared to be a virgin planet just waiting for us.

The solar system apparently had a close sister solar system that provided dual suns. Of course one of the suns was much farther away, but still bright enough to keep New Earth in varying degrees of sunlight during its entire rotation.

I faced a quick moment of panic. I thought, oh my, this is too much. I can't do this. How could I ever learn all these things I need to know and be expected to run the project in space?

Dr. Rossen must have noticed my panic and said, "Don't worry, Nick. You will know all these facts once you are integrated into the network. Actually, you will know everything programmed into the computer, including our research." He chuckled and continued, "You won't even have to study and learn it like we did. In reality, that's not fair." Again he laughed, and the others joined in.

Dr. Rossen continued, "General, we don't really have to be doing this at all. Capt. Johns really will know everything once he is hooked up. I know we are just trying to give him some comfort, but I think he is ready, and this time would be more productive with John in place." He then looked directly at me and asked, "You are ready... aren't you, John?"

Oh crap! I had already agreed and committed myself, but I was at the point of no return. If I say yes, that means cut my brain out and throw my body away. I couldn't run now if I wanted to. Somehow I found that funny and laughed with my newfound bravado and said, "Hell, yes! Damn the torpedoes, full speed ahead."

The general looked pleased with my answer and gave me a very respectful nod as did the others.

The general said, "So be it. I am glad I didn't have to push, because my trip to D.C. was disturbing. Some of the senators are starting to ask questions about us and what we are doing. The president is not about to tell the bastards anything, because they can't keep a secret. The president believes some members of congress are discovering the truth on their own, and all hell is about to break loose. I have used virtually every major company or corporation to supply various parts and services for this project. With some I spent taxpayers' dollars and others I promised patents. That alone would get me in trouble and get them looking. Bottom line - time is up."

"You should also know that I have already relocated my one hundred combat specialists within the final complex perimeter just in case they are needed for exit security. As of now, no one is allowed access to the ship area without direct approval from me. There could easily be panic at the end."

As he stared at me, he said, "There is only one thing left to do."

This last little speech revealed much. The general was going along, and he was bringing

44

soldiers. It was obvious he expected trouble, and now that I think about it, it was reasonable to assume this fact. After all, this was the last and only lifeboat leaving a sinking ship. Luckily, few knew the ship was sinking yet, but that was changing.

Genesis Log: 23 June 2015: (Transferred from journal of Capt. Nick Johns

This is my last log entry for a while. I hope it isn't the last one ever, though. Dr. Rossen and his team will do the surgery in the morning to remove my body. Somehow that sounds better than removing my brain.

If I am honest with myself, I am scared shitless. When I tackled the terrorist with the bomb, I didn't have time to think... I just did it. This time I have had too much time to think, and it is making it hard. My body is quivering with fear, but I will do my duty.

Late in the evening a Navy captain entered my room. I immediately noticed the cross on his lapel and recognized him as a chaplain. He was a tall, medium-built man in his late thirties with dark hair and olive complexion. His brown eyes were soft and gentle, radiating compassion.

He said, "Hello Nick, I am Capt. Klein, Chaplain of the Genesis, but you can call me Calvin."

Before I thought, I blurted out, "Calvin Klein, like the underwear?" I was never very subtle. Calvin burst out in a hardy laugh that was infectious and quickly had me laughing with him.

Still laughing he said, "Yes, just like the underwear. I am going to like you." Sobering, he continued, "Dr. Rossen suggested that I come and talk to you. He said you were feeling a little nervous. I have to admit, I would be too, but this team is very competent and confident that this procedure will work. I also believe that God would not let his great work be destroyed. I believe the Genesis is God's modern-day Ark to save his creations. If so, you must be his Noah, and he will not allow anything to happen to you."

I am not a very religious person, but somehow his words made me feel better. I guess I do believe in God, but I had not practiced any formal religion since I was a kid. The things I have seen in war and life didn't lend much to exposure to God, and it is hard to believe when you never see him.

I decided, however, I would take all the help and comfort I could get. If God still worked miracles, I didn't want to miss out. Calvin prayed for me and the project, and I finally slept in peace.

Chapter 3
(Alive and More)

Genesis Log: 26 June 2015:

I'm alive! The realization came slowly, like dawn slowly pushing the dark back. I became aware of noises slowly increasing and forming into meaning, but somehow they sounded a little different. With increased clarity came the realization that I was now conscious and must now be installed in the computer network. A moment of panic flashed in my mind until I realized that I survived.

The last thought I remember was fear, serious mind-numbing terror. That was just before the drugs kicked in and I sank into the dark abyss. I had never been so scared in all my life when they wheeled me into the operating room. I kept thinking, "Holy crap, I am letting them take my brain out, and they can't put it back. It's over. Thoughts of an autopsy flooded my mind, where the doctors saw the top or your skull off and pull the brain out. After a while it became a fleeting dream drifting away, then nothing.

Dr. Rossen's voice filtered into my awareness. I kept hearing him say, "Capt. Johns, can you hear me? Can you hear me? If you can hear me, speak to me."

Without any conscious thought about what I was doing, I spoke, "Yes, I hear you." I also heard my own voice, clear and resounding. Cheers erupted from the team, which surprised me, and my eyes jerked open. At least it felt like they did. I found myself looking slightly down on those gathered. It seemed that my vision was incredibly clear and focused as I watched them stare at me, or what must be me in the dome.

Again the doctor asked, "Can you see me?"

I nodded, but he didn't respond. I spoke again and said, "Yes, I see you." Again the cheers rang out.

Dr. Rossen said, "Good! The surgery went well, and you are connected into the life support system and interfaced into the computer, and everything is perfect. I just need you to rest and let the healing begin. It shouldn't take but a few days; then you can slowly begin exploring the computer. Your mind will figure it out quickly enough, so don't worry. Your days of instructions are about over. You will probably be teaching us soon."

That was two days ago, and I have learned so much since then. At first I felt little difference. I was simply me, the way I had always been, at least in my mind, but it seemed that slowly I was sensing more. I began seeing more, seemingly outside my own mind. Tentatively I could raise an invisible wall protecting me, my mind, and look beyond the barrier. It was amazing what I was seeing, and just as amazing that I could withdraw back within myself when I became dizzy or uncomfortable.

My eyesight was one such amazing example. Through outside computer programming, Dr. Rossen had limited my sight to only one vision center. He was careful not to disorient me too quickly. I use the identification of vision center as a way to describe it. There are actually two cameras

48

slightly offset to completely correspond and replicate my eyes. The vision center followed the instruction my mind would have used for my own eyes. I could move my gaze in every direction, even directly behind, and my vision automatically focused on what I was looking at, but it got better. With a little experimenting and practice, like learning to use a special muscle, I discovered that I could zoom in and out on anything, and it was always in perfect lighting and focus. I also discovered that, with effort, I could move the eyes in different direction in a full 360-degree range, but that made my head spin, and I quickly reoriented them to track together.

As I continued to experiment, I discovered that I could switch vision centers to thousands of others throughout the ship. I discovered this accidentally when I mentally blinked my eyes. When I used that response, my vision center switched to other locations, but when I thought about my original visual center, it changed back. There seemed some correlation to computers in that there were some hard Yes/No functions, yet my thoughts would override the computer programming. It was like my brain was learning and creating its own connections and thought processes and teaching the computer at the same time. Amazing! Now I understood what Dr. Rossen was trying to create and why he needed a human brain. The potential was astounding.

Once I began to find my way around in the computer maze, I created my journal again as a computer file and will have my original file entries transferred. I guess a simple download would work. Even learning how to make these entries was

49

inspiring. At first I thought letters and they entered like typing into a computer, but it soon progressed to thinking words, then the thoughts flowed into typed entries. This is the best of both worlds. I actually think this new brain would have recorded as a memory of thoughts and emotions; but I am a creature of habit, and a computer file is easier for someone else to find and read.

Genesis Log: 27 June 2015:

At some point I must have slept, because I suddenly became aware of Dr. Rossen and the general. One of them must have spoken to me, or maybe I simply became aware, but I was awake and looking at them. It must have been the general that spoke before, because he seemed to be looking directly at my vision center and spoke again.

"Good Morning, Capt. Johns. Doc says everything went extremely well. How are you feeling today?"

I meant it when I said, "I feel very well." I couldn't remember ever feeling this alive.

Dr. Rossen asked, "Did you sleep? I wasn't sure if sleep would be required in your new body."

Before I could respond, the general interrupted, "Enough of this chit chat crap. We are running out of time. Capt. Johns, the doc tells me you now have the ability to communicate and monitor world-wide communications. If you have not already discovered how, I would suggest that you learn it quickly. The world is now aware of the asteroid and the pending doom."

"The French could not hold back any longer. It seems the French government is so corrupt that secrets flow out of them like a leaky bucket. They lost their nerve under pressure from the bureaucrats and made the announcement early this morning, and that useless fucking U. N. immediately followed suit claiming a U.S. cover-up. The world is doomed, and the stupid bastards are still playing politics. Damn them! The world is already heading toward a sociological breakdown, and it won't take the world long to put one and one together and figure out what we have been doing here."

"This morning I put the whole base on alert, and I pulled the ship security team back within the final security barrier. All non-passengers have been expelled from the immediate area. I tell you, Capt. Johns, it's a good thing the news didn't break a week earlier."

I was in total shock, but I understood how desperate the situation was, even more so now with my intellectual boost. I started to ask when we would have to take off, but I realized that I didn't want to take off until the last possible minute. There were things I needed to check out and learn. Once we left, there would not be any re-supplies. This was our one chance to get it right, and I needed the time. I told him, "I understand, just give me as much time as possible to analyze any final requirements I might have." He kind of looked at me peculiar but nodded and left with Dr. Rossen trailing behind him looking somewhat terrified.

After I responded, I realized that this was the first time I had actually demonstrated any sort of need or authority. No wonder the general seemed shocked, but he was no more surprised than I. I realized that I just took the first step toward accepting and taking control.

Once I was alone again, I wasted no time in following the general's suggestion. Actually, I spent the day and late into the evening doing so. It was so simple. My mind thought about my desire, and I was instantly monitoring communication... not just any communication, but ALL communications, no matter what language or form. It sounded like a buzz of a million angry bees in my head. In reality there were hundreds of thousands of conversations and appeared as a blur of video and print media. What was more surprising was that I seemed to be following much of the flow, no matter what language. As surprising as that sounds, I understood the concise and extremely concentrated language flowing to me. It was not words or pictures, it was whole thoughts and meaning. I just seemed to understand. Words alone seemed only to be cumbersome and of little use. I had no doubt that my extended brain was deciphering the huge volume, filtering it, analyzing and converting it to abbreviated thoughts before allowing it to flow into my consciousness. So much was useless information, and I learned how to filter it down to only information I wanted. Eventually, I didn't even have to concentrate and could do other things. My brain was learning and controlling the flow of information, or maybe my awareness was expanding and absorbing more of the extended brain into mine. Whatever the case, it was amazing.

It was as the general had said. The world was in chaos and coming apart quickly. Panic was taking over. People around the world were angry and demanding action from their governments. We didn't have much time.

I knew I must be quick to identify my needs, before the madness hit the U.S., so I started analyzing the project. Yes, I needed to ensure my safety and survival. Without me this project was doomed, and so was the human race. I could see that now and understood the brilliance behind the plan. Unfortunately, however, the glaring need I immediately saw was personal defense. There wasn't any! Security aboard Genesis was centered in the security force. I, however, required personal security and the ability to control security aboard the ship. If I were to be in control, I must control the final security. History has always shown that control rests with the power, and I did not have the power. Hell, I didn't have any power!

It also became obvious that the ship was designed by pacifists, because there were no outside defenses or offensive weapons of any kind. Hopefully, we would never need them, but it is insane not to plan for that eventuality.

My first requirement for 2000 hand-held laser weapons and two high output lasers, the biggest we could get, was sent to the printer. I simply would not tell the general my planned use of the small lasers, but they would make a welcome addition to my visual centers.

Genesis Log: 28 June 2015:

As expected, morning brought the full team of the general, Kim, Linda, and Dr. Rossen. I knew the

53

general would be against my use of the hand-held lasers, but I knew he would welcome the larger ones for offense. I didn't know where Kim might stand, but I was relatively sure Linda would be against it. Her liberal Berkley education would assure she was thoroughly indoctrinated with the socialist peace agenda and no weapons. I just let them discuss the pros and cons of the request and offered no explanation. Honestly, I was doing several hundred other things while they were debating. The very fact that they were having the discussion in front of me put me in charge, but I needed to convince them to get the items aboard the Genesis. I waited to see their positions before I spoke.

Their positions were predictable but not all-inclusive. I spoke to get their attention. "I have monitored world communication and, General, your predictions are correct. We do not have much time. You need to get the equipment I require quickly, while money still speaks loudly. I have been listening to you express your concerns. Yes, the large lasers can be an offensive weapon, but there is nothing wrong with that. We don't know what we will encounter. But, that is not the reason I want them. I have analyzed the polymer metal, and it is quite invisible to a laser beam; therefore, there is no need for any heat factor concern. The lasers can fire through the bulkhead without distortion or damage. The units will fit in the engineering level quite well. I have the design worked out if you care to analyze it. There is more than sufficient energy from the reactors to power the lasers. Now, what you don't know is that my design and intended use is defensive. The purpose is for destruction of space

54

debris in our path at light speed, and yes, I have worked out the detection and monitoring system. Now, as far as the rest, we may need the small lasers on New Earth, and we can't go to a store once we leave. Now, if you don't have any other concerns, please get this going while we still can."

Talk about surprise! They were not expecting me to be so assertive, and I had counted on that, even though I had no idea how to exceed the speed of light with radar signals or even the laser beam, since the ship would already be traveling at the ultimate limit of speed. My story and confidence was total fabrication, a lie; but it sounded convincing. The general certainly was convinced, and the others were just confused but offered no further resistance. They only looked at one another and seemed to accept it. Now, I just had to wait and see.

I continued to analyze the design and list of supply inventories. Linda had been thorough in her design and inventory. The ship was powered by two nuclear reactors. One of the reactors was more than enough to power the needs of three ships like the Genesis, and she had installed two, with enough extra parts for a third.

The reactors were of the most advanced next generation design. They used plutonium in a reverse reaction, completely opposite to the action of a standard nuclear reactor. A standard reactor created plutonium as the waste. This new form of reactor actually uses plutonium isotopes as its power source and draws, in essence, from the power of a stored atomic bomb. This is a most efficient and reliable method of obtaining extremely long-term energy...

potentially several hundred years per isotope, and she had extra isotopes. This technology was obviously extremely advanced, probably experimental and custom built specifically for this project.

I would also venture to say that neither the design nor actual reactors were approved by the Nuclear Regulatory Agency. I say this with confidence, since my data indicates that it is decidedly illegal to use nuclear power in space, especially plutonium. It is sad to admit that, had this project conformed to all the bureaucratic bull shit required, they would still be at the paper drawing stage. Even then, it would not be approved.

From the design data, it is abundantly clear that the reactors were built from one of the polymers of Wonder Metal. Yes, that makes sense. No better radiation shield exists, not even lead; and certainly the polymer was stronger and safer than anything previously used. The result was an incredibly compact and versatile unit that took up relatively little space. The unit was obviously safe, since it was already online providing the power to the ship and the outside area as well.

I can't find anything I can improve on at this point as far as the power source for the Genesis. I just want to make sure we load up on the Wonder Metal ingredients. This metal is vitally important for our future survival.

Genesis Log: 29 June 2015:

I must have slept again sometime during the night, at least I felt refreshed and had some blank times in my memory. Every day my mind seemed to expand more. I knew so much I had never learned. It wasn't so much searching into files to find answers. It was more like I simply knew more and could do more, and I thought more deeply and almost constantly. Yet, I was still me... the lonely kid, the patriotic Marine that loved his country and believed in right and wrong... good and evil. I did not want the good of humanity to perish. If anything, I was even more dedicated to this project and would see it through no matter what the personal cost to me. I was adamant that my newfound intellect and power would not corrupt me.

I really didn't have to wait all that long to find out if the lasers would be ordered. I picked up on an early morning telephone call the general made to the CEO of Northrop Grumman. The security scrambling posed little problem for me to decipher. General McCullah could be very demanding, as I well knew Marine officers could be. The worse ass-chewing I ever had was delivered by a Marine colonel. I still cringe when I remember the feeling of total submission to his will.

The general lived up to this level of expectation. He worked his magic on the CEO, and I even felt sorry for the executive. The entire order would be en route by tomorrow evening from their facility in Arizona. We could expect the shipment within three days, and we could safely assume the anticipated societal breakdown would not have begun within this time frame to interfere.

Not only did the general get the equipment he wanted, but also the lasers he talked them out of were of the latest vintage of experimental design... top of the line and very Top Secret. As secret as the experiment was, the general clearly knew about them and demanded the lasers in return for an obscene check and a threat to financially bankrupt the company. The check was useless, and the threat was a bluff, but it worked.

It was publicly known that Northrop Gruman, under contract with Israel and the U. S. Government, completed and tested a weapons grade laser in 2004, the THEL (Tactical High Energy Laser). The THEL laser was capable of delivering a continuous output power in the megawatt range. This latest secret generation laser should be physically smaller with greater output power in the gigawatt range... superior in all aspects.

The smaller units were perfect for what I wanted: smaller and more powerful than anything previously built. Additionally, the two large units were much smaller and more compact than I had originally anticipated from the THEL project designs. From the general's conversation, I realized why. Northrop Gruman had evidently been one of the major defense contractors used to build and supply equipment for Genesis using the polymer metal. I also realized that they had used this technology, unauthorized, in the latest design of the lasers they were delivering. This was fortuitous for us.

This morning when the team came, I was ready. I had many questions for Linda. I met them with a hardy, "Good Morning. How is everyone today?" Pleasant smiles returned as they sat down in their customary places in front facing me. To me it was almost comical. I don't mean this badly. It's just that I can anticipate their questions and concerns. I have been following them as they work and by now, I'm beginning to understand their drives and motivations, not to mention their current projects. My projects must take priority of my time and theirs as might be necessary. My goals were becoming what theirs should be, but they didn't see them.

Our time was short and, although I could not identify any immediate needs, I continued to go over the plan and designs. I had already been planning improvement and projects for myself, but they could wait until after the launch. After all, I have to occupy two hundred years of space flight.

Before they could begin I said, "Thank you for making the proper decision concerning the lasers, and General, you did extremely well in handling the CEO. I am also most pleased that you were able to get the experimental models." The general's jaw actually dropped, leaving a wide-open mouth and surprised look on his face. Both Kim and Linda also looked shocked, I think mostly from the general's reaction. It was Dr. Rossen that surprised me. His face was radiating pride... pride in me! Doc knew exactly what was happening. He realized my intellect was expanding exponentially as my brain slowly absorbed the cells of the once master computer. Now I was becoming the master. After all, this was his plan. I think that at that moment Dr. Rossen became my brother.

I wanted to smile to show my understanding, but of course that was impossible. No, it was possible, and decided at that very moment. I asked, "Dr. Rossen, can you design and program a human video response network for me so I can appear to actually be here with you?" The smile never left his face.

Dr. Rossen thoughtfully said, "Hmmm, yes, I believe I can."

What I liked most about him was his ability to empathize with me and see things from my point of view. I could see the proverbial wheels turning in his head.

My attention turned to Linda and I said, "Linda, I reviewed your designs on the Light Wave Propulsion. I must compliment you on your great achievement." I watched her smile with the praise. Then I asked, "The results are great, but I need to know if you got it all right on purpose or by accident?"

Linda looked surprised and said, "What do you mean?"

I responded, "I see nothing in your notes to indicate that you are aware that the ship enters a new dimension once light speed is achieved, and I see nothing to indicate that you are aware that the artificial gravity must be off during the switch. So, that is why I must ask these things."

Linda was in shock and said, "I have no idea what you are talking about. It is what it is and nothing more. Please explain what you are telling me."

"I am talking about Albert Einstein, theory of relativity, the equation $E = mc2$, finite limits of the universe... and the like." I saw only a blank look on her face. I knew Linda was one brilliant and exceptional lady, but I was understanding far more than she could see. Was this added intellect going to be a curse? I knew then that neither she, nor anyone, would understand the depth I would have to go into explain it, so I gave her the shorter and simpler explanation.

"Okay, Linda, let me explain it this way. It has been theorized and mathematically supported that the speed of light is a finite number. Nothing is faster and everything that exists is subject to this limit. Assume that Genesis reaches the speed of light, then consider your sight for example. Since we have exceeded the speed of light we have exceeded the speed at which we receive vision. As a result, we would see nothing because that signal of vision is effectively behind us. Consider the fact that all functions have reached the finite level beyond which they cease to exist. The atoms cease to spin and everything dissolves. Are you getting the picture?" Oh, she definitely understood this. Linda's emotions were jumping from the fear that the project was doomed to the wonderment of learning something new.

Linda was now concerned and asked, "Are you saying this project is doomed?"

They all looked concerned, so I said. "Oh no, it is not doomed at all. In reality you have all the pieces in place to make it work. You are just not taking it far enough. Let me explain. Each universe has its finite limits, but each universe is part of a bigger universe with its own limits. Let's call these dimensions. Consider the moon as a universe, that universe is part of Earth as a universe, then consider Earth as part of the next universe with the center as the sun. See what is in common here?" I answered it for her... "gravity. A gravity source is the center of whatever universe you happen to be in. When we reach light speed for the first time, we use the sun's gravity as our universe. However, once we achieve light speed, we switch to the universe of the Genesis's gravity. Now we obtain new limits for a universe that is already traveling at light speed. We use the sun's limits as a booster from which we go forward." Yeah, she got it... told you she was smart.

Linda said, "Yes, I see. If Genesis's gravity was on when we first reached light speed we would be stuck in the sun's universe and not be able to switch to the Genesis's universe. We would not have a new universe until we came out of light speed at the next solar system, which would be about twenty years. We would probably all be long dead!" She looked suddenly serious and said, "This means we could exceed twice or more the speed of light by switching universes!"

I saw her logic and said, "Well, theoretically yes, but remember, if we exceeded the second light speed, we would still be in the same situation without a new universe to switch to. And, don't forget that at that point we would not have a light source to propel against. No, light speed is it, maybe a little past light speed, but we have the new limits, which allows us to live and have visual sight within that smaller dimension. Also, don't forget that our lasers and radar will now reach forward on the Genesis during light speed." Kim was in awe, Linda was totally excited now, and the general and Dr. Rossen were smiling.

Linda said, "Incredible! You have taken us into a higher level of understanding...new knowledge." Then she turned to Dr. Rossen and said, "Doc, you were absolutely right with your predictions. Capt. Johns is a new being and has left us behind."

I didn't know what to think about that statement. I still felt the same, but I knew nothing would ever be the same again.

Genesis Log: 30 June 2015:

I began to pick up bits of information from various sources through my monitoring of the worldwide communications. It was just bits of thoughts that would be added to from other sources. I then began researching contractors' past activities, following vast sources of money transfers back to its source and monitoring the activities and whereabouts of acknowledged experts around the world. Finally I was able to identify other secret locations with activities similar to what was happening at Area 51. I identified a location in Japan, another in France, one in Germany that seemed to be affiliated with Russia, and finally, one in China. Of the locations identified, only the Japanese and French activities seemed to have made any significant progress. The activity in France was massively funded by Mid-Eastern money, primarily from Iran. Both of these activities had done extensive financial dealings with many of the same contractors the Genesis team had used. From these dealing, I reasonably assume they have obtained the formulas for Polly Metal and possibly much of the other technology. It was inevitable, even the general knew it was just a matter of time. The important fact was, in all cases, the knowledge of the secret purpose had not been violated. All the activities shared the same fear that they would be discovered before the project could be finished. I have no way of knowing absolutely if any of the others succeeded, but of them all, France and Japan seemed the more likely.

There is no competitiveness, after all, I wish more would have tried and succeeded. At this point, I was thinking about collaborating with them. What do we have to lose? It is too late to worry about security leaks. They are either as ready as Genesis or they are not, but we can't afford to let the general population know or they would storm the facilities trying to get a free ride. That may happen anyway, but hopefully not too soon.

What I decided to do was post a coded message from a secure web address on web sites likely to be frequented by the experts working on similar projects. As I was planning this, the team came for their morning meeting. I decided to take a more direct approach instead. I decided to be up front.

As they settled into their chair, I dropped the bomb and said, "There are others like us." The reaction was profound and immediate.

The general barked, "What! Who? How do you know?"

I had plenty of time to analyze the situation and knew it would not be a problem for us. It could only be good for humankind. That, after all, was what it was all about. I explained what I had been researching and what I had found. The general's initial reaction was predictable, but understandable. He felt violated and was extremely angry. He wanted to attack his contractors for their treasonous actions.

I said, "General, I understand your reaction and under normal conditions I would totally agree, but remember, Earth is doomed and the more humans that can make an escape the better the chances of survival. We should secretly communicate with them and see if there are ways we can learn and help each other. It may be in our best interest and certainly the best interest of the human race."

He was thoughtful for a few minutes then said, "Yeah, I agree, but still the defense contractors are bastards." He chuckled and continued, "I guess they will get what's coming to them. Treason carries a death penalty. What is it that you suggest now?"

I explained about the coded messages I was considering, but offered, "I think you can get some satisfaction by busting those contractors and make them give up their contacts. That way we can contact them directly. That brought a smile to his chiseled face. I think we all laughed knowing how hard he would come down on them.

Kim said, "Our destination probably remains secret. The security on the alien information is locked down hard. Only some of the technology was released and not the star-maps and descriptions. I am most curious to identify their planned destination."

Hmmm, I hadn't even considered that factor, but he was right. I was also pleased that he reminded me of the alien computer and told him, "Oh, thanks, Kim, for bringing up the subject. I want to make sure the alien computer is brought on board and connected into my network."

It was Dr. Rossen that answered, "We have interpreted as much as we can, which is precious little. So far we have been unsuccessful in deciphering its language, but I will see to it that it is brought on board and I will connect the interface personally. Maybe you can crack the code."

"Well, at least it will give me something to do for two hundred years, while you sleep." That brought a laugh. It was nice that we were becoming comfortable with each other. I went on to suggest, "I think it would be a good idea to also stock some precious metals such as gold and platinum. With the antigravity system, weight should not be a problem, only space. If necessary the metal can be melted and fit into any usable space." I saw the curious looks and said, "I am not sure how we will use it, but I am thinking it might create some interesting possibilities mixed with the Wonder Metal to create additional polymers. Besides, we might want to stop at Walmart on the way."

There wasn't much else to discuss. Everyone had projects to do, except me, but I knew I would find my own direction. Dr. Rossen did comment that he was working on the visual display and should have it ready to install in a couple of days.

Genesis Log: 31 June 2015:

While I was waiting for things to happen, I decided to continue my review of the ship's systems. My life support was the first thing on my agenda. I mean, after all, it's my life I am talking about, and I want to live.

As I searched, I found artificial everything. I had artificial heart, lungs, self-cleaning filtering systems, temperature controls, glucose and nutrient feeders, and plastic blood vessels. I even had artificial blood made by some experimental research company in San Diego called Sangart. I checked them out and discovered that my blood was called by a typically obtuse and meaningless medical term of MP4. It did appear more than adequate for use as a blood substitute, and there was an exceedingly ample supply in two storage tanks on the next floor directly below my location.

I can't say I felt comfortable having everything artificial, but Dr. Rossen had chosen well and designed two of everything into the system, just in case. It is comfortable knowing I have a full redundant life support system, even if it is artificial.

When the team came today, I discussed my life support system, expressing my deep concern with the lack of human organs. I had realized several days ago that Dr. Rossen had left my inner ear balance nerves intact, or I would not have been able to decipher up and down. I wanted human organs to function as well as the balance nerves. I could always keep the artificial organs for back up, should that eventuality arise.

Dr. Rossen said, "Capt. Johns, I don't disagree with you, but it would have taken too long to do all the stem cell research necessary to build human organs. We simply didn't have enough time."

The general spoke up saying, "One other reason we didn't do that is the attention it would have drawn from all the damn watch dog groups in the country. If they even caught a hint of what we were doing they would have had teams of attorneys under congressional orders converging on us and our finances. Obviously, we didn't want to draw any unnecessary attention to The Genesis Project, any that we couldn't control that is. Stem cells, cloning, gene splicing, and the like are major taboo subjects."

I could see Dr. Rossen and the others nodding in agreement with the general, and had I thought about it before, I would agree too. I said, "Once we launch, they can't do anything about it, now can they?" Their smiles confirmed their agreement on this. I asked, "Dr. Rossen, I assume you have some of my DNA on file on Genesis?"

Dr Rossen said, "Yes I do. I have several liters of your blood. I even have your organs frozen in storage. I anticipated this subject might eventually come up."

It was my turn to smile; unfortunately they couldn't see it. I knew what we would be doing during the long flight.

Next, I both informed and questioned our security. I had continued to monitor the communication and could tell that the president was under extreme pressure from congress. It was just a matter of time before he would be forced to divulge the secret of The Genesis Project. Already expenditures were being analyzed, and it would lead directly to us. Our secret would soon be out, and I was worried that the Marine security personnel might hesitate to do what was necessary. Would they fire on their friends and fellow Americans if it came to that? I had no doubt that it would be necessary, however. The Genesis was the last lifeboat and the sea would be raging, but the Genesis must be protected at all costs.

The lasers were delivered today, and we skipped our normal morning meeting so they could attend to the unloading and storage. I breathed a sigh of relief, well, figuratively anyway. The general would not let anyone within the final security area, so they were delivered to the security gate. A team of his ship security brought them aboard, and Linda had her team immediately installing the two main lasers.

The main lasers were surprisingly small. The original vintage was almost twice the size, but the general had gotten the only two experimental models. At least no one else would have one of these anyway.

Once I had obtained the specifications, I designed the mounting brackets. Sorry, wrong terminology. Actually, nothing on the ship looked like a bracket. Everything appeared to be of one continuous structure, all flowing together directly into the bulkhead, floor, or ceiling. Even those corners were not at angles... more of a bend. Well, such that they were, the mounting structures were already in place from my design and the bulkhead had been modified to allow the Wonder Metal to become translucent. The bulkhead must be perfectly clear and offer absolutely no resistance to the laser beam.

Even the lasers were made of Wonder Metal, and the mounting structures flowed directly into them. Astoundingly, there were no mounting bolts, clamps, or nuts anywhere to be seen on the ship. Some of the equipment not made from Wonder

Metal was built using standard construction techniques, but that was a rare exception.

I checked the inventory and was pleased to discover that the team also relied heavily on Wonder Metal and had a major supply stored. In the course of 200 years, this supply could be very useful. It would certainly be useful on New Earth. It was not an endless supply, however, and would eventually run out. Hopefully, we would be able to find or manufacture the ingredients on New Earth. I will face that problem when I have to.

I was pleased and comfortable knowing that the lasers were on board. The plan was coming together... part of it anyway. It was time for phase two.

I said, "General, have one of my visual centers installed outside of the ship where I can monitor the gate and perimeter security, and general, have one of the new small lasers installed on it." Wow! His eyes flared and his jaw clenched. He instantly realized the total impact of my original request for the lasers, and he was pissed. I was not sure if he was pissed because he hadn't thought of it or because he realized he had been had. It might have also been because he thought I didn't trust them to do their job. Maybe it was all of the above. It didn't matter, I had known this would come.

The general barked, "Why?" His temper forced the word out a little too loud.

"I want to take on some of the defense responsibilities for myself and assist. Think about it. You and your men will eventually have to fire on a mob and maybe even friends. You know it will come to that just as well as I do. And they will have guns also. When that time comes, you will lose men, but I can hold them back until your personnel are safely on board."

That seemed to get his attention. He thought about it and nodded. Okay, good. I knew the first laser to deploy would be the hardest, but once it was installed, the next ones would be easier. The others were totally uncomfortable with the whole subject and offered no comment at all.

Chapter 4
(Final Days)

Genesis Log: 2 July 2015:

I met the main botanist today, and, of course, it was another doctor. I was beginning to wonder if even the soldiers had PhDs; I wouldn't doubt it. I will have to check it out. Anyway, Doctor Akiko Mitsuhara was a tiny Japanese lady and quite stunning in appearance. Akiko could not have been more than 5' 2" and probably under 100 pounds, but appeared very athletic and definitely curvy. Her long, shimmering black hair flowed halfway down her back. Her smallish round face was split by the darkest eyes you can imagine... black yet bright at the same time. The eyes captivated my attention. Her light, smooth skin accented her dark hair and eyes even more. I couldn't take my focus off of her. She was absolutely gorgeous. Her demeanor was very quiet and soft spoken, but when she looked toward my visual center I saw incredible intensity and intelligence. As she began explaining her area and responsibility, her passion surfaced and became quite evident. I was thinking how suited she was for this somewhat lonely responsibility. I mean, how exciting could it be watching plants grow?

Watching plants grow was a great oversimplification, and I knew it. It is an extremely important responsibility, and the lives of everyone on board, including myself, depended on her and her team's ability to recycle and maintain clean water, fresh air, grow food, provide waste management and all the many other life-support requirements. Two hundred years was a long time to maintain a complete and isolated ecosystem, which is what must be accomplished. Actually, when I thought about her responsibilities, I was somewhat awed.

Akiko is responsible for two entire decks of the Genesis and both are oversized in height, approximately twice the height of the other normal-sized decks. I had viewed the areas through my visual centers on those decks and found myself going back there often to enjoy the tranquil beauty of the thick tropical forest, lush gardens and beautiful ponds teaming with fish, and birds and wildlife of all kinds. Her Japanese heritage found its way into some of the designs utilizing small streams, waterfalls and walking bridges laid out in intricate patterns. Anywhere she could she added a touch of beauty and peppered the landscape with plants and flowers of every color imaginable. After all, an ecosystem required a delicate balance of animal and plant life to flourish, but a little beauty didn't hurt. She even had an abundant assortment of insects. I wish she hadn't brought flies on board, but even those pests served a purpose in breaking down decaying animals. I didn't see mosquitoes on the inventory list, and I was thankful for that. Hmmm, why would I care? They can't bite me now.

As a quadriplegic I had learned to hate the little bastards, because I couldn't swat them. When they attacked me, I would just have to agonize while they had their fill, and this had prevented me from indulging in many summer evenings outside the hospital.

Okay, okay... back to the log. Both decks, one over the other, were circular areas approximately the diameter of the length of a football field. This circular land area on each deck was a full two acres. These four acres were perfectly organized and totally maximized for absolute efficiency.

Of course the main purpose of the ecosystem was to produce oxygen from the plant's photosynthesis process and remove carbon dioxide, which required a total ecosystem to function.

Photosynthesis, is the process of converting light energy into chemical energy by living organisms, and the rate of photosynthesis is affected by the concentration of carbon dioxide, light intensity and temperature. All these factors were controllable with predictable results. Akiko also had built in climate controls. I don't think she could create weather within the decks, but she had certainly tried to simulate rain, humidity, and by varying the temperature and barometric pressure, she could create wind. The desire was to create an environment as Earth-like as possible, and I believe she succeeded.

A review of her inventory of plants and animals revealed an extremely encompassing variety. Not all types of plants were actively growing and not every animal. It wouldn't do to have dangerous animals roaming the internal forest, but like Noah's Ark, she had stored multiple embryos of most every animal, and there were complex storage areas of seeds of every conceivable plant. It was a very thorough and well thought out plan.

The secondary purpose, but equally as important of a requirement of the ecosystem, was

74

the production of food. It looked like the Awake Team would eat very well indeed.

Once we were in deep space there would only be a skeleton crew of about twenty-five maintenance and support personnel, which should be well within the ability of our man-made forest to support. Damn, I just realized I would not be enjoying the taste of food. Maybe in time I can do something about that.

As the general had said, they spared no expense. It made sense, as money would soon be worthless. At any rate, Akiko had brought in tons of rich soil directly from the Mississippi River delta, probably some of the best soil on earth for growing. She also wanted live soil, complete with all the necessary fungi and microbes necessary for healthy plant growth. Equally natural was the water. It was directly out of the nearest, relatively clean lake. Again, she had wanted the natural algae.

As Akiko described her department and long-range cycling plan, I was greatly impressed with her passion. My confidence soared the longer she continued. For someone to appear so unassertive, she had planned well and completed her task in record time. The crew was not completely living off the output yet, because there were too many awake and still working. Akiko, however, was quite confident that her department could maintain life support, and I was quite confident in her. I liked Akiko and her quiet ways.

Not only was she a botanist, but she was also an ecologist, zoologist, and analytical chemist. She knew it all and was typical of the others in the team... she was a whiz kid also. Akiko would need all her skills in this endeavor.

As she was winding down I asked her, "What else do you want?"

Confused, she said, "What do you mean?"

"I know you have everything you need, but is there something you still want or would like?" I don't know why I asked. I just wanted her to need or want something... so I could give it to her like a gift or reward for doing such a wonderful job. I guess I might have also wanted to impress her.

She was silent for a while, deep in thought, and then she smiled and said, "It would be really nice to have some soil from my native Japan. You know... like a part of home to take to a new planet to remind me."

I had to laugh at that request and said, "I believe the general will be greeting visitors from Japan soon. Maybe he can arrange for them to bring some. Would a potted Bonsai plant in native soil fill your desire?"

"Oh yes. That would be really nice. Thank you."

At first the general seemed surprised at my comment, but quickly realized that he actually would be talking to his counterpart in Japan as soon as I provided the contact information.

Akiko had taken up a great deal of time with her passion, but I enjoyed it and gained great confidence from this gentle giant. The others also listened attentively and had little to say at today's meeting. They must have heard it many times before and were still as impressed as I was.

Genesis Log: 3 July 2015:

The world is going crazy! I'm monitoring marches and protest demonstrations of hysterical people on almost every capital in the world. They were voicing their deep concern, fear and aggravation with their governments. Why, I have no idea other than just something to do, but there is nothing to be done. Maybe everyone is thinking about that emergency world-wide, last-resort, heroic, joint effort to save the world, like in all those doomsday movies. Unfortunately, missiles, space flights and atomic bombs will not be able to destroy this asteroid. It is simply too damn big. There is nothing that could be done to save the world... nothing! Those in the know knew it was hopeless from the start, and soon even those demonstrators will realize it, with the help of the news media giving all the facts and even pictures from space. The news media, as doomed as everyone else on Earth, was totally predictable, wanting that sensationalism to the very last, destroying any hope that remained. This, of course, will expedite the fall into total chaos and anarchy. Already about fifty percent of the work force has ceased working, and the remainder isn't far behind. Only the totally dedicated would continue, but even those won't last. The masses will soon take what they need.

Luckily, no world government, especially the United States, has admitted that there is no hope. The president has even alluded to plans in progress. The president is wise enough to realize that if the world has no hope, it will have no laws or resistance to total anarchy. So, he did like any politician would do. He lied and told the world of plans without saying what they were. Hope is a powerful tool.

During the night I was successful in tracking down the Japanese location for their space escape project. It was surprisingly easy. I followed tracking invoices of Wonder Metal (Okay... Polly Metal) and shipping locations. The whole Japanese project is under the direction of, ironically, the National Space Development Agency of Japan (NASDA) and located at the Tanegashima Space Center (TNSC). Its location is somewhat remote at the southern end of the southernmost island of Japan, Kyushu Island. Although remote, the facility is open to the public and even has guided tours. Their space craft is apparently hidden in plain sight. Fortunately, no one would know what they were looking at. Well, maybe they would know it is a space craft, but that is to be expected at a space center. How clever they are! The signature on the checks was Yoshiaki Sakata, from the space center. This is the highest level I can identify that would be positively aware of the project. I provided this contact information in secure communications to the general for his morning review. Then I waited.

Dr. Rossen woke me when he came in. It startled me, so I must have been asleep. My internal clock indicated 1:00 am.

"I have the visual center ready to install," he announced, "I have a surprise for you as well." He paused for effect. "We built a holograph system for you instead of simply a video monitor image. I think you will like it. We wanted to give your visual projection some personality."

"Excellent!" I responded.

It took him a few hours to install all the equipment, and while he worked, he idly talked about the computer program he created to give me realistic facial features. He had computerized all the video and picture data they had of me into the program data base. My actual recorded facial images were used to create the program for my holograph image projection. The body actions would obviously be simulated, but should appear realistic. Likewise, he created a program for my vocal responses. Theoretically, the results should provide a fair simulation of what I had looked and sounded like in the flesh.

He looked at me as he engaged the unit and said, "For better or worse... here we go! Oh, there will be some learning and experimenting to teach your brain how to make it work. So, give it some time."

He had installed numerous small laser projectors around the base of my dome, and they all flashed on at once. At first there was just a slightly blue cloud forming that I realized was under my control. I felt my extended mind slightly straining to control it. Without totally understanding how, my mind began forming an image. Suddenly, there I was, as I had been in life before my injury. The image seemed almost real and to scale. In my prime, I stood a muscular 6' 2", 250 lbs, with short military-cut brown hair, hazel eyes; and there I again stood in all my glory, complete with my Marine Corps dress uniform. That was a nice touch, and I loved it.

I never was what you would call handsome, so I didn't expect much on that account. I prefer the description of rugged, as opposed to ugly SOB that some of my fellow officers called me, in friendship of course... I hope. So, it was no surprise to see a rugged Capt. Nick Johns standing there.

There was a slight translucence to the image, but in all other ways, very lifelike. It was definitely me! I almost felt like I was projecting myself into the image and not just a picture... in reality I guess I was.

Looking at my image was like looking in a mirror as I watched myself smile, blink, frown. Like a child, I was making faces that appeared in my image. I spoke and it sounded like me. When I moved my arms and waved... well, I broke into tears. Seldom have I cried, but the emotions of seeing and feeling myself moving was more than I could take at the moment. I recovered quickly and hoped Dr. Rossen hadn't noticed. If he had he was hiding it. I thought, one day my dear doctor we WILL make this real!

I told Dr. Rossen, "I am extremely pleased. You did an excellent job, and I thank you so very much." I paused, "Thanks doesn't seem enough. This is incredible! I'm impressed." I truly was impressed. The holograph image was completely unexpected, but totally welcome and absolutely appreciated.

My mind continued to play with this new toy and, with some experimenting, I discovered that the image could be reduced to only a bust shot or expanded to a much larger than life image in various forms. I was reminded of the image of the wizard in the Wizard of Oz. It was awesome.

Observing myself from one of my remote visual centers was a little disorienting. The fact that I was watching myself move from a different reference point was somewhat confusing. I found it more comfortable switching back to the visual center at my same reference. The problem then was that I couldn't see myself. Combining both seemed to help. These were all strange new experiences, but no more strange than the other things that have happened to me recently.

By the time we finished testing the holograph extension, it was time for the morning meeting. I was anxious to spring our surprise... almost giddy in anticipation. I let the team get situated before I said, in my new holographic wonder, "Hello, good morning."

The reaction was worth watching, especially Linda. She actually jumped up and almost ran. Kim, Akiko, and Dr. Rossen broke out in laughter, and even the general's face broke out in a smile.

Dr. Rossen spoke up, "Let me introduce you to the new Captain Johns."

He then went on to explain his new invention, much to everyone's excitement, while I hovered over the group letting them admire his work and, of course, my new persona. Psychologically, it was as if I was now with them. Of course I had always been there, but now they had an image to focus on. Yes, this had been a good idea and Dr. Rossen had excelled in the delivery.

Finally, as the group settled down, the general surprised me by announcing, "The Japanese team will be here tomorrow."

Immediately, two options became abundantly clear. I had definitely been asleep to have missed the conversation, or the general had communicated by some form of secure communication designed to see if he could bypass my surveillance. The answer was likely a combination of both, but I had expected the general to attempt to and extricate himself from my monitoring. It was becoming a silent game between us. He was the type of person who didn't welcome losing control, even though the project was designed toward this goal. Time would take care of this, and time was on my side, unfortunately. I would be awake the entire flight.

The general was looking at my holographic image to judge my reaction. This could be a problem, since the doctor had programmed body language into my image. I knew he saw the surprise, and a smug look came over his face. I was annoyed that he felt a need for power, but I remained silent. It really wasn't that important, YET!

The general enjoyed telling the story of the contact. He kept watching me to see my reaction. I really would have liked to have eavesdropped on that conversation. He just dropped the hammer on them about stealing our patented Polly Metal, just to get their attention. Once he had their attention, he informed them that we knew what they were doing. Then he told them what we were doing and asked them if they wanted to collaborate. He took a chance telling them, but it really didn't matter much at this late date. We were ready to go, and it would take a lot to stop us now. The Japanese team jumped at the chance and left for Area 51 almost immediately.

"That is amazing, General." I said, "You really know how to work miracles." In fact, I really meant it. He excelled at getting things done. I almost missed it, but noticed that the general beamed at my praise. Awww, okay. He is starting to feel left out. Now I understood. He needs to feel useful now that his job is almost done. Maybe I misjudged him.

The morning meeting quickly broke up so everyone could prepare for the arrival of the Japanese delegation. I was excited also.

Today was a long and productive day.

Genesis Log: 4 July 2015:

While I had some time, I decided to search through the cryogenic inventory of stored souls. Just who was there? Almost immediately it was evident that some politically correct bureaucrat had compiled the invitation list. If ever the intent was to transfer all of mankind complete with all the social problems, this bureaucrat had succeeded. It also became evident that, as bureaucracies tended to be, some individuals had bought or influenced their way into the escape. There were some in frozen storage that had no purpose.

Beyond the obvious discrepancies, the plan was flawed. Every race was represented in equal percentages to that of the USA, not that that in itself was bad, but they had included every social standing, career, and age as well. How stupid was that? It really made a lot of sense taking up valuable cryogenic storage space with politicians, attorneys, bureaucrats, clergy, and uneducated elderly, or even the young. There were some whose only claim to fame had been collecting welfare. It was like they tried to ensure the new world would continue to have all the woes of Earth. What a missed opportunity this had been! Not only was the storage an identical stamp of a typical American city in people, but also religions, having carefully selected, not the typical, but somewhat radical religious leaders of all faiths. This could definitely be a problem, but what could I do now? Needless to say, I was upset.

It was also obvious that the team had been somewhat successful in influencing the list by including some very gifted experts in the sciences, trades, and academia. Skilled tradesmen were abundant and would be useful on the new world to train a new work force. Educators would also be necessary to teach the thousands of embryos that must be berthed in the nurseries before and after arrival at the new world. This was going to be a major challenge, and it was going to be my responsibility.

I toyed with the idea of thawing out some of the ill-chosen souls, but then what would I do with them? If I let them go they would be angry and go to the media or at the very least, tell everyone they met. No, that would not be a good idea. I was stuck with the fate I had been given and would make the best of it.

The hand lasers, all two thousand, had been stored in a secure area on board, and I had kept watch over them. As a result, I was aware when two of them were removed from inventory and taken outside. Two of the visual centers had already been installed and activated outside of the ship in the security area. Through these centers I watched as the lasers were installed. I ran an internal check to ensure they worked and even test fired one when no one was looking; no one will miss one rat. The lasers would work quite well for my purpose. The general had been true to his word, and I now had input and control of the outside area. The first step in my plan was complete.

Today is the 4th of July, typically associated with fireworks, and this was no exception. Unfortunately, the fireworks were not the good kind. Our counterpart facility in France was discovered and totally destroyed, ironically by the radical Islam population of France. The Islam nation of Iran had funded the space project, but the radicals within the Iranian government viewed Earth's destruction as Allah's will and informed those terrorist cells in France. The pending doom of Earth spurred the radicals to seek martyrdom, and they attacked the facility in mass numbers. Many died but many reached their goal. The attack was successful in destroying the facility, killing the scientists, destroying all hope of escape from that facility.

What a tragedy this had been. Although I was not aware of their plans or destination, they had demonstrated some major progress. It was so unfortunate. Only France and Japan had been successful in obtaining the Wonder Metal. Of all the others attempting an escape plan, France probably had the best chance. Germany and China had little hope of success at this late date. This left only us and Japan with any possibility of success. At this point, I was confident in the success of Genesis, but not so with Japan. I had decided that we should do everything possible to help Japan. Humankind deserved every possible chance of survival.

Genesis Log: 5 July 2015:

About 6:00 a.m. the Japanese delegation's Learjet was on final approach to the runway of Area 51... so much for Area 51 being a secret facility that, for all practical purposes, does not exist. The general had obviously provided the coordinates of the facility, but I strongly suspect the Japanese government knew more about this facility than most of our own politicians. They were escorted through security and into the final barrier to stand in awe in the shadow of Genesis.

I recognized Yoshiaki Sakata of the Tanegashima Space Center (TNSC) from photos on their web site, but there were three additional men in the delegation that I did not know. I assumed they had to be the Japanese counterparts of Kim, Linda, and Akiko. The general prodded them on toward the gangway into the ship, while speaking into his secure radio. The team and visitors could be expected soon. It was my belief that the general would bring them directly to me, because he would be unsure just what to do with them. It had been my idea so he would expect me to pursue the goals, whatever those were.

Kim, Dr. Rossen, Linda, and Akiko quickly funneled into the command center and were just

86

seating themselves when the general entered with the Japanese delegation. Introductions were made around the room. It saved time, that they all gave their name and function in their respective project.

The delegation consisted of Takashi Ishiguro (Life Support & Genetics), Jim Sharp (Engineering & Astrology), Hiroshi Tsuji (Engineering & Robotics), and Yoshiaki Sakata introduced himself as project manager, but it was soon evident that he was quite proficient in biology and botany. So this group had overlapping responsibilities comparable to the Genesis team, but Akiko and Sakata had much in common. With some regret I was thinking those two would get along well. Was I jealous?

The teams began to interface with each other as I observed. As it turns out, Jim Sharp is British and had initially been recruited for this project. He had done most of the design of their ship, with the help of Tsuji. I also found it interesting that Tsuji was one of the foremost experts in robotics. How interesting.

During a lull in the conversation, I took the opportunity to introduce myself. I loved the reaction of my holograph image. I said, "Good morning. My name is Capt. Nick Johns." The Japanese delegation was startled when I spoke, and even Linda jumped again, much to everyone's amusement. After a pause I continued, "I am the captain and pilot of the Genesis. Just so you know, I am very much alive and integrated into the Genesis. In fact, the Genesis is my body." I figured that was enough information to keep their minds busy for a while, and they were deathly quiet for the longest time. "Dr. Rossen can explain more."

The team already knew me as captain due to my previous military rank, but I had just introduced myself as THE captain. As we all know, the captain of a ship is the undisputed authority, and some might relate that to a dictator. I had officially taken control. Well, technically it could not be official until the Genesis was independent of Earth after take-off. The general looked a little disturbed, but he said nothing, and there was no reaction from any of the team members. It was as if this fact was assumed from the start, and maybe it was, except by the general.

For the next few hours, they talked and compared their projects. I mostly remained silent and observed and listened. It soon became obvious that the Genesis Project was far more advanced than theirs. I could only assume this was due to time or financial restraints. It certainly wasn't lack of intelligence. The Japanese space craft they called simply, Hope, was less aggressive and, as such, less likely to survive. They had developed Ion Drive for deep space propulsion to reach their goal of Mars, but relied on conventional rocket fuel and boosters to reach orbit. Even though they designed around rocket propulsion, they had made major advances in size and efficiency and were able to put a sizable ship into orbit. It was far smaller than Genesis but still noteworthy.

Even with Ion Drive in deep space, it would take years to reach Mars, and Mars was not habitable. Their plan was to attempt to terafoam the planet with an algae Sakata had developed that would grow in the Mars atmosphere to produce oxygen. Akiko seemed very impressed with his ideas. Unfortunately, it would take generations to build an atmosphere suitable for human life. It was as I suspected. They were destined for failure.

I wanted them to succeed and survive, which is why I had been thinking about an alternative plan. I planted my idea by saying, "I want both teams to consider an alternative plan. I believe we can develop a magnetic tow in orbit and pull Hope into light speed along with Genesis. We can all go to New Earth." I could see shock in everyone's eyes but also the dawning of realization that it just might work. "I suggest that you give the visitors a tour of the ship and discuss this possibility. Let's meet again in the morning to discuss it."

Everyone was in agreement. The brains were already churning over the possibilities. It was a good plan and workable, and they would come to this realization also.

I followed the tour throughout the ship by switching visual centers, which lasted well into the night. The whiz kids were already deep into the planning and the Hope team turned out to be equally as gifted. They seemed to like the idea. Tomorrow should be interesting.

Genesis Log: 6 July 2015:

My integration into the Genesis extended brain continues to advance. Thinking is far easier now, and I know so damn much without ever having learned it. My mind is also intertwined in virtually everything throughout the ship, monitoring and controlling. It is even becoming difficult to get down to a level where I can talk to the others. The team members are highly intelligent, even genius level, but it is almost like talking to a child. I am always way ahead of them, but I have to be careful and let them work things out for themselves, lest they rebel or become intimidated by me. I will just continue to plant new ideas in their heads and help them along the way. Like this plan! It has some obstacles to overcome, but it can work...they just have to accept it and bring their questions.

My thoughts were interrupted when Akiko burst into the control room.

"Hey, Nick. Look at this. Thank you so much."

She was beaming and holding up a planter with a Japanese Bonsai bush in it. "I got my Japan soil. Sakata just gave it to me."

Of course it was the sentiment of the Japanese soil that excited her and not so much the bush, but together the fact of having the soil seemed less silly.

Her smile was so big, making her pretty face shine. Her dark eyes seemed bigger and more intense. It made me happy to see it, and she had called me Nick! That open display of warmth is what I was pondering. It was said as one friend might say to another, and it pleased me enormously. It would be really pleasant to have friends. I responded with my own holograph smile saying, "You are very welcome, Akiko." She actually sat down, and we simply chatted for a while about menial things until the others came in for the morning meeting. I was happy and realized that I had not had a real conversation in days, and I missed it.

The general led off the discussion, "We have had a full inspection of Genesis and numerous discussions, and I think everyone is excited about the possibilities." It was almost redundant to bring it up. Even the general, if he thought about it, would realize that I had missed nothing. I was with them the whole time switching my monitoring sites to remain in the conversations. Oh well, bringing it up started the conversations.

I ventured forward and said, "So, can I assume everyone is in agreement that we should try?" Of course I already knew they were but allowed them to voice their opinions and make their commitments.

So many details needed to be addressed and worked out, but they were just details. The only real major obstacle that had to be worked out prior to launch was the towing procedure. I had originally mentioned a magnetic towing process, but in further research I had decided against that. It was possible, but I wanted a more direct interface with the ability to physically interconnect the two craft. Even more, I wanted to provide an interconnecting airlock tunnel between the crafts and full communication interface. It would be necessary to be able to monitor the internal functioning of the Hope, along with the Genesis. After all, their flight would now be extended to two hundred years, and they would not have procedures in place to handle that. What's another spaceship to control for a player like me? Ha ha

Fortunately, much of the immediate outside facility at this construction site had used Wonder Metal in its construction. It made sense. The polymer was so incredibly easy to work with, far stronger than steel, much lighter in weight and relatively inexpensive, once the ingredients had been manufactured. It was no wonder the contractors began using it. I had identified an outside water storage tank made of Wonder Metal that was perfect for what I have in mind. The tank was four feet in diameter and thirty feet long. It was as if it had been built for this use. The plan is to use the water tank to interconnect the ships, complete with atmosphere so personnel could move freely between ships. The strength of the Wonder Metal would be more than sufficient for towing, but both ships would need to install the interlock doors prior to launch I saw some surprised looks, even shock, but absolute agreement. They liked the idea.

It would also be necessary to monitor and control the Hope in flight. Linda was quick to mention the communication wiring modification that would be required, and I knew these whiz kids would handle all the details.

There were many more things to discuss, but I had to break up the meeting with some bad news. CNN has just broken the full story worldwide about the asteroid, complete with actual close up video. Somehow they had hacked into the Department of Defense's satellite feed monitoring the asteroid. True to form, CNN informed the world in complete detail of the anticipated impact and prediction of total and absolute destruction, complete with the exact date of impact. They were wrong on the date, of course, like they usually are, but that little fact didn't seem to matter at this point. They even provided the timetable of the approach with graph and live feeds of the asteroid from Palomar Observatory operated by the California Institute of

Technology. The vow of secrecy was obviously over. The thing that really pissed me off was the fact that CNN identified all the various entities that were building escape craft. Again, they were wrong with some of the locations, but they correctly identified Area 51 and Tanegashima Space Center in Japan. The bastards must have some excellent researchers, because they had discovered much, including the names and pictures of many of the top people. Leave it to CNN to be sensationalists to their last breath, but by doing this, they created disaster across the world. Then again, that was more news for them to cover.

I gave a brief description of what had happened and suggested the Japanese delegation head home immediately and be prepared to launch within days before the general public swarmed them. I didn't have to say anything to the general. He was already on his phone beefing up security and closing up the ship.

What I didn't mention was that the president had left Washington on Air Force One almost immediately after the news broke, heading directly to Area 51, and this had to mean trouble.

Genesis Log: 7 July 2015:

It took only a few hours for the president to arrive, but even the president couldn't get through the final security. As I monitored through the outside camera, the general came into view and could be seen arguing with the president. Finally, the president, less his Secret Service, was allowed entrance along with two small girls. I knew

93

immediately that these were his granddaughters, and they would be going with us.

I could see a hostile crowd building behind the President and realized they perceived the President was trying to escape Earth's destruction and save himself. I made my first hard decision! My loyalty now was to the Genesis and its survival.

I called the general on his cell. When he answered I said, "Do not let the president through. If you do you will have mutiny from the crowd."

The general responded by saying, "It's the president, for Christ's sake."

I said, "Tell him you will take his granddaughters, but he, personally, cannot come into the ship. The crowd will swarm the security. We will have a battle, and we need a little more time. You tell him I will shoot him if he comes into the compound!" The general started fuming and stuttering, but I screamed, "Tell him, NOW!" After a moment in silent thought he knew I was right, at least he knew I would do it. I could see him talking to the president and they both turned to see the agitation of the crowd for the first time. The president squatted to hug his granddaughters for one last time and turned back toward his security and let everyone see him leaving. The anger seen before in the faces of the crowd now showed confusion, maybe even pride that the President would remain with them to the end.

I never believed for a second that the President intended to join the exodus, but the doubt created by him entering the ship could not be tolerated. At least immediate danger had been averted.

What happened next completely surprised me and filled me with pride. The crowd followed him to Air Force One, and as he stood at the entrance, he gave an impromptu speech. I recorded it for posterity, and it will be forever remembered as long as the human race continued to live. He explained about the Genesis and thanked them for their contribution. He told them that due to their efforts humanity would survive. I don't know where it came from, but some of the final quotes went like this:

He pointed toward the ship for emphasis and said, "Genesis, we who are about to die salute you! You carry with you our future, our hopes and dreams... all that we are and have ever been. We gave you life, and you are our child and we sacrifice our lives so our child might live. As long as you live we will live in your memory. Like Genesis of the Bible, in the beginning... this is our new beginning. May God bless this new beginning."

"I am not leaving. I will stand with you and defend our child!" He stood tall and erect and full of defiance.

The crowd began to cheer, and I cheered with them.

Thanks to the president, I no longer worried about a mutiny at Area 51. They were now highly motivated to protect Genesis.

I made my second hard decision and paged Dr. Rossen. When he arrived I told him about the president's two granddaughters.

Dr. Rossen launched into a tirade, "We can't just add new people. Everything is carefully balanced into the life support, not to mention, we

95

don't have more cryogenic chambers. It jeopardizes the whole project."

I stopped him saying, "I have a change in plans. We will empty out a few cryogenic chambers." I provided a list on a monitor and printout indicating seven chambers I wanted emptied.

"You can't do that!" He said emphatically, "Two of these people are extremely wealthy people who contributed heavily to the project in the beginning, another is an influential politician and four are black. We will be crucified!"

I forcefully responded, "Who is going to stop me? I am responsible for the Genesis. Just do it! Tell the wealthy and influential to sue me. I also couldn't care less about being politically correct or what damn color they are. I made my choices based on age and redeeming qualities. These people are old, taking up valuable space, and can contribute nothing. Just get rid of them and find some others to take their place... quickly! I take responsibility." It was a hard decision condemning them to death, but it had to be made. This is why they picked me, even if they wouldn't admit it. Someone had to make the hard decision, and that someone was me. I just wished we had more time to clear more out.

Dr. Rossen knew in his heart I was right and left to comply.

Chapter 5
(Exodus)

Genesis Log: 8 July 2015:

The general didn't show the rest of the day. He was pissed and needed time to calm down, but in time he would realize what I did was the right thing to do. He just needed time to simmer.

At the morning meeting everyone seemed normal. The general said nothing about the previous day. He evidently wanted to pretend it never happened, and that was all right by me. The main topic was praises of the president's speech. The president's words affected all of us profoundly, as well they should. It was a great speech with feelings directly from the heart...motivating and inspiring. I vowed it would be remembered.

Dr. Rossen brought everyone's attention back from private thoughts when he said, "I have the new recruits already undergoing their physicals and will have them all in cryogenics by this afternoon."

The department heads secretly applauded my decision to vacate some of the chambers and immediately had replacements chosen, good ones this time. Damn, I wished we had more time. I would just have to make the best of our human inventory.

"Did you have any trouble with those vacated?" I asked. I already knew the answer, but wanted to get it out in the open to see the reactions.

The general chuckled and said, "Mostly they were a little slow to understand, due to the aftereffects of cryogenics. They will be bitching plenty later though, but I don't think they will get much sympathy from the others outside. The rich bastard was lambasting everyone and refused to leave, but I never liked the arrogant SOB anyway and had security drag his ass out past the gate and threatened to shoot him if he came back. The last we saw of him, he was leaving to call his attorney." Everyone broke out in hearty laughter. "The others were moved into the barracks complex. They will have a home until the end."

Linda reported next saying, "The outside hatch has been installed to interconnect to the Hope, and the connecting tube has been fused into the ship's skirt. I had my crew working all night on it. Engineering is ready."

After a pause for thought, I announced, "Okay, group, we launch into orbit tomorrow at noon. Make all the final preparations and countdown for that time. And please, don't be obvious. We don't want it known outside the ship except, of course, the guard." There was total silence. They just looked at each other with the realization that all their hard work and planning was now going to face the test; it was really going to happen. It was a solemn moment, but no one objected. It was time. The president knew it, they knew it, and so did I.

Another thing was becoming obvious. No one was resisting my taking charge. None wanted to make the hard decisions, and I smoothly slipped into the leadership position. Of course that was my purpose, but until just a few days ago, I was a useless quadriplegic in a wheelchair with no particular talents to justify being in command. I knew I was ready now, and I guess they did also.

We had been lucky, but we were out of time. Already, mobs were gathered outside Area 51 and isolated shots could be heard. It was enviable that a full-scale mob assault would be launched, but, hopefully, it would take an incident to trigger it. I hoped it wouldn't come before we launched.

All of the department heads continued to admit readiness, but with the realization of the deadline, their interest soon turned to thoughts of last-minute details and scurried off to attend to them. I was soon left alone with my own troubled thoughts.

Genesis Log: 9 July 2015:

Wow! It has been a long and eventful day. I doubt that anyone on board got any sleep last night. All functions of the ship were checked and rechecked, then checked again. Everything performed perfectly. What surprised me most was the fact that only a very few excursions from the ship were required to load the final supplies required into storage. The whiz kids had done an excellent job.

By 10:00 a.m., all consoles were staffed by the various department heads or their staff, waiting. Although I was now capable of doing everything myself, I allowed them to take charge of the launch. I don't think they even realized that possibility and it really didn't matter since I could always take control if necessary. I actually wanted them to do it as a reward and climax for all their efforts.

Once all systems were active, the pending launch could no longer be disguised. The outside hull of Genesis was beginning to produce a brilliant glow projecting into the sky that could easily be seen by friend and foe. The final indicator was when the security guards abandoned their position and hurried aboard. There was no final panic from the Area 51 workers as I had expected. Some were praying, while others were waving a tearful goodbye. We could thank the president for this. The access hatch lifted and sealed with a clank as the antigravity generators engaged, forcing clouds of dirt and dust to plume into the air. For an instant we felt the extra pull of the artificial gravity until it adjusted. After a moment, we felt the shift of lift-off and heard the landing struts close up with a slight shudder. Everyone aboard cheered!

We hovered briefly as Chaplin Klein offered a blessing, then Genesis began to rise.

As the ship slowly ascended, we watched through the floor cameras and saw the expanding view and eventually the turmoil beginning below outside the perimeter of Area 51. Something was happening! There was a major surge of people and vehicles bulging toward the fence. Guards were firing into the crowd, but what attracted my attention was a large diesel truck racing forward plowing through and over the crowd headed directly toward the fence. As I focused and zoomed the camera image, I viewed a flag flapping in the wind on top of the truck's cab. I instantly recognized the black flag of death with, what we GIs called, a burning white bomb. In Iraq, I had seen this symbol of Al Qaeda many times, and it was never good.

Suddenly, I remembered the destruction of the French spacecraft by radical Islam terrorists, claiming that it was Allah's will that none would escape his wrath and all would die.

Without warning, I immediately took control, focused the gravity repulsion drive to full force, and spurred the Genesis straight up. I didn't care where... just away. The sudden heavy acceleration forced everyone deep into their seats. Almost simultaneously, the dazzling flash below blocked all vision for seconds and was followed by a deafening boom. Genesis just barely outdistanced the concussion of the explosion by seconds, but it was still a rough ride. As we continued to soar away from the explosion, our cameras readjusted from the light shock, and we began to see the expanding ring of death rapidly encompass Area 51 and move in an ever-widening circle into the desert. The mushroom cloud plumed higher as we safely watched from above. I did a quick check of the systems, and luckily there was no damage from the energy burst. The polymer Wonder Metal had shielded us from the EMP (electromagnetic pulse) of the explosion, and we had only narrowly survived. Unfortunately, however, all those below, the remaining workers, support staff, and even the president had perished in an instant.

Those at their stations were finally able to regain control. They had seen and understood what had happened, but had not been able to react under the high Gs of accelerations. Shock still registered in their dazzled faces.

Kim was the first to speak, "Damn, that was close!" His oversimplified statement was followed by murmured agreements. He then said, "Thanks, Nick."

I responded quickly, "You're welcome, but contact the Hope and let them know what just happened. They are in as much danger as we were. The Hope needs to launch immediately!"

The general was quick to comply and was soon sending a coded message to his Japanese counterpart. His concern and panic was obvious.

The general's sense of priorities was commendable. Earth was doomed anyway, and he had chosen future life over the devastation and horror inflicted on his country, friends, government and president. His second message was sent to the Pentagon detailing the destruction inflicted and notifying them of the death of the president. He even transmitted the video we had just taken, which would probably be on CNN and all the other alphabet networks within minutes.

Kim resumed piloting the ship and calculating the maneuvers to obtain orbit. My unexpected acceleration had already taken us many miles in space, and, by my calculations, it would take some major repositioning to take us into orbit. Once in orbit there was not much to do but wait. I withdrew and silently reveled in the fact that Kim had called me Nick.

Genesis Log: 10 July 2015:

The Japanese Hope team went into emergency launch mode after hearing what had almost happened to us. Fighting had broken out outside their facility, but the Japanese security team used maximum force to repel any threatening activity. Their military police force used all of their might against their own people just to destroy any potential terrorist that had infiltrated. They no longer cared what the world thought... survival was the only thing that mattered now. But, the rest of the world had its own problems and took little notice what Japan did.

Within hours, total anarchy erupted all over the globe after the nuclear explosion in Nevada. The joint chiefs got pissed at the killing of the president and retaliated, without Congress's approval. The joint chiefs independently declared war on anyone they even suspected supported the terrorist activity. They figured there was nothing to lose anyway. Mushroom clouds sprouted over Syria, Iran and part of Pakistan, easily seen from orbit. Israel took the opportunity also to cleanse and settle all their disputes with the Arab world. Additional mushrooms clouds appeared all over the Middle East. I secretly cheered and felt satisfaction in the destruction of the enemy that had caused me to suffer in paralysis. Surprisingly, Europe and China did nothing initially. They had their own internal problems. I guess they figured as long as they were left alone they were happy. Obviously, the rest of the world would have no long-term oil needs to be concerned with; therefore, no more fears or restriction on targets.

What was pathetic about the world chaos was the typical media response. CNN had the Arab mouth pieces lined up to come on camera and denounce America. They would stir the pot until they all died, which wouldn't be long at this rate.

Earth might be dead long before the asteroid destroyed it. Unfortunately, we would live to see the self-destruction and record every detail for future posterity, assuming there would be one. We were also fortunate in that we were outside of the trouble on Earth and more fortunate still to be alive.

We anxiously waited for eighteen hours until the Hope finally launched. Even then there were battles raging on the complex. There was a huge sigh of relief as it rose into space beyond reach of attack. The Hope couldn't maneuver as well as Genesis, but did finally achieve orbit and slowly made rendezvous with Genesis some six hours later. During the long wait, Linda had dispatched her outside team and positioned the umbilical tube in place. It was attached and ready for docking as Hope approached.

Three hours later our crews were happily mingling and introducing themselves in the cafeteria. It was a solemn occasion for me... isolated and forgotten in my mechanical prison. It was even worse than being a quadriplegic. At least in a wheelchair I would have been noticed. I felt alone and left out, but at least monitored the festivities through my visual centers. I made a silent vow that I would somehow find a way to exit my prison and join the crew and never be left out again.

While the festivities carried on, I busied myself in monitoring Earth's communication, our own video from space, and, of course, CNN for the worst possible scenario. The world situation was worsening by the minute. The destruction had finally erupted in Europe, India, and Asia. Japan had been obliterated along with the Philippines,

Korea and large portions of China stood in ruin in retaliation. Even as I watched, mushroom clouds could be seen expanding over many of the major capitals of the world, including New York City and Washington DC. I was witnessing the beginning of the end and the fall of civilization.

My attention was suddenly shifted as the general made an audible moan. He had entered during my total focus on the activities below. He was as sad as I, and for once we shared a silent moment of understanding and agreement.

He also saw the futility of and insanity in the human race and asked, "How much more do we have to watch? When can we go?"

With those questions, he had finally given me full control and authority over the Genesis, both ship and project. Technically and legally, as captain of the Genesis in space, I was now commanding. He was now part of the team... my team. I knew we would continue to have differences of opinions, but those challenges I welcomed.

I brought my holograph image up and looked directly into his eyes. I said, "Let the crews have their moment of rejoicing, then call the team leaders of both ships here for a planning and instruction meeting." The general nodded and, for a second, I thought he was going to salute.

Genesis Log: 11 July 2015:

Today started very early. The whole international team of Whiz Kids brought me out of my thoughts and planning as they entered together. I wasn't sure if the general had told them what was

105

going on or if they just sensed it, but here we were all gathered in the middle of the night. Whatever the reason, they were concerned and solemn... wanting to know what was happening.

I believe in the old adage, A picture is worth a thousand words. I just brought up the view of Earth, at least what could be seen currently. The devastation was clearly displayed and even more mushroom clouds could be seen even though the atmosphere was becoming heavily polluted. The Japanese delegation looked deeply at me as if to ask, "What about Japan?" I just shook my head, at least that was the way it felt. Even through the holograph image, the gesture was immediately understood.

There was too much to be done to grieve so I said, "Don't act so surprised. We all knew Earth was going to die... it's just happening sooner than we expected. It's just us now, the survivors, to carry on, and we will do just that."

Their reactions indicated acceptance, but I didn't acknowledge the fact. I simply launched into instruction saying, "We need to finalize the communication interface between the ships. I need to be tied into all functions on the Hope as soon as possible so we can exit orbit. As you know, it will take many months, even years to completely exit our solar system, but more immediate, we need to obtain a very safe distance from Earth before the impact of Armageddon. I suggest we all get to work."

"General?" I waited for him to look, and then said, "I want security on full alert. We all saw what a few fanatics did to Earth. We don't want anything even remotely like that to happen here. Please don't say it can't happen here. The fact is we don't want any opportunity or chance to present itself... not for a while anyway. Let's play it safe. Oh, and General, please see to it that lasers are installed on all my main visual centers starting here in the control room." I watched him and the others for a reaction. I didn't expect any objections from the others, yet I was somewhat surprised when I got none, even from the general. Maybe it wasn't so surprising. The general was well-disciplined to follow the established chain of command, and, since launch, I was officially the top dog.

The general actually said, "Yes, Sir! Linda, can you get your crews on that immediately?" He then began scrambling his security force.

Linda nodded and started giving orders on her communicator. Most everything that must be done would be from engineering. It would be another long night for her and her crew, along with those of the Hope.

I didn't waste any time taking over command of the Hope. I turned my attention to the Japanese and their Project Manager and said, "Mr. Sakata, for us to operate in total harmony we can only have one chief and that's me. Do you have any problem with this?" All eyes turned to him and there was total silence.

Yoshiaki Sakata seemed to freeze under the proverbial spotlight, but only for a moment. His options were to take our help or proceed with his original plans to go to Mars, but that really wasn't much of a choice... almost certain death or follow us and potential salvation.

He simply said, "No, Sir, consider us under your command."

"Very well then. Coordinate with Linda and Dr. Rossen to interface the Hope's computer network into me as quickly as possible." I was somewhat shocked to realize that I had referred to myself as the computer by saying ME instead of the computer network. Oh well, I guess I am the computer network also.

I went on to say, "The interface of life support can be addressed later. I want to analyze Hope's engineering design first to determine the best way."

Mr. Sakata's response was almost funny. He must have been nervous, because he presented me with a formal bow and responded in Japanese. I don't think he realized that fact.

"Hai, wakarimashita. Mochirondesu isogimasu! (Yes, of course... immediately!)"

"Arigatougozaimasu. (Thank you.)" I said and returned his bow, but only a slight bow designed to show superiority in his culture. How did I know that?

It took me a few seconds to realize that I had understood his Japanese. I had even responded back in Japanese, a language I had never bothered to learn as Capt. Nick Johns. Obviously the Japanese language was programmed into the extended computer. It certainly wasn't in me. That fact made me realize that I might be more computer than I thought. That was kind of disturbing, and I pondered it throughout the night.

Genesis Log: 12 July 2015:

During the early morning hours and throughout the day, workers and some of the whiz kids came in and out of the control room. Dr. Rossen was on his knees much of the time with his upper body deep into the computer housing working on the circuit connections. For the most part, I knew exactly what he was doing, but he didn't ask me for help or advice, and I didn't offer any. Hell, he planned me and made it work. I guess I could trust him to make the modifications.

The Genesis had been built with abundant circuit redundancy. Anything the government does is overkill, so that fact didn't surprise me; however, Dr. Rossen did have to reconfigure the connections to the computer. So, the feeds from the Hope were coming online slowly one at a time, but they were coming.

By late in the afternoon, I was finally flowing into their computer network. The Hope's computer was far simpler than my network; even so, I was able to reprogram much of their network to make it compatible in speed and function to my own. After a few hours of this, it was finally interfaced and operating as an extension of me. Again, I use that word ME. I swear, if I ever start saying to a human, that does not compute, I will find a way to shoot myself!

By the time everything was completed, it was late in the evening, and many had gone without sleep for over thirty-six hours, some even longer. I called a halt and sent them off to bed, calling for a general meeting for noon the next day. There were no arguments, only sighs of relief. Should anything arise I could handle it myself or, if necessary, call one of the on-duty technicians, which were essentially all engineers with advanced degrees.

My night was spent reviewing the operations of the Hope and getting familiar with its functions. I must admit, for all the abilities of the Japanese, I was not overly impressed. I had to assume that the shortage of time was the cause. Also, I had to keep telling myself that they had designed the craft for a much shorter time in space.

First, the life support would never handle a two-hundred-year flight. I decided to, for the most part, shut down the Hope and put most of the team in Cryogenics, except for a small maintenance staff. Fortunately, between the two ships we had the facilities to support life for all. We would just have to keep a somewhat larger staff awake on Genesis.

I also realized early on that the Hope would never be able to descend into gravity remaining attached. Once at our destination, they would have to detach and make the landing on their own, but that should not be a major problem. The general hadn't leaked the technology of the gravity technology learned from the aliens; well, apparently he did leak some of it, since the Japanese had built a low force version of artificial gravity, but not nearly as functional as the one on the Genesis.

The general once told me the gravity technology was too dangerous to let out. The technology could be turned into a devastating weapon with little effort. To reduce this potential he had divided the contracts, thus the knowledge, among several corporations so no one corporation would have it all, only us.

Unfortunately, the Japanese had not been successful in obtaining all of the technology for full artificial gravity and two hundred years at low gravity would not be healthy. This was another reason to shut Hope down.

The redeeming factor about Hope was that it was built with the Polly Metal. Being virtually indestructible, the Genesis could just pull the Hope behind like a trailer without much concern of a hull breach.

It was to be expected that the department heads of the Hope would have many questions, and they would need time to interface with us. I was sure there would be learning on both sides, but that would come over time. The Japanese really didn't know the details about our trip. That would be the first item on the agenda in the morning.

Genesis Log: 13 July 2015:

The teams were gathered in the control room by about 11:00 a.m... having straggled in slowly, but looking refreshed. Coffee was made and most everyone was on their second cup. I silently wondered just how long the store of coffee would last. There were beans for growing, but it was unlikely that a supply could be maintained during the entire voyage. God, I miss coffee, and I think I would kill for a smoke to go with it. I had only had a very few cigarettes since my paralysis. I had been lucky to have an understanding nurse from time to time to hold it while I smoked. I caught my self-pity and made myself focus on business.

I wanted the atmosphere to be relaxed, so I waited for them to start talking, and I didn't have to wait long.

The general spoke first, "Welcome, everyone. Since we are going to be together for the rest of our lives, we should get to know each other and what area of expertise each brings to the table."

I listened as they went back and forth with job functions, expertise, plans, and questions. It was very much like the briefing I had received when I got here. Mostly I remained silent, but spoke up to clarify a point or inject additional information. In some cases I had analyzed and corrected calculations or assumption that were in error and hadn't informed the team as of yet. I got some astonished looks, but they were learning to accept my information as irrefutable facts.

During the conversations, I was not surprised to learn that the Japanese team leaders were all PhDs as well... big surprise! At that level, it was understood. They evidently were not quite as formal with their titles in Japan or their project at any rate. Even the Englishman, Jim Sharp, had stopped incorporating his PhD in his name there.

When the subject of alien technology came up, the Japanese team was all ears. This took them by surprise and generated all sorts of questions. There was no reason to hold back secrets now. The discussion covered the Poly Metal, gravitation technology, computer technology, but when they mistakenly believed Light Speed was alien technology, I said, "No, Light Speed technology is an original invention of Linda Clark. I am happy to say, in some ways, we are smarter than the aliens." I was pleased to see the pride in Linda's face as the Japanese team all turned their awed gaze on her.

The discussion moved back to the alien computer recovered, when Hiroshi Tsuji asked, "What happened to the information stored on the recovered computer?"

"It is aboard Genesis and already tied into my... computer for analysis." I said. Damn, I had almost said tied into ME.

"One of my fields of expertise is encryption. I would like to have access to it."

"Hiroshi, you are welcome to work on it with Dr. Rossen and myself."

It was pleasing to see his enthusiasm and assimilation into the Genesis. He was an obvious team player. I liked this little man already. I doubt if Hiroshi was over 5' 5", but he stood proud and seemed to radiate a greater size. Part of that was the confidence of his stance for someone no older than thirty. When he acknowledged me with a slight bow, the room light reflected off a balding spot on the back of his skull.

The conversation finally came around to the trip itself and its jumps and destination. Kim started into the dissertation presented to me, but I interrupted. "I'm sorry, Kim, but I have made some modifications to your schedule. Instead of the ten light year jumps chosen, I have cut some out and reduced the jumps to only six." Kim looked shocked, but remained silent... looking at my image. I went into my prepared description:

"Our first Light Speed jump will only be 4ly to our nearest neighbor, Alpha Centauri. This will be our shakeout cruse."

"Our second jump will be a 40ly span, traveling to Beta Trianguli Australis, a binary star in the constellation Triangulum Australe."

"The third jump will only be 25ly to a binary star Epsilon Scorpii in the constellation Scorpius. This will take us 65ly into our journey."

"The forth Light Speed jump will be for 36ly, destination Alpha Indi (Persian) in the constellation Indus. Persian is a Class KO, third-magnitude, orange giant star in a multiple star system. At this point we will be 101ly toward our destination."

"The fifth jump will be 26ly to G Scorpii, also in the constellation Scorpius. It is an orange K-type giant in the magnitude of 3.19. By this point we will be out 127ly."

"I had originally considered an additional hop in between our last and final destination, but it would only cut 13ly off the last hop. I seriously considered repeating again from Beta Pavonis in the constellation of Pavo (the Peacock). Unfortunately, there are not many stars on our path in this area without taking a major zig zag in our course. The other reason I am bypassing Beta Pavonis is due to the fact that it is a massive white star of the A-type. The high radiation coming from this star makes the risks too great for the little that could be gained, only a reduction of the hop by 13ly."

"The last hop will be our longest at 53ly. Our future home will be in the star system Alpha Pavonis in the constellation Pavo. We know from records stored in the alien computer that a habitable planet exist at this location."

"Excuse me for asking, but why do we need any intermediate hops? Why can't we do it all in one long jump?" Asked Takashi.

Takashi Ishiguro was a quiet man, but somewhat wild looking. It must be his unruly black hair. He looked a little younger than the others, which was a sure sign of his genius to be among this august group. With his quietness and average physical appearance, he could easily be overlooked. I had wrongly assumed he was only shy, but now it was apparent he just hadn't had anything to say so far.

Before I could respond Takashi's question, Jim Sharp spoke up with a very pronounced British accent.

"I think that is very obvious," Jim said patronizingly. "Since we are traveling with Light Speed Drive, we need light from a star. A very slight error of a fraction of a degree increases exponentially over distance. This cumulative deviation could be devastating over 200 light years. We could easily find ourselves trying to come out of light speed in a vast dark void without propulsion or not coming out of it at all. This means we die! By making the hops shorter we reduce the likelihood of error."

"Correctly so," Kim said.

Jim Sharp is a tall and lanky Brit with long brown hair pulled back in a ponytail. His prominent nose and Adam's apple reminded me of Ichabod Crane in the cartoon of Legend of Sleepy Hollow.

"I am also someone that doesn't accept other's conclusions unless I analyze them myself," Jim said. "What if we don't agree with your plan?"

"Who is WE?" I said.

"We... us here," Jim said, spreading his hands to encompass all there.

"Well... you can have your say and I will listen, but this is NOT a democracy. I am the captain and make the final decisions." He just stared hard at me and I heard him mumble under his breath, "We will see!" He didn't think I heard, but my hearing is very good. Crap, that's all I need... more politics. I was disturbed with his attitude and ended our session for the day.

Genesis Log: 14 July 2015:

Before I could begin the morning session, Jim Sharp launched into his assessment, and I let him vent.

"I have analyzed the locations of the light speed jumps and have some serious concerns. You have us jumping at some very inhospitable star systems (Giant stars, Orange Giants and binary star systems), most of which would have difficulty providing a planet capable of supporting life. This also includes Alpha Pavonis. There is little data on this planet, but what is known is it is a ClassB2 IV star and most probably a binary system. Gentlemen and ladies, this is a hot star. The likelihood of it having a planet capable of supporting life is remote, if not impossible. How can you rely on some obscure fable told by aliens?"

"Alpha Centauri is the only star system I agree with. It has the highest potential for a habitable planet of all of them. Point of fact, it is a binary system with two Earth like suns, doubling the

116

potential for finding terrestrial planets and possible life. Alpha Centauri is also the only star that provides spectral type G2 V (yellowish-white light). I don't know about you, but I don't want to settle on a planet that has blue-white light. I want my yellow sun!"

I didn't know whether to just shoot him on the spot or sew his mouth shut. I wasn't going to spend much time tolerating him, but I could see the others looking to me for a response. This arrogant ass hole was used to getting his way. Now I knew who the power behind the Hope project was. Project Manager Yoshiaki Sakata was only a figurehead to get the money. I decided to give it a little time and asked, "Kim, how confident are you in the alien data on Alpha Pavonis?" I knew the answer, but wanted to let my temper calm.

"I am very confident." Kim responded, "The coordinates match perfectly. I have seen aerial pictures of the planet, star maps, planet locations... it is very real! I might add, there is data on star systems within 500 light years, not all, but many. In all that data, only Earth and Alpha Pavonis have planets that would support life as we know it, and actually had life."

"Jim," I said. "Thank you so much for this lively debate. A devil's advocate is always welcome." This brought a hearty laugh from everyone... except Jim. "We are confident in the existence of a planet to colonize in the Alpha Pavonis system. You are welcome to review the data you haven't had access to before, but that debate is over. As to the other systems, we aren't looking for habitable planets on those systems.

They are for propulsion sources only. The only valid point you bring up is Alpha Centauri, there is no alien data on this system. It is possible there is a suitable planet. That is why we are going. If you had bothered to listen more and talk less you would have already heard this fact. I suggest you learn more before you wade in." His eyes were blazing into my image, but he remained silent... for the rest of the day he remained silent.

For all practical purposes, Earth was already dead. Sure, there were pockets of life, but few. It broke my heart to look, but the worst was yet to come. Armageddon was due within a week. It was time to leave orbit. I got their attention and said, "We need to leave orbit today to get a safe distance before the impact and Earth's explosion."

All departments were already ready. I watched as they gathered in the control room. Kim did the calculations and we launched out of orbit and headed OUT.

Genesis Log: 15 July 2015:

We continued to use the antigravity for propulsion to gain momentum, but it was time for the next phase. Dr. Rossen and Linda activated the Light Wave Drive (LWD) and did some final adjustments. The announcement was made to buckle in for a propulsion surge. The moment of truth was at hand as Linda nudged the controls forward. The sudden G force jerked them back in their seats. The forward momentum was excessive, as Linda decreased the controls slightly. Cheers rang out throughout the control room and I was one of the loudest.

The theory of the technology was flawless, but seeing and feeling the Light Wave Drive actually work was gratifying indeed. "Congratulations to you two!" I said. Linda and Dr. Rossen were exuberant.

"I love it when a plan comes together!" she said.

Chapter 6
(Alpha Centauri)

Genesis Log: 20 July 2015:

It has now been five days since we launched from Earth's orbit, and we are deep in space but still within our solar system. The ship is operating to perfection, but we will continue to operate at sub-light speed until we pass the asteroid belt. Unlikely as it is, there remains a collision threat from asteroids in our direct path. The asteroid belt forms a circular band, roughly located between the orbits of Mars and Jupiter, orbiting around the sun. Genesis has now entered the band, but it will take many more days to exit the belt.

There remains one final obstacle, the Kuiper belt orbiting beyond the planets extending out beyond the orbit of Neptune. Unfortunately, we would not be able to achieve light speed out so far from our light source, the sun. We will propel to light speed once through the first asteroid belt and take our chances with the other less threatening belt of asteroids. I have calculated the threat to be minimal. Even so, our antigravity force in the hull of the ship should repel any low mass asteroids, which the vast majority of them are.

I called a meeting of the department heads to convene immediately. It was time to watch the final destruction of Earth! Armageddon has been approaching steadily during our escape. As Earth is getting smaller in our viewing monitor, the asteroid is getting larger and brighter. A flaming tail lights the sky behind it.

They know why I have called them together and are solemn as they gather around the full screen monitors. One telescopic camera is focused on Earth, and the other is focused on Armageddon as they slowly merge into one screen. The huge asteroid is easily seen racing toward Earth. To make matters even worse, assuming that was possible, the gravitational pull of the sun increased the velocity speed of Armageddon to approximately thirty-five miles per second. As Armageddon is drawn toward the Sun, Earth orbit propels it toward and into the path of the oncoming asteroid at a speed of over eighteen miles per second. The calculated combined collision velocity is well over fifty-three miles per second. The combination of the extreme size and mass of the asteroid and the exceptional collision velocity will result in the total destruction of Earth many times over. Absolutely no hope exists.

From our viewing position, Armageddon is now traveling away from us and directly toward Earth. The witnesses remain totally silent and mesmerized, watching the impending impact.

When it happened it appeared almost in slow motion. The asteroid appeared as a fireball racing toward Earth just before it impacted. The initial impact could be seen as it physically entered and disappeared within Earth's crust. For an instant, it looked like nothing was happening. Earth seemed to absorb the asteroid within. As we watched intently, we could see Earth appear to bend inward at the impact point then bulge out on the sides. Suddenly, Earth exploded, shooting flaming magma spreading into space from the rear followed by a mass explosion in all directions. It reminded me of shooting a watermelon with a shotgun. After the initial explosion, what remained of Earth's mass seemed to collapse into itself and appeared to wobble. It was no longer Earth but an unrecognizable glowing glob with numerous new moons in wavering orbits. Dust, debris and water vapor stretched far into space clouding the view. It did not matter anymore... Earth was dead along with any and all life that existed. We all turned away and wept in silence. Eventually, everyone filtered out in silence to the solitude of his or her quarters... everyone but me that is.

Genesis Log: 22 July 2015:

We are through the majority of the asteroid belt now. At least we are close enough to risk jumping to light speed. The further we get from the sun, the longer it will take to reach light speed, since we get our propulsion from light energy. We must obtain light speed before we propel out of its reach.

I have already programmed in a temporary automatic gravity shutoff to insure we switch universes as we reach light speed. Gravity must be off as we reach this hypothetical physical limit. I want to accelerate to this magical number as quickly as possible but without harmful effects. I anticipate all bodily functions and physical senses will slow the closer we get to light speed. In fact, I calculate life would cease to exist if exposed for any length of time surpassing light speed without changing universes. The timing will have to be perfect, but my calculations are precise and flawless... hopefully.

I will stabilize our speed at twenty percent above light speed for the duration of the flight to Alpha Centauri. According to my calculation, we will remain at this speed for just under four years. By that time we should be close enough to the star to use its energy to slow the Genesis below light speed and establish an orbit in this solar system. This, of course, will position us to make the next light speed jump.

The department heads gathered well ahead of the scheduled time. Even so, Jim Sharp was the last to arrive, evidently a sign of disrespect to me. Big deal, I thought. I didn't like him much either. We were going to butt heads at some point. I found that funny, since my head was stainless steel. Seriously, though, he was going to be a threat to my authority, and I could not allow him to jeopardize my command. But, I chose to ignore his obvious insult.

Dr. Rossen and Linda were anxious. The Light Wave Drive seemed to be working to perfection, but reaching light speed was yet to be achieved and that was the ultimate goal. Kim had programmed in the calculations and precise heading, and I had confirmed his calculations. Surely, he suspected that I was overseeing everything... I think he even expected and welcomed confirmation, but we left it unspoken. It wasn't as easy to confirm all the complex calculations of the light wave drive program, however. There were so many factors that could go wrong. In addition, there could be glitches in the program, even though I had found none. We all needed the confidence of reaching light speed for the first time to assure us that all the planning and goals could be realized.

"Linda, you have control. Engage when you like," I announced. Kim, Linda, and Dr. Rossen were seated at the control console, their fingers flashing over the controls.

"Kim, set the countdown for engaging," she said. "Dr. Rossen standby for support, and the rest of you keep your fingers crossed."

The countdown flashed 4 - 3 - 2 - 1; then we felt the initial lurch of the propulsion, then nothing. I experienced an earthquake once and that is what it felt like... the ground moving under your feet. The only indication of acceleration was the speed indicator as it climbed. The rapidly flashing numbers on the right side of the indicator were unreadable. I was actually surprised at how fast we were approaching light speed, but I shouldn't be, since we were still reasonably close to the sun, thus abundant energy for the drive.

"Light Speed in 20.6 seconds," Linda said. "Prepare for zero gravity." This latter was announced over the ship's loudspeaker.

My automatic safety did not have to engage, as Linda manually shut it down ten seconds prior to achieving light speed. I felt the immediate assault on my system, which must have been far worse on the others. The abrupt loss of gravity had many on the bridge retching in their sick bags from the sudden nausea, but the speed indicator switched to light speed plus readings, and Linda switched the gravity back on. Cheers rang out on the bridge. I wasn't sure if it was from reaching light speed or regaining gravity. It really didn't matter... we survived and we were at light speed.

Linda began slowing our acceleration and shut it down at our target of 1.2 LS. "I am extremely pleased." I said. "Your design and program worked to perfection... even better." The smiles were contagious, even the general sported an uncharacteristic smile. I guess I was wrong; I always wondered if his face would crack if he smiled.

The general had been my nemesis, but in all honesty had done a superb job of assembling this team and getting the project funded, organized and built. It was, in fact, ahead of schedule. He deserved recognition, so I sported a huge grin of my own and asked, "General, what do you think of your team now?"

"They are incredible! I am proud as hell of all of them and all of my choices."

This last statement he made staring directly at my image. Well, I'll be dammed, I thought. I was giving him a compliment and he graciously accepted it and let me know... well, put me in my place by letting me know he picked me, too. It was a compliment though, masked as it was. I gave him a slight bow and simply said, "Thank you." Maybe he wasn't such an ass hole after all.

Genesis Log: 25 July 2015:

This is the third day since reaching light speed and not one glitch... not one single problem with the Light Drive or anywhere for that matter. Well, Akiko reported that the animals went crazy when the gravity was shut off, but there was no physical harm. Other than that, things are going incredibly smooth. This is a little unnerving because I subscribe to Murphy's Law... If it can go wrong, it will, and at the worst possible time. But, I will accept all the good and smooth operations that come my way.

If nothing occurs within the next week, I want to start retiring some of the department heads and staff into cryogenics, certainly some of the work force. When I brought this up at the morning meeting today, virtually everyone resisted. Jim Sharp was the most vocal.

"No! I am not going into cryogenics," Jim Sharp announced. "Not until after we explore Alpha Centauri."

Since this first hop was only four years and our shakedown cruise, most of them wanted to experience it. I didn't blame them; I certainly wanted the company, but it was a matter of resources. Not everyone could stay awake. The argument was that they could retire some of their designated staff, while they remained awake to address any problems immediately. All valid arguments, but this didn't necessarily hold true for Jim since Hope was virtually shut down. I knew what he was really after.

Jim Sharp held onto the belief that Alpha Centauri offered the best hope for finding a habitable planet, and he didn't trust me to wake him. This, of course, was ludicrous. I would be the happiest of anyone to find a planet we could colonize without me having to spend the next two hundred years awake.

I had every intention of exploring Alpha Centauri. Unfortunately, the alien records didn't provide any discernible information on this star system, which seemed strange, since there was an abundance of information on so many others. For some reason, the aliens had either missed or avoided this star system. Yes, I intended to explore Alpha Centauri.

After the morning meeting, the general remained. Most of the general's initial responsibilities were now completed, and well, I might add. Currently all he had to do was maintain order and security, and that included protecting me.

"Nick, you are going to have trouble with Mr. Sharp," said the general. "The sooner you deal with it the better."

I was flabbergasted! He was absolutely correct, but that was not what shocked me most. He was counseling me for my own good. He was trying to help... ME. I suddenly gained new respect for the man in that moment. I always thought he would be my problem. "What do you suggest, General?"

"It is hard to say for sure," he said. "But, you are the unconditional final authority... the captain, and your word is absolute. I will do everything within my ability to help you, but I can NOT do it for you, because that would undermine you more. I was the leader on Earth, but once in space, you became captain. A captain of a ship at sea, in this case space, is in absolute control. Now it is up to you... I am just advising."

"No!" I said, "You know exactly what to do, and I want to hear it."

"Okay, but are you ready for it?"

"Tell me!"

"Well," he said. "Kill him!"

"Are you fucking serious?"

"Yes," said the general. "Think about it. From a command logic position, it couldn't be better. First, he is asking for it. Secondly, you MUST establish supreme control, and Mr. Sharp has demonstrated that he will never submit to it. Many in an absolute authority situation look for a way to establish total control and discipline, which you must have. As you once said, this is not a democracy."

"The whole plan from the beginning required a strong leader, and you are it. I chose you because you were a Marine officer. You know these things already. Hell, I would have volunteered my brain myself, but I knew I wouldn't have been able to stay sane. You can! Now you must take command, totally, and I will stand with you."

Damn, he was right, and I did know this already, but kill Sharp? Could I just kill him? I thought back to what the president had said, your powers will be godlike. It finally hit me! Everything was up to me. I could do anything I wanted... anything! I also realized that they had picked me hoping for my self-control and self-imposed desire to serve. I had heard this repeatedly, but now I finally understood it.

I looked at the general, nodded and said, "Thank you, General." I could see in his eyes that he knew I finally understood.

Genesis Log: 30 July 2015:

Hope's team leader, Yoshiaki Sakata, came to see me very early in the morning... alone.

It occurs to me that I should stop using terms like morning to describe the cycle of the sun. We are now in deep space and out of the reference of the sun. I have maintained a twenty-four-hour cycle by dimming the shipboard lights during the designated sleep cycle. I have taken the light adjustment even further: Work time, the first eight hours, is now represented by a white hue of light above the yellow of the sun to closely correspond to the star system we will eventually colonize. Leisure and recreation time I adjusted to a bluish tint. Sleep time light I dimmed to half intensity and changed the color to a red hue. All of these hues will approximate the various star systems we will be encountering on our trip. All of these adjustments required me to alter and modify the programming and control of the Poly Metal light frequencies, which will be required in the future to generate Light Speed Propulsion from the various star systems.

Therefore, more accurately, Yoshiaki came to the control room during the middle of the Red Cycle when there would be no one else around. My light came on when he entered, and my image sprang to life. I knew this must be serious, and I waited for him to speak.

"I have discussed with the other Department Heads of Hope," He said, "We do not agree with Jim Sharp. He has always been an arrogant asshole, but we needed him. He is a brilliant engineer and we have put up with a lot from him, but we all agree that we are committing our future with you and

129

Genesis. We just wanted you to know. After the last spectacle he made with you, we were embarrassed."

"I appreciate you letting me know how you feel," I said, "Don't worry about it. I can handle it." I really appreciated the vote of confidence from him and most of his team.

I had spent no small amount of time considering Jim, and I still had no idea what I was going to do with him. I certainly did not want to simply kill him as the general had suggested. His knowledge and expertise were valuable, but his lack of teamwork and defiance of me will be a problem at some point in the future. The general was right about that.

Early in the White Cycle, the team came for the normal meeting. Mostly, we had little to talk about, since everything was going well. Today, however, I had made my decision. "Good morning," I said. "I have the Awake Team scheduled and all of the department heads will remain awake during this first short hop, with the single exception of Jim Sharp." I was looking for a fight.

"The hell you say!" Jim stood and screamed, "I told you I am not going into cryogenics until after Alpha Centauri."

Just as forcefully I said, "My order stands. You will go into cryogenics, and immediately!"

"Just who do you think you are to give orders to any of us? Fuck you! You are nothing but a computer. We tell you what to do!" Jim spit his response.

I could see Jim Sharp looking around the room for support, but all his associates were looking at the floor. Only the general stared at him indignantly before turning to me to see what my reaction would be. I was pissed at his arrogant disrespect and hurtful words but kept my image calm and said, "As I have told you before, this is NOT a democracy. We are a U.S. Government-sponsored ship, therefore military. I am the designated commanding officer or captain. I am the absolute authority of this vessel, and this authority was given to me and me alone directly by the president of the United States. This is the way I intend to command... as a military ship. Beginning now, the department heads, you folks here, will become officers of Genesis holding a military rank of commander. That is everyone, with the exception of Jim Sharp. Jim will remain a civilian until such time as I consider him a team player. Major General McCullah will be my first officer and second in command with a Navy rank of captain. First Officer McCullah will instruct you in all necessary military protocol."

Asshole Sharp was trying to talk over me so I announced, "First Officer McCullah, please have security remove Mr. Sharp from the bridge and hold him in cryogenics."

Jim Sharp's temper escaped, and he grabbed a chair, unhooked the restraining latch and came running toward my dome with obvious intent to smash as much as he could. I calmly fired my laser, slicing off his right ear. He stopped in his tracks, screaming and clutching the right side of his head just as security came running onto the bridge. After a few words with First Officer McCullah, they dragged Jim kicking and screaming from the bridge. I could not resist a parting shot and said, "If you are nice, I will get Dr. Rossen to sew your ear back on."

Everyone was aghast at my actions, but not a word was said. From the back of the room I heard laughter. The general, errrr, first officer, was hysterically laughing. This was the most visible expression of emotions I had ever seen from him. He looked at me, still laughing, and gave me thumbs up as he actually bent over, laughing so hard he was clutching his stomach. He was obviously happy with this turn of events.

"Cdr. Rossen, please go see to Mr. Sharp's needs and see that he is put into cryogenics as soon as possible." I saw a slight grin on his face as he picked Jim's ear off the deck on his way out.

Genesis Log: 1 Aug. 2015:

During the Red Cycle, I modified my image dress uniform per the general's suggestion. I replaced my Marine Captain's uniform with a blue uniform blazer, well more like a Star Trek blouse, complete with a wide gold band on each sleeve and gold shoulder bars indicating a Navy rank of admiral. First Officer McCullah suggested this rank, since I had given him the rank of captain. He said it was appropriate. He intended to wear the four gold Captain's stripes on the sleeves and shoulder bars and felt I should be a higher rank. It seems this had been his plan since the beginning and blue uniform jumpsuits were already standard issue. I guess it wasn't so ironic that they looked like a military uniform. Now the officers would modify their dress to include the blue blazer, black slacks and military rank insignia. The only other insignia on the

132

uniforms would be the gold and red Genesis emblem over the left pocket.

The emblem itself was quite impressive. It was an oblong red badge with gold border. It had a gold image of a side view of the Genesis and the name Genesis on the top. It seems the general had also stocked in inventory gold emblems for officers uniforms... both quite impressive.

At the early White Cycle, all the department heads (now commanders) arrived in full uniform. The first officer had definitely been busy. Everyone looked smart and seemed to enjoy the new dress. Capt. McCullah went around inspecting the officers, making slight adjustments to a crooked shoulder bars or wrinkled blazers. He seemed quite pleased.

Once the officers had their coffee and settled down to business, Cdr. Rossen reported that the security guards and he had gotten Mr. Sharp into the cryogenics chamber.

He said, "The security guards had to hold him while I gave him a sedative. Then I had no problem sewing his ear back on. It was a clean cut, and it should reattach without difficulty when he thaws out."

First Officer McCullah started laughing again, almost uncontrollably. The others quickly joined him, including the Japanese delegation. It really was hilarious the way Cdr. Rossen reported it... as if he was dictating to a medical log. Ironically, I joined in the laughter also. I had worried about their reaction, but, as the general had said, I needed an example. This was definitely a good one. I did not solve the problem, only postponed it, but it was better than killing him.

Genesis Log: 10 Aug. 2015:

As soon as possible I puts as many as I could in cryogenics. Only those who were absolutely necessary remained awake. As a result, little activity was occurring, at least among the Staff. The days were beginning to blur now. One day was becoming very much like the last. Each White Cycle meeting sounding very much like the last...no problems... no real activity to report on or do.

The only bright spot of the days to me was seeing Cdr. Mitsuhara (Akiko) in her form fitting officer's uniform, and what a form she had. God, she was HOT! Cdr. Clark wasn't bad either. Damn, I missed sex.

The Awake Teams spent much of their day in the recreation rooms or gym. I missed that too and often watched them exercise, especially Akiko. Damn, I am becoming a pervert, a computerized voyeur pervert.

This would never do. None of us could afford to become idle, certainly for two hundred years. We would have to have projects to occupy our minds. I decided right then to invent new needs and projects to work on.

Genesis Log: 15 Aug. 2015:

I kept thinking that for myself, I could occupy my mind on the long trip by learning new things, hell, even if it was French. When I tried, I discovered that I knew it already, hell, everything. All the stored knowledge of the human race was already in my data banks and integrated into my brain. It was just like the Japanese I spoke to Cdr. Sakata. I knew it without ever having to learn the language. I couldn't even watch a movie or listen to music... I also had those stored in memory with total recall. I realized this would destroy me eventually unless I could occupy my mind by creating new works of art, technology, or learning totally new knowledge. Some challenge! Dr. Rossen had never considered this, I am quite sure. Well, I had found the first problem, but why did it have to be one that affected me?

There was no reason to keep it a secret; after all, it affected everyone aboard. If I cracked the entire project failed. I decided to bring it up at our next cycle meeting.

As I suspected, Dr. .... Cdr. Rossen was shocked. The team of experts had obviously not anticipated or even considered this potential problem in the planning. I challenged the entire team with finding a solution for my problem. Now we have some focus.

Genesis Log: 18 Aug. 2015:

Today's meeting was very productive. The unanimous opinion among the Staff was to push me in directions of new science. "Tell me something I don't already know." I shot back, "Like what?" Dr. Rossen looked annoyed, but I didn't care. He would just have to get used to being annoyed and Cdr. Rossen would also have to get used to being called Dr. Rossen, somehow Cdr. still didn't fit. A medical doctor is still doc to me, military or not.

Dr. Rossen suggested, "Well... we could work on designing you a body that would allow you to escape the confines of your housing." A deathly silence followed that statement that seem to hang in the air.

That was one of the items already on my agenda from the beginning, but I wasn't expecting it to be necessary to maintain my sanity. I was, however, extremely happy to hear him bring it up.

"Are you talking about a robotics body?" Cdr. Tsuji asked, "If so, I think I can help."

Cdr. Hiroshi Tsuji was one of the engineering experts that helped design the Hope, but I had discovered he was also one of the world's foremost robotics experts. I guess now he is the only robotics expert, besides me... now. I had already been designing some new applications of Poly Metal, which I was anxious to share. My problem is no fingers with which to experiment. I needed him for that... that and to construct a robot.

Dr. Rossen said, "Robotics is certainly one method and probably the initial preferred option, but we might also consider a human body... Nick's body to be precise. We do have his DNA and could clone his body. But, this is not the problem. The real problem is communication between his brain, the computer, and the host robot or human body. Herein lies the problem. He can't be running around with a fiber optics cable trailing behind him. This will require some real research and planning. Nick, I assume you can help in this area with your intellect?"

"Yes, of course. Let me analyze your suggestions for a few days before I comment. Okay?"

This was already getting exciting.

Genesis Log: 20 Aug. 2015:

Our early meetings had reverted to mostly just coffee breaks, since there was little to talk about. Today would be different. My plan was finally ready to present. I had been working on it for days. The plan was far more complex than I want to reveal, but it should be exciting enough to hold everyone interest for a few years... I hope.

"Good morning," I said. "I have a tentative beginning plan. Hopefully, it will develop into many side directions that may or may not work toward the final solution... building a body for me. It goes like this:

"Genetics - (Dr. Rossen, Cdr. Ishiguro) This project will serve a two-fold purpose. It will research the development of human organs to replace or supplement my current artificial life support systems. Secondly, the research will produce a cloned body of me that will develop higher brain functions for telepathic communication. Even with a body, I will need to operate it as an extension of me, my essence as combined and expanded into the computer network. This engineered cloned brain cannot be self-aware if it is to serve as an extension of me."

"Telepathy - (Dr. Rossen, Cdr. Ishiguro) This project dovetails into the first project. Maybe there is a more appropriate name to give it, but telepathy works for me. That is the focus of the project... to develop and expand the telepathic functions of the brain, both for the remote body and for a neural network upgrade for myself. We will also be looking for a mechanical telepathic unit for the initial robotic effort. Dr. Rossen, this should be a challenge for your computer skills, but I can help."

"Robotics - (Cdr. Tsuji, Cdr. Clark) This should be pretty obvious, and I am sure you have many ideas already. You have already heard the need for a brain interface, and you can work with Dr. Rossen on that end of the planning. I also have some ideas and plans I can share with you when you are ready to consider them."

"Astrology - (Cdr. Kim) We need you to analyze the Alpha Centauri system for potential life and the potential of us being able to colonize a planet in that system. I realize that we do not have a telescope of any size aboard. I think some of your efforts should go toward building one. Since traveling above the speed of light, it was anticipated that we would not be able to see past this threshold, but this has all changed with our latest alteration of the gravity universe. You will now be able to study each solar system well in advance of us reaching it. Let's call it security. We don't want any surprises. If Jim Sharp joins the team, you can use him after Alpha Centauri."

"Botany (Cdr. Mitsuhara, Cdr. Sakata) I want this project to include the chemical and mathematical mapping of photosynthesis, among others. We want to create new knowledge on how to combine elements in plant life to create a predictable result. This will require massive amounts of data similar to DNA mapping. I will assist with this with my analytical processing capacity. Why, you may wonder?"

"Consider this. We may have been able to save Earth had we been able to create new plant life that, for example generated hydrogen and oxygen as its byproduct. Imagine cheap and abundant fuel that, not only burned clean, but also filtered carbon dioxide pollutants from our atmosphere. Think how much more new technology could have been discovered if so much of Earth's resources had not been expended in wars over fossil fuels and fighting Global Warming. Maybe it wouldn't have made any difference, but there was a chance."

"A single plant might have made the difference and given Earth time to develop new knowledge or weapons to fight the asteroid. In retrospect, I have seen some possible applications of our artificial gravity system that might have been developed that may have deflected the asteroid. See what I mean?"

"We have a new future to consider now. Armed with a total understanding of the chemical process and how to manipulate the biology of plants, we might be able to alter and improve our future. What if we need to alter the atmosphere of New Earth? What if our stored plants don't have the necessary element to grow? What if there is a toxic element? We will want to alter the plants to adjust for these changes."

"First Officer McCullah will coordinate the projects. Let him know what you need and keep him informed of your progress."

There was a heightened sense of purpose and excitement as they filtered out of the control room, and I had no doubt that these whiz kids could accomplish any challenge given them. Look what they accomplished with the Genesis project.

Genesis Log: 25 Aug 2015:

I had challenged Cdr. Kim to analyze Alpha Centauri, and he was ready for this cycle's meeting with a prepared presentation. From past experience I knew he loved the academia of his profession and was good at making informative and interesting presentations. He led off the discussion as if we were all in his classroom. We all settled back and got comfortable.

"As most of you may already know," Kim said. "Alpha Centauri is the closest stellar system to our sun at only 4.35 light years away and is one of the few known solar systems scientists believe is capable of sustaining life. This, of course, is one of the few close enough to study in detail."

"What many of you may not know is that Alpha Centauri is actually a binary system consisting of Alpha Centauri A and B orbiting each other in an 80-year cycle. This system could also be considered a trinary system, if you include a more distant star called Alpha Centauri C. For all practical purposes, this last star, also called Proxima, is a dim red dwarf with a spectral type of M5 and of little value for our purpose."

"Alpha Centauri A is a yellow star like our sun and has the most potential for supporting life as we know it. A yellow star means that the spectral type is G2, therefore its temperature and color also match those of the sun. It is slightly larger and hotter, however."

"Alpha Centauri B is an orange star with a spectral type of K1. As you would imagine, the spectral light appears slightly orange as opposed to the white-yellow of our sun. Alpha Centauri B is slightly smaller and cooler than our sun, but well within the limits of producing life."

"Both Alpha Centauri A and B have a higher metal content than the sun. The higher metal increases the likelihood of orbiting planets, but unlike the sun, the binary gravitational system would prevent larger planets to form at a large distance from either star. The interaction of the gravitational pull would tend to force them out of orbit. The good news is the stars are far enough apart that those closer planets orbiting either star would not be affected by the gravitational pull of the other star, and this is the location of planets capable of supporting life."

"Another interesting fact about this binary system is that both star systems are older than the sun by about a billion years. Any life on a habitable planet would have had a billion years more evolution. If we do find life, we might not be the higher life form."

"Both Alpha Centauri A and B meet the five test criteria for star systems capable of habitable planets, where most stars do not.

1. A star must be a stable main-sequence star fusing hydrogen and helium in the core to generate light and heat.

2. A star must be of the right spectral type to produce enough energy to sustain life. This is a requirement to permit the existence of liquid water.

3, A star must demonstrate stable conditions. It cannot vary so much that alterations will freeze or fry any life that manages to develop.

4. A star must be old enough to give life a chance to evolve.

5. A star must have enough heavy elements such as carbon, nitrogen, oxygen, and iron, elements necessary for biological life to exist.

As I have previously indicated, both Alpha Centauri A and B meet or exceed the criteria demonstrated by the sun. These systems are much older and have far more heavy elements. In short, this system is well suited to have planets orbiting them that could support life."

"Once I have developed a telescope capable of seeing that far, my research can progress further, and we will know for sure."

"That's it ladies and gentlemen... Alpha Centauri 101."

Chapter 7
(Void of Space)

Genesis Log: 29 Aug 2015:

Even though the teams had their projects and were hard at work, I was alone and bored. My mind was troubling me about something I had said a few days back. I had said that new technology might have been able to save Earth. I have spent the last few days going back and analyzing all the data concerning the death of Earth and running various scenarios on possible solutions.

All my analysis now confirms that I could have saved Earth! If we had launched three weeks earlier and met the asteroid far enough out in space, we could have used a combination of Light Wave Drive and a projected gravitational beam to force Armageddon off course. The data confirms this assumption.

The problem had always been the immense mass of the Texas size asteroid. In order to apply pressure against it sufficient to significantly alter its course would require pushing against something with enough appreciable mass to provide a force. The Light Wave Drive could provide that equivalent mass in a space vacuum.

True, the asteroid was huge... without a doubt the largest asteroid ever to impact Earth, but Light Wave Drive was a formidable force that could have been applied against the asteroid. Point of fact, it would have required only a very slight alteration in Armageddon's trajectory far enough out in space to cause it to bypass Earth. A minor change of trajectory over a large distance could make a major change in the offset course's distance.

I had since calculated and designed a modification to the gravity field generator that could project a beam of either polarity that could be used to push or pull the asteroid slightly off course. By using the full bottom surface of the Genesis as the beam projector, the stress against the Poly Metal surface would have been acceptable, assuming predictable limits of force could be applied for a sufficient amount of time at a calculable distance. Of course this distance would have had to be a point just past Jupiter and force applied to the asteroid for a minimum of 336 hours or 2 weeks. In all practicality, while the plan was flawless, the required timing was impossible; but what disturbed me most was the fact that I had never even considered this option until now.

The very thought that I might have made a difference, however remote, was distressing. Maybe I am not the right man for the job. Maybe someone else would have thought of it.

No! It was too late to be worrying about it now! I am now the only hope for humanity. It was up to me to council myself, console myself and forgive myself. How could I ever dream of mentioning this to anyone else? I must learn from my mistakes, accept the situation and move on, but it is hard. The pressure of command was crushing me.

Genesis Log: 1 Sept 2015:

I decided to take my own advice and delve into new research. Not only did I have all recorded knowledge in my storage, actually my active mind, but I had also stored all the problems humanity had discovered and experienced and not solved. The volume of potential problems was overwhelming. My choices were virtually unlimited. My only limiting factor was me. All I had to do was pick a subject.

Once I realized this, my mind was flooded with ideas and projects. Then it was a matter of prioritizing them. Luckily, I had already provided the most important ideas for the immediate problem to the team. That would be my focus... helping them.

Genesis Log: 1 Sept 2015:

I asked Cdr. Tsuji to remain after our uneventful White Cycle meeting. I had no secrets... it was just that the others had their projects, and what I had to share was more specific to the robotics project. I had been analyzing the needs and believed I had an idea he may not have considered. I didn't want to interfere with his planning process, but...well, I guess I did want to interfere.

"I have a suggestion for artificial muscles I want to share," I announced, "before you get too far into the planning." I provided the technical data and specs of my findings. As he was reviewing them, I continued with my summary. "The properties of Poly Metal continue to be surprising," I said. "I have discovered that Poly Metal, while it is extremely hard, changes its density and rigidity

145

slightly as voltage and frequency change. This is the nature of the polymer and source of its adaptability. What this means to us now is that we can manufacture an artificial muscle strand, not just a cell, but a whole muscle substitute. These can be grouped in a series or parallel configuration to make a complete muscle, depending on anticipated strength or flexibility required."

"If a long fiber of Poly Metal is wound like a spring and molded in place, when low voltage and adjustable frequencies are applied, the change in density and rigidity will cause the strand to expand or contract. Not only will you get movement, but the strength of the movement should be a thousand-fold stronger than a natural muscle. Even better, there is no stress. The strand will simply move to conform with the frequency applied and remain in that condition until it is again changed. Length of movement can be calculated and designed by stacking the fibers end to end or parallel for increased force. The best part is that this artificial muscle reacts instantly."

Cdr. Tsuji listened intently to my discourse without interruption and very uncharacteristically responded with, "No fucking shit?"

"No shit," I responded through my laughter. I could tell he was extremely excited with this new revelation.

"Thanks ... thanks! I need to analyze this data and work it into my design," Cdr. Tsuji said. He then switched inward into his mind and left in a hurry, like he had somewhere to get to in a hurry. He did, as an afterthought, turn around wave and said, "Bye."

I knew I wouldn't see much of him for a few days. I could help him more, but I needed him to ask. With my heightened intelligence, I understand the complex mind of these geniuses better. Cdr. Tsuji's mind would need to turn internal to organize his thoughts and understanding. He would not want further input until this new knowledge had been planned out in precise detail and applied to plans. I smiled to myself as I imagined his mental process now going on in his head, oblivious to all around him. Complex minds tend to move in this direction.

Genesis Log: 5 Sept 2015:

This is the third day in a row that nothing has happened. The meetings are coffee time only. They seem preoccupied with their own thoughts but take the meeting times to simply relax.

I have taken to traveling the ship via my visual centers. Of course, I constantly monitor, but of late I have begun to let my mind extend to the various visual centers. I am beginning to enjoy Akiko's gardens and spend hours each day there. It is relaxing, and on occasion I visit with Akiko. I never meant to interfere, but I had forgotten about the little red light on the cameras that indicates when it is on. On one such day when I was observing the gardens Akiko walked by, and she looked directly at me.

"Hello, Nick. Are you visiting me again today?

At first I was startled. How did she know? Duh! I briefly panicked wondering if she had known I had been watching her exercise.

"Yes," I said, "It is so peaceful here, and I enjoy watching plants grow." I laughed at my own joke... remembering what I had once said about her.

"Maybe one day you can actually come and sit with me on a bench and smell the scents and feel the air. It would be much more enjoyable then," she said.

I was thinking the same thing earlier, but now it had a much more profound meaning. Oh, how I would love to sit with her and just have a normal conversation... looking into each other's eyes. I ask, "Akiko, how does it smell and feel there? It looks fantastic."

With a deep warming smile she lost focus, as if experiencing it for me. Then, she spent the next fifteen minutes describing the smells and how they made her feel. She described the scents, the breezes, the squirrels chattering in the trees, birds chirping and flittering through the air. Her descriptions were remarkably detailed and made me feel like I was actually there experiencing it with her. I loved it, and I enjoyed her enthusiasm even more. Akiko had a profound love and appreciation of life. All I could think to say was, "Thank you, Akiko."

"You are very welcome, Nick. I also thank you for what you do for us. Please come back and visit me often."

You bet your ass I will, I thought, but what I said was, "I will, and thanks again."

Akiko was called away, but I remained and basked in the afterglow of the shared friendship. I really needed this break.

Genesis Log: 10 Oct 2015:

Boring! What can I say? I have nothing to report today...again. Nothing is happening... no problems... no activity... nothing! We just continue through the void of space that seems endless. I had more fun in my wheelchair. At least I had others to talk to in the hospital.

I continue analyzing data until my mechanical eyes cross, and then I roam the ship through my visual centers, watching the activities of others. At least they are busy.

Genesis Log: 20 Oct 2015:

Nothing!

Genesis Log: 25 Oct 2015:

Nothing!

Genesis Log: 27 Nov 2015:

I snapped out of my depression today, realizing that I had been acting like a spoiled child. It happened suddenly. For the last few weeks, I had not even activated my holographic center or spoke at the cycle meeting. If they gave me strange looks or even spoke, I did not remember or even care at the time. It was all a blur. I vaguely remember Dr. Rossen trying to talk to me at some point, but I have no idea what he said.

The deep depression I recently felt was as it was when I came out of my coma in a military hospital in Landstuhl, Germany. I remember the shock and fear of awaking and not being able to move. The nurse was there and caring, but there was deep sorrow in her eyes that spoke volumes. She was holding my hand, but I felt nothing. I felt nothing at all... anywhere.

I knew where I was, even back then. I had been there before on my first deployment to Iraq, recovering from shrapnel wounds. If you had ever been there, you would never forget the place. It was an excellent medical facility with fantastic and caring personnel, but neither the personal suffering of the wounded nor the horror of war could be forgotten. For many, life would never be the same. Some were missing limbs and/or horribly disfigured, while others were in shock from what they had seen and been unable to comprehend. I had been lucky the first time, but all those faces and memories flooded back to my mind with the recognition of where I was.

When the nurse confirmed that I was indeed at the Landstuhl Regional Medical Center in Germany, just outside of Ramstein Air Force Base, I lost all hope.

The last thing I remember was tackling a terrorist charging into my platoon. I drove us through a window into a building. I was the closest, saw the danger and reacted first. All I could think of at the time was protecting my men. "My men?" I asked groggily.

"You came in alone. They must be fine." she said, understanding my meaning.

Remembering back, I was at least relieved at that. It was the only good news I heard, though. She explained that I had suffered major muscle and organ injuries from the blast, but those injuries had been repaired. All my limbs remained, but I had sustained severe spinal injuries.

"You are very lucky to be alive," she said.

Big deal, I still had my arms and legs, but they didn't work.

I had been in a coma for weeks, but my injuries were so severe that they were afraid to transfer me. The care they gave me was first rate, but even that care added to my depression. I was totally helpless, captured in my own mind. They bathed me, fed me, cleaned my soiled sheets, scratched the itches on my face... it was embarrassing. Each day I felt worse... spiraling down into the darkness of self-pity. This was no life, and I wanted to die. I would have died if I could have slit my throat or wrists. I tried to will my mind to die and eventually sank into the abyss of despair. I didn't care anymore about anything and lost all track of time or the world around me.

I have no idea how long I was in that abyss, but suddenly one day I began to live again. The sun was shining, birds were singing and life seemed to have meaning again. There was a reason I was still alive. I had no idea what that might be, but my will to live sprang forth again to the amazement of my shrinks. I now understand that purpose was to BE Genesis.

Today reminded me of that day of awakening long ago. I have a purpose and it is an important one, a purpose I was saved to perform. Genesis is the hope of the human race, and I am Genesis. I must survive... I will survive... the human race will survive!

The stimulus I received back then is lost to me, but today's motivation is vivid. It is also surprising.

151

I was in the dark abyss again when spoken words finally filtered into my consciousness and my mind burst open.

"Akiko is dead! You killed her you son of a bitch!" said the general.

I clawed and fought my way back through the darkness and screamed, "What

did you say?"

"Welcome back boss. We missed you... you lazy bastard!" he said.

I looked hard at him and he was smiling. He wouldn't be smiling if Akiko was really dead. Would he? Did he actually say that? "What's this all about?" I asked.

Still smiling he said, "Well, I got volunteered to shock you out of your depression. Everyone has tried, but the team knew if anyone could reach inside you and piss you off or shock you enough to wake you up, it would have to be me. I guess they were right. Doc said you were severely depressed, and we had to bring you out of it before you got so deep you couldn't be reached. Are you okay now?"

"I guess so. What happened?" I asked.

"Doc said it was the boredom and lack of activity. You seemed to withdraw more and more each day until you were just gone. We tried to talk to you, but you ignored us," said the general.

"Why did you say Akiko was dead? She is all right?"

"Yes," he said, "she is fine. The reason I said it is because I know you love her and hearing that she was dead was the only thing I could use to reach you. Oh, don't try to deny it. It is obvious, because it worked. I have been trying to piss you off for days but to no avail. Only the thought of Akiko dying reached you. Before you panic, no one else knows. Well, maybe Akiko does, since she shares your feelings. She has been in tears for weeks. I am surprised you didn't see her crying over your dome when no one else was around. Maybe when you get to feeling better you can explain to me how the hell you two managed to fall in love."

Crap! What in the world is wrong with me? I am only a brain. Wait, he said Akiko was crying over me? Could this be true? We have talked many times in her garden, and I have enjoyed our talks, but love?

"Thanks, General," I said, "I will be fine now. And, the love thing... if I figure it out, I will let you know."

"You know I expected to get depressed at some point in the trip, but I never expected it to come this soon. Feel free to kick my ass again if I need it." As he was leaving, I halted him saying sternly, "Oh, First Officer McCullah, don't get in the habit of calling me a SOB."

The general burst out in laughter, and I joined in.

"Yes, Sir," he responded with a crisp salute, but the laugh could not be masked.

"Give me a little time now to catch up with everything," I said. He eyed me closely until I said, "Honestly, I am fine." He seemed satisfied and left.

If Akiko had been crying over me, I didn't want her to be sad any longer. Besides, I wanted to see her also. I went searching for her, but I didn't have to look far. She was sitting on the bench in her garden where we always talk. Her head was down

153

in her cupped hand, but she knew immediately when I logged on the visual center. I have no idea how, since there is only a small red light that comes on, but no sound.

"Nick?" she blurted. "Are you there?"

"Yes, Akiko," I spoke softly. "I am fine. The general said you had been worried about me so I came looking for you."

"I have been so worried about you," she said. "I... err... we thought you were lost to us. I tried talking to you so many times, but you wouldn't respond."

"I'm so sorry, Akiko," I said. "It was boredom and depression. It just sneaked up on me. I knew I would eventually have to fight it but not just months into the journey. I figured it would take years. I can fight it now. I know how." I really didn't, but she didn't need to know that.

I was so glad I came. Akiko was radiant now and obviously happy to see me, and I was more than happy to see her.

"Akiko, I have a question for you... something I am very curious about."

"Yes," she responded, slightly cocking her head and giving me a curious look in return.

"When I came in, you seemed to know I was here. How did you know?"

"I felt you. I always feel your presence when you are around me."

It was more than curiosity now. She had piqued my scientific interest. There were no scientific reasons for her to feel me. It would have to be unscientific reasons. She used the word felt as if it was a sense like sight, smell, hearing, touch, or

154

taste; but there was no sight (other than the light), no sound, no smell and no taste. Nor did I touch her in any physical sense. If she felt me, I must be projecting my presence. Is that possible? The only word that came to my consciousness was telepathy. This would take some analysis.

All these thoughts were instantaneous and for later consideration. Akiko was the focus of my attention now. I said, "Okay", letting her know I understood. We then began to just talk again like we have so many times, but I somehow felt we were closer now. I really enjoyed her company.

Genesis Log: 28 Nov 2015 (Thanksgiving Day):

The early cycle meeting was enjoyable. The team was pleased to see me outgoing again, even happy. Actually, so was I. It had been a close call, and I hadn't seen it coming. It is strange how depression can sneak up on a person. One moment you are busy and happy, and then something happens to change everything. I have two hundred years of this to look forward to.

First Officer McCullah was in an unusually jovial mood today. Wonders of wonders, he was even smiling. His attitude was contagious, even to me... wondering what was up with him.

"Happy Thanksgiving, everyone," he announced. "I ... well; we have a surprise for you. I have convinced Akiko to give up a few of her breeding turkeys, and the chef is preparing them now. Turkey and dressing for everyone today. Well, sorry, not everyone I'm afraid," he sadly said as he

155

looked directly at me. "Maybe by next year you can join us."

The general seemed genuinely sad. I thought he would be my nemesis the whole trip. How wrong I was. It is true that I would love to enjoy a Thanksgiving dinner with them, but contrary to his concern, I was extremely happy to see this celebration. Even the Japanese were happy with the celebration of this American holiday. The diversion from the monotony of daily life was more than welcome, and I would definitely join them there in spirit.

Saying the word spirit reminded me of Akiko again. Could she really feel my... for lack of a better word... spirit? How could she? I decided to test a theory I had been considering.

Extending my mind into the visual centers was routine now. I realized that instead of remaining stationary and simply switching the inputs of the visual centers, I felt like I was projecting myself directly to the chosen location, especially when I went to visit Akiko. I wanted to feel like I was standing there close looking at her; so, I perceived my mind at that location. This perception worked when I was monitoring only one location. As I analyze in retrospect, when I was monitoring multiple locations, I actually felt like I was at my main location, observing. Logically, if in fact Akiko does feel me, I may actually BE projecting my essence there. I have no idea how, but astral projection has been speculated and written about before. Maybe this was a form of that.

I waited until I thought they all would be in the dining hall. Purposely, I made sure to keep my reference in the control room and switched on the visual center. I observed Akiko visiting with Linda and eating. I silently retreated back to the control room. Okay, let's see, as I mentally projected to the visual center again as if I was standing there. Well, I'll be! Akiko looked up immediately and smiled at me. I could not believe it, but then I had to. She definitely felt my presence. To cover my spying I announced, "Happy Thanksgiving, all." Energetically, they turned, waved, and responded with their own greeting.

Damn, I had some real soul searching to do. Akiko had known all those times I had spied on her in the gym, her garden... hell all over the ship. Now that I think about it, she was the one who first spoke to me in the garden that resulted in the many conversations. I had been observing her, and she had known and spoke to me. She had known all the time. I should have realized it then. Damn, I felt embarrassed. Well, it was too late to worry about that now. There are bigger scientific issues that must now be researched.

Genesis Log: 1 Dec 2015:

After the early, uneventful staff meeting, he asked Dr. Rossen, Cdr. Ishiguro, and Cdr. Mitsuhara to remain. It seemed strange calling Akiko Cdr. Mitsuhara, but it was appropriate, considering the situation. Even though Cdr. Ishiguro was a medical doctor also, he would probably never come up to the status of Dr. Rossen in my mind. I guess it is the history we have together.

I was going to bring up the subject of telepathy, or at least Akiko's ability to sense my presence. I had mentioned telepathy before, and there had been no reaction; but I think Dr. Rossen was simply patronizing me. I don't think he believed it possible. I wasn't sure about Cdr. Ishiguro, but telepathy didn't really have much support from the scientific community. They lacked facts... something that could be measured and confirmed.

I was also a little apprehensive of talking about it, because I was afraid the doctors might dig too deep into the relationship between Akiko and me, or at least my spying on her. This had the potential of becoming embarrassing for me, but it was important and had to be pursued.

I noticed that the general also stayed. He should have been invited to stay anyway. As my first officer, he had a right. "Thanks for staying, General," I said, to which he nodded.

Reluctantly, I proceeded to lay out my finding of the last few days, complete with my test of Akiko in the mess hall. Everyone turned to look at Akiko. She kind of blushed, but nodded to the affirmative.

"It is true," she said. "I can detect his presence. I don't know how, but I do"

I could see the incredulity in the doctors' eyes, but they listened. "Test her yourself," I said, but I could already see the wonder of scientific curiosity blazing in their eyes. You bet they were going to test her.

After the doctors left, the general just looked at me then Akiko. His smile was huge as he also left. Damn him. He was enjoying my discomfort.

"I didn't know this ability was so strange," said Akiko. "I have felt you since the beginning."

"Really? You must have felt me watching you often." I said, greatly embarrassed.

Blushing she said, "I didn't mind. I liked it." She was quiet and shyly hung her head before continuing, "You know I have really cared for you since you got me the Japanese soil. That was such a sweet and caring thing to do for me. It meant a lot to me. The pot is in my quarters, and when I see it, I think of you."

"Huh? What do you mean?"

"You know, for having such a large brain, you can be really dumb sometimes," she said.

"Oh!" Just what was I supposed to say to that? Not only was I in shock, but my mind was having a hard time accepting the fact that Akiko could really love me in my condition. How could she? I was coming to the realization that I was also in love with her.

Neither of us knew how to proceed, so we reverted to our friendship and spent the next few hours simply talking as we have always done. This lasted until Akiko received a call concerning an urgent problem with rats in the storage area. My sentiments exactly... Rats!

Genesis Log: 5 Dec 2015:

Dr. Rossen tried to surprise me today, but I had been expecting it. Like I don't know just how cynical he can be. I knew he didn't believe that Akiko could sense my presence. He waited a few

159

days to catch Akiko and me off guard, but his communicator call was no real surprise.

"What are you doing, Nick?" he asked. "Can you project into the mess hall right now?"

The key word being project, and I knew what he wanted. When I projected into the visual unit in the mess area, I immediately saw him and Cdr. Ishiguro standing by the door observing Akiko from behind. She had no idea they were behind her and she immediately looked up at me and smiled. God, that smile just radiates into my soul.

"H o l y shit," came pouring out of his mouth, and the look on his face... well, it was priceless. He turned to the equally astonished Cdr. Ishiguro and said, "Did you see that? She did sense him." All he got in response was an animated nod that made his unruly hair wave.

"I told you she sensed me, but keep testing. I don't want any doubt in your mind when we talk again." It was Dr. Rossen's turn to nod.

He did, in fact, test her two more times today... once in the gym and another in her garden. I spoke to her in the garden and told her the doctors were testing her. I wanted her to know so we wouldn't embarrass ourselves. Akiko, normally shy and reserved, found this humorous and invited them to join us. She was starting to realize the uniqueness of our ability and was becoming as curious as the rest of us.

The doctors quizzed her at length, but Akiko could provide little additional information. She just knew when I was there, and that was it. It couldn't be explained; she simply felt my presence. They even blindfolded her and had me come and go, project and simply monitor, as I had done in my first test. Akiko felt me every time I projected, without fail.

The doctors were now believers, but astonished believers. It wasn't logical and didn't conform to any known science, but it was definitely real. They excused themselves to discuss and research this phenomenon. Our next meeting should be interesting.

Genesis Log: 10 Dec 2015:

Cdr. Kim excited the team today with his announcement, "I want to build a telescope." As is his typical style, Kim lectured the team, me included.

He took the center stage, so to speak, and said, "We, well, I, didn't expect to be able to use a telescope in space past light speed so we left it out. Obviously, this obstacle has been overcome. Since we can now operate a telescope past light speed, I want to build a good one to study our target jump solar systems before we arrive."

"I have been studying space telescopes and my chosen model is the Hubble Telescope. Unfortunately, I will have to design a reduced-scale version of the Hubble Telescope. The limiting factor of any telescope is the size of the primary focus mirror. The Hubble Telescope has a primary mirror of slightly over eight feet. I propose to build ours with a six-foot mirror. The original design and precision construction of the Hubble was extremely complicated, but we are fortunate that some factors, previously almost insurmountable, are far easier for us now. The extremely precise primary and secondary mirrors can be built using Poly Metal. A Poly Metal reflective parabola can easily be molded and polished to eliminate spherical aberration that might cause any image imperfection. Other advantages are its structural strength and ability to hold its form. Once built, it will not alter, changing its focus."

"I really love this polymer; but as fantastic as it is, we can't view through the ship's outer skin without causing some spectral changes. Each color has a slightly different light wavelength, which become separated by the effective prism of the Poly Metal. It is like viewing light through a prism. I am sure you have all seen the rainbow of colors separated through a prism. This is an undesired effect. Unfortunately, this will degrade the images viewed through a telescope."

"Therefore, because of this degrading quality, the telescope will have to be mounted outside of the ship in open space. The unobstructed vacuum of space provides a perfect environment for long distance viewing."

"Now, I have been giving thought about a primary location to install our telescope. I believe the perfect location is in and above the top dome right above our heads."

When he mentioned this, everyone looked up at the slow curvature of the ceiling, peaking above my central location. It is a perfect location and in fact is actually wasted space, not typical of the normal efficient economy of design of Genesis. After studying these facts, there were general nods of agreement, including mine. As normal, I was way

162

ahead of Kim in what was coming next, but this was his project, and I wanted him to take the lead.

Kim went on, "This poses many challenges to us, and I will need help." He paused for emphasis. "There are several problems that must be considered: First, the telescope will need to be designed in such a way as to collapse into a tight storage compartment that also must be constructed in the space above us. Secondly, and probably the hardest problem to solve, we must breach the hull of the ship in space traveling at light speed. And it would be nice if we could accomplish this without killing ourselves in the process."

"You sure don't bring us easy challenges, Kim!" Linda laughingly said. "This will take some thought and planning."

That was a gross understatement, but she didn't say it couldn't be done. That was encouraging. Linda was a very smart girl and she would accept this challenge with her normal vigor, and I would help but not interfere.

I was already running calculations. The telescope was the easy part, although Kim's desire was far more than I had anticipated when I originally planted the idea. Kim was right about the Poly Metal. Using this magic metal would make the design and construction far easier than the original construction. The space allocation would easily fit a design. All that would be required would be a retrofit to install a flatter ceiling and effectively a new pressure sealed outer wall to the Genesis. However, this was no small accomplishment. There would have to be an atmosphere evacuation chamber interconnecting to the telescope housing

163

area... two evacuation chambers when you considered the outside opening to deploy the telescope. Already it was getting complicated.

I could already see Cdr. Clark and Cdr. Tsuji in deep consultation, oblivious to everyone around them. Linda needed a challenge to keep her keen mind stimulated, but Cdr Tsuji was already working on my robotics so I had mixed emotions about that. But I was pleased how the team was challenging each other and working together without me putting any pressure on them.

My pleasure must have shown in my holographic image, because I noticed Akiko smiling, and when she caught my attention, gave me a wink. The little shit knew what I was thinking, but that pleased me.

Genesis Log: 22 Dec 2015:

Life is good. My team of geniuses, fellow voyagers and friends are making my life better. I don't feel so alone. They share the burden and challenges. This is so welcome to me, as I don't feel like everything is on my shoulders. I believe, if absolutely necessary, I could handle everything. I mean, I was designed and programmed to do so, but this burden is what set me on my path to depression. The general has tried to tell me many times to delegate; that's the secret of command. Make them feel part of the decision. Give them the information, motivation and goals; then sit back and let them run with it. Like he said, if you don't, you will be doing everything yourself. He said my job as admiral was to prop my feet up on the desk, figuratively, and supervise. That is exactly what is happening, and, like I said, life is good.

I also realized another factor: since my near disaster with depression, my mind had taught itself to compartmentalize and isolate itself somewhat from the vast increased intellect of my brain extension. Knowledge was still there at my grasp, but my core brain (ME) has established barriers to prevent overload. If anything, my intellect has increased, but I am more in control. I can remember when my intellect threatened to overwhelm my ability to communicate with other humans. I had felt overly superior... like I was speaking with children. It wasn't until recently that I discovered this change. I think it has something to do with my talks with Akiko. We talk as equals and mutual friends... lovers even to the extent this is possible. One day I simply realized I did not feel the vast superiority I had before.

As I said previously, life is good. Dr. Rossen accepted the silent challenge of believing telepathy was possible, lacking any scientific proof. He made it official at the early meeting by bringing it up to the entire team.

Just what should I call them: team, staff, officers, department heads? Of the three, I suppose staff seems more appropriate.

At any rate, Dr. Rossen brought the subject of telepathy up at this cycle's staff meeting, detailing the tests he and Cdr. Ishiguro conducted with Akiko proving its existence, at least to the extent telepathy announced my presence to her. There were many looks flashed to Akiko, but there were no questions.

I was thankful that Doc moved on after presenting telepathy as a proven fact.

"I believe in telepathy now," he said, turning to me. "We also believe we know how it happened, assuming it was never there before. We really have no way of knowing; but it certainly exists in you today; Akiko too, at least her ability to receive this ethereal energy. I can't speak for Akiko's telepathic ability. Maybe it was always there, or her mind is closer attuned to your increased theta brainwaves. It could be your focus on her. It could be any of these reasons or none of them. Whatever the reason, she can undoubtedly sense your mental force."

"As I said, we believe that I may have inadvertently created this projection ability in you when your brain was wired into the extended computer brain. As you know, I shunted silicon threads between your brain and the extended brain. The purpose of this was to provide basic interconnect paths between the brains that would allow them to grow together, making their own ties through the neurons' growth. This obviously worked, but what I didn't anticipate was that in doing so, we provided an extension of a little-known organ into the extended brain. There are several nerves coming from the eyes. These were interconnected directly into sections of the extended brain associated with your ability to receive video images, but one of the nerves connects directly to the pineal gland."

"This pineal gland is a pea size gland, some say organ, but little is known about it other than it is pretty much in the center of the brain directly behind the eyes. Actually, it seems closely associated with the eyes, but again, little is known about the functions of the pineal gland."

"We discovered in our research that old myths and some unsubstantiated theories call the pineal gland a third eye. Some believe it is a dormant organ that can be awakened to enable telepathic communication. The same sources also affirm that the pineal gland can be awakened by light or even a head trauma. Certainly, you have experienced both."

"If the pineal gland is the source of your telepathic projections, which we are inclined to believe, we have inadvertently connected this gland to a massive amount of higher function brain capacity. What this means, we have no idea."

"Is everyone following me?"

There were many awed looks and nods from the staff, but this was not really a surprise to me. I had already been engaged in my own research, with much the same conclusions. Dr. Rossen, however, provided some new aspects. I had not considered how it had happened. It all made sense now! My level of excitement was soaring, but not for the obvious reasons. I saw some incredible future applications, but this was not the time to bring them up.

Dr. Rossen continued with the discussion and answering many question, but little more information was gleaned.

Chapter 8
(More Challenges)

Genesis Log: 10 Jan 2016:

During our personal daily visits Akiko and I have been discussing the phenomena of our apparent telepathic abilities, among other things. Today we decided to begin our own experiments. Akiko surprised and intrigued me with her willingness.

Out of the blue Akiko said, "Nick, you know I have been thinking a lot about what Dr. Rossen said. He made a lot of sense about how it happened and all, but what he didn't say speaks volumes. Telepathy should be far more than just projecting your presence. It is the ability to project your thoughts. If so, I should be able to receive them don't you think? Maybe I do sense your thoughts but don't hear the words. Could it be that is what I sense? I wonder what would happen if you bypassed the communication network, the audio anyway, and projected directly to me. Maybe then, I could hear your words or thoughts directly and possibly, you could hear mine. Is that possible?"

That was profound! It really got me thinking. Akiko was right about telepathy, and she was right about the way I must be projecting. I was projecting to the visual center. Furthermore, I had never actually tried projecting to her directly. What if she was correct? We decided to try.

The first step was to withdraw from the visual center, which I did, not completely, however. I pulled back to a monitoring position only. I then focused on Akiko, concentrated my mind internally and then projected outwardly toward her. I thought the words, "Akiko, can you hear me?"

As I was monitoring the camera, I saw an immediate response. Akiko's eyes bulged and her mouth flew open in shocked surprise. If the scope of the situation hadn't been so serious, I would have laughed at her response. What happened next was a total revelation. I heard her response!

"I hear you, Nick!" she mentally said, but her response was far more than just words. I felt her shock and happiness. I felt her emotions! I saw images! I felt her thoughts beyond just the words. Most amazing of all, I felt her projected love. It was a total sharing of minds. This was the most fantastic experience of my life, but the shock of it caused me to withdraw immediately.

"Where did you go?"

"I am here," I responded, but my response was through the visual center.

"I felt you in my head, Nick! It was amazing."

I projected back again to the visual center in her garden, and we discussed what had happened in great detail. It seems we both experienced the same things, but we agreed to move forward slowly with this discovery. We also decided to keep this to ourselves, since neither wanted to share our thoughts with others.

Today was an amazing day.

Genesis Log: 15 Feb 2016:

169

Cdr. Kim and Cdr. Clark presented their draft plans for the retrofit of the control room and telescope today. I will only have some slight modifications I will inject into the plan.

For any future reader of these logs to understand the retrofit plan, it is necessary to provide a better description of the general layout of the control room.

The control room, my space, is in reality large, much less efficient than the rest of the ship. The control room, as viewed from outside, would appear as a raised dome, on top of the saucer shape of the ship. If you picture a cup turned upside down on top of an upside-down large saucer (no pun intended), you would have a general idea.

The diameter of the control room, which is the upper level, measures three hundred feet at the base and twenty-five feet at the peak, which is directly over the internal dome of the computer, ME. The majority of the outside of the bowl is configured with Poly Metal windows, allowing unobstructed viewing of space in 360 degrees. The view is quite impressive, and, I might add, intimidating. Fortunately, the view can be diminished or even eliminated by activating the Poly Metal lighting. This turns the transparency of the windows to an opaque white, depending on the level of light generated and segments activated.

Unfortunately, there is an internal semicircle of connected rooms positioned seventy-five feet behind me. These rooms follow the curved contour of the dome, obscuring the back 120 degrees and connecting to the top of the dome. According to Linda, the rooms also serve as support and structural protection beyond simply storage. The inside concave of the wall structure, facing me, is abundantly adorned with visual monitors and digital displays.

There is a semicircle of control stations one hundred feet out in front of me, spreading 180 degrees, but below my field of vision. Within this forward semicircle are three rows of swivel chairs used to man or observe the workstations when required or swiveled around for our staff meetings and gatherings.

Behind the structure to my rear is a single ramp leading up into the control room space. This ramp, as with all ramps between decks, is automatically lifted to form a vacuum seal and airlock as required. Speaking of airlocks, my individual computer dome has its own airlock as well.

The final fifty feet of the outside upward curving diameter is a cordoned off observatory circling the entire dome. Shipboard personnel use this as an observation deck, and the space is a popular place for jogging.

I am proud of the looks and layout of the dome, especially since the center's overwhelming feature is my silver dome... me. When my holograph image is active, it is the center of attention and quite impressive.

The control room dome is the only section of the ship without multiple airlocks. With this in mind, it can easily be understood that any retrofit that alters the air seal integrity of any part of the dome jeopardizes the entire dome, not to mention the aesthetics.

I have to say, though, the plans looked good. The plan calls for the reinforcement and conversion of one of the center rooms in the structure behind me to a transfer air lock. Since the structure went to the ceiling, a second airlock door would be placed at the top to open into the telescope compartment to be added. By having two stages of air equalization compartments to the outside, Linda was taking no chances.

The actual telescope compartment was also planned well. The walls will be double layered and internally pressurized, similar to the outside shell of the ship.

As it turns out, the compartment will not be directly overhead but attached to the revamped airlock compartment then extended overhead toward the center twenty feet with a vertical depth of ten feet. Surprisingly, the planned structure is not circular in design, more closely resembling a tapered square with rounded corners. A simulated view makes it look totally acceptable, even pleasing...like it was meant to be there.

"Why so big? It looks fantastic, but I was wondering why this large?" I asked.

Linda was grinning when she responded, "A couple of reasons: I want to build the telescope in place and need the room, but additionally, we can move one of the large lasers into the compartment and have 360-degree weaponry."

"Excellent," I blurted just ahead of the general. "Well done, Linda." I was happy with this revelation, and the general was ecstatic. I had never even considered this additional option. Improved weaponry was a brilliant idea, but with her Berkley pacifist influence, I was somewhat surprised.

"The design seems fantastic, but let the staff look it over before we commit," I said. "Barring any unforeseen problems, I think we have a GO on the project. I must insist on one thing, however. I want the outside hull door installed and checked before we breech the hull. I realize this will require installing it recessed, but if there are any problems with the breech, we must be able to seal off the compartment."

"For once I am ahead of you," she said, sporting a big smile. "I plan to install two doors, one initially and a second one after the breech... just in case."

"You are amazing!" I said, also smiling.

"You are amazing, too." Akiko responded telepathically.

She was grinning with our newfound secret, but the surprise almost made me lose my train of thought.

Genesis Log: 25 March. 2016:

We did not have a staff meeting today. Construction began instead... what a mess. Scaffolding was installed all around me as they began the work on the telescope room. This was the first time I actually had a chance to see the engineers work with Wonder Metal, and it was surprisingly easy. The electronic tools used to mold the Poly Metal worked incredibly fast. The walls were brought in already prebuilt and assembled in place. In one eighteen hour shift the entire room was constructed, and the crew had moved internally. The external visual portion of the retrofit was a work of modern art, seamless and symmetrical.

I asked Linda to install cameras inside both airlocks so I could watch the activity, and she was more than happy to comply. Visuals would be needed anyway, once operational.

The details of the complete construction and final testing would take months. The telescope would take much longer due to the precision required, but we had plenty of time before we reached Alpha Centauri.

Genesis Log: 15 April 2016:

Akiko addressed the staff today. She was usually so quiet, but when it comes to her responsibility, she can be quite vocal.

"Admiral," she said as she stood to get everyone attention. "I have been projecting the required food production, and we are coming up short. We have too many awake and living off our farm production."

Even though Akiko and I were far from just friends, she would never try to take advantage of me, quite the contrary. No one knew our telepathic secret, though I suspect Dr. Rossen may have guessed.

"How bad is it Cdr. Mitsuhara?" I asked.

"Well, it is not critical yet, but we are depleting our stores. We are just feeding too many."

"There are one hundred and five awake. How many can your farm feed?"

174

"Well, I originally planned for twenty-five awake, but I can provide for more... just not a hundred. I would like to reduce the number to seventy-five, at least until I can replenish the stores," Akiko said.

There were several groans, but it is what it is. Life-support must come first above all other functions. Staying alive is the highest priority.

Cdr. Rossen was quick to say, "We don't have that many cryogenic chambers free. Our plans have always anticipated more on the Awake Team. With what we have going, this is the required number to run and maintain the ship. We did plan for some contingencies, however. Currently, we only have fifteen open chambers. The most we can reduce the numbers to is ninety."

"We don't have much choice here but to comply with Akiko's request to our best ability," I said. "Additionally, we hadn't planned on Hope's Awake Team, but you are not counting the chambers still remaining on the Hope. They still have ten unused chambers so we can reduce the number to eighty."

They didn't like the rest of my speech, well, some of them. While we were having the conversation, I had already compiled a list of those headed to the freezer... well, the staff anyway. I announced them: Cdr. Takashi Ishiguro, Cdr. Hiroshi Tsuji, Cdr. Yoshiaki Sakata, Capt. McCullah, and Lt. Margret McKay. Although the Japanese team had an abundance of skills, they were part of the overpopulation problem. This made their choice easy, plus they were not part of any immediate solution to anything currently required.

With the addition of the lasers to my visual centers, I could maintain much of the security, so Capt. McCullah's responsibilities were not as important. Of course, there would still be an Awake Team level of security personnel. He gave me a look of concern, but smiled with my last choice.

I chose Lt. Margret McKay for a completely different reason. Lt. McKay was one of the general's security officers. She was also a beautiful young lady in her early twenties. I had noticed the attraction between her and the general. The old pervert and she had been sneaking around to be together. No one knew but me. On numerous occasions, I had monitored her sneaking into his cabin late and leaving early. Obviously, this was a mutual arrangement, and I didn't want him to have to make a professional choice of separation. I made the decision for him. The general gave me a knowing look and gentle smile.

The remaining volunteers would have to be chosen by the department heads, with the exception of Akiko's department. If food production was critical, all her Awake Team would be required to maximize the output.

I promised to wake them if they were needed or when we reached Alpha Centauri, whichever came first. That seemed to satisfy them, with one exception. Cdr. Kim suggested we wake Jim Sharp a few months before we reached Alpha Centauri.

He said, "I know he is a pain in the ass, but he is an incredibly talented astronomer, and we might want his expertise to observe Alpha Centauri prior to our arrival."

There were a few groans, even from the Japanese contingent, but admittedly, it was a good idea. I could imagine more pleasant thoughts than seeing Ichabod Crain bobbing around the decks, but I guess we could thaw him out and let his ear heal.

Genesis Log: 20 April 2016:

Okay, all the cryogenic chambers are full and we are now down to a minimum of eighty awake personnel, but our level of activity has dropped significantly. It is probably not going to be a problem. After all, we still have almost two hundred years to work on all the various projects. Besides, the whole object of cryogenic hibernation is to make sure the educated personnel remain young to settle New Earth.

Our staff meeting this cycle was the smallest yet, but we picked up a new member from the Hope. Even though all the department heads of Hope went into storage, they wanted a representative in the staff meeting. The Hope chose Cdr. Jane Jones, JJ for short, to represent their interest. I would have represented them since the Hope is part of us now, but they had insisted. I didn't really have a problem with it.

JJ had been recruited from the US Navy while serving in Japan. JJ was essentially still active duty Navy with the rank of full commander. JJ was, of course, a PhD with degrees in electrical and mechanical engineering. The Japanese government had requested her under the auspices of the US Government to work on a Top-Secret project. Being such, the US Government didn't know the exact project she had been working on. The Navy thought JJ was working on a completely different project. Once she had learned the nature of the Japanese project, she saw no future in informing the Navy. This was her ticket to survival and she took it. She was part of the Hope now. It was clearly apparent to the Hope Team that JJ, being American and an officer in the US Navy, could interface well with us and look after their interests as well. They would be right in this assumption.

Cdr. Jones is a gorgeous and shapely black woman in her early thirties, tall, about 5' 9", slim and muscular, black eyes and hair, dark ebony skin and assertive in demeanor. She meshed into the group immediately. We all liked her right away.

JJ's main responsibility as the leader of the Hope's Awake Team of five is maintenance of the Hope, but Linda liked her and her expertise and immediately took her under her wing.

With the general stored away in the freezer, I took the opportunity to assign the security detachment to JJ. She was, after all, a real Naval officer, one of the few onboard. She took the additional assignment without comment. I knew I had to assign the detachment to one of the staff, but was reluctant to use any of the current staff. Hell, most were pacifists. That would never work. I jumped at this chance, and I really think she will do a good job.

Genesis Log: 15 June 2016:

Akiko was mad when I projected to the garden today. She never spoke harshly... she was such a

178

gentle soul. With as much time as we had spent together over the last few months, I had learned to recognize when she was stressed or mad. During those times she reverted back to her native Japanese. Today she spoke Japanese when I entered.

"Doko ni imashita ka.? (Where have you been?)" was her greeting. "Anata ga inakkata aida samishikatta desu. (I was lonely without you.)"

Without thinking about it I responded back in Japanese, "Watashi wa kokoni imasu. Watashi wa anata kara tooku na idesu. (I am here. I am never far from you.)" I knew why she was mad, but I wasn't prepared to tell her yet why I had been absent the last couple of days. I didn't want to get her hopes up if I was unable to deliver. We haven't missed many days being together in the last few months, and I had missed her too. It was my favorite part of a cycle.

I had been researching and planning in an effort to find a way to project into a real body, my own. If this goal could be accomplished, Akiko and I could physically be together. God in heaven, I wanted that more than anything... not just to escape my prison, although that would be a wonderful freedom to enjoy. No, I wanted a body to be able to touch Akiko, look into her eyes directly, smell her hair, hold her in my arms and feel her warmth, taste her kisses, and experience physical love. How this beautiful woman loves me could not be explained, but I certainly love her, there is no doubt.

I think I have found a way, and became caught up in the planning. Time was short, because I needed Dr. Rossen to get it started before he had to go into cryogenics for the next hop. The downside,

Doc wouldn't be easy to convince. My plan would go against his training, but it was a sound theory. I would have to have answers to all his objections before I brought it up.

"I am sorry, Akiko," I pleaded. "I have missed you, too, more than you know. I am working on something for us. Please, just trust me. If it works, you will be happy... we will be happy. So far I had responded through the communication center, but the next response was telepathic and in Japanese for emphasis, "Aishiteru, Akiko. (I love you, Akiko.)" She rewarded me with a huge smile and shining black eyes leaking tears of joy. That was the assurance she needed.

We have perfected our telepathic communication, but Akiko never initiated a telepathic conversation. It could be disturbing to me, especially if I was already in a conversation. She knew that and always waited for me to touch her mind first. Well, almost always. Sometimes she enjoyed teasing me a little in the early cycle meetings, but I enjoyed having her in my mind on those occasions, even if she did tease me.

Akiko would tease me at other times also, but not telepathically. When she knew I was watching her exercise, sometimes she would put a little more sway in her hips and bend over just a little further. She even tried to shake her boobs, but as small a cup as she has, it was more cute than sexy. I loved it, and she enjoyed me watching her.

Genesis Log: 1 July 2016:

180

Cdr. Clark announced at our early cycle meeting that the construction and testing of the telescope room and airlocks were complete and she was ready to breech the hull and install the outside sliding hatch. Cheers and congratulations were offered, and she beamed with the attention; she deserved it too. It was a masterful design and accomplishment to retrofit an in-flight spaceship, especially trying to breech the hull traveling beyond light speed. Well, the final breech had not yet been accomplished, but if it went wrong, at least the damage would be minimal.

None of us really had any idea what would happen when the hull was breeched. Would there be super friction at light speed? Would it suck the workers out? Could a human cease to exist outside of the protection of the ship? I didn't think so, but it had never been tested, and I don't like surprises.

I keep thinking about space dust. When a person thinks about space, most imagine a void of nothingness, but it is far from that. Space is full of dust; although extremely small, it is there, nonetheless. At first thought, you might think, so what? Nevertheless, think about sandblasting. Sand propelled under high pressure is used to clean brick and stone quite effectively and fast. It can remove paint and wear down even metal. Take it a step further. Imagine particles, even dust, propelled at the speed of light; which is effectively what is happening, albeit the Genesis is the moving object impacting dust at the speed of light. The effects are the same. At that speed, a small particle could pass completely through an unshielded spacesuit and occupant.

Luckily, the Genesis is shielded with antigravity on the hull to repel any particles and even some larger masses of asteroids. This shielding, combined with the tapered shape of the hull, theoretically should knife the ship through space relatively safely, while pulling the Hope in its cleared wake. Hopefully, this wake would also protect our workers and equipment as well. That was the plan anyway.

Maybe I am just too damn paranoid. Sure, there is plenty of dust in space, but there is an abundance of wide-open nothingness, too...vast amounts. The odds are very good that no dust will be encountered during the short interval required, but I will feel much better when this is done.

Linda originally suggested retrofitting one of our landing shuttles to go outside to do the work, but I nixed that idea immediately. Without knowing what the effects would be, there was no way I would allow the bottom hatch to be opened, and certainly not exiting in a shuttle.

When it was time to begin the final stage, I insisted on volunteers only because of the potential danger. I also refused to allow Linda to be one of them, much to her annoyance. None were expendable, but Linda was totally irreplaceable. She was not happy about it but accepted my demand. As it turned out, there was no shortage of volunteers for the three workers required. Her whole crew wanted to volunteer, even JJ.

I was happy to see that Linda did let JJ join the team along with two of her engineering team. Everything was already in place, including the camera so I could monitor their activities.

The entire remaining staff and numerous other ship personnel gathered to watch the historic activities. We watched as the volunteers suited up in the first airlock then waited as the air was evacuated from the chamber. The workers then rode up on the small lift, entered the telescope room, and closed the second safety airlock. Just in case and according to procedure, they safety latched themselves to the bulkhead. The first hatch to the outside was electronically opened. As one of them stood by to immediately close the hatch again if necessary, JJ stepped up with the Wonder Metal cutting tool and stood ready. Linda held her breath and gave the order to proceed. Then all was quiet as JJ breeched the double hull.

Nothing happened! There were no disastrous mishaps as she continued to widen the opening enough to push a probe outside to test for safety. Again, nothing. It went quickly from there. The opening was cut and the hatch frame was set in place and molded in. The only concern was when JJ had to lean out into the opening to make the outside seals to the hatch, but that too went smooth. It was all done!

Genesis Log: 15 July 2016:

At our early cycle meeting, Linda reported that the long-term pressure test passed 5 by 5, which included several tests of opening the outside hatches and cycling the pressurization. She reported that they were now ready to proceed with the building and installation of the telescope and weapon laser, which they anticipated would take eight months to complete.

I was getting used to the overhead compartment. Truthfully, I rather liked it. I still had fifteen feet of space above the peak of my dome, and it tended to create a feeling of some enclosure, where it had been open before. Previously, when the Control Room dome had been translucent, there was a strong sense of vulnerability... as if I was exposed and alone in space. It is hard to explain, but suffice to say, I liked the new feeling of protection.

Genesis Log: 20 July 2016:

Not much has been happening, and I was beginning to enjoy the relaxed atmosphere of the meetings, but I had a feeling of the calm before the storm. What would be the next crisis?

I continued to research my project, but I was still not ready to take on Dr. Rossen yet. I needed him to be onboard with my plan... it was imperative.

Even though I continued with my research, and it was time critical, I never neglected Akiko again. I felt terrible having disappointed her in my zeal to be with her in body and soul. Akiko's gardens felt like my second home and sharing Akiko's passion of nature was very satisfying. I just enjoyed sharing anything with her, especially telepathically when our emotions and senses seemed to merge. We were, however, aware that we must handle our responsibilities, and it was becoming obvious to some around us that there was more to our relationship than met the eyes. We continued to meet in the garden but changed our time to late cycle when the activities around us were less. Of course, I continued to watch her exercise, and she continued to tease me.

Genesis Log: 15 Aug 2016:

I wasn't ready for this one. I don't like people problems, but it came anyway. Cdr. Jones waited around after the early cycle meeting to talk to me. I saw that something was bothering her and waited for her to come out with it.

"Admiral, I am sorry to burden you with this," she said. "I feel I have to report this." I nodded and she continued, "Cdr. Kim is making unwanted sexual advances toward me. At first, it was just comments and innuendos, but now it is touching, and it has progressed to groping. I told him I was uncomfortable with it and asked him to stop, but he continues. I don't want to cause any problems for him, but it is starting to affect my work."

Damn, I hadn't even considered having to deal with crap like this. Now it slaps me in the face. Pairing up on the long cruise was to be expected, even encouraged. There was an obvious effort to populate the ship with equal numbers of males and females toward this goal. This was, after all, a mission to settle New Earth and populate it with humans. Our mission was also to operate a military vessel requiring discipline and professionalism, and this must take priority.

I didn't really know what to do about it. I just knew I would have to do something. For a brief second, I thought about waking First Officer McCullah. I am sure he has had to deal with this

185

crap before. No, that would be giving up far too soon.

This is so unlike the professional Kim I know. He almost seemed shy around women, even a nerd. Maybe I have appraised him wrong.

I gave the standard stalling answer, "Okay, Cdr. Jones. Thanks for bringing this to my attention. I will deal with it." She seemed embarrassed to have brought it up at all and quickly nodded and left.

After she left, I kept thinking of all the questions I should have asked her. I was wondering, did she already have a male companion? Maybe she was gay. Why did she resent Cdr. Kim's advances? Why didn't she deal with this herself? JJ was assertive, and if she wanted to, could easily kick the crap out of Kim. No, that couldn't happen either. I even wondered if she was purposely trying to get Kim in trouble to gain favor with others or me. Could it be that she just wanted to keep relationships and professionalism separate, as it should be? Anything was possible. No matter what, it was in my hands now, so I had better start observing Cdr. Kim and Cdr. Jones to learn the facts. I had better know before I acted. It also occurred to me that I needed to take a more active role in what was happening aboard ship. If that required observing the rest of the crew, so be it.

Genesis Log: 16 Aug 2016:

I followed JJ around the ship for the entire cycle and saw nothing out of the ordinary. She appeared to have numerous friends around the ship, but none that appeared to be close or that might be considered a romantic attraction to her. Those times when Kim was around her, I did not see or hear him doing anything that could be interpreted as out of line, nor did she appear to be uncomfortable around him.

When I visited Akiko, I told her what was up and asked her if she was aware of any romance between JJ and another shipmate.

She smiled and said, "No, but then I am not around her much. I do know that Dr. Rossen and Linda are close."

"No shit, Doc and Linda?" I liked the idea of them together. They are family.

"It is not open for all to see, but you can see it in their eyes when they are around each other. I know what love feels like, and I see it in her when they are together," she said.

I really was going to have to keep my eyes open, if for no other reason than to watch the fun. I hate that everyone knows but me.

Genesis Log: 20 Aug 2016:

How could I have been so blind? Akiko was absolutely correct. There was something between Dr. Rossen and Linda, and it was easy to see if you looked, although their outward appearance was always professional. They always sat together in the meetings, ate together, exercised and played together, and, when I spied on them, could see them slipping into each other's rooms. As I said before, I liked the idea of them as a pair. They were like family to me. I wondered how I had missed it before and just how long it had been going on. They had worked together isolated in heavy security for years, so I presume it was a natural attraction that has gone on for some time, even before I came along.

I also continued to monitor JJ and Kim, without incident. Once I saw Kim touch her shoulder, but it seemed it was meant only to get her attention to address an engineering question. I saw nothing inappropriate in that action. I have to wonder what the game is here, but I will continue to observe them.

Genesis Log: 10 Sept 2016:

After our morning meeting I asked Dr. Rossen, Linda, and Akiko to remain. As JJ was leaving I asked her to inform the Marine guards at the two entrances that I was exercising security shield. This was their instruction to hold all admittance to the inner area. From this, everyone present knew this was to be a private and seriously secure meeting. I had seldom activated the full security measures, but after the area was clear, I brought up the visual and sound electronic shields. It appeared as a shimmering opaque dome surrounding the inner circle including my dome and the inner row of seats. When activated, the shield was physically impenetrable and totally blocked all visual and audio signals from escaping.

Linda had designed the shield for immediate danger and seemed concerned until I said, "There is no danger. I just want a private meeting between the four of us. You will understand soon." They relaxed some but still seemed tense with the pending seriousness of what might come.

188

I had decided it was time to present my case to Dr. Rossen, and since it affected Akiko, I wanted her here. I wanted Linda here in hopes she would support me with Dr. Rossen. Maybe Doc wouldn't have a problem with my request, but if he did, this was my only chance to persuade him to help...so I tried to stack the deck against him.

I decided on a straight upfront and honest approach and took a deep breath, metaphorically speaking, and said, "Doc, I have been working on a plan for some time, and I have been reluctant to bring it up; but I need you to help me, actually I need you to do it for me. I want you to clone a body for me." I watched for a reaction and saw no sign or indication in his expression.

I continued, "As you may have guessed, Akiko and I are in love." All faces turned to a blushing Akiko, but she met their looks with a nod of affirmation. "I want a body I can project into so we can be man and woman, as you and Linda are man and woman." It was their turn to blush, but they did not deny it. They looked at each other with affection and back to me.

Dr. Rossen, taking Linda's hand in his, said, "Are we that obvious?

"Of course not, but it can be seen if you look hard enough. I don't think others know, but Akiko pointed it out to me. We have a long trip ahead of us and there is nothing wrong with it. It is just, we want what you two have... physical love beyond what we already have." There were nods of understanding. Even Akiko was smiling and nodding.

"So," Dr. Rossen said. "You want a physical body, and you want me to clone an exact duplicate of you? You know there are many moral and ethical concerns about cloning, especially if it is used for body parts at the expense of the life created? Even if we create a new body for you, what makes you think you can project into it? Maybe you should just tell me your plan and let's go from there."

I was ecstatic that he didn't initially blow up with moral and ethical indignation. I think Linda's presence and the revelation of their love had softened the shock. I was happy at any rate. I knew he would listen to the plan. "Fair enough", I said.

"The whole plan starts with cloning a copy of me from my blood sample," I began. "You certainly understand cloning, but for the benefit of Linda and Akiko. This involves taking an egg from a female donor, removing the nucleus of the cell, and replacing it with a cell from my body, in this case from my blood, with my DNA. Once this is done and the cells begin to multiply, the fetus is then implanted in a host female to grow to full term. As the fetus grows, it will be an exact copy of my DNA, thus me. This is the essence of cloning."

"Let me answer your last question first. You asked about being able to project into the body. As you may have also already guessed, Akiko and I have been communicating via telepathy for months now. As we already discussed, for my part I believe the ability came from the expanded brain capacity programming itself to support a stronger functioning pineal gland. Certainly, it is fully awake and transmitting and receiving telepathic messages. As far as Akiko, I haven't a clue. Maybe as you

190

suggested, her theta brain waves are close enough to mine for it to work. Hell, maybe that is the reason we were attracted to each other in the beginning, an invisible attraction. We may never know why, but it works nonetheless."

"Now as to the plan, we won't have to wonder if telepathy will exist since the cloned body will BE me with exactly the same DNA and thus theta brain waves. Another factor that should increase this telepathic ability is the fact that the pineal glands in children are much larger. We can probably assume that the pineal gland shrinks in adults because it isn't used. I intend to use it and keep it exercised and active."

"I agree that there are some moral and ethical concerns, but I do not intend to destroy life. I intend to enhance life, my own. This sounds selfish and egotistical, but all life on the Genesis is my responsibility. If I fail, every soul on board will die. For this reason alone, this experiment should proceed in order to enhance my ability to remain sane and protect the lives of those in my charge."

"Having said this, my plan does not presume to kill the existence or soul of the new life. If all goes as planned, there will never be a consciousness to kill. The consciousness will be my own, extended into the new life."

"This is the hard part to explain. Theoretically, it should happen as I am presenting it. The human brain is continually learning, programming and reprogramming itself constantly. In the beginning, it is virtually a blank with no real consciousness. It is waiting to be programmed from inputs it receives from the senses of its body. The brain learns to be conscious, learns to be self-aware. I simply intend to teach it to be an extension of my consciousness."

"The frontal lobe of the new brain, let's call it Nick 2, normally used for higher functions such as thought, reason, decisions, etc., will learn to communicate instead. The vast capacity of the frontal lobe of the new brain will program itself to support the communication link through the pineal gland. My brain will be the dominant consciousness to direct its development and purpose. In essence, the new body will be an extension of my thoughts and directions; while the older, more primitive part of Nick 2's brain will support all the bodily functions."

My plan had changed much to the better as of late. Originally, I believed Dr. Rossen would be required to install silicon nerve connection, similar to what he installed to connect my brain into the extended brain, from the pineal gland to the frontal lobe. Additionally, and this was the sticky part of my plan that I thought he would balk at, I thought he would have to break (kill) the connections from the frontal lobe to the older primitive brain. This action could easily be viewed as killing the life or soul of Nick 2.

The more I researched the functions of the brain, the more I began to understand just how versatile a human brain is. I learned that the human brain would reprogram itself to serve its needs, especially in its development stage. That is when I realized it would not be necessary to surgically alter Nick 2's brain. Dr. Rossen would not be forced to struggle so much with the morality and ethics of the plan. This made my sales pitch far more plausible.

Akiko surprised us all when she blurted out, "I will contribute to this cause. I will donate an egg and host the fetus. I want to make this extra bond between myself and Nick." She laughed and continued, "I had always assumed I would first have sex before I gave birth, but I see now that I must first give birth before I can have sex."

In spite of the seriousness of the situation, we all broke out in laughter at Akiko's humor. Even so, the joke was factually correct.

I had not even considered this possibility, and I was flooded with mixed emotions, both love and concern. That she would want to undergo this hardship for us was fantastic and warming to my heart, yet the paradox of carrying her future lover in her womb was unsettling. The potential additional bond between Akiko and me in my growing physical form could actually be beneficial. Linda broke my thoughts with her comment.

"This is so fantastic and so incredibly romantic," Linda said. "What can I do to help?"

"I think you just did! And I must assume that, too, was part of the plan." Dr. Rossen laughingly said. "I am definitely outnumbered here."

"Actually, I think this is a realistic plan that can work. You do realize that the cloning is the easy part. All the work, well other than the nine months of carrying and nourishing the fetus and giving birth, you will have to do mentally. I do think your logic is on target, but we still run the risk of destroying life and there are those who will resent our interference in the evolution of life. Rest assured that this IS altering the evolution of life. If we were on Earth, I would be breaking the law, but I am in. Let's do it."

"I will probably make some demands as I think about it more, but the one thing that comes to mind immediately is this: I will insist that Akiko is separated from the baby immediately after birth. I think it is dangerous emotionally for her and the baby to bond. There should be no confusion in her mind as to who Nick 2 is then or in the future."

"My suggestion is that after birth Akiko goes into cryogenics for at least the next twenty years to allow Nick 2 to mature. She can't stay awake the whole time anyway. You can both then meet physically for the first time when she wakes."

"The baby can be raised in our nursery by my staff, and I will be able to help with the training and observe the progress."

I hadn't really thought much about that aspect, but it made sense, and Akiko was nodding in agreement. How would I be able to live without her around? I hadn't thought about this either, but it was inevitable that she go into storage at some point, anyway. This was going to get complicated.

Genesis Log: 12 Oct 2016:

The love of my life became pregnant today, but only the four of us knew. We would have to come up with a good cover story for Akiko, but what? Oh, I have been sleeping around and got pregnant? I don't think so. I didn't even like the thought of anyone thinking that about her. Oh well, we have a few months before she would be showing to think about it.

I spent the night with Akiko, projected into her mind. I wanted her to feel my love and I hers. These were precious moments.

Genesis Log: 25 Oct 2016:

Doc, Linda, Akiko, and I had another private meeting this cycle. After all the prior discussions, we decided to simply tell the truth about Akiko. Well, a partial truth at any rate. Dr. Rossen said he would mention to a few in confidence that Akiko had volunteered to carry a clone of me in order to have spare parts for redundant improvements. He would mention that my circulatory system was weak and could fail. This insurance could save the Genesis if problems developed in the future. Doc wanted to make it personal to their safety and head off any objections. If their life depended on it, they would be far less likely to have any moral outrage. He said he would choose some individual to accidentally overhear a conversation with Linda. They would have the word spread throughout the ship by late cycle.

We laughed at this revelation, as we all knew several onboard that would serve well in this task.

Chapter 9
(First Stop)

Genesis Log: 8 Jan 2017:

After almost three months, Akiko is beginning to show and draw attention, but she seems to like it. It doesn't take much for her to show with her petite body, but I think it is more that she wants to show and is beginning to wear maternity clothes. It does seem to become her though, and she is radiating with life and pride. She likes to say, "Nick 2 is our baby," which makes us both happy.

Dr. Rossen said, "I am concerned that other mating couples might also want to have babies."

This must be discouraged due to our limited resources and lack of additional cryogenic chambers. He suggested, and I agreed, that we must take steps to ensure no other pregnancies occur. The obvious answer is to add birth control additives to the drinking water supply and take any decisions away from individuals. This will be started immediately without any formal elaboration or even notification.

Akiko reports this cycle that, with the reduction of awake personnel, the food supply is now adequate, and she is building up the stores again. This is certainly good news and an obvious relief to the staff.

Genesis Log: 15 Jan 2017:

Cdrs. Kim, Clark and Jones announced that the telescope and laser were ready to install. Yep, I saw another lecture coming, but why not? They had obviously done well and deserved to toot their own horns, so to speak. I had a pretty good grasp of all the details, having followed their research and planning, but I was interested and wanted to hear the outcome. I knew the others were interested also; after all, it wasn't like we all had burning issues we had to rush off to handle.

Cdr. Kim droned into his lecture mode, "We had to back into our design. The outside sliding hatches have an opening of only five feet. This was the largest Linda had in inventory, and they are so complex that we didn't want to try and build one from scratch. Therefore, since the limiting factor on size for a telescope is the diameter of the primary focal mirror, we had to establish four feet as the beginning design criteria of the telescope. We modeled our telescope after the design of the Hubble Telescope, but unfortunately, ours is only approximately half scale. The Hubble Telescope has a primary mirror of almost eight feet. Nevertheless, our telescope, which my associates affectionately named Kibble, will be an excellent long-range precision telescope."

"How in the world did you come up with Kibble? It sounds like the name of a dog food," I said.

Linda burst out laughing and said, "Well, since it was Dr. Kim's project, we merged the names Kim and Hubble, thus Kibble."

After the laughter died down, Dr. Rossen interjected, "I hate to sound dense, but I know nothing about telescopes. I know you look in one end and view distant objects and they appear close, but I do not understand why you need mirrors and one so big."

Oh, crap. You could actually see Dr. Kim smile at that. Here it comes...the Telescopes 101 lecture. Akiko smiled at what she knew I was thinking. I really liked Kim and he was one smart SOB... hell, they all were. What's one more lecture? Besides, he did have the ability to take a complex subject and present it in simple terms so anyone could understand it.

"The theory of telescopes is relatively simple," Kim said. "The complexity comes from the precision required in the optics. Basically, the bigger area used to gather light, the better clarity you get and the more you can see. In this design, the Ritehey-Chretien telescope (RCT), we use what is called a Cassegrain configuration. This fundamentally uses a wide, in this case four feet in diameter, light-gathering mirror shaped in a hyperbolic or saucer shape. The primary mirror hyperbola is designed to gather light, reflect and focus it precisely to a secondary mirror, in this case approximately six inches in diameter. The secondary mirror is a reverse hyperbola, more like the outside of a cup, placed at an exact calculated location. The purpose of the secondary mirror is to reflect a beam of concentrated light through a small hole in the center of the primary mirror to the input of a camera."

"I know this sounds simple in theory, and it is, but it gets complicated when you consider that hardly any two angles on the mirrors are the same.

The reflecting angles must all be precise in order to concentrate the light. Think of it like calculating the bounce of a pool ball off the banks, but think millions of pool balls and double banks. If the angles are not all perfect, the viewed image appears out of focus, haloed or you suffer other forms of spherical aberrations. It was discovered that the Hubble suffered from this, which required a maintenance mission in space to correct."

"We had an advantage in our construction, our mirrors use the Poly Metal, which could be smoothed and altered as required to obtain perfection. Our perfection was far beyond the tolerance permitted on the Hubble's mirrors. This ability was impossible in the construction of the Hubble. Dr. Rossen, is this clearer?"

"Yes, much clearer... thanks."

Kim went on, "We have also designed an elaborate deployment arrangement. Both the laser and the telescope must be able to deploy through the outside hatch, but they both can't be deployed at the same time. The mounting structures for both are attached to a complex swivel arrangement, all automatically controlled."

"Well done!" I said... smiling, "I think I might be observing space as much as you." It would be a wonderful divergence.

Genesis Log: 20 Jan 2017:

The whiz kids completed installing the laser and telescope today. The mount and deployment procedures worked perfectly. Cdr. Kim had the controls wired into his control console, but in doing so, I also had complete control as well. I liked the idea of control, especially over the laser. Now I had security control inside and outside the Genesis. I hope I never need it.

My nights are long and lonely, living within my own quiet thoughts. Some nights it is as if I walk the corridors of the ship, secretly haunting them. I let my vision switch from camera to camera looking for life and entertainment... at least something to occupy my mind. Well, this new telescope will provide something new. I am sure I will become bored with it in time, but I will live for the moment and enjoy the new toy.

Genesis Log: 25 Jan 2017:

Doc wanted another meeting today, and I was a little apprehensive. Akiko had recently admitted that she had been having some minor problems, but she was fine. The solemn look on Dr. Rossen's face told me differently.

He started out, "I am afraid I have some bad news. As you know, I have insisted on frequent checkups to follow the progress of Akiko's pregnancy. I can't be absolutely sure, but Akiko is showing many symptoms of a condition called pre-eclampsia. Her blood pressure is high, and she has elevated protein in her urine, both indications of this condition. Since Akiko was in perfect health prior to becoming pregnant, I must assume she has pre-eclampsia."

"This condition is not even remotely rare. It is more common in women who are pregnant for the first time and occurs in as many as 10% of pregnancies, usually in the second or third trimester. It can happen earlier, but that is rare. Akiko is still in the first trimester, although toward the end. Since she is developing this condition early, it tends to indicate that it might be a more severe case."

"Pre-eclampsia is the mother's immune system rejecting the foreign DNA of the father's in the placenta. In Akiko's case, she didn't contribute any DNA to the fetus and its placenta. In the cloning process, the mother's egg that would contribute DNA to the fetus is removed and replaced with the donor, yours. Therefore, the very fact that she is carrying a clone of your undiluted DNA complicates the condition. In simple terms, her body is rejecting your foreign DNA."

"In normal pregnancies, the mother would have received small doses of the father's DNA in the form of semen during intercourse that would slowly build up her immunological tolerance. Again, there has been no prior exposure to your DNA."

"Pre-eclampsia can be a serious condition to the host mother. The hypertension can cause numerous problems along with permanent damage to blood vessels, kidneys, liver and other internal organs. This is what we are up against."

"I have explained this all to Akiko, but she waves it off as if it doesn't exist. That is why I am bringing it up now to all of us."

I knew what was coming next. I was racing through research studies as he was speaking.

Dr. Rossen continued, "The only known treatment for advancing pre-eclampsia is abortion or delivery, and Akiko is far from that point."

Akiko leaped to her feet and blurted, "Fuck you! I am not having an abortion... end of discussion. No one is going to take my baby." She then looked directly at me and screamed, "Not even you! Now, open the damned shield and let me the fuck out of here!"

That's exactly what I did. I opened the security shield and watched her stomp off. God, she was pissed. I had never heard her speak loudly, much less scream, and I had never heard her curse... ever.

I decided to give her space, but I couldn't stop thinking about the danger to her; worst of all, she was doing it for me. I was the cause of her sickness, and it was tearing me up. Regardless, we knew from her reaction that she was determined to go the term with the baby... live or die. She made that abundantly clear.

"I will do everything in my power to keep her safe," Doc said, "if she will let me."

Genesis Log: 27 Jan 2017:

Dr. Rossen and I keep attempting to talk to Akiko. We have tried separately and together to discuss the inevitability of an abortion, but she turns cold and harsh any time we get close to the subject. She won't even talk female to female with Linda. She acts normally in all other discussions and our personal time... just don't bring up her health in any form. I am so concerned for her.

Doc says Akiko is so petite and fragile with this condition that he is afraid the longer she carries the fetus, the more danger of her death or severe permanent damage to her organs. It doesn't matter to her... it is not open to discussion. She will carry the baby to term... no matter what. I wish we had not let her volunteer to carry the baby, but considering her possessiveness of the fetus, Nick 2, as she calls it, I can't imagine Akiko allowing any other female to have served in this capacity.

The whole situation gets so confusing. It's no wonder Akiko is confused emotionally. She has her maternal instinct at play, but when you think about it, Akiko would be her own mother-in-law. If the situation weren't so serious, it could be comical. Damn, I wish I had never brought up my plan to have a body.

Genesis Log: 10 March 2017:

Kim was obviously delighted with his telescope and had something new to report almost every cycle. So far there was nothing astonishing to report. He was making out a few more details about Alpha Centauri, but as he admitted, we were still too far away to expect much.

I believe Cdr. Kim lacked a little confidence in his astrological expertise, which surprised me. I had ultimate confidence in him, yet he asked again when we could take Dr. Sharp out of cryogenics. I was far from anxious to put up with his crap again and stalled Kim by saying, "Not until we are close enough to make out enough details of Alpha Centauri." The main reason was to give Dr. Sharp a focus to study and not harass me. I am not sure how tolerant I could be a second time. I might not be able to be as benevolent as I was last time. I had to smile at my own joke.

I did, however, agree to let Dr. Rossen bring Cdr. Sakata out of cryogenics to take over life-support from Akiko. She continued to try to oversee everything, but Dr. Rossen was forcing her into total bed rest, actually he was forcing her into a clinic bed with full life monitoring. Akiko knew better than to argue with him on this point, because the fetus was at risk as well. I personally had given up trying to reason with Akiko; she could be totally unreasonable. All I could do was support her decision.

I had already requested Linda to have an additional visual center installed in Akiko's cubicle. I didn't want to be far from her and, in her worsening condition, she wanted my support. It was nice to be needed.

Akiko and the rest of us had finally resigned ourselves to the fact that she would carry the baby as long as possible before taking it. Akiko realized that if she died in the process it might kill the baby and resolved that at some point the baby would have to be taken. She wanted to try to give it a chance at life and wait until the last possible moment. At four months' growth, it was yet far too soon, but we all worried that her body might not hold out long enough.

Genesis Log: 12 March 2017:

Cdr. Sakata reported back to active duty at the early cycle meeting. He was jubilant to be awake, although reported that it seemed like only yesterday he went to cryogenics. I am sure it was to him,

204

although it had been one month shy of a year, much shorter than it should have been.

At our meeting we explained why he was brought out, and I instructed him to spend time with Akiko to get up to speed on the requirements. In truth, those were Akiko's instructions to me. You bet I listened. In her condition she could be cranky.

She had accepted the temporary transfer of her department. As she told me, she had those on her staff who knew as much as she did and could keep things going with a new department head. I had my doubts that anyone could fill her shoes, but we had no choice.

Cdr. Sakata welcomed the attention and responsibility, but I noticed a change in Cdr. Jones. Since Cdr. Sakata was the Hope's team leader, JJ must have felt less important not to be representing the Hope. She said nothing, but I made a point of requesting information concerning security to remind her she was still a department head and expected to be at the cycle meeting. That seemed to help her disposition.

JJ still posed a potential problem to me, however. I have still not been able to validate her claim of being sexually harassed by Cdr. Kim. After all these months of observation, I had yet to see Kim do anything out of line. I don't know any more than before and continue to wonder what was up, but something continues to give me an uneasy feeling about her action. I wish something would have happened so I could stop puzzling over it.

Genesis Log: 19 May 2017:

I was shocked about mid-cycle today. I was projected into Akiko's hospital room attempting to reach her telepathically. Her body was failing her quickly, and she was floating in and out of an almost comatose state. As my mind was open, searching for Akiko's mind, I felt Nick 2. There was no communications per se, just a presence of his mind. He must have felt me projecting my mind and locked on. He began projecting what I might call emotions in small minute levels, but it continued. I also felt my mind responding. I have no idea what my mind was saying, but Nick 2 began sending information instead of trying to store it.

In a mind so small and fragile, I believe it felt my dominant mind and sought the comfort of its organization. It was easier for it to transfer the information than try to learn from it. Actually, there was no need to learn, my mind was storing and processing the information and giving responses. My mind evidently was automatically giving feedback as if it were a part of my mind, which it now was. This was easier than I had anticipated. Nick 2 was reinforcing the link and programming its small mind to communicate with mine.

After a few hours, it became almost routine, and I didn't notice it as much, but I was definitely aware of the input. It was projecting warmth, hunger, wonder, and it felt pain! Akiko's body was trying to reject it, kill it. Once I realized what was happening, I explained these new phenomena to Dr. Rossen. He was both elated and concerned.

"We have to take the baby," he said. "Akiko is dying from it. Already her poor little body is severely damaged. Honestly, Nick, she may not recover. I have only allowed it to go on this long to give the baby a chance, but from what you are telling me, it is also dying. We don't have a choice. We must take the baby now!"

"What about the baby? I asked, "Can it live if we take it now? You know that if Akiko lives and the baby dies, she will never forgive us"

Dr. Rossen was thoughtful and responded, "I know... I know. Well, it has a chance, but if we wait, she has no chance. We have the best premature birth facilities ever built. Keep in mind that birthing children is one of our main purposes, and we prepared well."

"The baby is about two weeks past the twenty-three weeks viable fetus stage, but it would still be considered a severely premature infant. These usually have underdeveloped lungs, but I started a regimen of glucocorticoid, steroid hormones, about two weeks ago. These steroids should speed the lung development and other vital organs. Hopefully, it will be enough. With your mental connection, you can reinforce the baby's breathing. Sometimes premature infants simply forget to breath. There is always this concern even in full term babies. It is one of the major causes of infant mortality."

After a moment's thought I said, "Okay, Doc. Do it while she is still out and can't stop us. I want her to live."

I watched the surgery like a nervous father and husband. It was a simple procedure and went fast. I swear Doc must have been able to sense my projected nervousness as well, because he talked to me all during the surgery.

207

Genesis Log: 21 May 2017:

Akiko came through the surgery well, but her recovery is slow... very slow. After two days she remains in a coma, but Doc says her vital signs are stabilizing somewhat.

I wasn't prepared for the next comment from Dr. Rossen. I have never seen him more glum.

"Akiko is in really bad shape, Nick," he said. "Her organs are really damaged. I am afraid she might not come out of her coma."

I was shocked and distraught. No, I can't lose her now. This can't be happening. No! I won't let it happen! All this intellect must be able to figure out a solution. All I had to do was turn it loose. That is exactly what I did.

I withdrew within my mind and opened all the self-imposed barriers I had installed to protect my sanity. Fuck it! I needed the intellect now. My consciousness was immediately flooded with the force of my expanded mind. I had been isolated so long now that I was momentarily dizzy and overwhelmed by its force, but it soon passed, and I was able to direct my full attention to finding a solution.

I researched medical records, gathered data, and launched into new science, all at the speed of light. I found an answer. It was a simple solution, but it was very complicated and far more complex than simply saving Akiko. She would be immortal. It would take an abundance of additional research and time, but it could be done. The hard part would be explaining it to Dr. Rossen on a level he could understand and assist me with the plan. It would also launch us into a new debate into the philosophical ramification of my actions and the morality of immortality. I looked forward to these debates. Regardless, I would save Akiko.

The more immediate problem was keeping Akiko alive long enough to accomplish my plan. This, too, was a simple solution. I broke my silent brooding and said, "Dr. Rossen, as soon as Akiko is stable enough, put her in cryogenics. This will give us time to develop my plan." A knowing but comical expression rolled over his face as if he could sense I was operating at full capacity and planning.

Genesis Log: 23 May 2017:

Nick 2's body is no longer under attack and has settled down some. He sleeps most of the time, but I feel the constant flow of data. As I suspected, his brain had made the conversion almost as soon as he felt my presence and sought the comfort of my consciousness. His brain was developing as a telepathic extension of my own. His brain would never learn or become conscious or self-aware, but function as an extension of me. I guess that is not totally factual; his primeval, older brain would learn the internal workings of the body such as muscle control, internal endocrinal network and the like, but the higher functions of the brain would link to me. I would be the one to learn from his sensory inputs. In essence, he was me, and I was him... we were one.

His frail little body was in an incubator, closely watched and monitored, nourished and cared for. I was, however, the far better monitor. I felt his discomfort and knew when he needed changing and fed. No feeding schedule was required. When he was hungry, I told them. When he was wet, I told them. It was perfect. I mean every mother or nurse has at one point or another wished their baby could talk and tell them what was wrong. It was my discomfort, so I was quick to tell them. I also realized with some satisfaction that once the muscles developed, I would actually be able to talk through Nick 2's mouth. That will surely scare the crap out of the nurses when I do. I could hardly wait.

Unfortunately, however, he was under two pounds and barely alive. Doc had been right about his underdeveloped lungs and potential infant mortality. Nick 2 has actually stopped breathing on several occasions, but I gently nudged his body along with his breathing. I project instruction to his voluntary muscles, augmenting his automatic breathing response. As a result, I am feeling more confident in his/our survival.

Also this cycle Dr. Rossen felt Akiko had stabilized enough to put her into cryogenics. There was only one chamber vacant, the one recently vacated by Cdr. Sakata. It is a good thing, too. I would have yanked someone, anyone, to make room for her.

Akiko never came out of her coma, but once Doc took the baby, her vital signs did improve. Unfortunately, her poor little body and organs had sustained major damage and Doc hadn't expected she would awake, maybe never. I will not allow her to die, ever.

I watched as her chamber filled and she was taken from me, possibly for years. Akiko had done so much for me, and I loved her even more for it. I spoke to her mind, "In time, my love, we will be together again, and you will be whole."

Genesis Log: 18 Aug 2017:

I thoroughly enjoyed this cycle. With all the seriousness, a good laugh can do wonders to lighten the spirits, especially mine.

Nick 2/we... our body is three months old tomorrow. I have waited this long to pull my trick on the attendants in the nursery. I have been exercising my muscles, learning how to move them. This includes my mouth and tongue, experimenting with random sounds. The beautiful part about this learning is that it is instantaneous. Once I discover the neural path of a muscle in Nick 2's body, that path is memorized in my mind and I can move it at will. The muscles are growing fast, but I have to be careful not to overextend them beyond the physical ability of Nick 2's body. His/my body was a total extension of me now.

By design, I had made it a point of not speaking other than "wet - hungry" and other bare minimum words. Mostly, I only made sounds that established the neural path. It was all I could do to remain quiet. I wanted to share with Dr. Rossen, but then I wanted him to be part of the butt of my planned joke.

That day arrived, and I was giddy in anticipation. I had waited for maximum results, and it came unexpectedly. I am not sure why Linda was

211

there, but this was the best time to spring it. She was there with Dr. Rossen and three of the attendants as they were conducting a three-months physical checkup on me. I was on the scale measuring in at just over ten pounds. All eyes were on me when I spoke, "I am a fat little fuck now, don't you think?"

I am sure happy no one was holding me, because two of the attendants literally ran screaming from the room. The eyes rolled up on the third one as she passed out and fell to the floor. Dr. Rossen immediately broke out in hysterical laughter. Linda just stared at me for the longest.

Eventually, she said, "Nick, you little shit!"

"Got cha!"

Doc was still bent over holding his stomach, completely incapacitated by his laughter, but the other two nurses tentatively returned to help the fallen one. Linda, well, Linda was beginning to chuckle at the situation and at Doc's antics.

Still laughing, Doc said, "I knew that was coming sooner or later, but it still took me by surprise. How long have you been planning this?"

Obviously, he had anticipated this development, just not the practical joke. Another fact that did not escape me was that he was talking to me and not a baby. He knew what was happening. I began kicking with glee and said, "Three months."

Linda, having figured out what was happening, said, "Nick, you are some piece of work."

All in all, it was the most fun I had had in years. It was a very good day.

Genesis Log: 18 Nov 2017:

The plan for Akiko I had devised would require some of Dr. Takashi Ishiguro's expertise in genetics and lots of new developments. Because of this, I had asked Doc to bring Taka out of cryogenics. He had been recovering the last few days and was now back to the staff meetings.

I didn't want to just come right out with my plan. First, it was too complicated and second, it would be a long term endeavor with many stages. I did, however, have an excuse to bring the initial part of the plan forward without revealing my ultimate goal. It was time to launch the first stage.

I asked for a private meeting with Dr. Rossen and Taka. Once we were alone I asked, "Gentlemen, we seem to have hundreds of thousands of human embryos in cryogenic storage. My question is, just how do you expect to turn these embryos into viable humans? Surely, you don't expect to use female hosts to carry them all to term. Please tell me you don't plan to do that, because the adult human females will be busy trying to populate New Earth with their own offspring."

I expected Dr. Rossen to answer, since I was referring to the embryos stored on Genesis. It was, however, Dr. Ishiguro who responded.

"Dr. Rossen and I have discussed this. We expect to develop what is called artificial uteruses," he said. "Major research was begun at Cornell University at the Center for Reproductive Medicine and Infertility, under Dr. Hung Ching Liu. They established the theory and basic research. Unfortunately, they could not move into the advanced research required because of the permitted

213

legal limits of in vitro fertilization legislation in the United States. Fortunately, the Japanese were not so encumbered by legal restrictions."

"Dr. Yoshinori Kuwabara at Juntendo University in Tokyo continued with the research in development of an artificial uterus. This uterus supports the growth of an embryo in tanks. I think I speak for Dr. Rossen when I say we fully expect to be able to develop this artificial uterus. Unfortunately, Earth side, controversy surrounding embryo research prevented full development. It will require much more continuing research before it is fully developed, but we feel confident that it will happen."

I looked at Dr. Rossen for confirmation, which he provided with a nod. "Very well, gentlemen. Don't you think you should get busy on the project? Otherwise, we will have transported a lot of embryos for nothing."

After a moment of thought, I continued, "If this were available sooner, we could have saved much hardship on Akiko." With the mention of Akiko, Dr. Rossen got this hangdog look, and his eyes cut to the floor. I know he felt responsible for Akiko's hardship, and it was maybe a cheap shot, but it was also true. There was no need to say anything further. They were sufficiently motivated to embark into this new challenge.

Genesis Log: 19 May 2018:

Today is Nick 2's first birthday, and Doc had a little party for us complete with hats and cake. It was funny seeing the cake with only one candle on it. I did manage to blow it out though. I was pleased with the attention.

Nick2's muscle development is coming along well, but there are no real shortcuts. It will just take time for my body to develop. I still can't really do much for myself and all my needs have to be handled by the nurses...they forgave me.

I was there inside his little body trying to eat some cake. God, it was good to taste food again. I can't wait until I have enough teeth to eat a T-bone steak. I know I have given my attendants fits with my finicky ways, but they are understanding and I can at least tell them what I like and what I didn't and how much to give me. I didn't cry. There was no reason to. All I had to do was tell them.

In many ways, it is rewarding to have a body. I was experiencing senses I had all but forgotten. As I said before, taste was one sensation I was enjoying again and smell, but having the ability to actually touch and the simple capacity to let your mind reach out, move arms, legs and fingers is exhilarating. If you have never been quadriplegic and physically incapacitated, it would be hard to understand. Imagine seeing something and not being able to reach out to it. Your mind says reach, but your muscles do nothing. It is enough to drive many insane.

I have the best of both worlds. The Genesis is an extension of my mind and now Nick 2 is becoming my physical sensory extension. My mind and body are becoming one in human form.

Genesis Log: 31 Oct 2018:

We had the normal routine reports this cycle, but nothing worth mentioning. Everything is still running normal and on schedule, but after the staff meeting broke up, Dr. Rossen and Linda stayed after. Something was up.

When we were alone Doc looked kind of sheepish and was sporting a barely controlled grin. "Ok, what's up?" I asked.

"We screwed up," Doc said. "You know we started applying birth control to the drinking water supply, but Linda was having an allergic reaction. She has been drinking distilled water. Well, she's pregnant, and after seeing Akiko's determination in having her baby, well, she won't consider an abortion."

Hell, I didn't know what to say. I couldn't make Akiko have an abortion, so I wasn't about to force Linda either. I just said, "Congratulations."

They both broke out in wide grins. I smiled and continued in a more serious tone, "But, you need to make sure others aren't drinking distilled water, and you better try and build more cryogenic chambers. Don't you think?"

"Will do, boss."

Genesis Log: 12 Nov 2018:

The research had taken a year, but Dr. Rossen and Dr. Ishiguro had been successful in inventing and testing an artificial uterus. They had total confidence in its ability to carry an embryo full term. They were in fact so confident that construction had begun in the nursery facilities with banks of hundreds of tanks. Their research was sound and quite inventive. In addition, as much as I had studied Taka's research on the miracle of life from fertilization to full term delivery, I was shocked to learn facts that had escaped me previously. They had done a fantastic job, and I asked them to give a full briefing to the staff.

Dr. Rossen happily launched into his presentation, "As Nick, I mean Admiral Johns, has announced, we have been successful in developing an artificial uterus. Surprisingly, this wasn't extremely difficult. We built upon research that had already begun, but we found better ways. Actually, the researchers were trying to make it difficult. As it turned out, the trick is not to try and replace the functions of the human reproductive process, but support it."

"An embryo is almost self-sufficient in that it will provide for its own growth and development. All it needs external to it is nutrients, oxygen and waste removal. These requirements can all be provided artificially to the growing fetus. These requirements are very similar to Nick's life support... artificial blood, heart, filters and nutrients. This is where the previous researchers were making their mistake. We want the embryo to develop a self-contained placenta."

"After fertilization, the cells begin to split and form a group of building cells called blastocyst. This early stage embryo attaches to the inner wall of the female uterus to obtain oxygen, nutrients and waste expulsion. The placenta grows from the embryo cells to become basically a self-contained bubble surrounding the growing embryo and isolating the fetus from the host. It fills with mostly

217

water containing proteins, lipids and electrolytes, which aid in the growth of the fetus."

"What many don't realize is the placenta functions as a barrier, which totally isolates the mother's blood from the blood developed by the fetus. The placenta transfers only the required nutrients and oxygen and expels toxic waste through this barrier. The umbilical cord provides the connection from the fetus to the placenta. Many think the umbilical cord connects the mother's blood directly to the fetus, but this is definitely not the case."

"Therefore, our process tries to completely duplicate Mother Nature and not interfere. The only missing link was the uterus tissue, which we engineered from cultures of endometrial cells to form a uterus material fold attached to external artificial life support. Previous research had proven this could be done."

"All we have to do is place the beginning embryo in the folds of the engineered uterus, and it will attach and grow. We float the uterus and developing placenta and fetus in a temperature-controlled vat of sterilized water and electrolytes and watch it grow. At full term, we open the placenta, which is equivalent to a woman's water breaking before birth. In this case, we bypass the delivery and simply take the baby."

This is the whole process... a baby machine. In this case we will have hundreds of wombs operating simultaneously. Mercifully, in the future there will be no need for any female to suffer through pregnancy unless they just want to. We can continue to operate at full staff once we land."

Cheers rang out in the control room, except for Linda who said, "My timing sucks!"

Genesis Log: 25 Dec 2018:

I put it off as long as I could, but I finally had to approve Cdr. Kim's request to bring Jim Sharp out of cryogenics. Since we were seven months out from Alpha Centauri, I figured we could use his expertise to study the solar system. It was also Christmas, and I was feeling generous.

Of all the solar systems we would be repelling from, this one had the greatest potential for life. This could be good, or it could be bad. Any planets orbiting Alpha Centauri A or B have almost a billion years head start on our evolution. If life exists there, it could be far more advanced. Who knows what that could mean, but we had to find out.

When Doc woke Jim Sharp, he would probably still be angry. He went into cryogenics fighting and screaming obscenities at me...go figure. Doc had stitched his ear back on where I had lasered it off, but obviously, it would still hurt and be a constant reminder. I had to smile, remembering the scene. I had already warned Cdr. Kim to get him calm before he came to me, because I would not hesitate to do it again, or even worse.

We could use his expertise, but I would not tolerate any disruption to our operation. Even at best, I would never give him any command control, and he would remain a civilian with no rank. That is something he would have to earn, assuming he wanted to, which I doubted he would.

I was right! When he woke, it was as if no time had passed. Jim started in again with his obscenities, expressing his desire to kill me. I mentally licked the sights on my lasers but resolved myself to wait. The general had wanted me to kill him, and I probably should have, but it wasn't too late. He would be trouble.

Kim and JJ were both with him, trying to calm him and catch him up on the activities of the last few years. Realizing he had been out for that long seemed to calm him some and even more so when Kim told him about the telescope. As I had hoped, Jim Sharp seemed to turn his attention to astronomy and the fact that we were only seven months out from Alpha Centauri. The potential research interested him more now.

In the back of my mind, I was troubled about something. Something was not quite right... out of place. I finally realized it was Cdr. Jones that was bothering me. She was head of security and could easily be expected to be there, but her attention to Jim was what was bothering me, plus the fact that she was with Cdr. Kim, her harasser, so she claimed. I had still not been able to substantiate her claim. Oh well, another puzzle to ponder.

The three of them came to the staff meeting together. It was like JJ and Kim were staying close to keep Jim from blowing up again. I noticed Dr. Rossen and Linda staying out of any target area. I even noticed a slight grin on Doc's face; he was enjoying it.

"Welcome back, Mr. Sharp." I said, "We have a challenge for you. Are you ready to go back to

220

work?" He said nothing and continued to stare at me. I then said, "I require an answer Mr. Sharp."

Jim blurted, "Fuck you, Infidel!"

His temper and hate had let it slip. Now I understood much. The shocked look on JJ's face and her tugs on his arm told me even more. That was their tie, and he had just revealed it. This is what had been bothering me. They evidently were both Islamic converts, not that this was bad, but I feel confident that these two are of the radical persuasion. It also became evident that JJ's motivation against Dr. Kim was to try to help slide Jim Sharp into his slot. Why had I not seen it before? There was no mention of it in their personnel file, but both had spent an unusual amount of time in the Mid-East for no apparent reason. They had also been working together in the Hope project as well. I saw it all, but I didn't let on. I just attacked his attitude, "You will show respect to me and the staff in these meeting, or you will go right back in cryogenics. Do you understand? Think before you answer, because this is your one and only opportunity to show that you can take orders and fit in."

He stared hard, but slowly relaxed and said, "Yes."

"As the captain, I will be addressed as Sir!"

"Yes, Captain, Sir, I understand what is required."

"I don't care if you like me, but you will obey me and show respect. Now go to work and report to me and my staff when you have something to report."

There was no doubt now. I would have more trouble with him. I would continue to push him and watch him very closely, and JJ as well. Actually, I was somewhat anxious to cut his other ear off.

Cdr. Kim was also far too trusting. I would have to educate him. I wish the general were here to help.

Genesis Log: 15 Feb 2019:

I had been hearing hints and rumors, and I had also been looking at the same telescopic views Cdr. Kim and Mr. Sharp had been looking at. Therefore, I had a good idea what he was going to say. I was, however, curious to know what they had determined. Cdr. Kim scheduled time for a formal presentation for this cycle date.

Jim Sharp stood to make the presentation. I had rather Cdr. Kim do the presentation, but as I had previously observed, he felt inferior to Mr. Sharp. I didn't understand why, though. Cdr. Kim is brilliant in his own way and certainly as knowledgeable as Mr. Sharp. He is either intimidated by or bullied by, of all people, an Ichabod Crane. I would get the general to work on his confidence at the first opportunity.

Surprisingly, Mr. Sharp was totally professional. He was even respectful to me, at least on the surface anyway.

He turned to me, nodded, and said, "Admiral." Turning, he continued, "Staff. We have been studying Alpha Centauri for the last two months with our advanced telescope, and we have some startling information to relay. Both Alpha Centauri

222

A and B have habitable planets orbiting them. It is better than we had even dreamed possible. Alpha Centauri A has two reasonably Earth like planets and Alpha Centauri B has one. There are other planets orbiting, but they would be comparable to our Mars, uninhabitable. Now, the surprising fact concerning the habitable planets is that they are already inhabited, and from what we can gather, the inhabitants have advanced technology. We can't make out any roads or ground traffic, but see the illumination of large cities. Point of fact is that two of the three planets are heavily populated, which is the basis we use to indicate an advanced civilization. The two planets are heavily populated, if lights are any indication. The third planet is not as populated but could be comparable to Earth's population. We also believe that it is reasonable to assume that all three are of common origin and fundamental race of sentient beings."

"How can you make that assumption?" I asked.

"Good question. We believe the similarity of the universal advancement of civilization and technology supports this assumption. If they were of separate origins, in all likelihood, they would not be at the same level of development. Additional confirmation comes in the form of a common communication, not unlike our own form of modulated signals, but in a higher range of frequencies. Of course, we can't interpret their communication yet, but we should be able to decipher some fairly soon."

"The conclusions we can make from this is that they do have the ability to travel in space as evidenced by the fact that they have spread out to the other habitable planets. This capability must have existed for thousands of years to have developed to this advanced level."

"We should soon be able to formulate a contact message to begin transmitting so we can open communication with them."

"There will be no communication message transmitted!" I interrupted.

"We must make contact with them!" he blurted out, "We need time to negotiate our colonization."

"No!" I said. "There will be no colonization either. Think about what you have already said. They are overpopulated now. They will not welcome more population, and even if they allowed it, we would be the subservient and weaker beings. We would be slaves to them. No. We will continue on our original plan."

"I am not opposed to communicating with them, but not prior to arriving there. Remember that we are traveling at greater than light speed. Theoretically, we should be undetectable, but if we transmit a message, they will be forewarned. We must use the Alpha Centauri stars to enable our Light Speed Drive to repel the Genesis on the next hop. We are committed to going there, but if they are hostile and warned, we would be coming out of light speed within their range and would be sitting ducks. No, once we are there we can try to open communications, but not before. At least if they are hostile, we might have an opportunity to escape."

God, he was pissed. The arrogant bastard doesn't have a lick of common sense. He wants it his way or no way. My logic flew right over his head and he stomped out of the control room. At least he had enough restraint to retain his ear this time. I really dislike this asshole.

Genesis Log: 20 March 2019:

I broke the language code during the late cycle. The Alpha Centaurians' language code wasn't that difficult. There was no encryption so they wanted it to be easy but not too easy. It only took me a couple of cycles to decipher and translate their language and message. They had even transmitted on Earth's communication frequencies to make sure we got it. The Alpha Centaurians called themselves, by my closest interpretation, The Enlightened. Their message was simple and straight forward, "What are your intentions in approaching our worlds?"

I am still pissed at Mr. Sharp. I can't confirm it, but I still think he may have managed to send out a message to them. It could also be that their advanced technology was able to detect the Genesis, even traveling above light speed. Oh well, for whatever reason it is useless worrying about how they detected us, only what their intentions were now. Their message didn't seem hostile, but not overly friendly either.

At least all the department heads, with the exception of Akiko, were removed from cryogenics and present at our early cycle meeting when I translated the Alpha Centaurians' message. Of course, First Officer McCullah was skeptical, but his military experience would pretty much dictate this approach. The others were in awe and had been since we received their transmission, remaining quiet and leaving it up to me to decide. Well, all but Mr. Sharp. He insisted we ask about colonization.

I had been contemplating our response and saw no other way than complete honesty, and at this point, we might as well broach the subject of colonization, although I was fairly sure of their response.

The following is the message I transmitted in their own language: "Message to The Enlightened: We represent the only survivors of our species (human) to have escaped our planet before its destruction by an asteroid. Our planet was located in the closest solar system to you in the direction of this transmission, which we call Sol. Our planet, Earth, was the only habitable planet in our solar system; therefore, we are seeking a new planet we can colonize.

Our propulsion is light, and we require the light of your stars to repel to the next solar system if necessary. We seek your hospitality and help for our survival."

Genesis Log: 22 March 2019:

After only two day we received The Enlightened's response. "Yes, we are aware of your plight and of your origin. Your Human species is obviously sentient, having developed rudimentary space travel. Your craft and inhabitants, however, would not be welcome in our solar system. Our level of evolvement far exceeds that of your human race. Your race could not co-habitat with The Enlightened nor survive. Your craft will not be

226

allowed to land on any of our planets in this solar system.

The Enlightened understand your primitive propulsion system and your needs. We will await your arrival and instruct you to orbit around the second planet from our brightest star. Your craft will be met and escorted during your brief time in our solar system. Again, you must not attempt to land. Your craft will be destroyed if you do. If you prove to be a friendly sentient race, we may assist you in your survival attempt as we sympathize with your plight.

The Enlightened will await your arrival."

After reading their reply, I felt like a first grader attempting to match intelligence with a college senior. Their manner of speech left little doubt in their superiority. The entire staff seemed to feel the same, even Ichabod Crane. For once he was speechless.

Genesis Log: 18 June 2019:

True to their word, The Enlightened met Genesis as we came out of light speed. Their two shimmering craft materialized on port and starboard as we slowed. We were still at the edge of the Alpha Centauri A solar system. As with our solar system, we did not want to risk travel within the solar system and run the risk of colliding with space debris. I had not expected The Enlightened to meet us so far out. It took us all by surprise, especially me. I called an emergency meeting of the staff.

Even before the staff arrived, we received a transmission: "Do not resist and cut your propulsion drive. Our escorts will deliver your craft into orbit."

Upon entry, First Officer McCullah ordered our laser deployed. I immediately belayed that order. When he turned on me, I said, "General, we must NOT show any aggression. If they wanted to destroy us, we would already be dead. We can't compete with their technology."

"Yes, of course, sorry, Admiral."

We did exactly as they asked and cut our drive. Actually, our drive was already switched to reverse to slow our speed, but I figured they knew that already. What happened next completely amazed everyone. The shimmering craft projected a field of energy that enclosed the Genesis in an encapsulating bubble of the same shimmering energy that seemed to surround their craft. Once it was in place we quite literally instantly appeared in orbit around the second planet. One second we were at the edge of the solar system traveling at near light speed. The next second we had traversed hundreds of thousands of miles through the solar system and were in stationary orbit around the planet. It was impossible, but it had happened. In my wildest imagination, I could not fathom the existence of such technology or power. We were totally at their mercy.

Linda was staring in awe. I asked, "Linda, do you have any idea what just happened?"

"I think we just traveled through time and space. There have been theories presented about Warp Speed where time and space are warped. I think we just experienced it."

All we could do was wait for The Enlightened
to make the next move.

229

Chapter 10
(Forty Years)

Genesis Log: 20 June 2019:

The Enlightened made us wait two cycles, all the time we were anxiously waiting and not knowing what to expect. Toward mid-cycle of the second cycle, we received a message: "We are coming." I did not know what to expect, but I summoned the staff that were not already present.

No sooner than all were present, a series of three concentrations of shimmering brilliance began to the side of my dome. They continued to get brighter as the lenses of my cameras closed and the staff began shielding their eyes. The lights suddenly dimmed their assault and three distinct entities hovered in a bright orange mist surrounding them. I realized that it wasn't actually a mist but a radiance emanating from their translucent bodies. Their nebulous bodies were not dissimilar in shape to a human, but they were taller and the features undefined with little physical substance. They had slender, elongated arms, fingers and legs. The heads seemed large in comparison to their bodies with large oval eyes and a narrow mouth. The dark eyes were the only feature that seemed to have substance. I could sense the vast intelligence like an energy force coming from each entity, concentrating from those penetrating eyes.

"Wa-welcome," I stuttered. "I am Admiral Johns, commanding this vessel." I spoke in English. There was never any doubt The Enlightened knew our language. The requirement to translate their language had only been a test to determine our intelligence. I guess we passed the entrance exam.

The entity in the center raised its hand as if to silence me and said in English, "We know who you are, all of you." The eyes looked around the room stopping on each person. "We have studied you and your data banks and know everything. Your complete mission is known to us.

We have no names... we are one. Our species has determined that you offer no immediate threat to us, or you would have been destroyed. We come to you in person to show you the nature of our existence so you will understand why you cannot be allowed to stay. Our evolution far surpasses your current level. We are a race of pure energy and common thoughts. Our consciousness would overwhelm your simple minds and your primitive individual emotions would invade and disrupt our common thought. Therefore, we will escort you to your next destination, from which you must not return to cause further disruption in our universal mind. We have downloaded information into your data banks that will aid you in finding a suitable habitable planet to colonize. Your emotions pain our entire species, so we leave now. May you find peace in your existence."

With the end of his/her... who knows, comments, the brilliance flashed again and they were gone, leaving us all in various stages of shock. Before we could fully recover, the escorts again captured Genesis in their bubble of energy. Like before, we flashed out of existence and back into a new existence in the light of a brilliant star.

231

"Where the hell are we?" I screamed.

Kim responded first. "Well, I would venture to say that we are at Trianguli Australis and some forty light years from where we were seconds ago."

I think the general summed up the way we all felt. "I feel like a damn caveman in the 21st Century."

Genesis Log: 22 June 2019:

It took me a while to find the files The Enlightened stored in the data banks. I had been looking, but had no doubt they had done what they said they would do. Finally, I found them addressed to me, Nick Johns. They clearly knew my nature of existence from their studies of our data banks, but I am still amazed I didn't detect them in my extended mind. I guess it is no big surprise, with their level of intelligence.

I reviewed the files during the Red Cycle so I would be ready when the staff arrived. Once they had arrived and before I could start, Cdr. Kim announced the obvious.

"We have confirmed that we are indeed in the Trianguli Australis Solar System. All star charts confirm this along with the physical evidence. I don't know how, but we are here and have just bypassed forty years of our travel."

Smiles and cheers greeted this announcement, even though we all already knew it to be true. Even a somewhat subdued Mr. Sharp seemed pleased. After meeting The Enlightened, I no longer believed Mr. Sharp had violated my orders by transmitting a message. I was positive their superior technology could have detected us, possibly from the beginning, but I am now more inclined to believe their common mind had felt our emotions from far in space.

"I have studied the files The Enlightened left us," I announced. "They confirm the existence of a habitable planet, several actually, at our planned destination. They provided extensive information on Alpha Pavonis and star maps of the area, which I have made available to you. The good news is that our alien Earth friends where correct in the existence of an Earth-like planet, but the bad news is that it is not exactly were they said it was. It seems there is another solar system just past Alpha Pavonis, which is obscured by it. It lays 3.6 light years past our planned destination. I have seen pictures of the system and planets, and they really look fantastic, but I will let the astronomers provide the analysis to us. The Enlightened provided additional locations as well, but they are at a greater distance. The Centaurians have been around the galaxy extensively, mapping and exploring. We owe them a lot."

Genesis Log: 4 July 2019:

I had brought First Officer McCullah up to speed on what I believed was going on with Mr. Sharp and Cdr. Jones. His first reaction was to suggest we execute them before they could cause trouble. He was confident that they would cause trouble sooner or later, and he was probably right, but I persuaded him to wait and see. He apparently did have a heart-to-heart with Cdr. Kim about the situation, because Kim had seemed more assertive of late. He seemed back to his normal self and more than ready to launch into his normal classroom lectures.

Cdr. Kim started, "We have completed our research from the data provided by The Enlightened, and we have wonderful news to present. To put it mildly, our target solar system is perfect for our purpose. As you already know, Alpha Pavonis is not our target. The star we seek is 3.6 light years past it. It has no official name and, with everyone's agreement, we would like to call this solar system Genesis Prime."

I said, "I think I can speak for everyone when I say Genesis Prime is an appropriate name and fitting choice." There were many nods of agreement from the staff.

He continued, "Great! OK, Genesis Prime is a newer single star system of yellow-white light very much like our own sun. The star is slightly larger than our sun, but this doesn't pose much of a problem as you will see. The star has seven planets orbiting it, three of which are habitable with moderate temperature and abundant water covering anywhere from 60% to 80% of the surface."

"The planet we believe is the best for us, the most Earth-like, is the center one of the three for various reasons associated with mass of the planet and gravity considerations. The center planet is also slightly larger than Earth, maybe 15% larger, but the orbit is correspondingly greater as well, making it very much Earth-like in temperature ranges. The gravity will also be slightly greater due to the larger mass. It orbits Genesis Prime in a twenty-nine-hour cycle. We can slowly adjust our shipboard cycles to this new schedule. By the time we reach Genesis Prime, our internal body clock will have adapted and will seem normal to us."

"The chosen planet, which we call New Earth, is lush and green, 80% covered with water, mostly tropical, with five major land-masses. Although Genesis Prime is only a single star, the neighboring Alpha Pavonis star is a super bright white giant, which will be prominently visible from New Earth. It will appear as a near star that radiates a significant amount of light, enough to color the normal black of space to a bluish shade in that direction. There are no moons orbiting New Earth, but there is a slight amount of gravity coming from Alpha Pavonis, enough to influence tides, which will be significant. New Earth appears to be perfect in all ways... so far."

"Now, according to the data records, New Earth has advanced life forms. Even more surprising is that the most advanced life forms are humanoid. This shocked us at first, but continuing research into the data gives references to interference by outside races having transplanted them from, of all places, Earth. There is no indication who stocked the planets, but I think we can safely assume it was those aliens who have apparently been visiting Earth for centuries, our friends. There is no clue as to the purpose."

"These current inhabitants of New Earth are of our DNA, possibly from tens of thousands of years in our ancient past, but they remain relatively primitive by our standard and sparsely populating the planet. It won't be like we are taking it away from them. It would, however, probably be best to try to remain separated."

"We have even chosen one of the smaller land-masses as our recommendation. If the records are current, and we don't know this to be true, this land mass is not populated and could serve us well for colonization."

Cdr. Kim had made an excellent and informative presentation. "Thank you Cdr. Kim and your team," I said. "If you discover additional information, please let us know."

I too was shocked to find out that humans had been stocked on all three of the habitable planets, but evidently not in any sufficient numbers to evolve beyond medieval or early pre-technology stages. There was no hint as to why or who had preformed the stocking, but I seriously doubt The Enlightened did it. Our existence was obviously painful to them in their proximity, and they would have no real reason to protect our existence. They had evolved so far beyond us that it would be hard for them to think of us as much more than ants.

No, I agreed with Kim, the aliens who had demonstrated interest in Earth must have transported humans from Earth to populate these planets. I might theorize that they had anticipated the destruction of Earth and wanted to ensure our species would survive. Any other theory would be far less appealing.

Genesis Log: 8 July 2019:

We remained positioned well out of Trianguli Australis' solar system, where The Enlightened dropped us off. They knew forty light years would be enough to keep us from coming back, but they had also correctly assumed being closer to the power of this star might be harmful to us. Beta Trianguli Australis is an F-type Giant star 40 times the size of our Sun and 450 times brighter. Even from this distance, our light filters of the ship's hull were mostly closed off. It didn't take long to determine there was little of interest for us here; therefore, we didn't waste any more time.

Due to the abundant available light outside of the solar system, we launched into light speed this cycle with relative ease. Our course was Epsilon Scorpii twenty-five light years away. Unfortunately, it was twenty-six degrees off our main course, but that could not be helped.

Genesis Log: 10 July 2019:

Once we verified we were on course, I did two things. I reactivated the buffers between my extended brain and me. I planned to slow myself again to avoid any self-imposed depression from setting in again. Fortunately, this was becoming easy to do. I could float in and out of my controls with ease and could bypass them as necessary for any extended research or thought. I just didn't want anything slipping out of control.

The other thing I did was order many back into cryogenics and added some new ones including Cdr. Kim, to fill the twenty additional chambers Dr. Rossen had built... well, all but two. Dr. Rossen had persuaded me to let him remain awake until Linda gave birth, which shouldn't be long now.

I had insisted that both Dr. Rossen and Linda go into cryogenics after the baby was born. I convinced them that it would not be good for them or the baby to bond. It would just make it hard on both them and the infant. I used the same logic Dr. Rossen had used on Akiko and me, and he was hard pressed to argue. We couldn't use up their lives in travel. They both were key to the colonization of New Earth and that took priority over personal desires.

I didn't much trust JJ, so she went into cold storage with Jim Sharp. I kept the general awake to resume security. That surprised him, actually me too, but it was logical; and since so many of the department heads would be asleep, I needed someone with me, someone to talk to that I trusted. That shocked me that I would say that after so many disparaging thoughts about the general, but it was true; I trusted him as much as I trusted Dr. Rossen, whom I would also miss.

Genesis Log: 18 July 2019:

Doc delivered his and Linda's baby today. It was a baby girl weighing 7 pounds 8 ounces. She had the Doc's dark eyes and sharp features but Linda's red hair. I had never seen Doc smile so much.

He came to the control room to announce and log the birth. Technically, this was the first actual birth; Nick 2 wasn't actually a new life. They had named the baby Kathern Lynn Clark, which I recorded in the log. I met Dr. Rossen with a smile and congratulations, but I felt bad, because I didn't want to encourage him too much. I knew it would be hard, in his eyes anyway, to abandon her, but it was best.

Genesis Log: 21 July 2019:

Linda and Doc went into the freezer today and Cdr. Takashi Ishiguro came out to relieve Doc. Linda left one of her team to head up engineering, Lt. Bill Boland. Like most of the other lower officers, Linda, as a Cdr. and department head had assigned officer ranks to her key staff. First Officer McCullah, since the beginning, had been instilling Annapolis officer training in these officers. He was hard enough to make it stick and make them live up to the standards and requirements, and he was back on duty.

Lt. Boland would fit the stereotype of a Big Swede Viking. He was tall, big, barrel-chested and blond. The only things missing in the description were a silver double-horned battle hat and axe. Despite being so physically imposing, he was a quite pleasant man and, according to Linda, extremely knowledgeable.

Taka was surprised to be awake so soon. I had put him back in storage after we embarked from Trianguli Australis, but I had plans for his expertise that I would finalize soon. Before that time, I wanted him totally familiar with the workings of Genesis.

Genesis Log: 19 May 2020:

Nick 2 turned three years old today, and I was beginning to live through him, but it was very frustrating. It was I in his body, but it was such an awkward young body and disturbed me that no one took me seriously. After all, I looked like a small child, but my demeanor was adult. As a result, I was avoided and isolated from the remaining awake crew. For now, it was far easier and productive maintaining my holographic image in the control room. Everyone listened to me there, but not in my three-year-old child's body.

So far, my focus was primarily keeping my body healthy and exercised. I remain constantly connected... how could I not? It was second nature to me now, controlling both bodies... Genesis and Nick 2.

About the only pleasure I was deriving was food. I love the taste of food and have really missed it. Having gone without it for so long, all the pleasures seemed far greater now. I had to fight with myself to keep from staying in the galley sampling all the food.

Genesis Log: 5 Dec 2022:

Something incredibly wonderful happened today. It happened suddenly, too. I must have been semi-asleep and was startled awake when the lights in the control room automatically came on and my holographic image sprang to life. I had learned to sleep for brief periods, but when I did, I felt vulnerable; therefore, I programmed both activities to come on if movement was detected. There I was, tense and looking for danger. Initially I didn't see anything; then suddenly there she was.

She was standing in front of my image. It was so comical. A tiny, little young girl... very young... maybe three years old, was staring up at my image. Her unruly flaming red hair was pointing in every direction, and her wide green eyes sparkled in wonder as she stared intently at me. What made the scene more humorous was the fact that she stood like a little princess in all her regal glory. Her legs were spread in a dominant stance, and her little hands were propped on her hips. She was not afraid of anything. It was precious.

In a high but commanding voice she said, "Who are you?"

It struck me so funny... the image, tone and words. I was laughing so hard inside I was almost unable to answer. Finally, after a few seconds of control I said, "My name is Nick. What is your name?"

"My name is Kathern Lynn Clark." She said it like she was announcing it to the world, and her smile radiated a force in itself...disarming and infectious.

"Can I call you Katy?"

"Yep."

I had her placed now. It should have been obvious. There were no other children awake on Genesis. This had to be Doc and Linda's baby. I had seen her in the nursery but hadn't given it much thought since. I wasn't even aware of the gender of the baby. Now here she was, staring defiantly at me.

Her expression slowly turned to wonder. After a few obviously thoughtful seconds said, "Are you a ghost?"

Oh, the pure innocence of youth; they have no secret agenda, no deep secrets to hide or complex strategies to exercise. They simply say what they think. I had no idea how this little girl found her way to me, but I was enjoying it immensely. I hadn't laughed so hard in... well almost ever. I was chuckling openly now and responded with, "Well, some might think so, but I am inside this dome."

As she looked for a way to open the dome she said, "Can you come out?"

"I am afraid not, Sweetie."

"Why not?"

Humm, I was at a loss as to how to explain my existence, so I just said, "I don't really have a body."

She asked question after wonderful question for what seemed like hours, but in reality was only a few moments. We actually talked, and I was amazed at her command of the language and large vocabulary for one so young. She was a sweet miniature person. It was so enjoyable, and I didn't want it to end. Finally, Katy moved to one of the chairs, crawled up in it and sat. She was so small, her tiny feet stuck straight out, but she acted as if this were normal and the chair was made just for her. She spread out and owned that chair, and we talked more.

At one point, she got quiet, looked thoughtful again at me again, and said, "I'm not afraid of you. Everyone says they are afraid of you, but I am not. I like you. Will you be my friend?"

"You bet I will, Katy."

242

I must say, in that moment, this little slip of a girl took my heart. I realized what I had been missing from my so-called life. Being in command is lonely, and I wanted true friendship. You bet I would be her friend, and she could come see me any time. I knew from this moment on I would have a little friend.

I had been monitoring and noticed that the medical staff were running around frantic, obviously looking for Katy. I have no idea how she came up the lifts between decks, but do we ever know how kids do the things they do? When I announced her location, they were shocked and apprehensive about that. The senior medical staff supervisor quickly came bustling into the control room, scolding Katy for bothering me.

Katy said, "Nick doesn't mind, do you, Nick?"

The nanny was very shocked when I said, "I don't mind at all, Katy, and you can come see me any time you want. Just tell your nanny when you want to come see me, and they will bring you up." I started to tell her she could just call out "Nick" and I would hear her but decided that was too much for her to understand.

Katy just reversed herself, slipped backwards down from the chair, and said, "Bye Nick. See you tomorrow, and we can play." As she was leaving, she suddenly turned, ran back, and spread her little arms in a hug on my dome. She then took her nanny's hand and left.

She was gone as quickly as she came, but she left with my heart.

Genesis Log: 6 Dec 2022:

After Katy left, I started thinking that she should meet Nick 2. Maybe she would understand that Nick 2 was I, but it really wouldn't matter. We could still talk, and I might be able to expand myself through the association with Katy. At the very least, I could still see her and enjoy her antics. I also wondered why we, she and Nick 2, had never met before. After all, we lived on the same deck. I suppose it was reasonable. She is a year younger than Nick 2's physical development. That would make her about three, while I am four. She, and I for that matter, had been isolated in different nurseries and quarters.

I waited until after the morning meal, which I take in the galley now. I then headed to her area in my Nick 2 body. Of course everyone knows who I am and are uncomfortable being around me, mostly because they can't decide how I should be treated, like an adult or a child.

As I entered her nursery area, the attendants got quiet and sort of pulled back, allowing me to do what I wanted. I saw Katy playing, went to her and said, "Hi, Katy." My child's voice must have captured her attention immediately.

She jumped up, her red hair as unruly as last night, and said, "Hi. Who are you?"

I didn't want to give her any deep answers. I just said, "I am Nick. You visited me last night, so I came to visit you."

She squealed with pleasure saying, "Oh yes... my friend that lives in a bubble. You got out!"

She ran to me throwing her little arms around me and gave me a surprisingly strong hug for such a little girl. She had never seen another person who was not adult, and she was radiant with energy and excitement and curiosity. She immediately accepted me for who I said I was. Her mind and heart were wide open.

"You and me are the same!" She squealed, "We can play"

That is exactly what we did. She took my hand and led me all over showing me her home. She demonstrated all her toys, and I loved the simple thoughts and just plain fun of watching and sharing Katy enjoying life. She had me laughing, running and jumping. By late cycle, we were playing hide and seek. I can't remember when I enjoyed life so much.

No one dared to interfere with us. After a while her attendants relaxed and even seemed to enjoy watching us play. At first I was a little embarrassed to get down on a three-year-old level, but after a while I just thought, "Hell, I'm only four. Fuck it."

She made me show her my quarters and was sad that I didn't have toys to play with. She insisted that I have some of hers and even gave me her favorite teddy bear to sleep with. I didn't even try to resist. There was no way I could say no to this sweet child.

The whole episode brought back memories of my own childhood, and I was reliving long forgotten memories of my own younger sister and myself, how close we had been. I remembered how sad I was when she died. At least her death came in her late teens. I was away in my last year of college when I was notified of the car accident that killed my parents and younger sister. I lost my whole

245

family at once and was devastated. I had nothing to come home to, so I joined the Marines after graduation and tried to bury those memories. I can handle them now, and I'm thankful to Katy for bringing them back. She was my new little sister.

As I lay in my bed late mulling over this cycle's thoughts, I sensed, then felt the little tyke, Katy, climb up in bed beside me. She curled up against me and went sound asleep. The attendants would be frantic in the morning, but I didn't care. I also knew this would not be the last time she would sneak in seeking the comfort of her big brother.

I had forgotten how pleasant it is to touch another in affection, feel the warmth of their body, the open affection and feel the warmth it generates in me. I am really beginning to live through my extended body.

Genesis Log: 11 Feb 2023:

I was now ready to start the first phase of my plan to bring Akiko back to full health and, more importantly, back to me. I had really missed her.

I couldn't keep Dr. Rossen awake the whole trip, although I could have really used him. Fortunately, Cdr. Takashi Ishiguro was out of cryogenics and back to full service. In some ways, Taka was better trained in what I need now. I would need Cdr. Ishiguro's experience and knowledge in genetics and DNA research to accomplish this goal. He hadn't been awake but a few days, but there was no time like the present to get him busy.

He was a little surprised that I asked him to stay after the early cycle meeting. There were more than

246

a few looks passed between the group members. From experience, they knew that being asked to stay usually meant a new project.

I knew it was my time to lecture and launched into it, "I know you have been briefed on the various projects Dr. Rossen has been working on. If not, I urge you to go through his files and notes and work with his staff, yours now. The project I need your assistance on is what I call the Immortality Gene, and that is exactly what it is. I know you have extensive experience in DNA and genetics research. What we are going to do is create genes that will code the development of a never before seen cell in humans."

"I will help you map out the DNA code in my computer network, which is by far faster and larger in capacity than any so-called Supercomputer that ever existed on Earth. Trust me when I say we can learn the language of DNA coding."

"The key to the Immortality Gene is unleashing the power that already exists in a human body, stem cells. As you know, embryonic stem cells are pluripotent cells that have the ability to develop into any of the 220 cell types of the human body. The cells, in fact, do differentiate to form a new human in the form of a developing fetus."

"Unfortunately, these stem cells are concentrated almost exclusively in the development of an embryo, fetus and then full-term infant. The main reason is that any loose stem cells would be attacked by the host's body because they are a genetic mix and not an exact duplication of the host's DNA. If these pluripotent stem cells were not rejected and were distributed throughout an adult

247

human body, they could convert to any type cell in the body to repair and revitalize any cell in the human body including organs, muscles, nerves, brain, etc. There would be no sickness, disease or infirmity. Injuries that did not result in immediate death would be corrected, and aging and dying cells would be replaced. The body would never grow old. These characteristics are what make them so important to our goal. This is as close to immortality as we could get."

I really had Taka's attention. He was wide-eyed and looked even wilder than he usually does. He pushed himself forward on the chair in an effort to totally concentrate on my dissertation. After a pause I continued, "The whole process begins with fertilization."

"I know you know all this, but you need to follow me. It will become clear why I am going over it again."

"Okay, the whole process begins with two haploid gametes (egg and sperm), both only having twenty-three chromosomes of the forty-six required in the necessary diploid cell. When these two haploid gametes (cells) combine, they form a diploid cell with forty-six chromosomes. This is the point of fertilization when the egg and sperm combine and mix the duel genetic codes. The diploid cell then begins to split through several cycles of reproducing identical pluripotent cells. These are the embryonic stem cells. These cells continue to multiply and form what is called a blastocyst or early stage embryo consisting of between 50 and 150 pure building cells. At this point the blastocyst attaches to the inner wall of the female uterus to receive nutrients and oxygen. From this position, these pure building cells start to specialize and form a fetus."

"For our goal, we are only interested in the process to this point. The embryonic stem cells, these pure building block cells, cease to be pure after the first few splits. They then begin to specialize and limit their ability to replace any cell in the body."

"My plan is to create a gene that will cause the human body to produce random haploid cells with twenty-three chromosomes identical to the hosts. These cells will be free floating within the blood stream as opposed to being implanted in the uterus. When any two of these cells meet they will be attracted to each other and adhere, as would sperm and egg cells, to form the forty-six chromosomes. This in essence simulates fertilization. This diploid cell would form a perfect genetic match and would not be rejected by the host's body. It would begin to split and release pure stem cells loose into the blood stream."

"It should be an automatic process from there. As the stem cells travel through the body, they would adhere to damaged or dying cells and replace them. As the body stabilized at peak condition and no longer required as many, the body would begin to reject the overpopulation of stem cells and expel the surplus."

"This can work. Now you see why I call this the Immortality Gene and the best part is that it is a genetic code that can be passed on in reproduction, at least for a few generations until it becomes diluted."

"Well, what do you think?"

Taka had slowly transformed into a comical picture as I had progressed through my thesis. He was now sitting on the edge of the chair with his mouth wide open and eyes big enough to swallow a coffee cup, but he said nothing... just stared.

Finally, he pulled himself back together and simply said, "H O L Y SHIT!"

I guess he liked my plan.

Genesis Log: 18 July 2023:

There is nothing like running and playing with your best little friend to keep you sane. We have the ran the corridors of the entire ship, and no one dares to interfere with our activities. They know who and what I am and aren't about to say no to us. Little Katy thought it was her with the power and was a terror aboard ship. There was no way I could explain it to her in a way she would understand. Therefore, I just run with her. She has even wiggled her way into that rock of the general's heart. Katy calls him Gramps, and he loves it. Every chance she gets, she crawls up in his lap to get some hugs. Having the general's backing made her even worse around the ship. I try to keep her under control when I can but mostly fail. I truly love her antics, however.

We had her birthday party in the galley this cycle and most attended. To be a terror, she is quickly becoming the ship mascot. Me? Well, most just seem to tolerate me, but I don't care.

Her fourth birthday marked the beginning she started coming to the staff meetings. Her Gramps

250

was there and his lap was her place. I was in my holographic wonder during the staff meeting, while also playing with her in my body. Suddenly, she took off with me in tow into the staff meeting. All I could do was follow. She talked to my holographic image and my physical body and never seemed to grasp that we were one and the same. Katy said to my body, "Let's go see your daddy."

Genesis Log: 29 Feb 2024:

I had volunteered to help map the genes and sequencing of Taka's project to create the Immortality Gene. After a year of full-time research, he came to report that he had made significant progress. So much progress, in fact, that he wouldn't need the vast computer process he originally thought.

He said, "Much of the mapping had been done previously in the Human Genome Project (HGP). The primary goal of HGP was to determine the genome, hereditary information, and sequence of the chemical base pairs which make up DNA. The project had identified the approximately 25,000 genes of the human. So, I basically know what genetic sequence to copy and where to inject or splice it in the DNA strand. Your detailed information and basic original idea was all I needed. That was brilliant, by the way, and amazingly simple in the overall scope of previous research."

"What has taken so much time so far is figuring out how to accomplish the production of haploid gametes cells, the twenty-six chromosomes, within the body and outside of the uterus."

I interrupted, "What did you come up with?"

He smiled and said, "Well, it is really sort of easy. I will grow another set of ovaries that attaches to the main blood stream and releases cells into the body's blood supply. They should work like you indicated. Even though the produced cells are identical, they will be attracted to each other to combine their missing chromosomes. Of course, I will have to slightly modify these ovaries to produce smaller cells. Normal ovaries produce a much larger cell, the egg."

"What is required is to copy the DNA gene that grows ovaries, modify it, and splice it in the sequence that tells it where to grow, then introduce it back in the body. I am still working on the best and fastest way to do that. My initial thoughts are to extract blood cells and inject the new DNA in them, maybe with a virus as the vector or carrier, grow them outside the body then reinsert them."

"What will take the time is the laboratory testing to verify the accuracy of my gene splicing. This will require time and will require actual testing, growing human embryos."

As he said this last statement admitting that this would be required, I just shrugged my holographic shoulders and said, "It is not against the law on Genesis, I am the law." I was thankful that Japan had less restrictive laws, and I wasn't having to get into a philosophical discussion on the morality of human embryo research, like would be inevitable with Dr. Rossen.

He bowed slightly and continued, "Nick, one benefit to all this embryo research is that I can store Akiko's stem cells from the test fetuses if we need to use it. We probably will initially, to get her healthy enough to go through this metamorphosis. She will be the first Immortal."

Damn, he was right, Akiko would be immortal with a capital I. This would take some getting used to.

"Thanks for the report, Taka. You are doing a fantastic job. If you need anything, just say so."

The general had sat in silence, but jumped up and said, "I'm next!" We all laughed, but he was definitely serious.

Genesis Log: 18 July 2027:

This cycle being Katy's eighth birthday... maybe I should be calling it birthcycle... I have decided to try to explain my true nature. Katy is a smart kid, but we have become so close, and I didn't want to scare her.

We had been running around the observation deck, one of our favorite places, and I took her hand and led us into the empty control room.

"Are we going to see your daddy," she asked.

"No, we are going to go see me." I said. "That Nick and I are the same. He is not my daddy, he is me. Remember what you said when we first met... about how I got out of the bubble?"

"Yeah."

"Well using this body is how I got out, but I am still inside that bubble and here too. We talk to each other." I thought she might understand that concept.

"Wow! How do you get back inside?"

"I don't go back inside. I stay outside with you."

"OK... let's go play now."

I guess that was it. She seemed to understand and not really care how impossible it was. She just accepted it, and we went to play.

Genesis Log: 11 Feb 2029:

The general wanted to talk at our early cycle staff meeting. He was tentative, quite unlike himself, so I listened intently.

"You know, a few years back when we were discussing the Immortality Gene, I mentioned that I wanted to be next." the general said. "Well, I have given it a lot of thought. I don't want to be the next after Akiko. I want to be first!"

"Before you think I am trying to delay Akiko's recovery, let me just offer my arguments. I don't care what doctors say. You can never be absolutely sure if a new medical procedure will work until after it has worked. Keep in mind that Akiko is already in bad physical shape, but she is safe while in cryogenic storage. What if the Immortality Gene doesn't completely work as planned and causes stress on her? It might just kill her."

"Now, I am relatively healthy. If something goes wrong, I am more likely to survive the physical stress. In addition, I am pushing fifty, the oldest person on the Genesis, awake anyway. I have the most to gain from the Immortality Gene due to my age. I am not sure if the gene can reduce my physical age from the time of activation, but if it can prevent me from aging further, please don't keep me aging any longer than necessary."

"The way I see it, let me be the guinea pig for the Immortality Gene. Once we have determined that it doesn't kill me and works as expected, then give it to Akiko."

The control room was silent. What he said made a lot of sense, but I waited for Dr. Ishiguro's comments.

Taka shrugged and said, "I don't have any problem with Mr. McCullah's request. Once the gene is perfected, we can splice into any donor's DNA."

I looked around and saw no objections. "OK," I said. "Done. Shall we change your name to Mr. Guinea Pig?" The usually prim and proper general simply gave me a one finger salute, but he was smiling.

Genesis Log: 14 July 2033:

During this cycle, Katy asked me about Akiko, and I was uncertain as to how to explain my relationship with Akiko to her. At fourteen years old, Katy was well into puberty and demonstrating many maturing physical signs in addition to her emotional development. She was growing up.

Over the last couple of years, we had talked about ever-increasing mature subjects. She fully understands who and what I am, but nothing would deter her from our growing friendship. She knew I was mentally an adult, and instead of that putting her off, she sought my wisdom.

I helped her with her school studies, tutored her when she needed it and tried to answer her always engrossing and challenging questions. I had even explained the birds and bees to her. I was tentative and inhibited at first, but Katy, well, nothing seemed to embarrass her or make her shy. We knew each other's secrets. Yes, I trusted her with many of mine. I could tell her anything and felt safe doing so.

Above all this, she made me laugh. Katy was the medicine and mental nourishment that kept me alive and sane. We had each other and were inseparable by mutual consent.

Lately, she seemed obsessed about Akiko and asked me many questions: what she looked like, what she was like, how old she was, etc. This late cycle, like so many others, I felt her slip into my quarters and cuddle up against me; but instead of her going to sleep, she shook me wide-awake and said, "Do you love Akiko?"

I sat up in bed looking at her and thinking. "Yes, Katy, I do love Akiko." I finally said.

It was time Katy knew everything, so we sat up most of the late cycle and I told her. I held nothing back and answered all her questions about my feeling toward Akiko, Akiko's feeling toward me, our telepathy, how Akiko had damaged her own body to provide me with this very body I was using. I told her of our desires to be together beyond the mental love we already possessed into the physical love. Even though it has been fifteen years, I told Katy how much I missed Akiko, and Katy wept with me.

After some time, Katy asked, "What about us?"

"Oh, Katy, how can you wonder?" I whispered, "You stole my heart long ago. I love you as much as I ever loved my own sister. We will always be together."

256

Katy smiled, squealed, and threw her arms around my neck in the biggest hug ever and said, "My Nick, I love you, too."

Genesis Log: 29 Jan 2034:

Katy and I went to Akiko's garden today. I loved this place, but I always tried to avoid it because it reminded me of Akiko, where we had spent so many days together. Katy insisted that we go, so we went.

She said, "You don't need to avoid her memories. You should embrace them."

Reluctantly, I agreed, but no sooner had we entered, I was thankful she had insisted. I had avoided looking and coming here so long. Now I was ashamed of myself for doing it. Akiko's beautiful gardens were in shambles. Where before they were immaculately maintained and a place of beauty, now it was unruly and overgrown. Weeds had overgrown the paths, the fields were poorly organized, and rats were abundant everywhere. How could this have been allowed to happen? How could I allow this to happen? Not only was this supposed to be a place of beauty and relaxation, but this was our source of life onboard ship. Hell, I didn't even see any workers. This was the only department I had not put on reduced staffing.

I started screaming, "Yoshiaki Sakata! Cdr. Sakata! Where the hell are you?" No one answered. My mind then started searching for him throughout the ship to no avail. In frustration, I announced over the shipboard Public Address system, "Emergency staff meeting in the control room. All department heads report immediately!"

I was trembling with anger by the time I stomped into the control room. I vaguely remember that I wasn't using my visual centers or the holograph. It was only my flesh and blood body. At the age of sixteen, I marched into the control room where most department heads had already arrived, all but Cdr. Sakata that is.

Katy was following closely but was very quiet and quickly found a seat with the others, as I angrily strode to the front and took charge. This was the first time I had done so in my body and actually didn't realize it. Again I screamed at the top of my lungs, "Where the fuck is Sakata?"

Remembering back afterwards, I can still see the shocked faces, even First Officer McCullah. To the general's credit, he took a position to my left in a protective posture and motioned the Marine guard to pace me on my right. At the time, I hardly noticed.

It was about that time Cdr. Sakata came out of the ramp and burst into the room. He was still trying to get his jump suit zipped. I launched into a verbal assault, "Where the fuck have you been? No, I don't even care where you have been. I want to know how you have managed to destroy Akiko's gardens and our life support." My anger was out of control, and I knew it but didn't care. I pointed my finger up into his face and screamed, "You bastard. You may have killed us. I am going to kill you, you son of a bitch." As I said that, I was reaching for the Marine guard's 45 still in his holster. It was a jumble of bodies after that as Sakata's face twisted in horror, and he tried

258

to run. The Marine managed to grab him at the same time I finally got the 45 out just as the general grabbed my arm. The general managed to wrestle the pistol out of my hands in time. The whole room was in stunned silence that seemed to last forever. Finally, my anger burst out in uncontrollable sobs.

Was I really going to kill him? You bet your ass I was, and everyone knew it. They also knew why. The general took over then. He led me over to sit by Katy, knowing she could calm me. He was visibly upset as well but was handling it better than my outburst.

"Officers, I think we need to find out what is going on here. I will organize the various aspects of our immediate investigation to determine all the facts and the amount of damage that has occurred. Cdr. Sakata, if we find you derelict in your duties, you will face my wrath as well. I just may give Nick back the 45. Sergeant, take Cdr. Sakata to his quarters and confine him there. I will be down to interview him in an hour. He is not to leave his quarters. The rest of you see me individually, and I will assign you tasks to investigate. We will find out what the hell is going on and exactly what has happened." He then came over to me and placed his big hand on my shoulder and said, "Don't worry, Nick, we will get to the bottom of this and report back. Katy, take him somewhere and try to calm him down. OK?"

Keeping the general out of Cryogenics was the smartest thing I have done, and I am thankful.

Chapter 11
(Life and Love)

Genesis Log: 30 Jan 2034:

At the next staff meeting, I sat in the audience since the general was making the presentation to the full staff and me. I remained in body form and didn't activate my holograph image. Cdr. Sakata was cuffed but present with a Marine standing behind him. The general obviously found fault with his performance. I was calm this time, so I remained silent, resolved to listen.

After I had calmed and was again rational after the earlier outburst, I was impressed by how the general had taken charge, organized an investigation, and formulated the reorganization of the Life Support Department. He had done it all in one evening and night, and I had not gotten involved, but I had observed.

It was the general's presentation and he began, "As you know, the conditions we found in the Life Support decks were horrendous. There were no workers and hadn't been for some time. Cdr. Sakata hasn't even been seen in the department in over a year, and with lack of tasking, the staff drifted off, only doing what was absolutely necessary. I am not happy with the staff, but the fault is with the department head. Cdr. Sakata has been shacked up with one of his staff and only coming out to come to the staff Meeting. I will have to assume some of the blame, because I did not supervise the department. This changes immediately. I will have weekly status

260

reports from all departments from now on and will personally verify the data.

The Life Support team is back to work at a one and a half work cycle schedule until such time as it is fully under control. We are reactivating one of Akiko's main line officers. I wanted someone of her team that was not involved in this debacle. Lt. Naomi Sami will be out of cryogenics and back to work in a couple of days to take charge. In the meantime, one of Cdr. Sakata's lieutenants will be in charge temporarily but under close supervision by Cdr. Ishiguro. Taka was previously in charge of Life Support aboard the Hope before we put it under Akiko. He is analyzing the needs and will report."

"The damage is not permanent. It all can be repaired, but it will take a lot of work. I think the biggest problem that exists is the rat overpopulation. The natural predators, namely cats, were allowed to dwindle in number and disrupt the balance. We are currently in the process of exterminating rats to return the balance. I am tempted to put all the excess rats in Cdr. Sakata's quarters with him.

Effective immediately, Cdr. Sakata will be stripped of any military rank, permanently. He has proven he can't be trusted with responsibility. As to further punishment, no one will object if you still want to execute him, but at a minimum, I recommend he spend the rest of his time in the freezer. No one wants him around."

This last statement caused Sakata's eyes to bulge, and he strained to fight against his binding, but the Marine forcefully pushed him back down.

I thought it would be more impressive if I spoke through my holographic image. It was more intimidating than my sixteen-year-old body. My image flashed into existence and I spoke, "Thank you, General. Mr. Sakata, you are very lucky the general stopped me or you would be dead. If Akiko were awake, she would kill you personally. If I ever see you again, I may yet kill you. If your incompetence has caused any permanent damage to Akiko's gardens, I will wake you up and execute you. You are a disappointment to me, the Hope, the Genesis and the human race; but I will accept First Officer McCullah's recommendation and put you away in cryogenics. General, get this bastard out of my sight." The general waved to the sergeant who was happy to forcefully escort Sakata out of the control room.

After the meeting broke up, the general took Katy and me to the side. He was smiling when he said, "Geez, Nick. You scared the crap out of me yesterday, and, at the same time, pleased me greatly. Do you have any idea how funny it was watching you shake your finger up into that muscle-bound asshole's face? It looked like David and Goliath. You scared the crap out of him, too. Hell, I thought you were going to shoot him. Knowing now what I discovered, I should have let you."

"Up until then I thought I had thought of every possible situation, but after that episode, I realized that you are vulnerable in body form. I am going to suggest that we get you, and Katy too, into martial arts training courses. You need training for your body for self-protection in case you try to beat someone else up." The latter was delivered with one of his rare laughs.

The general seemed to forget that I already had martial arts and weapons training as a Marine. He, too, was only looking at my sixteen-year-old body and not seeing the whole me, but it was a good idea. I could always improve my coordination for my current physical size, and more training couldn't hurt. In truth, liked the idea. It would be fun for Katy and me.

Genesis Log: 4 Feb 2034:

It took several days before the new department head in Life Support reported to me at the staff meeting. I didn't mind, because I had been observing her at her station. Once she had her briefing and heard what had happened, she headed straight for the gardens. She didn't even wait for the general to introduce her as the department head. She needed no introduction to begin imposing her will. Once she saw the chaos, she was as pissed as I was or Akiko would have been. Naomi started bellowing orders, as the general would say, kicking ass and taking names. She had no sympathy for any of those awake that helped create the problem and let them all know it.

Naomi is not an especially formidable looking woman. Her records indicated that she was originally from India but educated in the USA at the University of California San Diego with graduate studies at Stanford. Yep, she is another doctor. She stands 5' 9" and is a little on the pudgy side, but what she lacks in physical size she makes up for in attitude and assertiveness. Her dark complexion and deep-set eyes make her look like a tiger on the hunt.

The general had always liked her attitude... it was Marine.

Naomi had helped Akiko build and design these Life Support decks. She must have poured her soul into them, because she was livid with anger, even after several days. Unfortunately, she had been in cryogenics since before Alpha Centauri, back when the gardens were perfect. I have no doubt they would be perfect again under her command.

The general introduced her officially as the department head to the staff and me. I had only seen her in passing through my visual centers, but I don't think she had ever seen me here. No matter, she was not intimidated by me, but she was respectful and professional.

Lt. Sami stood and addressed me saying, "I want to thank you for bringing me back. As you know, the Gardens are in terrible shape, but the crew is and will be working around the clock in shifts to correct the damage. Unfortunately, we are limited to growth time of the environment, plants and animals, to solve the problems, but the crew WILL correct all the problems affecting the environment surrounding them. The Gardens were once a place of beauty. They will be again."

"The production has been drastically reduced, but a few months should see it improving. We just have to tighten our belts for a while."

As she began to sit, I asked her, "Is there anything we can do to help... anything you need?"

Naomi stood again and said, "Well, our population of predators, namely cats, has been greatly depleted. The past director had an allergy it seems to cats, and the bastard, excuse me, Sir, Mr.

Sakata, was actually shooting them, playing Indian with his bow and arrows; that is, when he showed up at all."

"Maybe you can get with Cdr. Ishiguro and discuss any possible help he may be able to provide," I said. We have birthing tanks and the ability to grow some of the animal embryos in inventory if that will help."

"Thank you, Admiral. I will do that."

"Thank you, Lt. Sami, for your report."

I felt much better knowing she was in charge, but I was still kicking myself for not discovering the problem sooner. If Katy hadn't made me go there, the problem might have been irreversible.

Genesis Log: 18 July 2036:

We had a dual celebration this cycle for Katy. Not only did she turn seventeen, but she also graduated high school. It was a small celebration in the galley with Gramps and me. There were various others there as time permitted, but mainly those closest to her. The general was so proud of his adopted daughter. Other than me as her constant companion, the general had always made a point of being in her life. Of course, Katy interfaced with many others every day. She had never been shy, and everyone liked her; but it was the general and me she sought most.

Taka had insisted that I exercise regularly. Initially, it was to strengthen the muscle coordination between my mind and body, but my bond was strong now. Now he insisted, simply because that is what doctors do. Of course, Katy had always been there doing whatever I was doing. In the last few years, this exercising had turned to racket ball, in which Katy excelled.

Mid-cycle, as was now our routine, Katy soundly trounced me in a few hard games of racket ball. I wish I could say I let her win for her birthcycle, but that would not be true. She was good at it and loved to rub it in, the little shit.

This is how we started out HER special day. The general gave a short speech, short for him anyway, congratulating her for completing her studies and, as he put it, coming of age. Katy seemed to really like the attention and acceptance of adulthood. There were gifts following the cake and ice-cream, which every girl loves, I suppose. I gave her a golden chain and locket I had special made. I had it engraved with: To Katy... my best friend... Love Nick. I was surprise when she read it. She burst out crying and threw her arms around my neck in a hug so hard it hurt, but I was happy she liked it.

Late cycle after dinner, she wanted to walk on the observation deck. It was a beautiful night, but she was strangely quiet. Normally she was giggly and always happy, but tonight something seemed to be bothering her, and I couldn't get it out of her. She was upset, and I couldn't help her and felt bad about it. We hugged before we went to our separate quarters.

I had a troubled sleep, my body did, anyway. My mind needed little. As I was monitoring the corridors, I saw her coming. Katy hadn't come to cuddle in a few weeks, and I had missed that. I saw her, then felt her slip into my bed beside me and spoon to me. Her little petite body felt good against mine, too good.

I care for Katy deeply, but of late, my mind senses a woman that troubles the raging hormones of this body of mine. Oh my Akiko, "Why did you leave me alone for eighteen years?" I knew it wasn't her fault, but I have missed her so. I must maintain control over this body.

I pretended to sleep, while I tried to control my desperate urge to take Katy into my arms. It was then that I felt her hand slide over my stomach and down to grasp my painfully erect penis. I jerked suddenly at her touch, but OMG, I didn't stop her. I was in a panic about what to do. She knew I was awake.

She whispered in my ear, "Nick, I know you love Akiko, and she loves you, but I love you too, and I know you love me also. I think I have always loved you. I will settle for only what you have to give, but I need you. I am a woman now, and I need a man, the man I love."

I had tried to prevent this from happening. I didn't want it to happen, but I knew I loved Katy too. I have just been trying to deny it, but I can no longer reject it. At that moment, my raging lust for her was devouring my conscious mind, but it was the lust of love. We needed each other.

I didn't want to hurt her any longer. I simply turned to her, took her face in my hands, and kissed her with all my passion, the passion of love. Our lust and love flowed together, and we became one.

Genesis Log: 19 July 2036:

267

I waited until a very happy Katy left to go to the training section. She was, after all, a freshman in college... no summer breaks at the University of Genesis. Once she was gone, my fleshy body grabbed the general for a private cup of coffee. I loved these coffee breaks, but today was different. I had very mixed emotions about Katy and myself. My love for Katy was not in doubt, but I was feeling guilty and somewhat like an old pervert for taking advantage of her. I had to talk about it, and the general was the only one I dared to confide in.

Once the general and I were alone, I blurted out, "Katy and I made love last night!" I expected him to chastise me, but instead he started laughing, and I mean laughing loud. Others within ear shot looked up to see what was happening but soon returned to their meals. His reaction was puzzling me.

After a moment he said, "Are you telling me this is the first time?"

"Well, yes. Why?"

"Geeze, Nick, you two never had a chance. You and Katy grew up together. We all knew it was inevitable. Hell, even Doc mentioned it before Katy was born. You look shocked." Spreading his arms wide he said, "Christ, look around you. Do you see any other children? It was always going to be just the two of you. What surprises me most is that you are just now figuring it out. I expected it to happen long ago. To be so smart, you can be pretty dense sometimes"

"But what about Akiko? What about the fact that I am old compared to her? I feel like a dirty old pervert."

Exasperated, the general sputtered, "Nick, shut the fuck up! I know you love Akiko, everyone does, but do you honestly believe she would expect you to wait twenty years for her? No! She loves you too much for that. Trust me... it will work out. Oh, she might be pissed at first, but Akiko is logical and reasonable. You lucky bastard, you will have two loves. Now, as far as you being an old pervert, hell, we all are. Look at me with my beautiful partner. I thank my lucky stars every day that Margret looked past our age difference and loves me. Besides, your body is only, what, eighteen? Your hormones must be raging in you. You are NOT old to Katy."

"There is another thing you need to know. I love Katy as if she were my own daughter. If I thought you did anything wrong I would still be kicking your punk ass. No, my friend, everything is as it must be."

I was so glad I had decided to discuss this with the general. He had a way of putting everything in perspective... forcefully. I suddenly began to smile and whispered, "About my hormones, after last night they aren't raging nearly as bad." We both broke out in hysterical laughter.

I felt better and more at ease about the situation. I decided right then that I was going to ask Katy to marry me... marry US, Akiko and me, assuming that I survived Akiko's awakening. I also decided that I would ask the general to marry us or preside over my funeral.

Genesis Log: 14 Feb 2037:

269

Lt. Naomi Sami reported that the Gardens and Life Support were back to Akiko's standards and full food production was restored. This was welcome news indeed, but I was already fully aware of the situation. After the last debacle, I monitored the situation constantly.

After almost two years, she had finally taken the staff off time and a half work schedule and relaxed her stringent work pace. What impressed me most was that she didn't replace the negligent staff with others from cold storage. I asked her once why she didn't replace them and she said, "They helped create the problem. They will fix it." I knew then that Lt. Sami was the right one to head the department in Akiko's absence, and this has proven to be correct.

Naomi was also clearly loyal to Akiko, and I respected her for that. She also took Sakata's dereliction of duty personally. I had once observed her in cryogenics, apparently searching for Sakata's chamber. I didn't know what to expect, but once she found it, all she did was spit on his chamber and call him a few unladylike names. At the time, I found that vastly humorous... still do. She was never aware that I had seen her, but for months I couldn't help but smile when I saw her.

After the staff meeting, Katy and I took a tour of the Gardens, and they looked almost exactly the way Akiko left them. Lt. Sami could have installed her own personal touch, but she had recreated the original design right down to the Japanese rock and sand art. The only thing that was different was the prominence of Akiko's prized Bonsai plant, still growing in her precious Japanese soil. The pot was centered in the Japanese garden close to the bench she had used when we visited each cycle.

Katy and I sat on this very bench, and I was silent in my memories and Katy was strangely silent, as if she didn't want to intrude on my thoughts.

Genesis Log: 19 May 2039:

This was my twenty-first cycleday in the flesh, and it had been a very good day. As always, Katy and I have been together except for the few hours she spent in the learning center.

Like her mother, Katy had chosen engineering as her vocation and has excelled in her learning. I think secretly, Katy wants to impress her mother when they finally meet, at least she never ceases asking questions about her: what was she like, how did she look, what did she sound like when she laughed, did she love her father, etc. Sometimes it was questions about her father, but mostly it was Linda that fascinated her. Sometimes she drew from my recorded memory bank in the form of video recording. It was one of her favorite things, watching videos of her mother and father.

This late-cycle was different. We were resting after having made love. Our passion was especially strong this time. Katy's emotions were strong, and as we lay spooning in our bed, she turned in my arms and held me close, her dark green eyes looking deep into mine.

Katy's eyes radiated her love as she said, "Nick, I feel your love. There is no doubt in my mind, but there is something we must talk about." She paused

271

as if trying to find a way to say it. "Sometimes I feel how sad you are, missing Akiko. No, don't deny it. I feel it, but I understand. I really do. This is what I want to talk about. I have always known how you felt about her and that you miss her every day. I don't want you to hold it inside yourself. I want you to let it out; let it out with me. Bring me into your sorrow so I can help. Let me be all things to you. I know you and I will be together always as you and Akiko will be. Let me share your thoughts about her, and let me share your love for her so it will be mine, too. No, please don't try to talk yet. Let me get this all said first."

"There is a part of you that you don't share, but I want to share it with you. Honestly, I think it will make our love stronger if that is possible. Maybe you think it will hurt me, but knowing there is a secret part of you I can't share hurts me more."

"She will come back to you one day. This scares me, but not for the reason you may think. I know you will never give me up, but I don't want you to have to make that choice. I am secure in this, but I worry about what this stress will do to you. I feel it tearing you up inside, and it hurts me to feel it."

"This is why I want you to be open with me about Akiko. I have always accepted this part of you, that Akiko is part of you. Now let Akiko be a part of me... us."

"I have thought about this a lot and I want your promise. When Akiko returns, I want to go into cryogenics and give you time to teach Akiko to love me too. I know this will be a big surprise to her, but if she loves you, she will accept the situation as I do."

"To be honest, another reason I want to sleep through this period is because there will be some initial jealously and pain involved if I am awake thinking about you and Akiko making love. Akiko will also have to accept the jealousy and pain of our love while she was asleep. I think this is the best way to handle the situation. Don't you?"

How did my Katy get so damn smart in only twenty years? She showed profound wisdom in her statements, wisdom far beyond her years. Even so, she was not being fair to herself, but she was right, I didn't want to lose her and wouldn't. I didn't want to lose Akiko either. Even after twenty years of her absence, I still missed her. Granted, after so much time the memories were dimmed, but they were there, and the deep love was also there. I also realized that once she was back in my life again, all the memories would come flooding back to drown me. If I had to be honest though, as it stands today, I would have to choose Katy. She was right about that, but it would be extremely painful. Katy was taking that choice away from me and giving me options. I loved her even more for it.

I took her in my arms, kissed her, and opened my heart for her to see inside. My secrets were gone, and Katy was right again, our love grew stronger.

Genesis Log: 12 Aug 2041:

Due to the reduced awake crew, our staff meetings were small and, luckily, we didn't have

273

much to report. Reporting most anything meant trouble, and we didn't have any, nor did I want any. I was happy to keep it this way.

It was the customary I in the flesh, Katy, the general, Lt. Sami, Cdr. Ishiguro (Taka), and Lt. Boland. As we were having our morning coffee, my favorite part of the cycle, Taka surprised me, and I almost choked.

Taka just blurted out, "The Immortality Gene is complete!"

Maybe it was the way he said it, sort of like, I just finished breakfast, that shocked me. Maybe it was that he had been working on it so long that suddenly today stunned me. No matter, I was staggered, and it took a couple of minutes coughing and a few good slaps on the back by Katy to get me going. I said, "All the testing is complete?"

"Oh, yes. Everything checks out, and I am completely satisfied. I already have the cultures growing and equipment set up. We can start whenever you are ready."

"Damn, Taka. You could have given me some warning," I choked out. With his quiet manners, he just looked at me. As I stared back, it struck me how comical he looked with his unruly hair matted like a shaggy dog. I wondered if he ever combed it with anything but his fingers.

Finally, I said, "Well, this is great, but the first thing we need to do is wake up Dr. Rossen and Linda. We will want him to verify your data. I don't want to make any mistakes. Taka did his combination bow and nod to indicate his agreement.

Katy's gasp attracted my attention. She was breathing hard with wide eyes and sort of shaking.

274

What in the world? Oh crap, I realized I had just said we were bringing her mother and father out of cryogenics. At the age of twenty-two, she would meet her parents for the first time in her memory. Hell, I should have warned her, too.

I ended the staff meeting, then took Katy in my arms to comfort her. Then it dawned on me that I would have to explain to Doc and Linda that their daughter was my partner and lover. I wondered how that might go. Panic also hit me, wondering how I could explain all this to Akiko. I loved them both.

Genesis Log: 15 Aug 2041:

Taka took me at my word and brought Dr. Rossen and Linda out of cryogenics. He put them in the clinic to recuperate for a few days while he allowed them to be slowly briefed. They were the longest, twenty-two years, to be in storage and then awakened. Taka said he was curious to see if time in storage had any long-term effect. That was his stated purpose, but in reality I think he wanted to give Doc and Linda time to grasp the loss of twenty-two years. I think he also wanted to give me time to prepare to meet them. I still had no idea how to discuss it.

As it turned out, the general gave the briefing to them in private. I knew he would bring everything up, but even the general spread it out over three days.

The general entered the control room and said, "Doc and Linda are ready to re-join the team. They are up to speed on everything. I might suggest that you first present yourself to them in your physical

275

form and that you take Katy with you. I think it will be easier for them to accept seeing you as a twenty-three-year-old alongside their daughter."

"Thanks, Mac." This marked the first time I had used the nickname Katy had given him. She either called him Gramps or Mac. He smiled at the familiarity. He would have allowed Katy to call him most anything, but I believe that few others would have been allowed. "I think that is an excellent idea," I said.

It was mid-cycle, and Katy and I were in the gym practicing judo, while my holograph image was talking to the general. I said, "Katy, it is time."

Katy had been anxious to meet them and at the same time apprehensive, but nodded in the affirmative. I gave her a reassuring hug, and we were off.

When we entered, both Doc and Linda were in adjoining beds. They looked up and stared. Katy and I were holding hands to give each other support. Yeah, I was nervous too. I said, "Hello, you two. I'm Nick, and I think it is about time you two meet Katy." They stared at me only briefly then turned their attention to Katy in open mouthed awe. There was an awkward silence for the longest.

Katy spoke first, "Mother?" When Linda nodded, Katy ran to her and they embraced.

I watched as Katy was torn between embracing Linda then her father and back. They were all talking at once. We all had tears at the emotions shared. Katy was all smiles when she turned to me holding out her arms. I quickly joined her embrace.

"Nick, is that really you? Doc asked

"Yes, Doc, It's me in the flesh."

276

Once the ice broke, we all settled down and began talking. We talked for hours, trying to catch up. I had really missed them, but we talked as friends, not as admiral and staff members. It only got sticky once when Katy mentioned that she and I were getting married, but we had waited for them. I was a little surprised when they congratulated us, but relieved as well.

Genesis Log: 20 Aug 2041:

My next meeting with Dr. Rossen was in the more formal setting of the control room and my holographic image. I was learning to uses both personas to my advantage. It amazed me how people tended to see me as two persons. In the control room, I was the absolute leader, while in physical form I could be a friend. This dual personality allowed me to have the best of both worlds, and I liked it this way.

At this staff meeting, I chose to be the admiral, even though I sat in the audience beside Katy. My holographic image flashed into existence, and I said, "Welcome back, Dr. Rossen and Cdr. Clark. You have been missed." To them it was as if they had been gone only a couple of days, although most of the department heads had changed and twenty-two years had transpired. It must have been a shock to them. I continued, "As you have already been briefed, we brought you back early to review the astounding research Cdr. Ishiguro has completed on what we call the Immortality Gene. Taka is confident that his discovery is ready for the next stage of implementation, but before we do that, we want you to review and verify his findings."

"Yes, I have been reading some of his research, and I must say it is very impressive." Dr. Rossen said, "You know me though, we must be very careful before we start manipulating DNA. Some would say we are breaking the law, and others would say we are playing God, but then you are the law in space, and we started playing God when we escaped Earth. Now that we have begun, we might as well take it as far as we possibly can."

"I will give Dr. Ishiguro's research my full attention, but, as I said, we want to make absolutely sure we don't create a monster in the process. It will take some time. Can I assume we have a first volunteer?"

The general raised his hand and said, "Yes, I volunteered. I am the oldest and growing older every day." This generated laughter through the staff.

Dr. Rossen next said, "Dr. Ishiguro, I still have volumes to read, but I am curious how you plan to introduce the Immortality Gene (IG) into the host body."

Taka stood and said, "I haven't locked down any single procedure, but I have been considering two methods. One method involves using an RNA modified virus as the vector carrier to inject the IG into a supply of blood cells, then re-injecting them in the blood stream. This is the fastest method because the virus will grow in the host and spread the DNA. I am, however, reluctant to introduce a virus even though it has been proven safe. What happens over the long term has not been tested."

"The method I am more inclined to use is stem cells from embryos of the modified DNA. It will take longer, maybe years, but it would not involve injecting a virus. It may not take that much longer either. As the stem cells are injected in the host's body, they may tend to concentrate and grow the extra set of ovaries sooner. Once developed, this new organ will produce more of the stem cells and accelerate the body's conversion. These are my thoughts, but if you have other ideas we can certainly discuss them."

Normally I would say the staff would find this medical discussion somewhat deep and boring, but not this subject. They all knew immortality was something they wanted for themselves and were extremely attentive. I also knew it was something I wanted, too, not only for my physical body but for my human mind as well. Unfortunately, adapting immortal organs to support my brain would have to wait for a while.

Genesis Log: 10 May 2042:

Dr. Rossen surprised us all at the staff meeting. He asked, "May I address you and the gathered staff?"

"Certainly," I said, "Go right ahead." I was anxious at what I thought he was going to say, but I couldn't be sure.

He announced, "I have completed my analysis of Dr. Ishiguro's research and physical tests. I have even conducted some of my own, and I am ready to endorse the Immortality Gene project. I believe it is completely safe to implement, and we are prepared to begin. First Officer McCullah, are you still willing to be the guinea pig?"

The general looked shocked, leaped to his feel and blurted, "You bet your ass I am. Let's do it."

The general's enthusiasm sparked a round of laughter, but I could tell he was serious and more than ready to proceed. I also knew that Dr. Rossen was comfortable with the procedure. He is overly careful, to a fault; therefore, if he was endorsing the process, I could assume two things, it would work and it would be safe.

I said, "Very well, you certainly have my blessing. Go at your own pace and good luck."

Genesis Log: 15 May 2042:

Both doctors refused to let me into the sterile room to observe, but I was monitoring through my visual centers and reviewing the data the doctors were working with. As a result I could follow what was going on quite well. Unfortunately, I kept having to report to those behind the viewing window of the clinic. Katy was standing between her mother and me as we watched. This was her Gramps after all, and she was concerned.

The procedure was actually simple. The general was resting back in a recliner and Dr. Rossen slipped in an IV needle and hooked it up to a solution bottle. The process took only three hours for the drip bottle to empty. This was not the scary part. The scary part was what was now going to happen in the general's body, and only time would tell about that.

The actual work began months ago when the doctors drew the general's DNA. The DNA strand was then chemically cut, altered to specifications, and spliced back into the DNA strand. Once this was achieved, the altered DNA was inserted into eggs in the same manner as a clone. It was in fact a clone of the general with the altered DNA containing the Immortality Gene. I am not sure where the eggs came from, but it didn't really matter because they would contribute nothing to the cloned embryos.

The fertilized eggs were then placed into the tanks of artificial uteruses to develop to the point they produced stem cells with the altered DNA. These stem cells were then collected to make the IV solution that was now being dripped into the general's arm.

What is expected to happen inside his body is the miracle of the Immorality Gene. The doctors believed that these released stem cells would begin to develop the modified ovaries at the location the gene mapped it to grow, attached to the main blood supply. The stem cells would also begin to replace dying cells in the body also, but they should interpret the missing organ of the modified genetic code as being in need of repair, building another one. The cells would attach to the coded location and begin multiplying. This was the theory and expectation. If the organ grew, the process would be a success.

Just how long this process of growing a new organ would take was unclear. It was not expected to take more than one injection of stem cells, however. If one treatment didn't work, no amount of new treatments would help.

There was only one concern that the doctors worried about, but it wouldn't be life threatening. Even though the DNA of the injected stem cells was a duplicate of the original host's body, it was not an exact duplicate due to the modification in the new DNA. As such, there was a remote possibility that the host's body might reject the stem cells. If this happened, the host's body would attack and expel the injected stem cells. They said this was not likely, but remotely possible. They would be able to tell by monitoring the urine and excrement for the injected stem cells. They would keep the general in bed for the next few days to make this determination. Knowing the general, this would not be pleasant for him.

I tried to explain all this to Katy and Linda, but they were expecting something much more ominous. Katy remained a bundle of nerves until it was over. Linda wasn't that concerned. I suspect she was here more to support her daughter than anything else.

Katy finally said, "Is that it?"

"Yes, dear. That's about it. Now we just have to wait to see if it takes." That was it, the first Immortal.

Genesis Log: 1 July 2042:

After a month in the clinic, the general was going stir-crazy and wanted out, but the doctors had refused up until this cycle. The general finally told them he was checking himself out if they didn't let him out. Reluctantly, they finally agreed, knowing it would take a squad of Marines to stop him, and since the Marines reported to the general, it was senseless trying to keep him.

The general wasted no time getting back into the mix of activities, such as they were. Actually, he was the center of the activities going on. Every staff meeting concentrated on his progress, and this was no different, but I asked for a full status report on the progress of the Immortality Gene project.

Dr. Rossen took the podium to address us saying, "Well, after five weeks, I think we can safely report to you that the Immortality Gene project is a success." He waited for the cheers to die down before continuing, "We have found no evidence of body rejection of the modified DNA stem cells. There is even evidence from ultrasound readings that First Officer McCullah is definitely growing what we now call the Immortality Organ." Again the cheers rang out.

I took the opportunity to ask, "When might you start on the next patient?"

Dr. Rossen said, "If what you mean by the next patient you mean Akiko, this is a little more difficult to answer. Akiko, even though in cryogenics, is still effectively in a coma. Her condition was stable, though critical, when she went in. When we bring her out of hibernation, she will still be in a coma. Taka and I have discussed her treatment and believe the best way to proceed is with stem cell infusions, but NOT the modified DNA stem cells. The procedure would be the same as the general's except we would use her exact DNA from the donor embryos. Since her body is already barely fighting for life, we think it unwise to ask her body to fight the change of her altered DNA initially. The stem cell treatments in themselves, and yes, there would be several required, should replace her damaged cells of her organs and bring her back to health. Once she has returned to good health, we can inject the Immortality Gene therapy."

"We would like to wait a few months to follow the progress of First Officer McCullah. We don't expect any side effects, but exercising caution seems more prudent."

During the staff meeting, I maintained and spoke through my holographic image, but at the mention of Akiko's name, Katy gripped my physical arm... hard. I loved her so. How could I ever hurt her? How could I ever hurt Akiko? This was going to be difficult for all of us.

Genesis Log: 1 Aug 2044:

We approached Epsilon Scorpii, our third leg of our journey, this cycle, and brought Genesis out of light speed. I had to recalculate and adjust the frequency of the light drive more into the infrared range in order to work more efficiently within this star system. Once we had the necessary reverse thrusts, we were able to stop well out of the system to observe.

I had not expected it, but then I wasn't all that surprised either that by readjusting the light frequency for the drive, our visible light within the ship also shifted somewhat. Our lighting changed to an orange red range within the ship, but I was able to compensate it somewhat to a yellow orange. It was noticeable, but not that objectionable. We would have to tolerate it until we were back up to light speed and on course to our next hop.

Epsilon Scorpii is a K2-III star, meaning the visible light was dim orange red in color. The star is slightly larger than our sun, but the temperature somewhat lower. Even though the visible light was much dimmer, the majority of the generated energy radiated in the form of infrared above and beyond our visible range. Most disturbing was the amount of energy, measuring some seventy-two times that of our sun. These conditions made this star system uninhabitable for almost any life form, much less human.

I had decided months back that, with the unimpressive structure of this solar system, it would be unnecessary to wake anyone to study it. It would just be a further delay. I recorded as much data about the system as I could for later study, should Cdr. Kim or Mr. Sharp want to review it.

I plotted the coordinates to Alpha Indi, set our new course, and, without further delay, launched Genesis to light speed for the next thirty-six light year leg of our voyage and continued adventure.

Chapter 12
(Menage A Trois)

Genesis Log: 15 Aug 2045:

The doctors declare that the Immortality Gene project is a resounding success. They went into great detail that, in many ways, was extremely boring, which I will try to summarize for the sake of saving log space. If the subject hadn't been so important to everyone, the doctors would have lost their audience during the two-hour presentation.

All the test results, X-rays, MRIs, and Ultrasounds supported their endorsement of the project's success. The bottom line is, the general now has a fully functional Immortality Organ and it works.

They presented the staff with hundreds of images and reams of data... all proving the organ existed. Naturally, they wanted to document this medical miracle for posterity, but it was totally unnecessary. There is no world medical association that needed to be sold. It is only us... my staff and me, and I have total confidence in them. If they said the project is a success, then it is. It is as simple as that.

They had tested and retested and knew positively that the IG organ was producing the twenty-three chromosome cells at the modified size, these cells were in fact attracting to each other and merging, and producing pure stem cells within the blood stream. Everything was working as predicted and designed.

The general's body was in fact rebuilding damaged cells. Already, even to casual observers, changes could be seen in his body. The grey in his hair was replaced with his natural red, a previously prominent scar on his cheek had disappeared, and he was looking noticeably younger, much to the pleasure of his partner, Lt. Margret McKay. Judging from Margret's increasing smiles of late, it can reasonably be assumed the general's sex drive was greatly improving as well.

The doctors' major concern was only recently satisfied. Stem cells were newly found in his urine, which proved that the stem cells multiplying in his blood stream were being expelled if they were not used. This was the final indicator that all was functioning perfectly, which prompted the final endorsement.

Many questions came from the staff and me that generated enlightening answers. From all expectations, the general's body would settle to a stable appearance of about forty-five years old and remain there permanently. He was not expected to be subject to illnesses, diseases or aging. The doctors were adamant, however, that he was not totally immortal. His body could die from serious injury or acute medical trauma such as poisoning, just like anyone else's. The major difference was his body would repair itself from any injury or trauma that did not initially kill him, even to the point of regenerating limbs. This brought many ohhhhh's and awwww's among those present.

This discovery was simply too major of an event to remain secret. It was probably too late to even try. This situation could get out of hand quickly, so I decided to take control of the project. I said, "Before the doctors are swamped by requests for the procedure, I will control the schedule, and I will tell you now, not everyone aboard the ship will receive it." Allowing time for this to register I continued, "Now, before you panic, I intend that all department heads that want the procedure will have the opportunity, basically everyone present here today. First priority will be given to Akiko. After all, she is the reason this project is a reality. I will insist the doctors go next. They are spending far too much time awake on the trip. After that, I will analyze and assign priority based upon the needs of the Genesis. After the initial first run, we can then consider recommendations for your staff. Becoming immortal is not going to be a right. It will be a responsibility that should be carefully considered and controlled."

I didn't see any major objections, not that I would have been overly concerned with any. If anything, I saw relief in the doctors' faces. Choosing the Immortals was, as I said, a responsibility, a major responsibility only I could assume.

Genesis Log: 24 April 2046:

The alarms in the Hope went off during the late Red Cycle, automatically closing the air locks. The alarm said it was the air-seal between two decks. Luckily, it didn't affect the life support decks.

I dispatched Linda's duty crew in environmental suits to investigate the alarm. Linda was now ready to report their finding.

Linda said, "I think we might have a serious problem aboard the Hope. Our crew reports finding evidence of deterioration of many of the air lock seals onboard the Hope. There seems to be an algae or mold of undetermined origin growing on the seals. We can't determine if it is the algae affecting the seals or the seals creating the algae, but it must be stopped. The crew found one seal that leaked and repaired it temporarily, but many others need attention."

"Our problem is that we don't have the specification used in their design and manufacturing. I am going to suggest that we wake up the designers and engineering team of the Hope to work on this problem. They built them and should be able to repair them much faster. Additionally, we should do this quickly before we lose the Hope."

Oh crap, this means bringing Cdr. Tsuji, Mr. Sharp, Cdr. Jones, and maybe some of their crew, and possibly even Mr. Sakata. If the problem has anything to do with algae, it would fall into Sakata's expertise of botany and biology. I hoped I wouldn't have to see him again. Just in case, I calibrated the sights on my lasers.

Genesis Log: 11 May 2046:

I watched as Dr. Rossen removed Akiko from cryogenics. The process involved in going in and coming out of cryogenic is fast. The theory and engineering is complicated, but, for the most part, routine technology and has been for years with only slight improvement from this team.

289

The cryonic chambers themselves look somewhat like clear glass tubes filled with water, but in this case a special water called Glassy Water. This molecule-altered water has special traits in that it does not form crystals when supercooled to -196F. It remains in a thickened state approximating the texture of thick honey.

The human subject is immersed in this liquid with an attached umbilical breathing and resuscitation tube along with an IV to feed a special type of antifreeze (cryoprotectants) primarily consisting of glycerol or glucose. The cryoprotectants circulate through the blood to remove excess water in the cells to reduce the formation of crystals that can damage the cells.

The outer portion of the chamber circulates liquid nitrogen that supercools the Glassy Water to -196 F, where it is maintained throughout the hibernation period.

Basically, the reverse is true when a subject is brought out of hibernation. The difference is the resuscitation process, which involves sending electrical pulses to the lung muscles and heart to stimulate them as the body's temperature rises to the level they can begin to function. The whole process is automatic and reasonably quick.

During hibernation, the subject is not visible due to the circulation of the cloudy liquid nitrogen that masks the subject from view.

As we watched the reverse process, Akiko slowly became visible for the first time in twenty-seven years. Katy was with me to share the moment and support me, and I was thankful, as my emotions were soaring. As the liquids were evacuated,

Akiko's naked body became visible. It struck me as strange that this was the first time I have seen her naked beauty.

As Katy had wished, there were no longer any secrets between us. Katy knew all my secret thoughts and feelings and, true to her word, she truly shared this moment with me. Katy truly accepted the triple nature of our relationship. Either that or she loved me enough to share. Either way, I loved her for it all the more.

Katy said, "She truly is beautiful isn't she?"

Slipping my arm around her I said, "Yes, and so are you."

Katy smiled and said, "You don't have to worry about me, but thanks anyway."

The awaking process went without a hitch and her vital signs began to strengthen. The doctors had done this many times, but this was the first time I had watched the process. As Doc said, "It's routine."

We watched as Akiko was removed from the chamber and moved to a room where she continued to be warmed. I suppose I had hoped that she might wake, but she remained in her coma.

She would now go through a series of stem cells IV's that might take several months, hopefully not that many. It was up to her body to repair itself with the help of the Stem Cells.

Genesis Log: 17 June 2046:

While Katy was at her learning center, I had been roaming the ship as I always did. We were so used to being together that I became easily bored waiting. As I returned to our quarters looking for her, I was surprised to see Doc and Linda there talking with Katy. In my preoccupation with my boredom, I had lost track of them, not that I always knew, but I tried to keep loose tabs on many. At any rate, it was a surprise in several ways. To the best of my knowledge, they had never been to our quarters, nor had Katy ever invited anyone here. This was our private sanctum.

She looked a little sheepish and said, "Hi Nick, I invited Mother and Father here to discuss some things."

I had no idea what was going on, so I just went with the flow. "Oh, okay. What's up?"

"I have been explaining about our arrangement between you, me and Akiko, how we are all going to be together, how I would not let you give her up, and why I want to go into cryogenics now."

"Hon, NO! I don't want us to be separated." That was the damn truth, and I really didn't care what anyone thought.

"I know you don't, and I know you will be lonesome, but it will help you connect again with Akiko. I want her in our lives, and I need you to make it happen. Father says she will be waking up any day now. She will need you, and I need to be absent for a while." I started to object, but she said, "No buts! That's the way it's going to be." Looking at Doc and Linda she said, "Tell him."

"That's the way she wants it, Nick," Doc said, "She has got it in her head that the three of you can work it out, in fact, I think you had better work it out while she is in cryogenics or you may have some answering to do."

Damn, I finally realized she was absolutely serious, and it clicked for me. Katy knew everything about Akiko that I did, all our talks, shared feeling, our love. Katy had experienced all these emotions with me. Knowing what she must know and feel, she would almost have to love her as much as I do. There was no jealously ... none! She wanted this, and I was being told in no uncertain terms to make it happen. My kinky little Katy actually already loved Akiko and wanted her in every sense. I suddenly remembered Katy's looks when she saw Akiko naked. I remembered the affection I saw in her eyes. Katy even mentioned how beautiful she was. I thought at the time, how strange, but now I understand. Now this would take some getting used to, but really, how could I complain? Fact is, I didn't want to.

I began smiling and nodded my understanding. I then took her in my arms, knowing that she realized that I, finally, fully understood. She had even brought her parents into the discussion, I think partly to help her explain and partly to get them to understand. This was something she wanted for us and for her. Yes, Katy is always a bundle of surprises.

Genesis Log: 20 June 2046:

Katy went into cryonics last cycle. This is the first time in twenty-seven years we have been apart, and the last ten years she had shared my bed. My physical body did not sleep at all from missing her smart-ass remarks. She always made me laugh, and I felt the loneliness of command begin to fall upon

293

me again because of it. I had plenty of associates but no real friends. Katy had been the only real friend, well, there had been Akiko before her, but Akiko and I had blossomed almost directly into love. I am still amazed how that had happened.

Damn, Katy knew what she was doing, the little shit. She knew that as long as she was with me, my thoughts would be on her. She was right about that, and maybe she was right about the rest of her plan. For whatever reason, I was missing Katy but bringing Akiko back to the forefront of my thoughts because of it.

Suddenly, I felt it before I heard it in my mind. "Nick?" I had almost forgotten how it felt, telepathy. It could only be Akiko. "Akiko? Is that really you?"

"Where am I?"

"Oh, Akiko, I am coming to you now! Wait."

"Coming? What do you mean?"

Oh, I said too much already. There was no way Akiko could know that twenty-eight years have passed. To her she just had the baby, the baby that is now a twenty-eight-year-old man. I can't just rush in there and hug her, but as I said it, I was already running down the deck screaming, "Akiko is awake!" I must have been a sight to see. Doc and Linda came running out of their quarters half-dressed to join me in my sprint. I did have enough foresight to stop myself from barging into her room.

Doc got my attention asking, "She is awake? How do you know?"

"She is talking to me in my mind." He then understood.

"Wait out here and let me check her out. Keep talking to her, but go slow, Nick. We don't want her going into shock."

I could now see her through my visual center in her room. I was so shook up that it took me a few minutes to remember the visual centers. She was lying in her bed with her eyes still closed, but her mind was waking up. I watched as Doc came into my view and began checking her out and talking to her. Slowly she responded, and her eyes began to blink unseeing as her vision blurred in and out of focus.

I felt her telepathic link strengthen as her mind gripped mine. It wasn't the mind in this body, it was my mind in the control room, I realized. I said, "Welcome back Akiko. Don't panic, hon. You have been in a coma, but you are coming out of it now, and you are going to be fine."

"How long?"

"A little while...Doc will explain."

Doc was apparently pleased with her vital signs and removed her life support tubing. Akiko watched with interest and seemed to be staring at him.

She spoke for the first time and said, "Who are you?"

I realized the mistake too late. Although Doc had been in cryogenics for years, he must still have visibly aged, and Akiko was not making the connection. Maybe she was still a little groggy, also.

Doc said, "I am Dr. Rossen. Don't you recognize me?"

Her eyes grew wide with recognition and said, "How long have I been out?"

295

"A few years. You have been in cryogenics, because we didn't have the technology to bring you back until now. We now have the ability to repair your body, and we have in fact done so. You are healthy now and will stay that way."

"My baby?"

"Your baby is fine. You will meet him soon, maybe tomorrow after we have had a chance to talk some. What I need you to do now is rest, truly rest, and then we can talk. Okay? All you need to know now is that everything is fine."

She seemed satisfied, plus she must have been tired, because she nodded and promptly fell asleep, a true sleep and not that of a coma.

When Doc came out, he seemed happy, saying, "I think this worked to our advantage. She accepted the passage of time in terms of years. I must look older, but due to my stint in cryogenics, I don't think I could look more than ten years older and probably less. Once she has accepted the fact that she has been out for a few years, the hardest part is over. The next step is actually establishing the numbers of years. It won't be as big of a shock now."

Akiko was back, but this late cycle I would have neither her nor Katy. I would be alone again.

Genesis Log: 22 June 2046:

Akiko slept straight through a complete cycle and halfway through another. She woke up about mid-cycle hungry. I know because I watched her the whole time. Doc was called immediately before she could start asking questions. Doc wanted to be the one answering them.

296

I listened as Doc started slowing bringing her up to date, very slowly. He sort of went backward by talking about her treatment with stem cells and just how badly her body had been damaged. Akiko kept interrupting to ask questions, but Doc kept her focused. Doc even tackled the explanation of the Immortality Gene and how I had come up with the theory to save her and how that would be her next treatment to make her immortal. Next, he described the encounter with the aliens (The Enlightened) and how they had instantly transported us forty light years.

I saw his plan, to occupy her mind with the new wonders so she could more easily accept the challenging ones like, oh you have been asleep twenty-nine years. The amazement in Akiko's eyes indicated his plan was working.

Doc said, "You will also be happy to know that the Nick 2 project was completely successful and everything worked out as Nick planned it. He is anxious to see you, but you must understand some years have passed."

"I understand. How many years?"

Doc said, "Well, let's just say the project is full term. Nick is a grown man of almost thirty years old. He is that young man standing in the door waiting to see you."

Doc had lessened the shock, but Akiko's eyes visibly bulged with the realization of the amount of time passed. When Doc pointed me out, her eyes shot to bore into me. I tried to smile, but I was so nervous about her reaction. I projected, "It's me... honest." Her stare remained for a few seconds then softened, as her face broke out in a huge, almost comical smile and her arms spread to beckon me into her embrace. I didn't need to be asked twice. I ran to her embrace, almost tripping over all the life support equipment. I projected, "I have waited so long for you." For such a petite woman, her embrace was so strong, it almost hurt, but in a fantastically good way.

I was vaguely aware that Doc slipped out the door leaving Akiko and I in privacy to finally meet in person. If I had any concern that Akiko might think of me as her baby, they were quickly dispelled by the very unmotherly kisses she was giving me.

I was finally physically holding her in my arms, smelling her intoxicating aroma, and tasting her warm, sweet kisses. This had been the height of my desires since I first met her, and now it was happening. It was definitely worth the long wait.

We spent the entire late cycle talking, intermingled with fits of touching and kissing. We had years of catching up to do, but I would save Katy until later.

Genesis Log: 4 July 2046:

Mr. Sharp asked for a meeting with him, Cdr. Tsuji, Cdr. Jones, and Mr. Sakata. Taka had remained onboard Genesis working with Dr. Rossen. Mr. Sharp wanted the meeting to discuss the air-seal problems found on the Hope.

They had been sequestered on board the Hope, living, working and remaining there throughout their stay. The reports they had made indicated the problem was mechanical and not biological, as Linda had feared. Linda had her staff manufacture the replacement seals and the Hope crew had systematically replaced them, including some of the outside seals. According to Linda, it had been a mammoth job, but there had been no choice if the Hope was to be salvaged.

I had asked Linda what they wanted to meet about, but she had no idea, "Probably to get praise and recover some lost prestige." I didn't have a problem with that as long as they earned it. Honestly, I would love to see them back in the fold, so to speak.

As the team entered, Cdr. Tsuji was suspiciously absent. In his place was a large man I had been introduced to in passing, Abdul Karim. Something was not right here, and I sensed the general felt the same. He was beginning to look toward the Marine guard as I began activating my lasers, but before either of us could do anything, gunfire erupted from the .45 cal automatics they had smuggled into the control room.

I hadn't noticed that the Hope team had spread out until it was too late. The initial targets had been my lasers. Mr. Sharp and JJ took out my main two lasers, while Abdul took out the rear one. They attacked simultaneously and without warning. Sakata took aim on the Marine and sealed off the access ramp, as JJ turned to cover the remainder of the staff. The coup was complete almost immediately.

I was thinking quickly, and my military training kicked into gear. This was an obvious coup, probably radical Islam motivated. I didn't think Sakata, JJ, or Sharp were professionally trained, maybe at most a six-week course at one of the Al

Qaeda training bases in Iran. It couldn't be much more. I wasn't even sure that Sakata was Jihad motivated or trained. He was just stupid, more of a follower, an easy convert. These men were amateurs in warfare at best. I assumed Abdul was a professional soldier, because they took a chance even bringing him. Unfortunately, it was a risk that worked.

The first thing I needed to do was get them talking and buy some time. I activated my holograph image to draw attention away from my physical body. I said, "What is this? What do you want?" I knew Sharp, the arrogant bastard, could not resist the opportunity to gloat.

"We are taking over the ship," he said, "This is jihad! You will all die for your abomination against the will of Allah."

"What have we done?" I knew that would launch him into a tirade and focus his attention upon my holographic image.

"What have you done?" he screamed, "It was Allah's will that we all die when he destroyed Earth for its wickedness. You have also presumed to act as Allah's equal, as only he can give life." He turned to stab a finger at my physical body, "You and the Jew have created an abomination in this Satan body." Turning to now glare at the general, he said, "Only Allah is immortal. My hand will destroy these abominations. It is Allah's will."

"Will you also destroy yourself?"

Sharp whirled back on my image screaming, "No, we now know it is Allah's will to survive and keep his word alive. We will continue the journey,

300

create an Islam world and destroy all those that don't convert to Allah's truths."

"You stupid bastard! I control the Genesis, and I do what I want, not what you want."

"We will hold those important to you at our mercy. If you do not bend to our will they will die."

I had succeeded in buying some time. Unseen, I had already dispatched Marine security guards to guard Akiko, the cryonic lab, the umbilical connection to the Hope, and the ramp to the control room. I didn't want to take any chances in case there were others involved in the plot. During this stolen time, I had also managed to piss them off enough that they were all staring at my image. During Sharp's rant, I had managed to get the attention of the general, Marine guard, and Lt. Boland through my physical body and mimicked looking at the ceiling lights and back down tightly closing my eyes. With my eyes, I looked at them, then looked at their intended target with a slight nod. They understood.

Many things happened all at once. I yelled, "Now!" and simultaneously briefly flared the room lights to maximum, which is an extreme brilliance. It had the same effect as a flash grenade going off. The sudden flash can incapacitate all for approximately fifteen seconds. With my warning, we had our eyes tightly closed and looking down when it flashed. We all moved immediately toward our targets.

Unfortunately, Sharp started firing his weapon blindly, but he was lucky enough to catch the general in the stomach with a shot and me in my right thigh before I managed to knock the gun away and drive his prominent Adam's apple almost through the back of his neck. I felt his throat collapse, but proceeded to drive his nose bone up into his brain with the palm of my hand. Mr. Sharp was dead before he hit the floor.

The general had managed to break JJ's neck before he was shot, and I looked around to see Abdul down with Lt. Boland standing over him holding Abdul's gun. I didn't know if Abdul was dead, but Sakata certainly was. Too bad, I wanted to kill him myself. He was lying with his head at an unnatural angle, even as I saw the Marine kick it to the other side just to make sure. It was all over within seconds.

The general croaked out, "Next time I tell you to kill someone, do it!"

Even in my pain, I found that comical and began laughing, as did several of the others. Linda had been shaken during the episode, but she even managed to smile at that.

Once Dr. Rossen regained his sight, he had the general and I rushed off to the clinic for treatment. Neither wound was life threatening, and I was eventually wheeled into Akiko's room to recover. It was almost worth getting shot.

Doc said the general would heal fast, due to the IG. His wound was far more serious, but he would probably be up long before me.

After the initial action, I dispatched the Marines to enter the Hope in force to discover Cdr. Tsuji and two others tied up. They had not gone along with the mutineers, much to my pleasure.

I have to admit, this cycle was not a boring one, and our 4th of July celebration was the most exciting ever.

Genesis Log: 7 July 2046:

Akiko was pronounced healthy enough to begin her IG treatment this cycle. The general came around to give her a pep talk. Yes, he was already up and around after only three cycles. He was still a little sore, but functioning quite well, better than I was. My thigh still hurt like the devil.

The smiling general said, "I think the abominations should all stick together. How is your devil-spawned body doing today? Mine is pretty good."

"Well, not as good as yours, but I will make it."

"You know, you handled yourself well in there against the radicals. You saved us all." Mac said. "I knew I was right to pick a Marine for your job."

Turning to Akiko he continued, "I really came in to see you, dear lady. I wanted to make sure you are comfortable with taking the IG and joining the Immortality Club. It has really worked out for me, as you can see. I was never handsome, IG can't help me there, but I look and feel younger, and I have been told that I will remain this age. Well, unless some asshole shoots me dead."

Akiko said, "It will take some getting used to, the not aging, but yes, I am okay with it. I'll join the club."

"Good! Taka, Doc and Linda will be next, and then we need to get Nick here onboard. You never know when he might have to fight terrorists again."

I had been thinking the same thing. I thought it might be better to get a few more years on this body first, but who knows, maybe Akiko might like a younger man.

Later during the cycle, as Akiko was taking the Immortality Gene IV, she turned to me and said, "Nick, tell me about your lover."

I can't be sure, but I think I had to swallow my ass about that time. I had dreaded this moment. I didn't want to lose Akiko. After a moment, I said, "Has someone said anything?"

"No, quite the opposite. No one at all talks about your life on board ship, not even you, and that speaks volumes. Your body is almost thirty years old. Are you going to tell me you are still a virgin? That is not very believable. From all the silence, there has to be someone."

"No, I won't tell you I am virgin, but I know you are."

"Just tell me about her."

So, I did. I was finally happy to get the secret out. It had been tearing me up inside. I told her everything: who she was, how we had grown up inseparable since we were children, how it was so natural for us to fall in love, how it had finally happened, and how we had been together as lovers for over ten years. Akiko listened as I rambled on for hours. I even went into Katy's plan for the three of us to live together. From her lack of reaction, I could tell nothing about what was going on in that beautiful oriental mind.

Finally, Akiko asked, "Where is she?"

"When you started showing signs of coming out of your coma, she wanted to go into cryonics.

Katy has always known I love you too. We have no secrets. She wanted to be out of the way for a while so, as she put it, so we could have our honeymoon."

"Katy did that for us? She wants to share?"

"Yes, even more. She wants us all to share."

"Oh! Tell me, is she pretty?

I said, "Oh yes, Akiko, she is as beautiful as you but in a different way."

"Tell me, Nick. What do you want to do?"

Was she asking me to choose? How could I choose? I think it would kill me. In desperation, I just blurted out, "Well, can I have you both?" I waited for a reaction, but she just sat there thinking, while my stomach churned and threatened to empty its contents.

Finally, her face cracked open in hysterical laughter so loud that it attracted the attention of everyone in the clinic. They looked at us, but eventually went back to their work. I had never seen her laugh so hard, and I didn't know exactly what she was laughing at. Did she find it funny or hysterical? Therefore, I maintained my troubled silence.

After a few minutes she turned serious and said, "I haven't been completely honest with you either, Nick. I have said that I am a virgin, and I am, in the sense that I have never been with a MAN before, but... I have never found a man that I liked enough before you. I fell in love with you almost immediately and wanted you, and I still do."

"I even have an ex-lover on the Genesis. Before you ask, no, I won't tell you who, but it was over when I met you. I just never knew how to tell you until now."

"In reality, to join the team I had to lie about my sexual orientation, they only wanted straight people that could help populate the new planet. Before meeting you, I considered myself a lesbian."

"I tell you this now because I think Katy has come up with a plan that might just work. I don't want to give you up, and I can tell you don't want to give me up either. From what I have heard, I already like Katy and the way she thinks... a very wise woman. What she did, giving us our honeymoon, shows a very loving person, someone I think I could also love. So, I guess maybe you CAN have both of us. But, not until after a little time for just the two of us. Agreed?"

I jumped up, dragging my IV and stand with me, to embrace my Akiko. We even managed to get both of us in the same single hospital bed, at least until Doc came in and sent me back to mine, something about kinking up the hoses and setting off alarms. Oh well, soon.

I am the luckiest man alive. I have two beautiful and smart women in my life. With this realization, I suddenly wondered if I could handle both.

Genesis Log: 15 Aug 2046:

The day finally came when Doc released Akiko from the clinic. He pronounced Akiko Immortal. The IG worked perfectly according to all tests, but the announcement itself had little importance to Akiko and me. We just wanted her out of the clinic.

We had built up a great deal of excitement with the anticipation of us finally being alone together.

We wasted little time and were almost running hand-in-hand as we approached my quarters. I was giving my sound command to open the door even before we reached it, and we rushed inside. Once inside, we were all over each other like animals in heat. I wish I could say our first time was slow and romantic, but delayed desires for each other drove us to raw lust. It was rough, but I withstood her attacks. I can't help laughing at my own joke as I write this log. But our lovemaking, if truth be told, was primitive.

The anticipation and level of desire we had for each other, compounded by the years of waiting, drove us to extremes; but our second time was as loving and romantic as the first was primal.

I wish we had room service, so we could stay in each other's arms forever. It is certainly a nice way to make a long space voyage.

Genesis Log: 22 Dec 2046:

We have our first setback on the Immortality Gene. Dr. Rossen, Linda, Lt. Margret McKay, and Taka all took the IG on the same day. Doc, Linda, and Margret handled the IG well and were pronounced successful recipients, but Taka's treatment was a dismal failure.

His body defenses attacked the small difference of the Immortality Gene's DNA. This was evident from the start when they found expelled stem cells in his excrement. They tried drugs to reduce his body's rejection defenses, but even that failed to work. Sadly, Taka would evidently be one of the rare recipients that this technology would not work on. Being a statistic is bad enough, but when it is you, it is much more devastating.

How ironic that the inventor of the gene can't make it work on himself. It almost seems sad, even though he should have a long full life, and with stem cell injections, even longer. At best though, he will have a finite life expectancy. This can be viewed as disappointing when compared to virtual immortality.

Taka had been extremely important in the development of this technology, but we all realized his years awake would now have to be rationed. He would be direly needed on New Earth. It was decided to put him into cryonic storage until such time he was needed.

Dr. Takashi Ishiguro was not one of the original Genesis team, but he became extremely valuable toward our betterment. The Genesis was fortunate to have him.

Genesis Log: 18 June 2047:

Over the last year, Akiko and I have gotten so very close in mind and body, finally consummating our love. Akiko, eventually returned to her duties as department head and returned Lt. Naomi Sami to cryonic storage with a Well done. Other than her involvement with her department, we had become as inseparable as Katy and I had been, and it felt so natural.

Akiko had also continued learning about Katy. It was obvious that Akiko greatly respected Katy's wisdom in what could have normally been considered a complicated, if not impossible, situation. When we were together, Akiko would ask different things about Katy, getting me to remember and talk about her. She was by no means obsessed with Katy, but often after we made love and were enjoying those special quiet moments, she would bring her up, maybe wondering about the three of us and how it would work. On other occasions, we watched videos of Katy and me as we grew up together. Unfortunately, it was making me miss Katy that much more.

Finally, tentatively, after one such discussion I said, "Are you ready to bring her back? I think it is time."

Turning to face me, she looked deep into my eyes saying, "Yeah, I am a little apprehensive, but I think you are right. I know you miss her, and it's time to wake her up."

"I have really enjoyed our time alone, but I understand it can't last forever. Let's do it."

Genesis Log: 25 July 2047:

Katy came back today after a year in the cryogenic chamber. Akiko and I watched her in recovery as she regained consciousness. It is somewhat like waking up after a minor surgery, you're a little groggy, but that passes fast enough.

Pushing me forward, Akiko said, "Go to her. Stay with her tonight and get reacquainted."

"No! None of us will be separated again."

Katy saw me coming and threw her arms open wide for me, almost as wide as her smile. We embraced, and I tasted her kiss again. Oh, how I had missed them.

"How long?"

"A long year."

She nodded and said, "Where is Akiko?"

I motioned for Akiko to come in. As she approached, Katy's smile spread as she pulled Akiko into a bear hug that seemed to be equally reciprocated. They began chatting like old friends who had been separated, and, much to my surprise, they ignored me.

Finally, Katy said, "Nick, give us a kiss and get lost for a while. We want to talk about you." At that they both laughed.

Feeling somewhat dejected and left out, I did exactly that. I left and visited Doc for a while and told him what they said. I didn't think it was so funny, but he was enjoying my discomfort greatly. He just told me not to worry, that it was a good sign. I don't know how he could say that. From my look, he correctly interpreted my discomfort.

"Look, my friend. Don't blow it now. Look at them. They both love you enough to make it work, and it looks like they are working it out, so don't let your jealously get in the way now."

What? Jealousy? Damn, he was right. I could see them talking and laughing, probably at me. They were completely at ease with each other and enjoying each other's company. They had overcome the jealousy part obviously quite well. What right did I have to feel rejected and jealous? This was now a three-way partnership, and I would have to accept that also. I hadn't even considered this aspect, but it was time I did.

I was feeling some better when I went back in, but it didn't last long. Katy was getting dressed with

Akiko's help. They stopped long enough to take me in a three-way hug, kissing both my cheeks. The bomb landed then when they told me to take Akiko's quarters tonight. They felt they needed to spend some time together, getting to know each other better.

Here I was nervous about sleeping with both the women I love and at the same time anxious to experience the so-called Menage A Trois. Now I find out I am the one left out. What a shocker, but I created this mess and left it up to them to solve the problem. It was as Doc said, "Don't blow it now." So, I forced a smile, kissed them both, and went back to cry on Doc's shoulder.

I truly was happy to see them getting along so well. The only problem I had was, they didn't even look back... they were so busy talking, staring at each other, giggling, and walking off hand-in-hand. I doubt if either will ever tell me what they talk about this late cycle.

Genesis Log: 26 July 2047:

I wasn't interested in much of anything else on the Genesis this cycle. I did finally get control of my emotions through reason and logic but still managed little sleep. I would just have to wait until they came back to me on their own.

Finally, they came into the galley while I was eating. I almost didn't see them until they were plopping down on either side of me. The big hugs and kisses lavished upon me made everything all right. They were all smiles and giggly, but this time I was included. They were like twins, finishing each

311

other's sentences, and what wonderful sentences. They told me everything was going to work out. They suggested I take a nap today, because they had big plans for me this late cycle. Like I said, I was included in the smiles and giggles this time, and I could hardly wait until later.

Chapter 13
(Deja Vu)

Genesis Log: 23 Nov 2047:

After the near successful mutiny, I have been poring over the history files of those in cryonic storage, searching for any indication of additional potential Muslim radicals. I concentrated on those stored on the Hope, since that is where these radicals came from. I have identified many Muslims, but that fact alone does not make them radical or even undesirable. I have had many friends, especially in the Marines, that were Muslim. They were very close friends and had volunteered to fight the radicals to help purge their religion of these fanatical murders. I do not want to assume that just because they were Muslim and Islamic they are dangerous, but it is one major common factor that must be considered in profiling for potential radicals. I have never been politically correct. It would be pure insanity NOT to put these characteristics first on my profiling list. The Islamic religion is, after all, a common association for all the radicals.

Mr. Sakata did not fit in any of my profiles, though. I was unable to find any potential suspicious background on Mr. Sakata. He was even a professed Catholic. Considering the snake Sakata was, I finally just wrote him off as just plain stupid. I figured Sharp told him what to do, and he simply did it.

In my research I was able to identify several in storage on the Hope that would warrant closer observation. Being Muslim and from the Hope met two of my profile categories.

As for as the Genesis, a full 10% were Muslim, but I suspect they had passed the general's security check or they would not have been able to be on board. Being PC only went so far with the general. Of these, I reviewed passport records to identify any lengthy stay in questionable areas where they may have been indoctrinated in the radical teachings of Islam. I picked five from the Genesis complement for the security watch list, ten in all.

Of the original four mutineers, none remained alive. I had originally thought that Abdul Karim might have been alive, because I remember seeing Mr. Boland standing over him, pointing his weapon at him. After Sergeant Major (SgtMaj) Andy Gomez and the other Marines removed them all from the control room, SgtMaj Gomez reported all were dead. I chuckled to myself at the slight grin SgtMaj Gomez had when he made his report to my holographic image. I never bothered to question him or Mr. Boland. All I knew for sure was I didn't care that they were all dead.

Genesis Log: 26 July 2048:

Katy and I went into the clinic this cycle for an extended stay. It was finally our time to take the Immortality Gene. We had stalled and pushed Cdr. Tsuji and Lt. Boland ahead of us. We even brought Lt. Sami and Cdr. Kim out of storage to push them ahead of us, but we couldn't put it off any longer.

This would be the first time Katy and I would be separated from Akiko since we came together. None of us liked it much, but Akiko said she would visit us every day. Smiling to myself I was thinking, "I could use the rest."

Conspiratorially, the general had once mentioned that the IG would help me in the bedroom, while making a gesture of slapping his bicep and raising his clinched fist and forearm straight up. This had struck me funny at the time, but now it seemed comforting. He should know though, with that little nymph he was paired with.

The general had really changed from the stiff-necked Marine senior officer he had once been. I actually think he liked not being the final authority. It let him relax somewhat. All he really had to do now was support me, which he did extremely well. He was the driving force in getting my body protected. The persistent bastard was here now, making sure I didn't back out.

Genesis Log: 12 Sept 2048:

I didn't know it was possible to weep in a telepathic message, but it is. Akiko's weeping came through loud and clear, "Katy's body rejected the Immortality Gene, Nick! What are we going to do?"

Akiko's heart was broken, as was mine, and I had no idea what to do. My mind went racing. It wasn't like she was going to die tomorrow. Katy would continue to age, but with stem cell treatment, her life could be extended greatly. We can still have many years yet together.

Then again, compared to immortality, an extended life would still seem far too short. Eventually, Akiko and I would lose her. It may take eighty or so years, but we would most assuredly lose her, and after so many years of being together, it would be even harder then.

I didn't want us to have to face the problem so soon, so I decided to take a lighter approach. Maybe I could yet find a way to make it work on her. I tried to soothe Akiko saying, "Hon, it might not be as bad as it seems. Katy is still younger than you are. Maybe this will give her a few years to catch up with you before we can fix it." I discovered that it is also possible to telepathically transmit weeping and laughing at the same time.

Akiko burst out with radiated humor at my joke, while saying, "Nick, you shit!"

Akiko seemed in better spirits when she came in. Together we told Katy what the problem was and how I was going to fix it. Katy wasn't as sad as we thought she might be, certainly not as sad as Akiko and I were, even though we were hiding it.

Katy said, "It's strange, a year ago living to a ripe old age was considered a fantastic achievement. Nothing has changed. I intend to live a full and active life. I will just have to get used to having a couple of kids in my bed." This generated uproarious laughter from all of us.

How could I... we, ever hope to be without Katy? I promised myself that I would find a way, no matter what it took.

Genesis Log: 17 Jan 2049:

316

Katy accepted the fact that the IG did not work on her, but Akiko and I did not. My mind had continued to research and seek a solution to the problem, but was unsuccessful so far.

The girls have had to put up with me for the last few months since I relaxed my self-imposed baffles between my extended brain and me. I wanted to apply my full mental capacity to a solution. When I removed the barriers, my consciousness seemed to run faster, which tended to make me grumpy.

Fortunately, the girls don't allow me to get too far off track. They have a way of bringing me back to their reality. Our late cycles tend to always wind up in a tangle of arms and legs and sweaty bodies. Our love, passion and lust for each other seems unquenchable. Often I remembered the general's comment about how the IG improved things in bed and how thankful I was that it had.

At our staff meeting, I broached the subject of the failed IG again with Taka and if he had discovered anything new with the IG. He stared at me for a while, as if he was trying to decide if he wanted to say anything. That really got my curiosity up, and I waited for a response.

Finally, Taka said, "Well, I have found the gene that creates the higher function of rejection in both Katy and me. It's ironic, though. Before IG, this gene would be highly desirable; but now it causes the rejection levels to attack the minor alteration of the IG. Unfortunately, I can't even alter our DNA to eliminate the accelerated rejection gene, because our bodies would reject that change too. So, it is catch-22."

"What can you do?"

"Oh my, its complicated, maybe too complicated and it would only resolve part of the problem." At my continued staring, he continued. "OK, OK... the only thing I can do is start at the very beginning. Since I can't alter the DNA in our existing bodies, all I can do is create a new body with the altered DNA. I can alter the DNA and use this new strain to clone a new body that would be able to accept the IG. This is the only way. Are you following me?"

I nodded, but I was leaping far ahead and saw it coming. "Fantastic idea!" Doc had scooted to the edge of his chair, also in anticipation.

Taka went on, "As you can see, this only solves part of the problem. Now we have an altered body that would be able to accept the IG, but the new body is a new consciousness. Take Katy for example; there would be a new Katy, but it wouldn't be the same Katy... unless... we somehow find a way to transfer her mind to the clone. I have no idea how this could be done... not my expertise. But, assuming we could copy the existing memory, there would be two identical Katys complete with memories and self-awareness as Katy. Yeah, it gets really complicated. Her mind, who she is, would be living in two bodies. The only differences would be the new experiences lived by the individual bodies once copied, which would be vast. One would be immortal, while the other would grow old and die, but it would be the same mind sitting here staring at us now. It might be easier to understand if you look at it from her perspective. Years from now, she could look back and remember sitting here today from either body."

"Yeah, I have thought about it from my perspective also, and it gets really confusing. I would not have brought it up, but you asked. Of course, it all assumes the mind download could be possible."

I knew Doc and I would be working on this part, hell, I already was.

We all agreed to kick around all these ideas and discuss them when we had more to report.

Genesis Log: 1 April 2050:

I had spent the last few months trying to digest the concept Taka presented concerning the failed IG solution for Katy and himself. Taka did not give Doc and me an easy task, but I finally came up with a plan. It was a difficult plan.

A human brain is nothing like a computer, where you can simply copy all the files and transfer to another computer. Even if you could, you must consider a human brain has over 100 billion neurons that connect to 10,000 others, equating to maybe 1,000 trillion connections. Computers just don't come that big... well, other than mine.

Add to this the fact that human memories are extremely complex. A single human memory may involve visual, audio, smell, touch, emotions and a variety of different categories, all potentially stored in different sections of the brain. As an example, consider a walk through a park. The memory records thousands of intertwining inputs: Possibly the chirping of birds, the feel of grass between your toes, the smell of flowers, the feel of wind on your face, the color of the trees, words being spoken, a feeling of peace and harmony, etc. All these different data inputs come together to form a memory that is stored in multiple areas of the brain.

Even the encoding of sensory inputs falls into numerous categories such as visual encoding to process images; acoustic encoding to process sounds, especially the sound of words; semantic encoding processes the meaning of words; tactile encoding to process the feel of something through touch, and we must assume emotions are encoded in a similar process.

Even if it were possible to copy the entire data of a human brain, it would be jumbled, without a way to reconstruct a memory. As an example, smells would be recorded in the olfactory lobe of the brain that deals with smell, likewise with audio, touch, feeling and emotions, etc. Bringing the hundreds, maybe thousands, of data inputs back together to remember the event would be impossible to reconstruct from computer organized files.

The human brain uses a form of computer router called the hippocampus (meaning "sea horse" because of its appearance). This organ encodes and routes the various sensory inputs to the appropriate part of the brain that can best store the data. As near as I can tell, the hippocampus codes the inputs and records them in such a way that they can also be retrieve and recombined in the same order to reform the memory. The hippocampus plays an important role in recording and retrieving memories. As I said, it is extremely complicated... beyond even my ability to understand, and I am operating at full mental capacity.

Having said this, sometimes extremely complicated solutions can be found by allowing the brain itself to serve as the solution. Since the hippocampus is already performing these functions, my theory is to simply tap into it, not in the traditional sense as splicing a wire, but in the sense of detecting the minute electrical signals as it communicates with the brain. If I can link the hippocampus of the source brain to the hippocampus of the target brain, they could work in tandem. With this communication established, we wouldn't have to be able to understand how memories are stored, all we would have to do is let the target hippocampus view the memory from the source and store the same sensory inputs in its appropriate location. The source memory would now exist in the target brain's memory, theoretically in the identical same location, effectively copying the memory.

I have even devised a method of establishing this link. There are two hippocampus organs, one in each hemisphere of the brain embedded deep in the brain folds approximately center behind the ears and eyes. I designed a helmet using a series of extremely sensitive detectors precisely placed and focused on the main impulse stream of the hippocampus. If my calculations are correct, the helmet detectors should sense the small electrical signals flowing through the hippocampus. Retrieving this information from the source brain, amplifying it and transmitting it through an identical helmet to the source brain should transfer the virtual memory.

A person's consciousness, who they are, consists of the sum total of their memories. By duplicating those memories, assuming they can all be captured, in the target brain, would effectively transfer the consciousness. Transfer is not the proper word... let's call it copying because both brains would have the same memory and consciousness. The end result would be a cloned body and mind. Problem solved... theoretically.

This simple approach and solution, unfortunately, remains complex. I will be required to develop a massive computer program of sensory stimulations and verbal questions geared to stimulate the hippocampus to retrieve memory, virtually all memory. This in itself will be a massive undertaking. Not only must every memory be stimulated, but they must be stimulated from multiple directions. For example, the memory of the walk through the park might be stimulated by the mention of the park's name, the color green of the grass, the sound of a bird chirping, the feeling of peace and harmony or any number of other triggers. All the cross references must also be stored in the target brain. The only good aspect to developing the program is that it could be reused on any subject. The downside is it will take some time to develop the program and administer. The process of gathering memories from the program could take months, even years for both the source and target.

This procedure is far too complex to present at a staff meeting, so I presented all my data and backup information in white papers and schematics so they could study it to whatever depth they might wish or could. I knew Doc, Taka, and Cdr. Tsuji

(Hiroshi) would pour over it in depth, but much was still beyond their ability to understand. I was not sure if I understood it completely, but the theory seemed sound. One thing for sure, they would build the helmet and begin experiments to prove or disprove my theory.

The collective expertise of these three in medical, computer and encryption technologies, combined with their scientific curiosity, virtually guaranteed they would not be able to resist the challenge I gave them. Of course, the personal need of Taka wouldn't hurt either.

Genesis Log: 4 Feb 2051:

As spokesperson for the combined medical department, Dr. Rossen was ready to present his findings concerning the copying and transposing memory to cloned brains from the host mind. From all my analysis, the only possible weak step was the brains interconnect apparatus. Everything else was proven out already: my body is living proof that cloning works, the IG is proof that gene splicing works and the IG itself proves that genes could be manipulated. All that was left to prove was the hippocampus interconnects.

Linda, with Katy's assistance, had recently completed the building and installation of a captain's chair I had designed. The structure was adaptable in that it could refold itself and reconfigure into a podium, which it was now doing in preparation for Doc's presentation.

I had recently begun to preside over the staff meetings in my physical body. Even though everyone knew my relationship between my mind and body, it was still sometimes confusing. It was not much of a problem when my physical body was young, but now that I was an adult, they were not only treating me as an adult but ship captain as well. I had noticed many times that the staff couldn't seem to decide which persona to address. For the most part, I tried to remain quiet in body form during the meetings and preside over the meetings in my holographic image; still, some would turn to address my physical form. The chair was the general's idea. He had noticed the confusion and suggested I begin the captain's role in my physical form and establish a command chair. I decided he was right, and it would be best to remove this confusion and asked Linda to build the captain's chair for me.

Since the captain's chair would be somewhat elevated and centered in the control room, I designed it to serve multiple purposes.

As I took my usual place between Akiko and Katy, the podium completed its realignment. As Doc stepped to the podium, he had a pleased smile as if he was the messenger of good tidings.

Doc began, "Most of you here know the experiments we have been conducting over the last year with thought transfer. We built the helmet design Nick provided to accomplish the interconnect. It was crude, but we have refined and streamlined it. This is what it looks like now."

Doc was smiling when he criticized my design, but what he held up was an infinite improvement over the clumsy helmet I designed. The improved version was a streamlined space age adaptation that looked like something out of a Star Wars movie. This version was a form fitting, studded belt that slipped around the head like a golden crown. Attached to the crown were small wing-looking flaps that wrapped back around and behind the ears. The largest part of the apparatus was a golden visor that slipped down over the eyes to provide the controlled visual stimulus. Another slim belt extended over the head to adjust and hold the headband in place and ear cups to provide the audio stimulus. It was a work of art as well as a functional apparatus... at least I hoped it was functional.

It was earlier decided that both the source brain and the recipient brain should receive the identical stimulation. Doc believed the target brain would be better able to reference the same memory and speed up the process by receiving the same stimulus. I believe he is right.

Doc continued, "A great deal of the time we have been analyzing Nick's program to interrogate the source brain. As I have already said to Nick many times, it is exceedingly comprehensive. We have added very little to it. What is surprising about the program is its size. The program is just over one petabyte of information stored in the thought transfer program. You might say, "Yeah, so what?", but let me put that in perspective. A petabyte is a thousand terabytes (one trillion bytes), this is fifteen zeros! It is a massive program, bigger than any program ever ran on Earth."

"The program was designed to stimulate thought and recall memory in multiple formats and combinations: sound (words, music, raw random sounds, etc.), visual (images, words, colors, shapes, etc.) questions (questions of everything imaginable, no answers, just questions to stimulate memories from various directions. You get the idea. These memories can then be picked up and transferred to the target brain. As I said, it is complicated."

"Our experiments have been interesting, to say the least. The outcome is that we have determined that it will work, and the team is endorsing the project; but we have found some other interesting benefits as well."

Once we built, what we now call, META (memory educational transfer apparatus), we discovered some interesting facts. Information transmitted directly to the hippocampus is immediately stored in permanent memory and bypasses the short-term memory. This expedites the process of learning. Also, it apparently does not go into conscious thought for analysis in the receiving brain, which means the transfer process is much quicker.

We also learned that the human brain can process the program at super-fast speeds, which means the META transfer process will be far less time consuming. We are not quite sure why, but we have learned to accept the gifts as they come.

Skills and knowledge can be separately transferred. By limiting the stimulus program to certain files only, we can effectively transfer specific knowledge or skills. As an example, I have learned Japanese from Taka via the META. It took us a single day for me to learn it, and I am now fluent in the language. We feel that we can use META to educate; we just have to be specific on which interrogation files to use. Emotions and other deep memories are not required to learn skills such as this, so they are disabled. At some point we will be able to use the META to teach skills we may need on New Earth. META may eventually replace some of the tedious and time-consuming education."

The staff was as impressed as was I. I loved these whiz kids. Even with all my unbridled intellect, abstract thought remains the spark of the human spirit and these kids had the spark. High intellect does not guarantee this abstract thought.

Genesis Log: 6 April 2051:

At our staff meeting, Taka reported that the cloned embryos for Taka 2, Katy 2, and Nick 3 were placed in their artificial uterus tanks last cycle and were doing well.

The cloned DNA for Taka 2 and Katy 2 had, of course, been slightly altered to allow the IG to work, but Nick 3's DNA had not been altered. Nick 3 would be an exact duplicate of myself and Nick 2.

The whole idea of Nick 3 had been a shock. I was already living through Nick 2, so I hadn't even considered another body. I mean, how could I live through two bodies? When Doc and Taka came to me with the suggestion, I was surprised.

Taka said, "I think we should clone another Nick!" After a long pause to allow me to get my mouth closed, he continued, "There are two major reasons: one, for the sake of Katy's developing memories, we should try to duplicate her early childhood as much as possible by allowing the two of you to grow up together like the last time. Two, it would be prudent to have a spare body. Imagine how you would feel now if the radicals had killed your body. Doc and I have talked about it and believe you might have gone insane if your mind had been thrust back into the confines of your dome prison, especially after having escaped into a body."

I had thought about it, also. I can't imagine having to live in that prison again. Well, actually I can, but I don't want to. It would be so much worse now, losing the physical love of Akiko and Katy. I think it would be too much to bear. Therefore, they sold me on the idea of a spare body... easily.

Doc picked up where Taka left off, "We have it all figured out. Clearly, you can't occupy both bodies at the same time. To eliminate this possibility, we have designed another type of META to induce a deep sleep so only one body will be awake at a time. The device is much simpler than the original METAs. They can even be surgically implanted so only you can control them.

Since your mind virtually never sleeps, you can occupy a body twenty-four hours a day. The body you currently occupy requires sleep so the result of having two bodies can only be better for you."

Like I said, it was an easy sale to me. I said, "You don't have to continue with the sales pitch. I'm sold. Good job, guys."

Genesis Log: 1 Jan 2052:

Taka 2, Katy 2, and Nick 3 were removed from their artificial uterus tanks this cycle. The infants were past full term and healthy. The ward was echoing their healthy wails of rage at being forced to enter into life.

As before with Nick 2, I had established contact with my clone early. Also as before, Nick 3's brain was hungry for the organization of my consciousness and made the conversion easily and quickly.

I had always intended that the babies should be raised in the nursery together. Those times with Katy and myself growing up had been very meaningful to me and obviously to Katy as well; it was part of who we were. Unfortunately, I lost that argument early on.

Linda was adamant, "I missed out on Katy's childhood the first time... I will NOT miss it again. It will be as if we have a second chance. John and I will raise Katy 2."

I looked to Doc for help, but he shrugged as if to say, "You can't win this one."

Even more surprising was Akiko. Katy and she had decided between themselves to raise Nick 3. I tried to explain that even though it was a small person, it would still be the adult me in his head. That didn't seem to make any difference.

Akiko said, "We know that, but we still want it that way, besides, I feel sort of like Linda. I carried the baby for nine months and almost killed myself in the process. I even have the stretch marks to remind me. I miss the bonding I should have had. It will just make us all closer. Don't you think?"

Taka coughed to get my attention and said, "Ioa wants the same thing."

Ioa Ito was one of Taka's staff and they had been together for some time. They would obviously be mates for life, and he had already pushed her high on the list for the IG so she would have time to raise Taka 2, then be with him in adult life again. Immortality created its own set of problems, but in a good sort of way...hopefully.

"Cripes, I give up!" I was way outnumbered here.

Genesis Log: 1 Jan 2055:

In our previous life, Katy and I had not even met before the age of three. This time we are being raised together. Akiko attends to my physical needs and treats me as a child, her child. I like her attention and allow myself to be the child. She dotes affection on me, and I eat it up. I don't even fight the opportunity to be Akiko's child and the child Katy 2 wanted me to be. It is satisfyingly fun, being without worries as a child, at least part of the day anyway.

Akiko would take me, Nick 3, to her gardens with her while she worked. I played the role and enjoyed it. I enjoy her gardens and playing with the animals. When I needed to talk to her as Nick, I trained myself to only use telepathy in communication to her during those times. We both played our roles in life.

Katy spent many of her cycle hours in the education facility. At the age of thirty-six, she was becoming quite accomplished as an engineer and was working closely with Linda. Since Linda had ceased aging, they were now approximately the same age physically. They have also become close friends, more like twin sisters than mother and daughter. I still found it strange that Linda was raising the clone, Katy 2, as her daughter, but she actually was her daughter. Katy was in reality helping Linda to raise Katy 2. I still take a double look every time I see them together.

I have my special chamber, where I rest in deep sleep as Nick 3. At those times I occupy my other adult body in Nick 2. It works out remarkably well. I preside over the staff meeting in the early cycles as Nick 2 and attend to any business that needs doing. Afterwards, I retire to my quarters and the special sleeping chamber Doc built for me there and transfer to my Nick 3 body. I am still available through my holographic image to address any of the staff that requires it. By the end of the late Blue Cycle I would re-join Katy and Akiko for a late dinner.

It took some getting used to, but I was sharing the meals with both my bodies. They both had needs, and it seemed I was constantly hungry and eating. I remembered how I had once felt cheated by not being able to enjoy the taste of food. Well, now I was making up for those lost times.

Fortunately, our late cycle time together never grew old. Akiko, Katy and I continued to enjoy those times together while Nick 3 slept. This was our special time.

All our lives seem so very complicated, but they really weren't. This cycle, however, things happened that might be the beginning of the complications, if there were to be any. Doc, and Taka decided that at the age of three, the memory transfer should begin.

The two teams of Katy - Katy 2 and Taka - Taka 2 began their sessions this cycle. At only three, the children didn't seem to be getting a lot out of it but more than you might have expected. Doc was limiting not only the session length but also the depth of the program. Luckily, the program was divided into increasingly difficult levels, which lent itself to the children. Additionally, the program ran at fast forward, so the children did not have to analyze any thoughts they might receive. The limiting factor for the children and the program was the level of the development of the young mind. If there was no reference data in the mind, incoming data did not stick. It was simply rejected, but some data would remain to begin building a greater reference. Doc believed the process was worth the effort as the young mind would learn and add reference data that would aid the next session.

Genesis Log: 17 July 2060:

I woke the girls up very early. Something was wrong! I knew what it was. One of my artificial hearts was failing and my internal alarms were going off. Doc had designed two artificial hearts for just this reason, but the failed heart was throwing off the rhythm of the second one and threatening to make it fail.

I woke up the Doc through the intercom alarm, but I also sent Katy to get him and tell him what was going on. Akiko and I rushed to the control room to get my dome open. We had just gotten the dome open as Doc and the others burst into the control room. I yelled, "Hurry, Doc! The second heart is beginning to fail."

Doc dove under the dome and began turning valves to isolate out the failed heart. I felt the immediate release of pressure and the rhythm of the second heart smooth out. That had been close... very close. I had begun to feel my mind getting dizzy and had almost passed out. I had been lucky that the second heart had not failed as well from the extra strain to maintain my artificial blood flow. The Genesis Project might have failed and everything to date lost.

After the initial concern over the stability of the second heart, Doc woke his team and went to work replacing the failed heart.

Doc said, "I can't believe this happened. There should have been more warning. I have never known an artificial heart to fail in this manner, so suddenly. I designed the system with two hearts to prevent anything like this from happening, but I never considered a total valve breach. I can promise you it won't happen again. I will install automatic artery cut-off valves that you can control in any such future emergency. This was just too close."

By this time Taka had arrived and said, "Dr. Rossen, you know we really should consider replacing the artificial hearts and blood with a real cloned heart or hearts and actual blood."

I could tell Dr. Ishiguro had been thinking about this for a while but had been reluctant to bring it up, probably because this would be way over the normal bounds of morally acceptable research in cloning. It would be criminal in any country on Earth, but then Earth was no more.

I have to admit that I had thought about human replacement also, even from the beginning. The obstacle I always encountered was not my brain, but the extended brain. Could it accept my DNA blood? Making the conversion might doom the extended brain and thus the entire Genesis Project. I decided to remain quiet and see how their discussion progressed.

Taka continued, "If we can make the conversion, we can introduce the Immortality Gene and drastically increase the longevity of Nick's brain and supporting body organs. The organs will self-repair along with any lost brain neurons."

Dr. Rossen was silent in thought then spoke, "Honestly, I have thought about a conversion, also. I have never mentioned it before, but one of the qualifying factors we used to pick the possible candidates for the controlling brain was blood type and tissue matching. Ideally, the extended brain would have been cloned from the controlling brain and it was. Unfortunately, the original donor died. Nick was a last-minute replacement, but the original donor and Nick had already been type matched. Both were blood type O, which as you know is the most compatible blood type. They were also matched on the standard twelve-point gene match done for potential organ donors. I guess what I am saying is there really shouldn't be any potential rejection problems. I think we can do more research and see if we find any potential problems. Taka, genetics is your area of expertise; therefore, I support your desire to consider it"

I was shocked with the revelation Doc had revealed. I had not found this information in my archives and wondered if it was intentionally withheld. I know initially Doc had been concerned about me due to the suddenness of my involvement. He had not been able to prepare me for the shock. I am not even sure there would have been any way to do it. It was probably better that I hadn't had a lot of time to think about what I was doing. The stress might have killed me like my predecessor.

I have learned to accept the constant changes; it is a way of life now. This would only be another event in my apparently long life. I had no doubt that it would happen. My brain would become immortal along with my two bodies.

Genesis Log: 1 Jan 2062:

We had a celebration in the cafeteria this cycle. It was Taka 2, Katy 2 and Nick 3's tenth birthcycle. Almost the entire Awake Team was there, partly to partake of the rare cake and ice cream being served, but mostly to enjoy the special event and activity that seemed ever rarer on our voyage.

I was enjoying my third childhood and playing my role as a child. I was better at it the third time around, running and playing with the others. Akiko enjoyed being the mother and I never missed the opportunity to receive her hugs and kisses. It was an understanding we had, and we never spoke about it, but sometimes I believe Akiko was so comfortable in the role she probably forgot. I did my adult communication either telepathically or through my Nick 2 body and remained the child in Nick 3.

Katy was a little different. She always took a special interest in Katy 2, like she wanted Katy 2 to experience things she had experienced, maybe better. Often, however, Katy would pass a knowing look at Nick 3, as if to say, "I remember when you and I did this." It really was wonderful to experience these things for a second time. It also reinforced my affection for Katy, reliving it again. Mostly, it was the little things, many I had forgotten... something like running through the ship holding hands and squealing in delight, or teasing the general about something.

Of course, Katy 2 was every bit the general's princess that she was the last time, and Doc and Linda doted on her. None of us had a chance. We all fell in love with Katy 2, some of us for a second time.

I truly do enjoy being free of responsibility, even for a little while. I am also enjoying being Katy 2's best friend. She was as perky and bossy in this life as she had been in her last. It was deja vu of past times. Akiko even commented about it once as the three of us lay in bed.

Akiko said, "Is this the way Katy was when you were growing up? If it is, I can understand how you fell in love with her."

As Katy hugged her, I said, "Yep, she was a bossy little shit like this the last time, too." They both jumped me in a mock attack, but I let them wrestle me down. I think I won, too.

In this second life, I had the advantage of knowing where this was all leading, and I didn't miss an opportunity to encourage this friendship. Often, I even recreated some of the past events we had experienced in the last life. It was fun.

336

The only difference was the presence of Taka 2, but he was shy, even with us. He was content to be our shadow, but we caused him to get into as much trouble as we did, like last time.

Katy 2 and Taka 2 learned at a much-accelerated rate due to the mind link sessions. Doc had explained the process and it was proving to be correct. The young mind could only absorb what it understood, but the young minds were absorbing data that was accelerating its understanding. It was like each session understood more based upon what it learned from the previous sessions.

Many times I could see recognition in Katy 2, dejà vu, as she was recalling some of Katy's memories. At those times Katy 2 would give me that look that told me she remembered our past lives.

Genesis Log: 13 July 2063:

The transition to my new body was complete this cycle. I am not sure what I expected, but certainly not what I got. I kept envisioning some sort of partially human-looking body, as ghoulish and hideous as that may sound, but the actual body they were referring to was a series of plug-in modular containers. They were shiny Wonder Metal interlocking sections that formed a low semicircle ring around my central brain within the dome. The containers were all the same size, measuring about twenty inches tall by twelve inches wide and ten inches deep at the base. The measurements were not precisely rectangular, since the containers were formed with slopes and curves to match the space

337

requirement and curve of my dome. When I say they were modular, I mean they plugged into a housing receptacle that automatically rerouted the blood flow through the module when they were plugged into the receptacle.

One container housed cloned bone marrow carefully arranged to flow blood into and out of the container. This marrow would produce the red and white blood cells required to serve the extended central brain and body modules.

Another module contained the actual heart to pump the blood throughout the system. Again, it was cloned from my DNA and altered to a larger size to handle the projected load. The heart itself was suspended in fluid with little constriction to hamper its operation. Doc had designed two such heart containers with an elaborate redundant operation. Both hearts pumped in rhythm but at a reduced volume. Either heart would pick up the load demand should the other fail to keep the blood flow steady.

Yet another container housed most of the other organs including the liver, spleen, pancreas, a reduced-size stomach and intestines, kidneys, and the other torso glands and organs. The digestive organs interfaced with the filtering, blood generation and waste excrement organs and could not be separated. The digestive organs were not critical because the nutrients could easily be provided through the artificial network in almost pure form. Unfortunately, however, they were part of a balanced whole-body network interconnected with the necessary ones. Even so, food could still be provided in a balanced and near pure form, which reduced any requirement for any normal size requirements.

One other container housed a placenta type blood barrier to tie into the artificial blood system that was intended to be maintained, at least as a back-up. The placenta barrier would allow the artificial life support to continue to provide oxygen, nutrients, and waste removal to the blood supply if required. The artificial system will remain as backup only once the total system is operational. The body systems could draw from the artificial network as needed; otherwise, it will draw from the body system.

Doc said, "Initially we believe that nothing much would be gained by creating a human stomach, lungs, and intestines functions, but after long consideration, we found so much interconnection between the organs of the body that we decided we would be forced to supply those organs. Another reason was that the IG organ might possibly try to re-grow them anyway.

Taka believes that some functions can be eliminated from influence by the IG organ if blood flow never reaches it. I hope he is right.

"The Wonder Metal housing will also, hopefully, eliminate any need for the body system to seek further protection or requirements outside of the enclosed system. That is the plan and design anyway," he said.

"You will notice there are two additional plug-in receptacles for future use. One is simply a spare for any potential future need that might arise. The other is designed to support a lung container. It is one body function that doesn't readily interface with the other organs and can be handled separately. Currently the oxygen is supplied through the artificial network and through the placenta barrier. Not much would change with a lung module. Oxygen would still be forced through the body lungs from the artificial network. There would not be much of a gain, but we will eventually activate it."

As he was talking, he was activating the modules. Actually, they activated when the module was plugged in. I did feel the switch when the heart modules were plugged in, but only momentary. There was a noticeable irregular beat and then a slight change in rhythm. It also seemed to be a slightly smoother internal life support flow, but the feeling quickly passed. My only question was, "When will the IG be introduced?"

Taka answered, "It already has been introduced... just now. I convinced Dr. Rossen to allow me to use your Immortality Gene altered DNA for the clone growth of your cells. Your IG organ is already developed and installed in the modules along with the other organs. This way your system will convert much faster. The artificial blood will eventually be filtered out and replaced with your own blood cells and the system will be complete."

I was somewhat shocked to hear I was immortal already and wouldn't have to wonder if it would take or not, but I enjoyed surprises. I said, "Thanks." I couldn't think of anything else to say.

By now I was quite used to viewing myself through Nick 2's body. I had planned to sit up all night with myself... just in case, but pleased that

Katy, Akiko and Doc sat up with me throughout the late cycle. I am not sure what I expected to happen... maybe watch myself die, but nothing at all happened besides having a wonderfully long conversation.

Chapter 14
(Katy times Two)

Genesis Log: 5 Sept 2063:

Akiko, Katy, and I seem to have a wonderful life. We get along perfectly in every way. We complement each other and truly enjoy being together, amazing for a three-way relationship. Lately, however, Katy seems to be a little withdrawn, like something is bothering her. Akiko noticed it, too. One late cycle Akiko transmitted her secret telecommunication, "What is wrong with Katy? Is she upset about anything? Have I done something?"

I transmitted back, "No, you haven't done anything. I wondered if I did."

Akiko rolled over me and squished Katy beneath for a brief moment before she snuggled in on Katy's other side. We pressed against her, staring at her until she broke into laughter.

Almost simultaneously, Akiko and I said, "OK, prune face what's wrong?" We continued to stare at her, and Katy knew we would keep after her until she told us.

After a long pause Katy said, "Well, I feel left out." She quickly added, "Not between us and our relationship but within the Genesis. Genesis is all I know. Hell, I was born onboard Genesis and will most likely die here, part of me anyway, and I have no purpose. You two were born on Earth, lived on Earth and experienced life on Earth. You have memories of another life. I do not. You have

342

important functions onboard Genesis. I have none, and I feel left out."

"I am forty-four years old and I have spent my entire life learning. I have degrees in Electrical and Mechanical Engineering, Political Science, Management, Computer Science, Biology. You name it and I have a doctorate in it or at least some major knowledge. That is what I do... learn, but I don't use the knowledge. You two get up in the morning and go to work. I go to the Educational Center. Akiko has her gardens, Life Support and great responsibility. You run Genesis. I hope you see my point. You have a purpose. I have none."

"I get some satisfaction in knowing Katy 2 and my essence will live on through her. I will pass on all this knowledge to her... and in essence, me. Maybe Katy 2 will have a purpose on New Earth, but I will never see it. Well, maybe I will. Oh hell, it gets so confusing. Me... this branch of me will eventually die, and I will have served no useful purpose."

Her revelation shocked me. She was absolutely correct. How had I failed to consider this fact? Katy was correct in stating that she was extremely well-educated, probably more than anyone on the Genesis. She was also correct in that all this education was not being utilized. Well, all this would change. I made up my mind. Now all I needed to do was come up with a responsible function and challenge for her. I said, "Katy my love, you are absolutely correct. Give me a few days, and I will make you a department head and give you a challenge worthy of your talent and drive. Just remember, when you come to our

343

quarters with your butt dragging, you asked for it. Another thing, tomorrow I am expelling you from school."

We all began laughing at that, and Akiko and I embraced her and sandwiched her between our bodies, our love and our passion. Katy welcomed our passion and reciprocated our affection with renewed energy. Katy was back with us in body and spirit.

I already knew what function she would serve, but it would surprise her, maybe even frighten her with the responsibility it would entail. I had already been considering the need and who might be able to fulfill the role, but I was guilty of not recognizing Katy's ability to serve in that capacity. She was perfect for the position, but I didn't want to spoil this night of passion. It would have to wait. Plus it would be more dramatic to let her find out along with all the other staff. I looked forward to seeing the expression on her beautiful face.

Genesis Log: 13 Sept 2063:

With Dr. Rossen and Linda as her parents, Katy was always destined to become a whiz kid too. This genetic mix of superior intelligence and IQ, combined with a lifetime of education, produced a highly efficient and motivated dynamo in Katy. Unfortunately, this energy had no outlet. If I had given it much thought, I would have understood Katy's increasingly brooding demeanor, but I had not. I think her age was also forcing the peak in her frustration. Katy was aging, and without an outlet for her energy, she was beginning to feel useless, like her life would pass without contributing anything. I really could understand her frustration.

Slowly, over the last year, Akiko and I had noticed Katy's decreasing sexual drive, whether it was her biological clock ticking or the building frustration, we were not sure, but at least I could resolve one of the problems.

The challenge and responsibility I was going to assign Katy was a true need, not just a made-up job. In truth, the job is perfect for her. I had already been pondering how to solve the problem. The responsibility would be great, and I had been reluctant to bring up the subject, because those I depended on most were already involved in their own challenges. The solution to the problem was sleeping beside me every night, and I hadn't recognized it. I am glad Katy finally brought it up.

At the early staff meeting, I strolled to my customary Captain's Chair and took my place. As all settled, I held my hand up to get their attention and said, "I have a promotion and a new department head assignment to make." Silence and rapt attention met my roving stare. "Miss Kathern Lynn Clark, Katy, is being promoted to full commander and department head of New Earth's Planning Department. It will be her responsibility to coordinate with all department heads and devise an overall plan of colonization of New Earth. This will include the settlement location, how the settlement will be organized, governed, operated, and defended. In short, she will plan everything."

"I will continue to be the supreme authority along with First Officer McCullah as second in command, initially anyway. Over time, as the population grows, branch-off settlements may be allowed, but initially I will assume overall control."

"This is a daunting task, but someone has to do it and Katy is, by far, the most qualified. We have many years to work on the overall plan and massage it to fit the needs of all departments. Are there any questions or comments?"

Tentatively, Cdr. Tsuji raised his hand.

"Yes?"

"Well, as you describe the position, it seems that the responsibility carries over to New Earth after we settle, like a governor. Aaaa... well... sorry to put it bluntly, but Katy will most likely die of old age before we reach New Earth and won't be able to continue to serve there. Again, I am sorry to bring it up so crudely."

Katy responded, "Only one copy of me will die. I will continue to serve Genesis through Katy 2."

The realization of this fact seemed to hit everyone at once. Everything Katy knew, learned, did, experienced or had every experienced, would be fully copied in Katy 2. Katy 2 WAS Katy, or will be. Katy would begin the work and the same mind through Katy 2 would see it to completion on the new world.

Cdr. Tsuji summed up everyone's feeling, "Oh, yes... I see."

I said, "Cdr. Clark, do you accept this responsibility?"

Katy was stunned, but nodded and said, "Yes, yes... I accept this position and responsibility and thank you and the staff for this opportunity."

The general was the first one to cheer, followed by a sudden chorus of the others.

346

Akiko transmitted, "Well done, my love. That was a brilliant move. Katy will do a great job, but I can't wait to see how she thanks you...tonight."

Genesis Log: 11 July 2068:

I should have felt bad the first time, which I did, but the second time I really should have been shot for being a sexual pervert and having absolutely no will power to control the situation. Honestly though, neither of us had a chance.

Katy 2 and I in my Nick 3 form have fallen in love again. Of course we did. It was planned from the beginning, and the memory transfer from Katy to Katy 2 was working. I loved Katy and was watching her carbon copy grow up all over again, which reinforced my already strong love for her, but I was still the adult here and Katy 2 was just a kid of sixteen. Well, she may have been a kid of sixteen, but she was receiving the memories of an adult Katy who has been and still is a very sexual Katy of forty-nine. Katy 2 was still not quite yet the same Katy but was remembering many of the experiences we had already lived. Trust me, I was too, but I am supposed to be the adult in this situation, even though my Nick 3 body is also sixteen and screaming for attention.

Like I said, we never had a chance and when my mind transferred to my prone Nick 3 body, I knew it was too late. Katy 2 had slipped into my bed to await my mind's arrival and surprise me. "Surprise me" is an understatement. When my Nick 3's eyes opened, I looked down into Katy 2's open eyes staring up into mine. She already had me in her

347

mouth and, with my sixteen-year-old hormones, I was lost again forever. I took her virginity for the second time.

Thinking about it now, I am surprised how she had been able to plan it so completely. Splitting my mental activity between two bodies was becoming hard to coordinate. It was easy when Nick 3 was young, but now that he was active, it was keeping my mind occupied, and I was constantly switching bodies. Katy 2 would have had to keep close track of both activities to be able to launch her surprise, but she had it timed perfectly. The surprise was total and extremely welcomed, but it did pose a new problem. How could I maintain an active sex life with three beautiful women? I guess it wouldn't be that difficult... I do have two bodies.

Later this cycle, as I was lying with Akiko and Katy in my Nick 2 body, I told them what Katy's carbon copy had done, and they broke out in hysterical laughter.

Akiko said, "Well, that sounds like our Katy for sure."

It was one of the few times I ever saw Katy blush, but what a lovely blush.

Life is sure becoming complicated.

Genesis Log: 18 July 2070:

Katy 2 and Nick 3 are now eighteen. We have given up all pretense of hiding the fact that we are lovers and eventually moved in together. Doc and Linda begrudgingly gave us their blessing, much to my surprise. Katy never had any doubt... she was used to getting her way. With Katy's memory transfer almost complete, Katy 2 truly WAS Katy in a different body. Well, that's not true. It was the same body, just a younger version.

Another result of the memory transfer was the knowledge and life experiences. Where Katy had spent every day learning in the education facility, Katy 2 already knew what Katy had spent decades learning. The result was that Katy 2 had much more free time. She spent all her time with me when I was occupying Nick 3's body, but that was never enough. Her boredom began to surface and of late began to seek the company of Nick 2. Katy was spending increasingly more time involved in planning New Earth's settlement. As a result, Katy 2 was beginning to take her place in the threesome.

Often, as was our custom, Katy 2 would come to Akiko's gardens where we tried to spend a few hours each day. The first time she joined us, Akiko and I exchanged puzzled glances, but to Katy 2 it seemed quite appropriate and natural. My male ego initially assumed that she couldn't get enough of me and that was probably true to a certain extent, but it quickly became evident that Katy 2 (Katy's memories) was missing Akiko. The young Katy needed Akiko's attention and love also. I almost felt sorry for her. She had me in my other form but nothing of Akiko.

Akiko's love was evident also, since Katy's age and waning sexual needs and desires were beginning to affect our relationship. Akiko welcomed Katy 2's affection. Akiko transmitted, "We will have to discuss this with Katy. Katy 2 needs us, and I need and want her too."

349

"I know... me too. It isn't fair to Katy 2 to give her all the memories and love and not let her have them. We will have to work things out."

Akiko transmitted, "Oh shut up! You are already having her, you little shit."

Between my chuckles I responded, "Not me. It's that other guy. I haven't had her."

Our laughter caused Katy 2 to stare at us, and when we told her she joined in our merriment. The levity lasted only a few moments until Katy 2's frustration surfaced again, and she embraced Akiko and buried her face into Akiko's neck and burst out with short sobs.

During the late cycle Akiko and I told Katy about Katy 2's visit. Katy was quiet for a while then said, "I understand how she feels. I would feel and did feel the same way. She IS me! She, I, should be with you two. I, she, love you both. Hell, this was the plan. I have been recreated in Katy 2. That part of me wants to be with you and will be virtually forever, thanks to the Immortality Gene. This part of me, the aging part, still loves you both very much, but you both know that I no longer have the strong sexual desires I once had. No, don't object. I am a realist, besides, thanks to you, I have responsibilities that I take very seriously. They occupy much of my mind now, and I can begin to pull back some and make room for Katy 2."

"I know neither of you want to hurt me, but we need to make some plans for the future that we all know will only get worse as I age. Actually, I have given this much thought already. Taka and I have discussed it at great lengths, since we both are in the same situation. We have planned to eventually pair up to live out our old age together and make room for the new version of us, but we still have many good years before that comes to fruition."

"Katy 2 is already me. The memory transfer is going very well. I know she wants what she, I, knows she should have. I want her to have it, but I am not yet ready to give it up either." She paused to laugh.

"Here is my plan. It is coming a little early, but it will have to do. Nick 3's physical body is a little young yet, but he is man enough. My suggestion is that you retire Nick 2's body to cryogenics and live through Nick 3's body. I know it is difficult for you trying to maintain two lives. Age this body until you can take the IG, then you will have two spare bodies."

"Next, bring Katy 2 into your lives and bed totally... now. I am not going away... yet, so get a bigger bed. I want to continue to share your lives as long as I can, and I can also continue to share some through Katy 2. Remember, I am also Katy 2, and I want that for us, her and me."

Katy seemed to fall into deep thought for a moment then smiled and said, "You know what, Akiko? You will have to get used to being the older women in the threesome now."

After a hearty laugh from all, she continued, "So, what do you think?"

How could we argue with the plan? It really was the only solution. All we could do was sandwich Katy between us in a loving embrace that lasted all night.

Genesis Log: 20 Aug 2070:

I have postponed the transition Katy suggested for as long as I could. I wanted us all to ease into it, but this cycle I requested that Doc put Nick 2 into storage.

The first time Katy 2 and I, in my Nick 3 form, slipped into bed beside Akiko, she looked shocked, but it quickly passed, as the held-back passion of Katy 2 was unleashed. It was the same threesome as it had always been. We said the same things, touched the same and loved the same. We were, after all, the same people. The only thing different was Katy. She pulled back as a participant, but seemed to take great pleasure in observing her carbon copy melt into the love and passion.

Since that first time, we began increasing the visits until this cycle. Nick 2 was now in storage so it was necessary to permanently move Katy 2 and my Nick 3 body officially into our quarters. Katy would continue to share our quarters, but she always withdrew somewhat when Katy 2 was there. We believed she would continue in this manner in spite of our objections. She was not anxious to make the total change and neither were we, but it was inevitable, and we all knew it.

Somewhere along the line I had started referring to Katy 2 as simply Two and it stuck. It had become confusing because every time I said Katy, both looked up, and I had to point out which one I was talking to. Others began doing the same to eliminate the confusion. I should have seen it coming, but Akiko quickly dubbed me as Three, but, fortunately, that did not stick, since there was only one of me active. I remained Nick to everyone

352

but the general. He always calls me Admiral in public.

Genesis Log: 15 Feb 2071:

At the early staff meeting, Taka announced that the memory transfers were complete and further sessions would be unproductive. He declared the process a complete success. It had taken nineteen years, which was honestly far more time than necessary, but I think he was reluctant to give up his project. He probably felt the same as Katy had about a productive project.

I think Taka also had another reason to delay it so long. Katy and he had spent a great deal of time together during the sessions, and I think both of them were getting attached. Katy was now fifty-two, the oldest person, physically, on Genesis. Taka would have been the oldest except he had spent many years in cryonics; they are now approximately the same age. Both were beginning to feel isolated due to their age, and it also was forcing them to gravitate toward each other.

My suspicions were realized in the late cycle when Katy told Akiko, Two, and me that she was going to move in with Taka. Akiko and I both said, "NO!"

Katy said, "I know how you feel, but you have to understand. I need to make room for Two, but remember Two is also me. I want to make room for myself, the other me. Can you understand? This is not all bad. You know this branch of me will always love you two, but it is inevitable. I am aging. My desires are different. Thanks to you, I have my work and it is important."

"Now before you start considering me dead and gone, I want you to know that I have many years left, and, honestly, Taka and I can make a life for ourselves while we are still young enough to enjoy our time together. We have talked about it. Taka is also making room for his double. We have much in common and have become more than friends during the years we have worked together on the memory transfer. We haven't become lovers, but we are close. We both knew this time would come and have decided to make the switch at the same time, now, for both of us."

"I do have one request though. I know this branch of me will miss you both terribly, and I don't want to give that up. I request that Katy 2 and I continue the memory transfer sessions for a while but in reverse. I want to receive her memories of life with you two."

Akiko and I were at a loss for words. We knew she was right, but it was hard to accept.

Two embraced her double and said, "I understand completely, and I will be happy to let you have my memories."

Of course Two understood. How strange it must be to view the situation as the same person from different perspectives. I would never be able to fully comprehend this, but we all must accept it.

Genesis Log: 23 Oct 2074:

Cdr. Tsuji announced at the early staff meeting that he had broken the code of the alien computer.

354

To be more precise, he had translated the language of the aliens and was now able to convert the language to English. I knew he had been close, because he had been using a large portion of the computer capacity to do so.

I still found it strange... well, almost violated when users, especially large users, enter my mind. My mind is extended into the ship computer. In reality, the ship computer is my extended brain and mind when I have removed the barriers. Even when the barriers are up, I am aware of the activity, especially if they are using a large portion of its capacity. It feels like someone else is in my mind and, of course, they are. It doesn't cause me any difficulty, but the very action links my mind into whatever a user is doing.

As a result of his research and translation, I was aware of his progress, but not totally. If I wanted to follow his activity completely I could keep up, but there is no real need, as I can go back and review it. Again, there was no real need... the translation and encryption was complete. The alien computer could now give up its secrets, which I was now exploring.

Genesis Log: 12 June 2077:

At fifty-eight, Katy made her first presentation to the staff this cycle, and I was wishing she hadn't. She truly established herself as a department head, but the seriousness of her presentation took all pleasure out of it for me.

Katy stepped up to the podium and announced, "I am sorry to be the bearer of ill tiding, but I am afraid that I must. I have been working with Cdr.

Tsuji interpreting some of the data in the alien computer. I have mostly been interested in New Earth... its layout, climate, indigenous life forms... anything that might affect our colonization of New Earth. In doing so, we have discovered some disturbing facts."

"We all know the aliens have been to Earth and New Earth. This is how we learned the location of our destination, but we never knew why. We have also discovered that the aliens at some point transplanted humans to the planets of our new solar system. This never made sense either. Why would they do this? Well, we have discovered the reason, and it is not so benevolent."

"Before I explain, let me go back and cover some things that we do know. One of the most fantastic inventions we obtained from the aliens is the metal polymer Nick so affectionately calls Wonder Metal. Without it, we would never have been able to create Genesis. Once the original teams found the repair kit and was able to break down the ingredients, they were able to recreate the polymer from minerals and ingredients found on Earth. Three of the more important minerals include molybdenum, columbite, and titanium are somewhat rare on Earth but nevertheless available in sufficient quantities to supply our needs and apparently the aliens."

"We still don't completely understand the interaction of the polymer mixture... just that it works. We do know molybdenum is used to make steel hard, it is impossible for columbite to absorb water and Titanium is extremely hard and light weight."

"Here is what we learned: the aliens apparently came to Earth to obtain these minerals. New Earth evidently has an abundance of these minerals, possibly greater quantities than available on Earth, or the greater population on Earth was becoming a deterrent to the mining of them. We believe that humans were taken to this solar system to mine these minerals, possibly as slave labor. We must assume that those minerals are no longer available on the alien's home planet, and they needed a continual supply, at least they did tens of thousands of years ago. We have no way of knowing if the aliens are still active on New Earth, but I am quite sure they would not welcome our interference. I am suggesting that we assume the worst and prepare for conflict when we arrive."

Katy then really did take charge of life on New Earth, and I was extremely proud how she did it.

"General, I would love to hear your suggestions on how to prepare for our defense."

The general had sat straight up in his chair at the mention of hostilities and was listening intently. Katy had done it perfectly. She had taken a political approach to the problem. Her duty was to provide an overall colonization plan which now included a military presence as part of the plan. She knew as well as the general and I that she would be presenting the plan to us, but the general would have to directly provide the military aspect to the plan as a part. So, Katy had subjugated the general under her authority, for part of it anyway. It was masterfully done from a political perspective and delicately presented on a personal basis. The general would understand and accept the procedure as necessary. There was no way he would ever get mad at Katy, his adopted daughter, anyway. Even since she was a child the general believed his sweetie could do no wrong.

The general said, "I will begin planning immediately."

Genesis Log: 1 Aug 2080:

After thirty-six light years, we approached our fourth stop on our voyage and began repulsing the Light Wave Drive to slow and finally stop at the Alpha Indi solar system.

All total, we have been traveling in space for sixty-five years, but thanks to The Enlightened, we are 101 light years from our home solar system and 40 years ahead of schedule. Four stops in sixty-five years is not much to break the monotony of space. As a result, we were all looking forward to a change of scenery. Unfortunately, this system did little to excite us except the sheer size.

Alpha Indi is different from the other systems in structure, but that is not the reason we stopped. Alpha Indi is huge. This star named Persian is, in itself, eleven times the size of our entire home solar system. Unbelievably, this star is cooler than Earth's sun at 4,860 degrees, but 62 times brighter due to its immense size. We had to stop well out of its overwhelming brightness.

Alpha Indi is obviously an orange giant with its light radiating a deep orange, almost red in color. This system has multiple stars with two smaller dim companions on opposite sides. I suppose most any star would seem small in comparison. The closer of the dim stars is still distant and barely visible in the overpowering light from Alpha Indi, but close enough to be in a 55,000-year orbit.

Surprisingly, there were two planets orbiting Alpha Indi, but due to the huge size of the star, the orbits are so large that the nights would last thousands of years, and that in itself would destroy any life, even if they were potentially habitable, which they weren't.

We drifted and observed the solar system for a complete 29-hour cycle, while maintenance crews took the opportunity to inspect the outside hull of Genesis for any damage or problems. We hadn't expected any and were correct, but it is not often we are not traveling at light speed, and it is always better to be safe.

After the inspections, we plotted our next 26-light year course to G Scorpii and reengaged the Light Wave Drive.

Genesis Log: 1 Aug 2082:

It is amazing how time just plugs on along. The bodies of Nick 3, Taka 2, and Katy 2 were now thirty years old; more amazing was the fact that Taka and Katy were now sixty-three. The whole team, especially Taka, had decided that thirty was the perfect age to remain for immortality. He said Katy and he were old enough to retire and let the next generation take over. Of course, the next generations he was talking about were the copies. I knew he was being facetious... there was no chance they intended to retire. They had way too much energy, especially with the stem cell treatments they began taking.

The age of thirty was a good age, but the real reason was that Taka was anxious to complete his plan and the final stage of seeing the IG work. I was positive it would work, but until the gene was accepted by the clones, there was a remaining question mark in the plan.

The three of us - Katy 2, Taka 2, and Nick 3 - were put in the clinic for the treatment. As with all recipients of the IG, we would be monitored to make sure the gene was not expelled.

I had ultimate confidence in Doc and Taka; however, I was nervous. How would I ever be able to accept losing my Katy twice to age? That would be too much to take.

Genesis Log: 11 Oct 2082:

We knew after the first three days that the IG was not going to be rejected, but we were waiting for Doc and Taka to verify that we were all growing the IG organ.

At the staff meeting, Taka took the podium and announced, "I am proud to declare that the IG is a total success on Katy 2 and Taka 2. They now join the ranks of the Immortals."

Cheers rang out, but the proudest faces were Taka and Katy. The impossible had been achieved. The Immorality Gene Project had taken almost fifty years, but it had been completed and they would survive... in their copied form.

It had been a massive undertaking, and I had exercised my power to make it happen, but I didn't feel guilty. I kept telling myself I would have done it for anyone, but I am not sure I honestly would have. The only thing that mattered was that Akiko was alive, and I had my Katy back.

Hopefully, I would never have to face that decision again. Ironically, of all the other recipients of the IG, only Taka and Katy had rejected the gene. If someone rejected the IG in the future, he would have no choice but to allow another cloning... maybe.

Genesis Log: 23 Feb 2085:

Many of us had been waiting anxiously for this staff meeting. Katy had planned a major presentation on some of her research for New Earth. She had set up audio visual projection on the main screen. Many of the department heads had invited some of their staff as well. The normally tight group had expanded to fill the small auditorium. Katy was by no means nervous with the large group, quite the contrary.

Katy took her place on the podium and began, "Thanks for the large turnout. In this first presentation, I wanted to go over some of the general details of what our initial settlement will look like, assuming all approve of it. I have worked with most of you to come up with this plan, but few have seen it all tied together."

"This first view, thanks to our elusive alien friends, depicts a view from space."

The picture flashed on the large screen showing New Earth from space as it rotated in orbit. It was a beautiful and green planet. New Earth was very much like Earth with vast blue oceans, and five large land masses, with floating clouds in various stages of weather conditions. It was easy to see areas of dense tropical forest along the equator and also some arid deserts.

The picture began to zoom in on one of the smaller land masses positioned centrally between three of the larger ones, but not connected. The land mass was not really large enough to qualify as a continent, more like a large island. I was trying to get some perspective on the size of the Island, and in Earth's perspective it would be approximately the size of Texas.

As the zooming continued, we could see dense tropical forests covering over half of the southern end, along with steep rugged mountains. Toward the northern end of the island, the terrain changed to rolling hills and open plains broken up by spattered forests.

The picture enlarged on a section of the northern coastline with tall hills surrounding a large natural protected harbor.

Directing attention to the map with a red laser pointer, Katy continued, "According to First Officer McCullah, this natural harbor and surrounding mountains provides a perfect defensible location for a settlement. The harbor can support our future shipping to outlaying colonies, fishing and industrial activities. Here on this tallest rise," she paused, pointing, "is where we propose to land the Genesis. We call this Mount Olympus, home of the Immortals." She stopped, smiling, while the laughter exploded.

"From this vantage point, we can defend the settlement spread out on both sides of the mountain below and also the harbor. The ship's laser can defend against anything approaching from ground, sea or air."

"In addition to the shipboard laser, we propose to move the second laser to a permanent location, here, adjacent to the Genesis's location."

"We also propose to use the spare parts we have aboard to build a nuclear power plant deep inside caves in the mountain. If there are no caves, we will build them. Initially the plan calls for tying into the Genesis' power plant. It is large enough to supply electrical power to a city much larger than we will have for many years. The Genesis has never used more than a tenth of the available potential, and I might mention that we have two power plants."

"We can thank the aliens for identifying the locations of mineral deposits on the planets. Many are on the larger land masses but accessible for mining. This is where the shipping comes into play. Our harbor is ideal for receiving ore from ships that we will construct. The good news is that there is an abundant supply of minerals to make Wonder Metal for much of our construction. Initially, much of our construction will be made from stone from quarries here (pointing). Lasers should work well to cut the stone, of course, we will have to build them, which I suggest we design and build while we are en route."

Katy superimposed a layout of the complete settlement over the picture, complete with docks, buildings of all kinds, defense walls, gates on both sides, fields, factories, utility distribution, etc. There were multiple levels and an organized system of roads, stairs, and railways interconnecting them. Ironically, virtually all roads eventually led to Genesis on Mount Olympus. I could see the vast work in the planning. The buildings were labeled, and I could clearly see military barracks, housing, sewage plant, water treatment plant, refineries, hospital, a community center, a large cafeteria, motor pool and even a cemetery. It was a totally well-thought-out design of a complete operational city. I knew she had thought of everything. I was impressed.

Katy continued answering questions and explaining various parts of the plan until the questions were exhausted. There were surprisingly few questions, though, as most had been involved in the planning to some degree. Certainly, she had used their input in the planning.

The only question that surprised me was from one of the Hope team asking where the Hope would be located. I hadn't seen it in the plans, but Katy quickly pointed out the location of the Hope's resting place next to the community center. It had been covered or hidden with a large stone roof.

Before breaking up, Linda asked one final question, "Do you have a name for the island?"

"I was reserving naming to solicit suggestions," said Katy.

"Good." Linda said, "Might I suggest Atlantis?"

There was no necessity to wait for other suggestions, everyone loved the name.

Genesis Log: 1 Aug 2106:

After another 26-light year hop, our sixth stop at G Scorpii was hardly more than a slow down to reposition our course toward the next stop. Cdr. Kim had been studying G Scorpii for months, as had I. This system was hardly impressive. It was very much the same as the last one, maybe the size was smaller and slightly more yellow than orange in color, but nothing caught our attention that we wanted to spend any time observing.

The only thing exciting about the stop was the fact that it marked a 127-light year distance point from Earth in our voyage, with only one more major hop to go. This in itself was cause for celebration, but this fact was diminished by the great length of the next hop.

This last major jump to Alpha Pavonis would be, by far, the longest one at 53-light year, which caused us to double and triple check our course plotting. A slight error in the beginning plot could cause a major distance error at the 53-light year point, a fatal error if there were no light.

Genesis Log: 12 Sept 2111:

At the staff meeting Akiko, requested the podium. Akiko was not shy, but she was quiet and reserved. She spoke only when she had something to say, so she had my complete attention immediately.

"I have been reviewing some of Dr. Yoshiaki Sakata's work, some with great interest," she began. "He may have been easily duped by the dark side, but he was a brilliant botanist, and some of his experiments proved this fact. He had been working

365

on several projects, but one of them really caught my interest. Sakata had, with a little help from Taka, created an Orange Algae. That in itself is unimpressive, but what I have discover it can do is quite impressive."

"To understand I need to describe some basics of photosynthesis. This is the process of a living organism, plants, using light energy to convert carbon dioxide and water into oxygen and sugar. This is done through a chemical process using enzymes to rearrange the molecules (protons and electrons) to form new chemical equations and by-products. This is the process we have used to maintain life during this long voyage."

"Mr. Sakata altered the pigment in this algae and thus its properties. The photosynthesis process continues to function as normal unless the building blocks change. In this case, depriving the process of carbon dioxide alters the by-products. In most cases this would destroy the plant, but this strain is resistant and adaptable to the changes."

"Dr. Sakata designed this Orange Algae to process raw sewage. Unique to this algae is an altered hydrogenase enzyme that makes this a very special algae. When the sewage plant is enclosed and deprived of carbon dioxide, the algae adapts to chemically feed on the host, in this case the raw sewage, to rearrange molecules. In this altered state, this strain of algae in essence reverses the photosynthesis process and uses light energy to convert carbohydrates (sugar) and water into hydrogen and oxygen and produces a sulfur waste. This waste actually helps the chemical break down of the raw sewage."

"By using this algae in Katy's sewage treatment plant and enclosing it in a bio-dome configuration, oxygen and hydrogen are released into the dome and captured. Hydrogen is heaver and forces the oxygen to be released into the atmosphere from the top of the dome, leaving hydrogen to be collected and stored."

"Bottom line, Dr. Sakata solved the fuel problem that plagued Earth. He made it possible to create a hydrogen fuel manufacturing plant using algae that will provide unlimited fuel for us on New Earth."

The room was totally silent... shock. Slowly the staff began to smile realizing the future impact. I hated the fact that Dr. Sakata had any redeeming qualities, but I was so proud of Akiko for bringing this all forward. I transmitted, "Very well done my dear. Good job. I love you." She gave me a private smile.

Genesis Log: 4 July 2113:

We celebrated doubly this cycle. As was our custom onboard the Genesis, the crew always celebrated the American Independence Day holiday (July 4th). It was always a happy and welcome break from the boredom of space. Unfortunately, Katy had announced at the staff meeting that she was retiring from her duties, effective this cycle. She had spent a lifetime aboard Genesis, but she was tired. She was, after all, ninety-four years old.

Akiko and I were somewhat prepared, however. Two had been working with Katy the last few years taking over increasingly more of her work. Katy and

Two had even begun the memory training again to get Two completely up to speed on the work. We saw it coming, but hated to face the truth.

Late last cycle Katy came to our quarters. It was a surprise, but we welcomed her warmly. She began by saying, "I wanted to catch you all together." After getting settled she continued, "Kids, I am old and tired. My mind is faltering, and I can't remember things. It is time I turn everything over to Katy 2. She is ready."

We were silent for the longest time. Finally, I said, "We understand, but continue to stay involved as long as you want to. We will really miss you."

Laughing, Katy said, "You won't miss me, love. You still have me, I stand right there in Katy 2's shoes, but I know what you mean. It is still confusing, but this branch of me is starting to make mistakes. Trust me; it's time to make the switch."

"Taka's health is going fast, and he won't last much longer... Doc agrees. I want to spend more time with him while he is still with us. He has already turned everything over to Taka 2 months ago. We just want to rest and enjoy life for a while."

"I only have one regret; I wish I could see New Earth with my own eyes before I die."

I hoped she could live to see New Earth... she had earned it.

Chapter 15
(Black Hole)

Genesis Log: 12 April 2115:

Cdr. Kim seemed worried at the staff meeting. I gave him every opportunity to come forward, but he remained silent and reserved. Finally, I just blurted out, "Kim, what the hell is wrong?"

After a long wait he said, "I am not sure. I'm not sure if anything is wrong or not, but I am getting some strange measurement. I can't be sure. I just don't know."

"Well, just tell us what you DO know."

"I have been studying space along our trajectory, and I am getting strong readings at all frequencies: radio, infrared, gamma, you name it. What is strange is the fact that I can find no stars or planets where I am reading the bursts of energy.

"What could it be?"

Again Kim paused then said, "The only thing I can think of is a black hole."

Oh, crap! Astronomers knew of the existence of black holes for years and could even prove their existence. They even knew they were far more prevalent than previously believed. Black holes are dangerous to space travelers, and if one were close to our trajectory we could be in deep shit!

A black hole was the result of a burned-out star that collapsed under its own gravity... gravity so dense that nothing escaped it, not even light. They sucked everything into their intense gravity field to disappear forever. What Kim was describing was how astronomers proved the existence of a black hole. The superheating of gases along the outside edges of its event horizon, gravity suck zone, generated the bursts of energy like he was describing. Black holes cannot be seen, but their effects can be measured.

I said, "What else can you tell us?"

"Well, assuming it is a black hole, it can't be one of major size. If it were large, it would have already sucked Alpha Pavonis in... I think. It appears to be about 15-light years out from that system. The black hole is not in our direct path, but dangerously close... if it is a black hole. Our current trajectory will take us through the energy burst and thus the gravity reach of it... if it is a black hole. I'm just not sure."

I could see why he had hesitated to say anything. If what he was saying was true, we were truly doomed. We were already out of star light range of G Scorpii and our course was set with no way to alter it. No! This just can't be happening... not after all we have endured. We must be able to do something.

I said, "OK, let's assume Cdr. Kim is correct. What can we do? What options do we have? Linda?"

Linda was panic-stricken. She had already recognized our fate. Linda said, "Our Light Wave Drive is useless in deep space. We do have antigravity we can apply against the black hole's gravity pull, but it has to push against a gravity source. This means we couldn't use it until we actually reached the black hole gravity... far too late to do us any good against the gravity of a black hole. It would be ineffective against any massive gravity. It would be like a fan blowing against a tornado. We really don't have any other drive we could use to take us off course."

Cdr Tsuji coughed to get our attention and said, "That is not entirely correct." He paused, while the staff focused on him. "For what it's worth, the Hope does have Ion Drive. It is not much in comparison to the Light Wave Drive, but we might be able to apply Ion Drive at full force at right angle to our trajectory to force us off course. If we begin immediately, we might be able to gain enough distance from the black hole to by-pass its pull. If we are lucky enough to get past it, we can then apply Ion Drive in the opposite direction to get us back on course or at least close enough to use the Light Wave Drive at Alpha Pavonis. That star is a Super Giant, right?"

Linda was excited and said, "I hadn't thought about the Hope's propulsion. It is not a great amount, but quite possibly enough combined with our antigravity. Hiroshi, let's crunch the numbers and see what we can do."

I loved these Whiz Kids. They truly are the best of the best the human race had to offer.

Genesis Log: 13 April 2115:

I immediately started poring over Kim's research. It really didn't take me long to discover that he was precisely correct. There was definitely a black hole near our path. He had also correctly estimated its size, strength and location. It was so evident from the data that I couldn't help but wonder why he was hesitant to announce it.

The black hole was slightly over fifteen light years out from our target destination of Alpha Pavonis, and The Genesis was slightly over nine light years out from G Scorpii. This meant that we had twenty-nine light years before we encountered the effects of the black hole. This is not a lot of time, relatively speaking, to take us the estimated 5-light year alteration in our course.

Any alteration in our course must be done quickly, because a slight change, even a fraction of a degree early, would be multiplied and expanded over a longer distance. Even so, five light years is a huge distance. A major change must be completed quickly.

Employing the Ion Drive from the Hope might just do it, but the change in course from it would take a long time. Ion Drive required a slow build up of force, and we needed it early. Granted, it made our chances better, but I calculated the delay and amount of force required to be inadequate... sadly. I wanted a second opinion from Linda, which I could expect soon in the staff meeting.

I had remained in my captain's chair perched like a statue of the "Thinker" throughout the cycle, while my mind calculated options. All, including the girls, had left me alone, knowing I was working on a salvation plan and hoping I would find one.

I slowly focused as I became aware of the department heads entering. They were also strangely serious and quiet, as if they didn't want to disturb my thought.

Akiko transmitted, "Are you all right my Love?"

"We will know soon enough!"

I broke the silence, "Linda, did you get the data on the black hole, and have you completed your calculations?"

Solemnly, Linda said, "Yes, to both questions." After a strained pause, she continued, "Well, there is no easy way to say it, but our opinion is that, even with the Ion Drive and Gravity Drive, we will not be able to avoid the pull of the black hole. I'm sorry we have run out of ideas."

"I was afraid of that. I came to the same conclusions," I said. "Okay, here is what we are going to do. Come up with a plan to move and attach the Hope to the bottom of Genesis... quickly. We are not going to give up. We will apply the Ion Drive as quickly as possible. As you know, the Ion Drive takes time to build up speed... too long to make the sudden course change that we need, but it will be significant. We can't survive without it."

"Secondly, devise a plan to launch projectiles from the bottom hatch. It will be necessary to launch them with massive force. We will use this force to thrust the Genesis off course by pushing against the mass we launch. Calculate projectiles of 1,500 pounds. See what you can come up with... quickly. This only stands a chance if we do it early enough to make a difference. Let me know what amount of force you can produce, the speed of launch and approximately how many projectiles you would need."

I saw the recognition in Linda's face, Katy's too. I knew they would be working together on this project. It was a matter of physics; push against enough mass with sufficient force, there would be a corresponding shift in the mass of the bigger host. It would be a minute shift, but if we did it enough times, it might just be enough to alter our course... hopefully.

I didn't want to think about what I was committing to do, but it was my problem and my responsibility to bear. I didn't want any to know my total plan... yet.

Genesis Log: 14 April 2115:

I spent the late cycle with Akiko and Two. They knew I was stressed almost to the breaking point and did everything to keep me calm. There were no questions, only comfort, and I loved them for it. I even managed to get some sleep, which I desperately needed in this body.

I was up early and in the control room well before everyone. I had already done the calculations and knew it could work if Linda could create enough force in the launch. If so, I had some hard decisions to make.

The general was the first to arrive. I suspected this was no accident, and I was happy to see him.

The general said, "OK, Nicky boy, what's up? I know you are stressed, but this goes beyond that. You want to talk?"

"I have a very hard decision to make, something that will make me very unpopular, even to myself."

He said, "Command is very lonely. Someone has to make the hard decisions, and you are the one that must make them. My advice to you is... do what you know must be done and to hell with what others think."

"But, how do I live with my decisions afterwards? I mean when it cost lives?"

The general said, "My advice is still the same. Look, the president, America, the world... hell the human race put the survival of us all in your hands. You have those god-like powers the president mentioned. You must honor your commitment, and, right or wrong, you must do what you think best. No one else can make those hard decisions... only you. Now, get with it, Son, and make them."

"Thanks. I will."

When all were there, I nodded to Linda to begin.

Linda took the podium and said, "I can modify the lift system in the bottom four decks to provide a hydraulic catapult system that can launch a 1,500 pound projectile out at 70 mph every hour. Based upon all data, I believe this additional propulsion will clear the 5-light year safety margin from the black hole, but we must begin within five days. I project we will need 1,250 projectiles at 1,500 pounds, but to be safe we should plan on 1,300."

I bellowed, "Excellent!" My praise barely came through the cheering from the others.

Linda was smiling but continued, "My only concern is the projectiles. Where are we going to get this much mass to pump out?"

I did not want any further discussion or speculation, so I ended the meeting abruptly by saying, "You just concentrate on the modifications.

I'll worry about the projectiles. I suggest you get your team working, since you only have five days."

Genesis Log: 18 April 2115:

At the staff meeting on the fourth day Linda announced, "The modifications are complete, all but the projectile release device. I need to manufacture a catch and release for them."

I took a deep breath and said, "We will be using cryogenic chambers as the projectiles."

Doc said, "What do you mean we will be using the chambers? They are all occupied. I need time to vacate them."

"They will not be vacated "

Doc screamed, "But they are full of human beings!"

I could see the horror in their eyes, and I lost it. "Don't you think I fucking know that? The Genesis must survive at all cost! This is the only way. Adding 1,300 eating and breathing bodies to the Genesis's life support would kill us as surely as the black hole would. So, don't give me all the indignation of questioning my ethics or offering alternative options. I have considered them all, and there are none! I carry the burden of my decision, and I am the one who must live with it. Now... all of you shut the fuck up and follow my orders."

It was the hardest decision I had ever made, but the general was right. Someone had to make the hard ones, and it was my responsibility. I would have to carry the weight on my shoulders of all those innocent humans I was sentencing to death.

After my outburst no one spoke and soon left to execute my orders.

I remained in the control room throughout the late cycle. I didn't want to hear from anyone. I was not sure I could stand any criticism. I was critic enough.

Hardened as I felt, I continued the calloused duty of choosing those who would be sacrificed. I could not choose any that I had personally met; that was just too hard. I started with the elderly, then progressed on to politicians, attorneys, those on my terrorist watch list, the uneducated and continued through any others that would have no immediate purpose in the new world. I tried to keep all the tradesmen, soldiers, at least a representative of each religion and the highly educated; but in the end, I still had to pick at random. I finally came up with 1,300 sleeping souls to surrender.

Lastly, in total exhaustion, I slept in my chair. At some point, I was vaguely aware of Akiko and Two leading me to bed and finally feeling the comfort of their embrace as I slept.

Genesis Log: 19 April 2115:

Prior to joining the staff meeting, I had provided the inventory cryonic list and launch schedule to all the department heads. I purposely entered late to avoid the small talk. I was having enough trouble sticking to my decision, but I need not have worried. Silence greeted me as I entered. I took my position and said, "I am sure you have all reviewed the list. If you feel anyone on the list is indispensable, as department heads, you may make a substitute change. Now, is everyone ready?" There was no reason to say just what they were ready for. Quiet nods were given.

"Then my orders are to commence the launch." When they were slow to react, I barked, "Now! Time is critical."

I wanted to assume all responsibility to make it easier for them. Hopefully, it was working as they left me in the Control Room with my own troubled mind. Akiko was the only one to remain. She approached me reluctantly.

"Nick, I know you have much on your mind, but I want to make a change. I know you are doing what must be done... I understand. In the gravity of the situation what I am asking may seem menial to you, but it is important to me."

"Spit it out, Girl."

"Your list includes Lt. Naomi Sami, and she is important to me."

Oh my, Lt. Sami was one that I had elected to save. I knew and respected her. She must have been one of those I picked at random to fill out the list. I hadn't wanted to know, so I literally picked numbers. "Of course she is important. I hope you understand, but you will have to pick a replacement. I can't deal with it right now. I am at the end of my personal resolve."

She was shaking her head and said, "No, you don't understand. She is very important to my department, but there is more. As you know, before we met I had a lover... I am sure you always wondered who. Well, it was Naomi, and it is hard for me to see her die. She is in the past, but it is still

378

hard... the memories. I just wanted you to know why I am asking."

"I understand, Love. Do what you must." She kissed me as she left. She was right. I had always wondered who her female lover had been, but somehow it didn't seem important to me right now. I was appreciative that Akiko had finally told me. Too bad it wasn't under better circumstances.

Cdr. Hiroshi Tsuji and Cdr. Takashi Ishiguro (now Taka 2) were the only remaining department heads still alive from the Hope that knew how to operate the Hope. Luckily, they were all cross-trained in the Hope's operation. They took the few Hope crew members awake and boarded the Hope to begin the maneuvering.

My monitoring ceased as the umbilical cord was disconnected, along with the hatch attachment on the Genesis. Soon they were using precious rocket fuel maneuvering to reattach to the new hatch seal Linda's crew had installed on the bottom of the Genesis. She had positioned it slightly forward of the main hatch so as not to interfere with the projectile launch. Remarkably, it only took them thirty minutes to get the Hope in place and reattached.

There was no need to re-establish monitoring. Unfortunately, the Hope would now have to be staffed while it was in full operation. Taka 2 and Doc had already pulled a couple of the Hope's crew out of cryogenics prior to getting my list. I noticed that one of them had been on the list, but Taka 2 had replaced him on the list with another of the Hope's crew. Now he had a taste of what I had gone through. I know he would never speak of it, nor would I.

Once the Hope was reattached, I felt a slight surge as they fired off the Ion Drive. I just wished it would have been enough.

Once the Hope was attached and out of the line of fire, Linda announced over the ship's loudspeaker that the lift area was being engaged and was off limits.

The process of launching a projectile required the sealing off of the bottom four levels of the lift system and a series of air evacuations. Once the projectile was loaded, these levels must be evacuated of air to match the vacuum of space before the outside hatch could be opened. While this was happening, pressure was being built up in the hydraulic system to provide the thrust for the projectile. Once the launch was complete, the whole process must be reversed to load another projectile. The whole process would take just under an hour

After about twenty-five minutes Linda announced, "Launch!"

I felt the shudder as the lift drive engaged. It probably wasn't the launch but the deceleration that I felt, but the first projectile was fired, the first human sacrifice.

My Nick 3 body was crying, and I felt sick... I was sick... sick of myself, but we continued firing projectiles around the clock. The process would take 6.4 weeks, launching a projectile every hour for 29 hours per day around the New Earth clock.

Genesis Log: 2 June 2115:

The staff continued to attend the staff meeting but little was said. The general became somewhat talkative, uncharacteristic for him. I knew it was his way of showing support for me. Akiko and Katy also acted normally, but the others expected them to support me. I didn't let it bother me. I was the focus for their repulsion at the moment. They needed to blame someone else, and I purposefully set myself up for that role.

I was startled when Linda spoke, "Nick, I have run the numbers, and I believe we have expedited the launch and gained an extra margin of safety. The teams have excelled in efficiency, and we have reduced the launch window from one hour to forty-five minutes, consistently. This has effectively increased the projected torque by launching the projectiles earlier. As you know, the earlier the torque is applied, the greater the effect at the far end. I request permission to cut the projectile numbers from 1,300 to 1,250."

She got my attention, along with all the others. I had noticed the reduction in launch time. I didn't mention it, but I was also aware that she had slipped other projectiles into the launch besides the cryogenic chambers, several actually. For one, my gold supply had been melted out of the storage room. All the gold was not worth one life, but it took a lot of extra work and time that I didn't think we had. She found the time, and I secretly applauded her, even though she circumvented my orders.

I quickly did the calculations. She was correct to a certain extent, but her numbers were more aggressive than the facts allowed. I knew she was trying to save lives, and those souls on the end of the list were the best of the lot, those I had to pick at random. The numbers were close, and I really wanted to agree. If I opted to be safe and demanded the full 1,300, they would hate me all the more. I needed to support her, and I also wanted to show the staff that I had a conscience after all. Reluctantly, I said, "Permission granted."

Linda's face beamed when I agreed, and the staff cheered. There was a look of understanding that passed between us. She knew that I knew she had stretched the envelope with her numbers in making the request. She had taken a chance, and it had worked. I wanted it to work. I hoped it was the right decision.

Genesis Log: 2 Feb 2130:

Cdr Kim was smiling when he came to the staff meeting, so I knew he had good news. I said, "Okay, Kim... what's up?"

He came to the podium and began, "Well, I have been carefully monitoring our progress and course, comparing star locations. I can safely report that we are on our required course to bypass the black hole. According to projections, we will be 5.1 light years off our original course and should be safely out of the gravity pull of the black hole by the time we reach the closest point."

There were others who realized what I recognized long ago. Luckily, they had not broached the subject in open conversation. It was knowledge that weighed heavily on my mind. The Genesis was nine light years out when we began altering our course. It would take us twenty-nine light years to deviate the five light years off course. The numbers were there for anyone to see. Maybe they chose not to see the facts, but the fact was, there were only fifteen light years remaining to get back on course. By my calculations, that is about fourteen light years less than what we need to reach Alpha Pavonis. This, of course, assumes we could duplicate what we did before and sacrifice another 1,250 souls. No, at best we will fly by Alpha Pavonis at a distance of 3.2 light years. This is almost the distance of our first leg to Alpha Centauri, far too distant to obtain light energy for our propulsion... not even close. I didn't want to face the fact that the Genesis Project was doomed to failure. Evidently, none of the others wanted to accept the facts either.

The staff cheered Cdr. Kim's information, and none mentioned the next phase of the operation. I didn't bring it up either.

Genesis Log 14 Sept 2140:

I was startled awake when Taka 2 came into the control room. My Nick 3 body was resting soundly in my quarters, and my mind had dozed off, apparently. When the automatic lighting came on, I was instantly awake, and my holographic image burst into life. I could tell he was upset, and I knew it would have to be something extremely important to bring him back from the Hope, where he had been living. I said, "What's wrong, Taka?"

Through his tears he said, "Taka is dead! He died in his sleep."

There was no way I would be able to comprehend how he must feel. Taka 2 is/was Taka. To Taka 2, it must be as if he watched himself die, yet he was still alive and among us. He had to be experiencing feelings totally unique... never before experienced. On one hand, he could be feeling great that he had cheated death, on the other, he might be experiencing a death far more personally. I really didn't know what to do or how to help him, but my mind suddenly jumped to Katy. Oh my God, she must be devastated.

My Nick 3 body roused Akiko and Two and told them what had happened and that we needed to rush to Katy and comfort her. They understood immediately.

Taka 2 continued, "Doc called to tell me; Katy called her mom and dad first. I am sure you will be contacted soon. I rushed right over. I really didn't know what else to do. I will head over there now."

No sooner than he said that, Doc burst into the room. He saw Taka 2 and realized I already knew.

"Katy is fine. Well, not fine, but she is as good as can be expected," he said. "Her mother is with her now. I came up as quickly as I could."

"Thanks. Akiko, Two, and I are already headed there."

As was customary for Katy, she was the emotional rock and comforted us, especially Taka 2 and Katy 2. I am sure her embrace was as comforting to herself as it obviously was to Taka 2 and Katy 2, but Katy had a special bond and seemed to understand, as only she could, what they were experiencing.

As always, the assertive Katy insisted that Taka be cremated right away and his ashes spread in Akiko's gardens. She said, "That is what he wanted, and when my time comes, I want the same."

Even though the cremation was completed by mid-cycle, most of the Awake Team wanted to attend. As a result, we finally gathered in the garden and reverently watched Taka 2 spread his ashes.

Everyone owed their immortality to Taka. Even I silently thanked God and Taka that I would never have to die like he did... a decrepit old man of 115 years. I am sure most gathered had similar thoughts.

Genesis Log: 15 May 2142:

Doc came to me and said, "Nick, I know you don't want to hear this, but Katy is not going to last much longer. She is failing fast, and her poor frail body is simply used up."

I had been expecting it for some time. I knew she was in pain, but I wanted her to last long enough to give her her final request... to see New Earth with her own eyes. She deserved it.

The Genesis Prime solar system is hidden by Alpha Pavonis, or was anyway. Since we are now off course by five light years, I had been hoping it might come into view around the edge. Cdr. Kim had been watching for it and recently reported that it was just barely visible. I was delaying showing it to her, hoping for a better view. Hearing Doc's report, I decided to go ahead.

I had Katy wheeled in to the staff meeting. It hurt to see how frail and sickly she looked. It was all I could do to keep from bursting into tears.

Two squeezed my arm and whispered in my ear, "It is hard to imagine this is the same Katy that marched into the control room and demanded you come out and play. Don't forget, I was there too. I remember everything, and I am still with you."

I knew she was right, but it was just unsettling. I was thankful that Akiko and Two were with me.

I had the telescope already focused and was thankful that there was a surprisingly good view of Genesis Prime. More surprising, we could actually see the planets, including New Earth. Of course, there were no details, but the actual planet could be seen, thanks to Kim's telescope.

Katy focused hard on the video screen. I was standing behind her with my hands on her shoulders. Her little bony hand reached up to touch mine as she turned her head to speak. I leaned down to listen to her whisper.

Katy asked, "Is this New Earth?"

"Yes, Love, this is our goal."

Smiling, she said, "Thank you."

Katy gently squeezed my hand; then I felt her hand go slack and fall to her lap. I didn't need to look to know she had passed. I didn't care who saw me... I burst into gut-wrenching sobs. But I was not alone. I could hear others; the deep rasping sobs of the general were the loudest. The tiny red-headed little princess who had stolen so many hearts had now broken them.

Genesis Log: 16 May 2142:

Katy had reached the ripe old age of 123 years. I was so incredibly happy that she was able to see

New Earth before she passed. I will never forget the pleased look she had on her face when she died. Katy was such a fighter that she may have lasted longer if she had to, but she had accomplished all her goals. I think she simply stopped fighting and let her soul pass on.

As per her wishes, her body was cremated. We all gathered in Akiko's garden to watch her ashes being spread. Akiko did the honors and spread the ashes in her special garden by the bench we used so much. It was a sad time, but Two comforted everyone by reminding us all that she is Katy, and the memories remained.

Katy said, "You are not getting rid of me that easily. Just because my body is gone doesn't mean I am. You will have to put up with me in this body. All those secrets you have... well, just keep the blackmail checks coming."

With that, we all laughed and life went on.

Genesis Log: 12 Oct 2144:

I have been tense for weeks anticipating the approach of the closest point to the black hole. As it turned out, the event was almost anti-climactic. The ship felt only a slight pull, well within our ability to compensate with antigravity. Never at any point were we in any real danger. Of course, we were over five light years from our original course, which would have been disastrous. Had we not changed course we would have been sucked into its pull like dust into a vacuum. There would have been no chance of survival.

Now that I think about it, the black hole did kill us just as surely as it would have if it sucked us in.

The Genesis currently has absolutely no chance of regaining our original course no matter what we do. I could launch all the rest of the cryogenic chambers on the Genesis and the Hope and there would still be absolutely no hope. I had even considered propelling against the Hope's mass itself, but then I would lose the Ion Drive. No matter what we do, the Genesis will pass Alpha Pavonis, and it will appear as only a tiny light in the vast void of dark space.

The only good thing about our predicament is that Katy died believing we had survived the long journey, and we had succeeded. I am glad she died happy. Unfortunately, everyone else will die, eventually, knowing the truth. I didn't have the heart to tell them either.

I went through the motions and instructed the staff to rotate the Genesis 180 degrees so the Hope would be applying Ion Drive thrust in the opposite direction to bring us back on course. Maybe they believed it would work, maybe they didn't want to know; maybe they thought I could save them again. Whatever the reason, no one asked, and I didn't volunteer. Life went on.

Genesis Log: 1 Jan 2147:

It took two years and two months before anyone mentioned anything about our course change, or lack thereof. Surprisingly, it was the general. He lingered around after the staff meeting until everyone was gone. I noticed he seemed to have something on his mind, and I told Akiko and Two I would catch up with them. They gave each other a knowing look and left. What is going on, I wondered.

"Nick, some of the others and I have talked. I was volunteered to talk to you." He said. "It is pretty obvious that the Genesis Project is doomed. We were wondering when we can discuss our options."

I responded too quickly saying, "There are NO fucking options!"

"No, no, we have figured that out, but that is not the options that are being discussed. We know we are going to die. We want to discuss how and when we die."

"I suppose everyone is outside waiting?"

"Yes."

"Okay, bring them all back in." I said.

It didn't take them long to reassemble. I looked them over and saw rapt attention. I began, "Well, I guess it is no big secret that our chances of getting back on course in time to reach Alpha Pavonis are so slim that it's virtually impossible... in truth, there is NO chance at all. Additionally, there are no stars on this current course, even with the slight course modifications of Ion Drive that we can reach. Well, at least for the next 1,000 light years or so. There you have it... the truth. So... what did you want to talk about?"

It was the general who spoke, "We had pretty much come to the same conclusions. If we are destined to travel, virtually forever, since we are now immortal and won't die of old age, we feel that at some point we might want to end our lives. I

389

think most of us would like to consider this option and others. At some point, life would cease to have meaning. We would have no purpose, just living in our small bubble of an artificial world going nowhere. Life without purpose is not worth living."

"What is it you want?"

"Well, we want to explore the theology of life or maybe death or maybe even the life after death." He paused and finally blurted out, "We might want to ask for Divine intervention. We want to wake up Chaplain Kline and get his thoughts."

I am not sure what I expected to come out in this discussion, but this was certainly not it. At this point I would have gone along with almost anything and definitely would go along with this, but it was surprising. I was half expecting them to suggest we make up a lethal batch of kool aid. I really wouldn't blame them, but this was a much better idea.

I was never a very religious person, but I think I am a moral person. I was raised in a Southern Baptist home, but losing my whole family so suddenly the way I did, I blamed God and pulled back. I blamed God again when I was injured and turned into a quadriplegic. I guess I do believe in God, or I wouldn't have blamed him. Suddenly, I realized that I would not be Genesis if those things had not occurred. I probably would not have joined the Marines if my family hadn't been killed. I certainly wouldn't be Genesis if I had not been injured. Could this all be by design? No, that is too much to accept or believe. I was just the victim of random chance... the luck of the draw.

So far we had relied on science alone, and it had served us well. We had created Genesis and almost succeeded, but science could not save us now. I just hadn't considered God as a possible solution. Oh well, what do I have to lose?

The whole group seemed to be in agreement, even my girls. I decided to wait and talk to them in private, but I found it more than curious that Taka 2 also seemed to be in total agreement, even eager. Taka 2 was Taka reincarnated. As such, I knew he was Buddhist and wondered how he interfaced with the others. Dr. Rossen is Jewish, while Linda, Akiko, the general and several others are Catholic. Still others represented different beliefs and verifications, but I was curious about Taka. I said, "Taka, do you believe in God?"

Taka appeared deep in thought for a few long minutes then said, "That is hard to answer. When I was young, I was taught there was a higher creator and I accepted this and believed it. After I studied science, I was convinced there was no higher being, and life is what we make it. Now, after my extensive research on DNA, I am convinced that life is far too complicated to have just emerged on its own. The billions upon billions of genetic codes in only a single strand of DNA just can't randomly align themselves together in the exact right sequence to create life. The mathematical odds of this occurring randomly are astronomically impossible! An inadequate and grossly poor example would be like asking someone to believe that the Genesis aligned itself randomly from the elements of the Earth on its own. No, my friend, the Genesis was designed and created, and so was life."

"So, life must have been designed and created by some infinitely intelligent force, beings, entity or something else far beyond our ability to comprehend. If I believe this to be the case, and I do, than a higher intelligence, exists or did. This could be God. Yes, I guess I must believe in God."

"Now, having said this, I am not sure if God can or will intervene to save us, but I am willing to explore the possibility."

From the looks on the others' faces, Taka seemed to mirror the feeling around the room, mine too.

"General, What about you?"

"I might be a crusty old fart, but I have always believed in God."

"Very well. Bring the underwear salesman back." This was followed by uproarious laughter at my joke. They remembered the jokes Calvin Klein and I had bantered back and forth in the beginning. I had always called him underwear salesman, because of his name, and he called me grunt marine. We had never spent that much time together, but those times I had found him to be pleasant, outgoing and humorous.

Genesis Log: 10 Jan 2147:

Capt. Calvin Klein (Chaplain) reported for duty at our staff meeting. He has been awake for several days, and I assume he has been busy being briefed on what has transpired during the last 130 years, and presiding over various services in the Chapel. As the sole Navy Chaplain of the Genesis, Calvin had been cross-trained to be able to conduct services in the various religions of the diverse crew. I would imagine, though, that he has received a major shock with the liberties we have taken in science.

When he entered, my Nick 3 body was sitting in the captain's chair. This was the first time I had seen him since he was awakened and the first time he had seen me in body form. "Welcome back, underwear salesman." I said.

Grinning, he said, "Good to be back, grunt."

I was not comfortable meeting him, because I knew, well, suspected, he would take exception to the cloning, embryo research, stem cells and Immortality Gene, among others. That was one of the reasons I had kept him in cryogenics so long. I would have done it anyway, given the circumstances, but having him awake would have made it more difficult. I did, however, relax some after his levity.

I said, "I suppose you have been brought up to speed, somewhat, on the last 130 years and why you have been awakened? As you probably know, the Genesis Project has failed, and we are doomed. Some have suggested that our only hope now is Divine Intervention. What do you think?" As I said this, I activated the podium and indicated he should take my place while I moved to take my seat in the audience.

Calvin did take the podium with ease. He looked very comfortable there, even though I could see tightness in his lips. I had put it pretty bluntly to him and put him on the spot. I was puzzled with myself as to why I had done that.

I had admitted to myself that I did believe in a creator, God, but I had never seen God or a burning bush to know beyond doubt that he/she/it lives. I

393

remained skeptical that God could or would save us if we prayed for it.

I think the thought that there is a living God must frighten me. If so, I must feel a little guilty for my past actions. If God still exists and can provide a miracle that will save us, what must God think of me? What of those 1,250 defenseless souls I sacrificed in vain?

"Hmmm... there is nothing like being put on the spot so quickly," Calvin said, "but, let me try and respond."

"Yes, to your first question. I have talked to many of the staff and different members of the Awake Team, and I have a fairly good grasp of the last 130 years, the major events anyway."

"I must say, you have all been busy and very creative. Due to your efforts and ingenuity, the Genesis Project has survived to this point. I believe God has blessed you."

"As to the second question: can Divine Intervention save us? No one can presume to know God's will, but I have to believe God has gotten us this far and will not let us fail. I do not believe God has finished with humans, and we are all that is left. If Divine Intervention is required to save us, it will happen. We will certainly ask for deliverance."

"I also believe that God has used our entire lives to prepare each and every one of us to be here today at this exact spot in space and time. Yes, I believe in Divine Intervention."

"Are you saying that God prepared me by killing my family and putting me in a wheelchair to suffer just so I would be ready for the role I am now in?" I blurted.

394

Calmly, Calvin responded, "Nick, again, I cannot presume to know God's will, but that may be the case. God is ageless; he can take generations to move his chess pieces on his board of life. Another thing to consider: taking your family home is not the same as destroying them. Sometimes things must be done for the betterment of all. For example, sacrificing those stored in cryogenics to avoid the black hole, or developing the Immortality Gene to ensure the salvation of the project."

He had me on that one. I was speechless, well, almost. In some frustration I said, "Why can't God just snap His fingers and make things happen?"

"I suppose he could if He wanted too. It has happened before, but remember, God is all things, He doesn't need humans... humans need God. What happens in our lives is all about us and how we become what we are. God wants us to experience life and learn how to become better. If He snapped his fingers, like you say, we would not have learned from the experience... we would not be better for it...we would not have evolved."

"Aren't we now asking God to snap His fingers and make it right?"

"No. We are asking God to save us. How he does that is His choice, but I believe God will save us, and we will learn and grow from it. Maybe He will allow you to see a way to save us, as he did before. Only He knows how, but it will happen. I believe, and so will you when it happens."

Chapter 16
(The Miracle)

Genesis Log: 13 Jan 2147:

It has been three days since Chaplain Klein first address the staff and me and began praying for salvation. I have even joined in the daily prayer sessions and meant it, but I still remain skeptical. I have given what he said a lot of thought. Some of it makes sense, yet it is hard to accept that God could or would save us. I have even considered what Calvin said about God allowing me to see a new way to save us. I have removed all my barriers into the extended brain, but, operating at full capacity I still come up without a solution. There simply isn't one.

Two has been full of questions about God and the Bible. It is no surprise, since neither Katy nor Katy 2 had been exposed to religion. Akiko has helped answer many questions, and I have referred her to the general or her mother with the harder questions. I didn't want to try and answer them... I am having trouble enough with my own questions.

It is my fault Katy and Katy 2 had not known religion. I had always been fearful to allow organized religion onboard due to the potential radical Islam influence. I didn't want that hate to spread within the Awake Team. To eliminate the possibility, I didn't allow any services. Maybe that was wrong, since there are a few Muslims in the Awake Team, and they were praying for salvation just as hard as the rest. Oh well, too late now.

Genesis Log: 16 Jan 2147:

This cycle it happened... a miracle! As the staff was filtering into the control room, a brilliant light encapsulated the Genesis. The light seemed to be everywhere, outside and in. Our eyes were momentarily blinded, including my cameras. When the light dimmed again, the Genesis had stopped, and we found ourselves in orbit around a beautiful blue and green planet. It could be none other than New Earth. In the blink of an eye, we were there.

The Light Speed Propulsion was off, and the ship was stabilized in orbit. Silence flooded the control room for long seconds until Linda voiced everyone's thoughts.

"What the hell happened?"

Chaplin Klein said, "I don't think hell had anything to do with it. What happened is the miracle of Divine Intervention we have been praying for. Ladies and gentlemen, let me introduce you to our new home, New Earth."

I must say, I was in total shock. Had God snapped His fingers and saved us? How else would you explain it? Our prayers had been answered, and we had been saved from an endless life racing through the void of space going nowhere.

Just when I was coming to the conclusion that God had indeed saved us, my attention was drawn to three shimmering lights growing in form beside me. As they took shape, there was no mistaking The Enlightened. The orange glow of The Enlightened brightly illuminating the space around them.

As it was the last time, the center being spoke in English, "We are The Enlightened. Your species has caused great harm to our universal common mind. Our tranquility has suffered a major setback from our short exposure to humans. Over the eons The Enlightened have purged all forms of evil from our common mind. It is difficult for us to comprehend lust, vanity, hostility or any thoughts of individuality. We find these qualities vile and repulsive. But, your species has also demonstrated some worthy qualities such as compassion, love and belief in the Supreme Creator. These qualities we find worthy of saving.

As The Enlightened evolved and advanced in knowledge, we became more assured of the existence of a Supreme Creator and the ancient teachings of its prophets. We learned that life is no accident. Life is planned by design. Once we proved this mathematically and accepted it as absolute truth, we began our journey toward enlightenment...to unite in purity of thought.

We have been monitoring your doomed voyage, but once we heard your prayers to the Supreme Creator, we had no choice but to aid you in your journey toward enlightenment. This is the teaching of the Supreme Creator. Primitive as you are, your species has begun to evolve. When you reach our level of evolvement, maybe in a few million of our years, we will welcome contact. Until then we must remain apart. Behold your new world, a gift of compassion from The Enlightened, servants of the Supreme Creator. Use our gift wisely."

Again, The Enlightened had transported the Genesis some twelve light years instantly. More importantly, they had saved us...or was it Divine Intervention?

I was almost disappointed, not because we were saved, but in the way we were saved. I wished God would have revealed himself in a burning bush or parted the sea. That way there would be no doubt of His existence, but it had been just as Chaplin Klein had said... God doesn't necessarily work directly but through others and would let the individual decide and learn...evolve.

The devout would see the salvation as Divine Intervention. The skeptic would see it as The Enlightened's Intervention. It would depend on the individual's belief and faith to decide. I am sure Chaplain Klein and I will have some interesting conversations about this.

Genesis Log: 17 Jan 2147:

It didn't take us long to get back to business. Now that we were back on schedule, actually way ahead of schedule, the staff was energetic and eager to move on to the next stage, colonization. Unfortunately, we were not ready. We could not just land and wake everyone up, what was left of them. There simply weren't enough food stores to support that many. I also knew I would not have to work it all out; this was Two's area of expertise. Katy and Two combined had spent decades refining the plan, and now it was time to execute it. "OK, Two." I said, "How do you propose we should begin the colonization?"

Two took the podium and began, "Well, I suggest we remain in orbit and study the planet in detail for a while, identify the native population centers and search for any potential dangers. We know the aliens who visited Earth also visited here. That is the potential danger... that and remaining distant from the native human populations. They will most likely be somewhat primitive and frightened of us.

The next stage is the actual landing. Once we know our chosen location is clear, with no immediate danger, we can land.

One benefit we already have, The Hope is still attached to our undercarriage. In this position, the Genesis can ease the Hope to a landing, and they will not have to land under their own power as we had expected.

Security is our first concern. The general suggests that we first wake all the security force and establish defense and security posts around the inner valley where we will initially begin colonization.

Our next concern is food. I propose we send out teams, with security escorts, to identify native plants and animals that we can use as food. This will determine the size of the awake personnel. Hopefully, we will be able to feed many more, maybe all those in storage, long enough to establish our own Earth crops and animal herds.

Our major limiting factor is housing and support facilities. Luckily, our location is semitropical, so we really don't have to worry about freezing, but it's not advisable to awake more than we can feed and house comfortably. It will be a delicate balance, but it appears New Earth can support us.

Late-cycle as I lay in our quarters, my mind was spinning... thinking... remembering. We, these whiz kids and I, had accomplished so much just to have survived the long journey. It seems strange to say it only took us 132 years to get here, but now it is a short time compared to immortality. When I consider the additional challenges we will face on this new world, we may need to be immortal. We will face those new challenges and will continue to survive. Earth will live on through us, and all those long dead will be honored in our continued existence.

Two nuzzled me out of my thoughts and seductively whispered, "Can we have children now?"

Akiko nuzzled me on my other side and said, "Me too!"

Did I mention challenges?

The End
or
The New Beginning